ERA ONE

BOOK ONE

FOREVER IN A

DAY

Kitty Lancaster

CHAPTER ONE

The sun didn't rise with the birth of a morning, but with the fear of death rocketing through me. Before the horizon fully gave way to the mark of a new day, I found myself plummeting into what I imagined would be my instant demise, the bottom of a ravine much too close for comfort. I never could have imagined any feasible ways I could have been saved, but the universe loves to surprise you when you're not expecting it. Nothing seemed special about the circumstances, but what happened was, quite literally, magical.

Everything seemed to have started normally; the crisp, dewy air was always putting a positive spin on the beginning of a week day, even though I had woken up way too early. I couldn't help but find myself in the woods again, venturing away from my house before anyone noticed. We didn't have to leave for a little while, but I still didn't want to risk getting chewed out.

The peaceful green leaves shone like small emeralds above my head, the barely visible sunlight filtering through the trees. The gentle chirp of the birds' melody was calming, and the spring wind ruffled my hair as I breathed in the chilly air. I dashed through the woods, sliding down a hill and stopping just as I reached the babbling creek that led as far as the eye could see. My friends and I had tried to explore it, but after all of our adventures—falling into the cool water, stomping around in boots, climbing up hills, over rocks, and through the entire forest to try to find the end (or the beginning) of this intricate maze—it was still a mystery to me and all the people I knew. It was nice to look at the flowing water rising above the rocks that were trying to block its path.

I slowly rose, taking in the fresh smell of air one last time before strolling back up the hills, slowly walking amongst the familiar canopy of trees that I could never forget. I've been in this forest so many times I could walk through it completely blindfolded. Every tree, every stone, every path was marked out in my mind, etched there forever. The only part I hadn't memorized was across a large ravine.

I obviously couldn't cross it; the gap between my land and the other was much too wide, but the view I had from my end always made me curious of what laid on the other side. I sprinted through the forest, my tennis shoes digging into the soft ground, gripping every surface they could. I kept running, squeezing through the narrow paths the trees laid out, over fallen logs and around dead bushes. I ran up to one of the highest areas in the forest, towards the spot where the ravine branched off from its jagged line and curved into my land. There, right at the edge of the cliff, was a fallen log, slowly decaying every second. As I stepped onto the soft bark, it crumbled slightly beneath my weight, and I had to shift my weight to catch myself from falling. Struggling to balance on the uneven and precarious bark, I stared out into the fields across the divide. Past the large decline of the ravine, there was a large patch of tall, dead grass that led into a forest that echoed mine. The other side was a mystery to me, sometimes creepy and intimidating, but the expanse of land had always peaked my curiosity.

The other side...

I wished that I could go there. To see what it was like, experience the forest that was so similar to my own, but was something I'd never stepped foot in. Sometimes I would see strange things that didn't seem explainable, like animals disappearing into thin air or creatures that didn't look like they could be from this world. It was one of my greatest wishes to find my way over there, a burning desire that wore at my soul every living second. No matter how much I loved the forest here, it felt like a cage, trapping me everywhere I seemed to go. This place had been with me as long as I can remember, but it never let me out, either. To be able to travel carelessly to the other side of the ravine was a story that would only be rooted in fantasy and fiction. An irresistible urge came over me, longing for a place I could just barely touch... I reached out, imagining a world where I could leap over this barrier to a land that was so close yet so far when I remembered I should have been watching my balance.

One distracted moment was all it took. Panic spiked through me, fear cut me in half as my foot slipped and my heart skipped a beat. The tree bark fell away, revealing a colony of ants that spewed forth, awakened and frightened by the light. I screamed as I fell backwards, my body becoming weightless. I plummeted off the side of the cliff, terror consuming every single bone in my body.

A second felt like a lifetime. My hair flowed out in front of me as I twisted in the air, and at that moment I knew I was going to die. I would hit the ground far beneath, and it would be over. My life didn't flash before my eyes like the books and movies always say; every fiber of my being was so enveloped in panic that I couldn't even seem to think. My worst fears suddenly came to life: dying young, especially in such a painful way. I would never see my friends again, never laugh with them, never smile with them, never cry with them. My life couldn't just be... over, could it?

Tears seeped out of my eyes, the droplets ripped off of my cheeks and into the air. My vision blurred and I tilted my head to see the ground approaching quickly. I sniffed, bracing myself for a painful death as I finally touched the rock below...

A warm feeling passed through my body, and I sunk through the floor like it was made out of sand.

The world reversed, and as quickly as I fell, I was rising into the air. I screamed, expecting to be shot into the trees, but my momentum was slowed from falling through the floor. I passed the edge of the ravine and I thought that this was my chance; I could save myself! I tried to grab onto a tree, a rock, anything, but I was too slow, and I started to fall back down. I braced myself again when I felt hands wrap around my wrists. I looked up at my savior, seeing a hooded figure pulling me into the woods, swinging me over the edge.

I landed on the floor, almost crashing into a tree. I coughed; dirt had somehow gotten into my mouth. I glanced up at the person who saved me, vaguely realizing that I was in the same forest as before. Every detail I recognized, processing in the back of my mind. What had happened? Was falling just a dream? A rustling sound caught my attention as I looked over to see the cloaked person hurriedly scuttling away. The sweet scent of cinnamon seemed to fill the air around me, assumingly coming from the person in front of me, and I watched as their cloak blended in with the trees, a dark green that seemed to shimmer with every move. Bright green symbols were embroidered on the edges. It was a beautiful garment, but one I didn't have time to appreciate.

"Wait!" I called out, realizing that they were almost out of sight. I scrambled to get up, brushing the dirt off of my clothes. It was almost difficult to see their figure at this point. "Stop, please!" They looked back, we both paused, and our eyes locked. I was suddenly at a loss of words, confused as to what I should say. But then they blinked and turned away, shaking their head. "Please, stop! What just happened to me?"

"Not now!" I heard them mutter, disappearing through the trees. I was alone in the forest, once again.

I could feel a cold breeze sweeping over me. I tried to stand, but my legs could barely hold me. I suddenly felt very weak, but I didn't know why. It was as if all the strength had left me when I passed through the ground. That still made no sense to me, but I figured that was a problem for another time.

"Hello?" I cried, hoping for a reply. The person couldn't have gone that far... right? But I knew it was useless to chase them. I had one more chance, though. If this was like my forest at home, my house would be in the opposite direction than the figure disappeared in. That was my best bet. It had to be.

Through all the confusion and chaos, I had a reassuring sense of hope, so I decided to follow my gut. Once again, I was traipsing through the leaves, the forest coming alive around me in an instant. There were birds chirping in the highest parts of the trees, bugs swirling around looking for their next meal, and a slightly ominous feeling that hung over my head, the depths of the darkness holding terrors that followed behind my every step. I didn't know where I was, or even how this world worked. I didn't know what was out here; I could be in actual danger. The eyes that I felt on the back of my head may not have been paranoia taking effect, but a predator, slinking through the woods, waiting for the perfect moment to strike...

Needless to say, I started to walk a bit faster. Weaving through the paths of trees and logs I know so well. Taking in the fresh air, appreciating the beauty of the earth. The floor suddenly curved down, into a small ditch filled with mud. I quickly hopped over, and started up the hill on the other side, expecting to look over the landscape and see a house, surrounded by flowering bushes...

But as I went up, something didn't look quite right. It was the same hill, going down and coming back up again. It led right back to the log I fell off of. How did I go backwards? I... I didn't. The feeling of being watched intensified. Fear started to take root and spread, making my steps quicker, my breaths shorter, and my brain run faster than it ever had before. What was lurking in the shadows? Why was the land repeating itself? What sort of horror-story wonderland had I found myself trapped in?

After a few useless attempts to actually cross the hill, all failing and leading back to the same place, I decided to climb back over the hill to the log, and I sat on the edge of it for a moment. I was extremely upset, and panic was beginning to set in, clouding my mind of all rational or cognitive thought. I had nowhere to go, no one I could trust, and no knowledge of my surroundings other than the general landscape. I was trapped, and I didn't want to risk falling off the cliff again. I might not be so lucky this time, and could end up actually dying. My best chance was to find that strange person in the green cloak, but... how?

"Hello? Please tell me you're still there!" I yelled. The forest stayed stagnant, and my only reply was faint birds chirping high above me. "Please! I'm lost and I don't know where to go! Nothing makes sense right now!" Even though I felt like no one could hear me, I still wanted to scream into the empty land, getting the trees to hear my fears even if no one else did. But this time, I heard the rustle of leaves. I looked around, excited for a moment, hope spreading through me, but nobody was there. "Hello?"

I screamed as something pitch black landed in front of me. My shriek carried across the forest and echoed, showing just how vast the land was. The thing in front of me rose, its eyes glowing a deep purple. Evil radiated off of its large body, encased in shadows so I couldn't make out any features. Its breath steamed in the crisp air. A mammoth-sized claw reached out to grab me, and I closed my eyes, trying to block it with my hands in front of my face, knowing that the feeble gesture wouldn't be enough to keep the creature away.

A blast of light hit the monster in the chest. It stumbled back, its stubby legs flailing as it fell. I looked back to see the cloaked person holding out their hand. Blue energy circled their palm, encasing a small wooden object in their grasp, the power from it heating up the air around me, emanating warmth. The thing seemed stunned from the blast, but that didn't last long. The giant creature suddenly rose, screaming in anger, a malicious, vibrant red steam seeping into the air around it. The leaves gave way to the sun, letting light in from above so I could see the thing clearly. It was twice the size of me, with a pig's head and hooves. Thick, coarse hairs sprouted off of its arms and head, and as it roared, I could see tusks sticking out of its mouth, all of its teeth distorted and crooked. Its stomach was swollen and red, covered in a thin layer of hair.

"You need to run," the cloaked person said calmly. "You can't be here."

"I don't even know where here is!" I yelled in frustration. "Where am I supposed to go? The land just… *loops*!" I doubted my legs would even work if I wanted to flee. I couldn't help but stare at the creature in front of me, my breath shaking in fear. I was surprised I was even able to speak.

"It does?" They looked confused, their voice questioning. "Oh, I see. That—"

The pig decided it suddenly didn't like our conversation, and attacked once again. Running forward, snorting and spitting, its claws finally met its target. The person was distracted by me, and the creature used that to attack. It batted them away, their limp body flying through the air and landing several yards away. Then it turned on me.

I could feel the heat of its foul breath as it drew closer. Time seemed to come to a stand-still, and for the second time, I knew I was about to die. It raised its vicious, clawed hand once more, and slowly moved in to strike. All I could do was shrink away, though I knew my attempt to flee would be completely useless against the brute force of this monster.

Suddenly, I felt warm, like the person was standing next to me again. It filled my entire body, a sweet sensation like the calm in the storm. Fire roared out of my palms, a blast of heat so strong it knocked the monster over the cliff and into the deep ravine. I stared down, terrified of my own hands, and the power I was suddenly able to wield. I could hear a thud at the bottom, and a shrill scream, and I knew that the pig didn't go through the portal as I had, but landed violently below. Somehow, I had been the one to prevail in the fight.

Through the hazy cloud of shock I was suspended in, I heard a small, quiet groan, and snapped out of my stupor, remembering the cloaked person. I looked around until I found a small spot of green, just slightly darker than the other leaves. I ran over, and winced as I assessed the situation. His hood had come off, revealing sparkling, crystalline green eyes and a small splash of freckles across his nose, with a mop of dark, tousled hair, but his face was marred by scars and blood. He was covered in newer cuts, too, and probably many more injuries hidden from my eyes. I reached down to gently take his hand, pulling him up as delicately as I was able to.

"Are you alright?" I said softly, still trapped in a sense of surprise. I could barely believe that anything in the past few minutes had actually happened, but despite whatever had just gone down, I wanted to help, and I couldn't do that if I was freaking out. I'd have to stick with internally screaming for now.

"I—yeah. I'll be okay. Th—thank you." His voice was almost sweet, not very deep. It was nice to listen to. I nodded, smiling slightly in what was hopefully a comforting gesture, then glanced at his marks. I couldn't tell if the scratches were from the monster attack, or him running into a few trees after he was flung away.

"We need to get a doctor or something, you look... no offense, but you look awful," I laughed nervously. Now it was his turn to smile.

"Well, those things are difficult. Where did it go? Did I intimidate it enough that it just turned around and left?" He said confidently, his grin quickly turning into a smirk. I rolled my eyes, giggling.

"Yeah, I'm sure it was terrified after it poked you and you flew all the way across the forest." I watched his cocky expression melt into a shocked amusement.

"I wasn't that pathetic, come on! Cut me some slack," he sighed, glancing around. "You... You didn't happen to kill it, did you?" I shrugged, unsure of what had transpired, and lead him over to the edge of the cliff, pointing down into the ravine.

"You tell me. That's where it landed, but... I don't see it," I commented, glancing down the steep walls. He stifled a yelp.

"How... what—huh?" He looked at me, extremely surprised. "And yet... you're not from here? What did you do?"

"I don't exactly know," I admitted, feeling that mixed sense of dread and panic creep up on me again. "I felt warm, and suddenly... a blast of fire came out of my hands, and it threw that... thing off the cliff."

"You did?" I nodded again. "That's... absolutely amazing! The General needs to see this! Or... you," he laughed.

"The General?"

He held himself up, and pointed over the hill.

"No, that won't work," I shook my head, reliving the trek I had made a few moments ago. "Like I said, it just... loops."

"That's because you didn't know what to look for," he winked, and tried to move forward, but his leg wilted beneath him and he crumpled to the ground. I almost fell over trying to pick him up.

"That made no sense, but... lead on!" I laughed, holding him upright, his arm draped across my shoulders. "Just don't—I dont know, kill me? I feel like this is a start to a bad horror movie."

"A what?" The guy looked at me in confusion, and I glanced skeptically back at him, unsure of how to respond. My mind was still racing, but I took a deep breath, swallowed the feeling of fear building up in my throat, and focused not on what had just happened, or the strange supernatural occurrence that allowed me to wield fire and for that monster to exist in the first place, but rather set my sights on what lay ahead. This feeling was mostly panic, but also some sort of giddy, child-like joy and excitement to find this magical world right under my nose, like a dream come true. Except it started out as a nightmare.

We hurried forward, a sudden, strong breeze picking up, the wind lashing at us from either side. As we walked through the forest, the cold started to get worse, seeping through our clothes. We barely made it up the hill, shivering and struggling to keep standing. Every step was a battle, trying to overcome the harsh wind, the cold, and this stranger's injuries. Not to mention the silence that hung between us was intensely awkward, almost painful, like the air had frozen between us. As we slowly weaved our way to the bottom of the ditch, as I had done before, I decided to break the ice and introduce myself.

"I'm Amber, by the way," I yelled over the wind. The guy looked towards me, his green eyes shining in the light.

"I'm technically not supposed to even show my face to outsiders," he said sheepishly, eyes turned to the ground.

"Oh? Why not?"

"If I can't tell you my name, I don't think I can tell you my backstory. I promise. Everything will be revealed at camp."

"What cam—oh."

We reached the top of the hill, and stretched out before us was a gigantic castle. A stone wall encased the building, towers sitting on the edges, about a dozen people with flaming bows positioned at the ready. Two oak doors barricaded the entrance to the magnificent fortress. Cannons lined the walls, each manned by a person with a cloak similar to the stranger's. I was so shocked by the beauty of this amazing place, the wind almost knocked me over.

"We just have to get to the doors. This is a defense mechanism!" he yelled, pushing me back before I fell.

"How do you use *wind* as a defense?"

"How did you shoot fire out of your palms?"

"Touché."

We kept going, the cold almost unbearable now. I felt like I was going to completely freeze! But every step brought us closer. The doors started to screech, and as they slowly opened, they revealed what looked like an entire town inside. The wind suddenly dropped, and I could hear music, smell delicious food, and heard the sound of metal clashing together along with small explosions. My jaw literally dropped as I took in the sight. What looked like hundreds of people milled around, chatting, sword fighting, throwing blasts of light at each other and giggling. There was a long stone path that lead to the castle at the back of the wall. Buildings lined the street, taverns, inns, and training arenas all decorating the camp. It looked like it came out of the medieval times, except for the Waffle House, the bright yellow building looking very out of place right next to what looked like a stone castle. I started forward again, still helping the stranger walk, and suddenly, everything stopped. The music trickled down, the roar of laughter died, the swords and magic halted, and then they were aimed right at my neck.

"Whoa!" I backed up, startled, my hair standing up from the sudden burst of energy and electricity around me. I could feel the tension build up, all sights set on the newcomer. I really hoped they didn't have company too often, or that would be awkward.

"Guys! It's okay. She's with me." The weapons were lowered, and I allowed myself to breathe. "This is Amber. She helped me get back here after a Zanzagar attacked."

"They," I squeaked, nervous about correcting him. I wasn't even sure if he had heard me before the questions arose, gasps and murmurs filling the air.

"Where is it?"

"What happened to it?"

"Did it run away?"

"Did you defeat it?"

"What's a Zanzagar?"

The last question, of course, was asked by me. I decided to ignore my discomfort, and at least chime in with something I knew they could hear. I would have to deal with my personal comfort later.

I was extremely lost in all of this, in a place that looked like my home, but felt so... cold. Isolated. Different from what was once here.

"A Zanzagar is that pig-thing we were fighting. That's why I brought them here. I didn't defeat it, but... Amber did."

A large gasp came from every person in the crowd, and I quickly noted his immediate switch. I guess he had heard me after all.

This newcomer, a stranger to the people and the world of magic, defeating an enemy such as that? Unheard of! An incredible feat thought to be impossible! Or, so I assumed by their reaction. But I was standing right here, defying all odds, even though I was confused while doing it. I smiled shyly, the entire camp looking at me with wonder and amazement, their mouths hanging open.

"Move out of the way!" The crowd parted, a wave in reverse, sweeping itself back to reveal a small, old man walking down the aisle of people. He had a slightly hunched over back, and pure white hair. His dark face was covered in wrinkles, and his eyes drooped. He wore a simple outfit, a brown cotton shirt and a pair of pants that was a paler brown. Two guards stood by his side, covered from head to toe in thick armor, carrying sharp staffs glowing with a purple aura. As they approached, everyone got onto one knee in a bow. I, however, did not kneel. Not out of disrespect, but out of confusion. My mind couldn't process what was happening, and before it got a chance to catch up, he was standing right in front of me.

"General, I made it back, and... accidentally brought a friend." Mystery Man beside me commented, and I realized that he was trying to kneel, not just entirely going limp and attempting to slide off of my arm.

"Accidentally?" The old man laughed, his voice as fragile as his body looked. Scratchy and rough, just like you'd expect an old person's voice to sound like. He kneeled over a cane, his back arched, his skin thin and his eyes soft and kind. He had a certain sense of peace around him that made me want to smile.

"Hello, sir. I'm Amber, I—"

"I know. J! Come here!" A kid slowly made his way through the crowd. He looked a little older than me, with short, curly brown hair, and brown eyes. His skin was really dark, and as I looked around I noticed that most of the people here were either very tan or had dark skin. He was also wearing a cloak, with the hood down against his neck so I could see his face. "Do you remember the prophecy the Oracle gave us many years ago?"

"Prophecy?" I whispered to the Mystery Man, who I was still holding up.

"You'll see," he whispered back, smiling... mysteriously.

"I do," J said, his voice cracking a bit. I could tell he was slightly nervous, and I was beginning to be as well.

What prophecy? Did it have something to do with me?

"You don't think...?"

"Yes, we were visited by an Oracle," the General began, turning towards me. "She came sheathed in green smoke, floating above the ground with lightning crackling around her. It was absolutely magical, nothing like any of us had ever seen. She told us that the end of my reign was coming, and this place would be taken by an outsider, whose home existed from another world. We thought she meant someone from the Kingdom, or even further within the reaches of our universe, but now her words seem to have taken a new meaning. Amber, is it? Perhaps it really is you that will… Preserve our camp."

CHAPTER TWO

"What?" I exclaimed, shocked. "How am I supposed to help? I don't even know what this place is! How can you even decide that so quickly? I just got here, what if I'm not actually who you think I'm supposed to be?"

"Four hundred years ago, I said the same thing. Now, look at me!" The General gestured to himself and around the camp, but I couldn't help focusing on the first part of that sentence.

"Four hundred years? Why is this place still so... rustic if it started over four hundred years ago?"

"Hey, we've improved!" Mystery Man laughed at my side. "We have a ton of modern things. Do you not see the Waffle House?"

"Yup, that totally brings all of it together," I jokingly scoffed.

"You two already seem like old friends!" the General croaked, his voice shaking.

"We've been through a lot together, fighting pigs, shooting fire, and pushing things into ravines! Yet, I still don't know your name..." I looked over to Mystery Man, his green eyes lit up mischievously, like a child getting his first toy, the same impish humor flitting across his face.

"Well, I think it would be best to tell them your name, as they've told your theirs, and I have a feeling you two will remain close. All leaders need a friend by their side, after all, perhaps... a right-hand man," the General spoke up, smiling softly. I looked on in confusion, not knowing exactly what he meant by that.

"Well, if it's that important to you... I'm Damien. Nice to meet you, Amber. Or should I get a head start on calling you

General?" I laughed, shifting my weight from one foot to the other. Damien started slipping off my arm, and I pulled him back up just before he could fall into the dirt.

"Oh, yeah, we should... probably get you checked out."

"I know someone who's already doing that," I heard someone mutter in the crowd. I looked up in confusion, trying to pinpoint the source, but the sound simply blended in with the ambient noise.

"Ignore them. We're not used to outsiders. R! Please, get him to B. Amber and J will be coming with me to talk." I quickly noted the strange names, wondering what that meant. The General nodded to one of the guards by his side, taking a small red stick out of his pocket. He waved it, and a blast of energy shot out towards Damian. A purple bubble encased him and lifted him effortlessly into the air. The two guards marched off, the bubble trailing behind them.

"Get well soon?" I smiled at Damien, who was slipping and sliding around the inside of the sphere.

"Whatever you say, General." He winked at me, waving. I rolled my eyes and waved back, then my focus turned back to the crowd, all eyes on me.

"Well, uh... hi?" I said, wilting under the confused gaze of all the people around me. J stepped forward, holding out his hand, a smile on his face.

"Hi, and welcome to our camp. I'm J, and I'll be your tour guide today," he joked, speaking slowly and calmly, but he seemed a bit different from before. His vaguely bubbly personality made me smile as I shook his hand. The crowd still looked uneasy, but since all the interesting people were gone, everyone slowly started peeling away, dispersing to go back to their jobs. J and I were quickly left alone with the General.

"Wow, I guess I'm not very popular," I muttered, examining the camp.

"They'll get used to you soon. We don't get many visitors, or new people at all. How... how did you get here anyway?" My stomach started to growl before I could get a word out.

"How about I tell you over lunch. Breakfast? What time is it?" I laughed. J shrugged.

"Time doesn't work correctly here. We basically judge on how high the sun is and if we need to get inside. The night brings a lot more creatures of darkness. Things worse than even the Zanzagars, demons from different realms. So, if you see the sun setting... run."

"Noted," I said, unsettled by that. What kinds of horrors were lurking in the woods? I was apparently in much more danger than I previously thought.

"Before we continue, we need to talk," The General reminded us, waving his hand to get our attention. "J, I want you to remain here so someone else remembers this. Obviously our new friend here entered this world in a very... Unusual way. You don't know much about magic, do you, dear?"

"Nothing other than what I've read in books. This is all really new and... Overwhelming." I couldn't help my voice from getting quieter, as I started to feel small, like I was a lost child.

"Where do you come from?" He whispered, like my answer was supposed to be a secret.

"Uh... I thought the same as you? Earth? More specifically... America? Oh no, am I not even in America anymore? Actually, that wouldn't be so bad."

"If I'm being honest, I'm not even sure what America is," the General responded. "Please... Take your time to adjust here. I won't bother you anymore. J, my boy, please help them explore." With a pat on J's back, the General hobbled off, muttering under his breath.

"Well, I suppose I should go ahead and show you where you can sleep, then. Tomorrow will probably be a big day." J nonchalantly started leading me around the camp. I took in everything as quickly as I could, the cabins, the training arenas, the weapons rack, and the Waffle House. "Oh, and be careful in training. Even if you're new, the General might test you."

"Wait, training? Training for what?"

"Well, you're at least a possibility for the new General, according to the prophecy. You have to train for that. You don't know what you're doing yet... do you?" He turned around, one eyebrow raised. I laughed nervously.

"I know I can shoot fire out of my hand, but that's about it, so I guess you're right."

"Wait, you can what?"

"I... can shoot fire...?"

"Without a wand? Or a staff, or anything else?"

"Yeah. It just kinda happened. I was fighting that pig thing—"

"Zanzagar."

"Right. And I felt... warm. Then I held my hand out and fire just appeared. That's what killed the Zanza-thing." J looked shocked, overcome with a mixture of fear and confusion, so blatant you could see his mind racing. "Is that bad?"

"No! Actually, the opposite. Possibly. Unless you turn evil," He said it so casually that I almost glossed over the last part.

"*What?*"

"Well, one of the first few Generals, after we established the concept was a mage who could use elemental magic. But... he kinda turned evil and tried to destroy everything. The power is also rare. From what we know, only villainous people have seemed to hold it. And here, history has a bad habit of repeating itself. So, you can use elemental magic and are destined to become General, which may be fatal to the camp... Not that you're evil, but it… was a concern in past centuries." He said quickly. I couldn't help but smile as he sighed at himself. I knew he didn't mean to offend me, but he seemed nervous.

"It's alright! I promise... that I won't turn evil?" I said, shrugging. He chuckled, but I could still see the anxiety in his smile.

"Come on, I should get you to the cabin you'll be staying in. Then we can get over to Waffle House. Tomorrow will be… fun." He said hopefully.

"Are there gonna be people watching?"

"Maybe. It's a big deal, a new General. But most likely it will just be you and Damien."

"Damien is gonna be teaching me?"

"No, but if he's gonna be your right hand man, he'll be there."

"Who says he will be?" I crossed my arm defensively. It seemed like everyone was trying to determine exactly what I wanted to do. But I wasn't sure of anything; I barely even knew what this place was!

"Hey, Amber!" I turned to see Damien, supporting himself with a makeshift wooden crutch (which was basically a glorified stick), and hobbling across the camp. I was surprised to see his cloak was entirely gone, replaced with a green button-up flannel shirt and black, casual jeans. A large cast hindered his ability to walk. He was still smiling impishly, despite all of that.

"Damien! That was really quick. Are you alright?" I walked over, stifling a laugh as he stumbled across the camp.

"Yeah, it'll heal in a few days. Hopefully in time for your coronation!" I wasn't eating when he said that but if I had been, I would have choked on my food.

"*Days?*" I shrieked. A few people turned around to look at me with a sideways glare. I felt my cheeks grow hot under their angry gazes. "Sorry. What do you mean, days?"

"Think that's pretty self explanatory." Damien hopped over to stand beside me and J. "I heard the training only takes a few days."

"But I don't know anything about magic, or leading a place like this at all! Wouldn't that be more like a few months to get me into it?" Damien smiled, shrugging.

"The General works fast. He goes at his own pace, and makes us either catch up to it or quit. If you're gonna be the General, he's not gonna wait." I looked over to J for confirmation, and he confirmed my fears with a nod. I inhaled sharply, trying to calm my nerves.

"Hey, you're already doing pretty well. I'm surprised you haven't completely freaked out, if you're new to all the magic stuff," J shrugged.

"Did you come over here just to get me even more anxious about all of this, or did you have an actual reason?" I turned back to Damien with a stern frown.

"Oh, yeah. I was gonna ask if you wanted to take a walk in the woods. You know, get a good look of your soon to be territory," he winked, and started to trot off. I sighed, but I couldn't bring myself to be annoyed with him. I waved to J and jogged after Damien, quickly catching up. The cast and crutches made him walk significantly slower. As we walked through the fort, I noticed more people smiling at me and less staring than before. Three people waved to me as Damien and I passed through the gate.

"Well, their mood seems to have changed quite a bit," I muttered, surprised at the sudden friendliness.

"We get used to new things pretty easily. I mean, we haven't had a visitor in centuries, but we're basically trained to adapt to our surroundings immediately. It's how we survive out here."

"Well, yeah, that would be useful. Hey... where did the wind go?" I held my hand up, not a single breeze rushing by even though less than an hour ago the air had turned to ice and attempted to impale us.

"Oh, yeah, that only activates when there are monsters nearby. Humans like us can pass through easily, since the dark forces are usually monsters or some other non-human entity. The Zanzagar must have triggered the trap, and we had to get through it instead of him." He said with a shrug. "But anyway, about the woods—whoa."

As we went over the hill, away from the fort and deeper into the forest, I noticed that it was changing. The trees were shimmering with a thin blue sheen, glowing and slowly sinking into the ground. Yellow grass grew in its place, covering the entire forest floor, small green shrubs popping up here and there.

"What's happening?" I asked, my voice shaking. It was strange and terrifying, yet somehow... familiar. I felt a strange sense of security and comfort in this place, like I'd lived here my entire life, like it was my home.

I didn't understand how this place could feel more like my home than the forest, where I actually lived, but there was no doubt in my mind that I had been here before. Where and when were the questions that evaded me.

"I—I've been here before," I said nervously, taking a shaky step forward. Damien reached out and put his hand on my shoulder, pulling me back.

"Wait, we don't know why this is happening, it could be dangerous," he looked around suspiciously, worry very blatant on his face. "We should tell the General."

"Hey, aren't I gonna be the General soon? Time to make a difficult decision, that's what they do." I smirked at him, turning his joke back on him. He looked extremely surprised, and I shrugged his hand off and stepped into the grass. The woods and plains were divided in a straight line as far as I could see. Every step I took made something rustle or crunch, my gray tennis shoes absorbing the dew that had somehow already accumulated on the blades of brittle, wilted grass. I turned to see Damien, stubbornly standing still, refusing to move across the line. "Come on, how bad can it be? It's grass," I rolled my eyes at him, baffled by his attitude.

As I stepped forward, worry started to creep up on me. What if something was actually out here? Could I be in danger? What even was this place? I gazed out into the forest, slowly transforming into this weird grassland that seemed so familiar. I turned back to Damien, still standing behind the line.

"Do you have any idea why this could be happening?" I shouted over to him. He simply shrugged.

"I mean, before I found you, the woods changed just slightly. It was mostly the same, only the fallen log appeared." That got me thinking. If it changed when I came through, maybe someone else was going to be here soon.

"I think I know what's going on, but... I'm not sure," I confessed. This all was extremely confusing, but only time would tell. This place seemed so peaceful, and real, not like it had appeared just seconds ago. I wanted to stay, figure out where this was, and who it might link to. A small guess was all I had to go off of, and I didn't know how accurate it would be. The golden light of the sun danced between the fading trees, slowly disappearing behind the horizon. I jumped, remembering what J said. *The night brings a lot more creatures of darkness.*

"Damien, we should—" I turned around to see... nothing. He was gone. "Damien?" Not a trace was left behind. The woods that weren't affected started turning black, wilting and dying instantly. "What...?" I muttered to myself, slowly approaching the border. The trees crumbled apart, turning to dust that was swept away by the breeze. "Damien!" I shouted, starting to worry again.

"Amber!" It was small, barely a whisper, and it sounded very far away, distant and quiet, but I knew it was Damien.

"Where are you?" I yelled, fear replacing the worry. The world around me was suddenly decaying, disappearing before my very eyes. I was alone.

"Amber! Wake up!"

Wake up... this was a dream?

"Come on! We need to go back!"

Back to where? The camp is gone. The forest is dead. Soon, I will be too.

"That isn't real!"

Wake up... I snapped back to the real world, groggy and half asleep, my limbs numb and my energy depleted. I looked up into the blazing red eye of a monster, plant-like vines wrapping around me, dragging me closer and closer to a spinning saw of teeth. It was like a tree octopus. I shrieked, adrenaline flooding through my body as I ripped the vines off of me, stumbling away from the dark silhouette of a demon, nearly falling down a hill.

The monster hissed as it backed up, staring at something behind me. I looked back and screamed. A giant hellhound was standing there, baring its large teeth, snarling and barking. Sleek black fur rippled as it lunged forward, claws bared, grabbing the tree. I watched in horror and amazement as tree bark went flying, the demon demolished in minutes. The hound looked back at me, murder in its small, dark eyes, but it didn't charge. It stiffened, and suddenly started to change. Its snout melted back into its face, its four legs shrunk into two and shortened, its ears fell to the side of its head, and Damien stood in its place. I was speechless, my mouth hanging open as I stared at him, completely astounded. He just looked flustered and embarrassed.

"Sorry, I was gonna show you that at training, but you being in danger kinda made it a better time," he laughed as he stepped forward, offering his hand to help me up. I took it, still shaken by what just happened.

"What was that thing?" I whispered, my voice hoarse.

"A night demon. Those types are really rare. It's lucky I was there. They grab you when you're distracted, and they use needle-like thorns to inject venom into your bloodstream, making you hallucinate a nightmare situation so they can eat you. They don't have an official name yet," he shrugged. I looked down, and noticed his cast was missing.

"Your foot..." my throat hurt, I could barely talk, and now all the adrenaline had washed away. I was weak, and felt empty.

"I'm okay now," Damien said softly. "We need to get you back. Come on." I tried to take a step but my legs crumbled beneath me. My limbs failed me, not responding to my desperate attempts to move them. My vision started to blur, and I felt myself being lifted off the ground. Damien picked me up as I lay there, not able to move a muscle. The frozen wind of the night once again attacked us, as Damien ran through the forest. I saw the large oaken doors to the camp slowly creak open. The rest was a blur. A blur of faces, noise, every moment was blended together. It felt like I had been drugged, my mind not working properly. This was the full effect of the demon's poison, as I would soon learn.

I woke up before the sun. I groggily opened my eyes, lightheaded and feeling weak. I slowly turned, every muscle aching as I stood. I was shaking, but I finally found the strength to stand. I walked forward, examining the room I was in. The bed behind me was gray and dull, but soft. A dresser stood next to me, and a wardrobe loomed in the corner. A long mirror was hung on the wall, one I barely even wanted to look in, but figured I should dust some dirt off, erase a few of the marks from the days of adventuring.

Before I could get up the courage to face my own reflection, the cabin door swung open with a light creak. The General stepped in, waving kindly.

"Amber! Glad to see you're awake. I understand that last night was a bit of an… unexpected challenge, so take a few moments to yourself if you need it, but we're having a small meeting in the Mess Hall. We'll be eating soon if you're interested," He said cheerily, waving once again. "Oh, and there are new clothes in the dresser if you need them." He backed out of the doorway, and I stood awkwardly in the corner, waving.

"Okay…" I muttered, my throat still sore and my voice still scratchy, but I decided not to waste any more time and hurry to breakfast. I looked into the small oak dresser at the side of my bed. A plain, long sleeved blue shirt and soft jeans lay on top of shoulder pads, fingerless gloves, and a leather vest that almost looked like armor. I pulled everything on and took a bobby pin from on top of the dresser. I put on and laced up black combat boots near the door, and took a deep breath, glancing back at the mirror to make sure I was presentable.

My hair, of course, was a bit of a wreck. I tried to brush through the curls, but the tangles seemed almost impossible to unravel with just my hands. I had a bit of dirt on the top of my head, but I quickly brushed it off, almost shocked to see my hair lighten into a softer brown. That was a lot of dirt.

I adjusted my glasses, pushing the black frames back, farther up on my nose. I let my hair splay over my shoulders, the length just barely reaching. My eyes drooped, and I tried to stay on my feet but I ended up stumbling back to the bed, still glancing at myself in the mirror. My eyes looked… dead. Maybe I hadn't entirely recovered from the attack. I at least thought I normally looked awake, but now… the color had faded in my eyes. The hazel seemed to fade down to brown. Just like the dirt.

I couldn't really focus on that now. All my worry disappeared as hunger took over, my stomach complaining the entire way down. I passed through the camp, barely anyone else around. I was at one of the buildings at the beginning of the path, near the doors. As I looked down the road leading to the giant castle, I saw a large group of people gathered around the Waffle House, which was apparently the "Mess Hall". I fought through the crowd of people, through the doors to see Damien, the General, J, and someone I'd never met before. He turned to look at me with a soft smile. He had dark, wavy hair that was cut short, sparkling blue eyes with detailed flecks of gray and green, and a round face. He had pale skin, and a streak of white went through his hair, all the way to the back of his head. He looked about my age, fourteen or fifteen, and greeted me with a friendly wave.

"Amber! Welcome to the Mess Hall. I'm assuming you two haven't met?" The General nodded towards the boy, who held out his hand in greeting.

"No, we haven't. It's a pleasure to finally get to know you! I'm H," he said with a nod.

"It's nice to meet you, too!" I said, holding out my hand as well. I found it strange that most of the people I'd learned the names of only had letters, not an actual name, but I figured that was a query for another time.

He took my hand with a firm, friendly grip. H seemed nice, but I couldn't tell just yet. He was quiet, avoiding my eyes, head turned to the table in front of him. "So," I said, turning back to the General. "Do we eat first or start training?"

"Eager to get going, I see," the old man chuckled, his eyes sparkling with glee. "We can eat first. No use fighting on an empty stomach. It could cause distractions."

We quickly whipped up some food. Instead of a server like in a regular Waffle House, we had to make our own food. I wolfed down a plate of eggs and a waffle, quickly throwing in some hash browns before we left. My stomach full and my mood and energy significantly higher, I was ready to face the challenges that the training may present.

As I walked out the door, the same crowd was around, excitedly waiting for the show to start. I was greeted with friendly smiles and hellos, a much warmer and nicer greeting than I expected. These people didn't know me at all, yet were already kind and supportive. It made me smile—this little, nearly insignificant part of my life made me so happy. I didn't understand why, but I was glad it was there. I followed everyone across the camp, to a large, gated arena. The stone walls stretched up to a caged dome above. Bleachers surrounded the building, and the door was barred with a metal pole. I wondered if that was to keep the people in or to keep the monsters out of camp. I could hear the rumble of the crowd as everyone settled into their seats. I felt a bit self conscious, knowing hundreds of eyes would be on me. The General suddenly appeared next to me, and I jumped. He simply stepped forward, leaning heavily on his cane.

"Today, we will practice with combat-related training, honing your agility and skill. First we will test your abilities with humans, and then move on to some… aggressive monsters." The way he said it made me nervous, but the challenge in general didn't seem too complicated. Damien also suddenly materialized, popping into existence next to me, which also came as a shock.

"You'll need this," he whispered, handing me a wooden sword. The handle was covered in a very plush material, so it was comfortable to hold and wouldn't hurt my hand. Damien also held one that seemed to be a duplicate. He was wearing armor similar to mine, so I suspected I would be dueling him. My suspicions were confirmed when he held the sword in front of him, shifting his stance so it was wider, and then looking at me expectantly. "I suggested you fight me first, so I'll go easy to warm you up."

"You think I need practice first?" I said with a smirk. I had taken many martial arts classes throughout my summers, and I had some experience with a sword.

"Hey, you're lucky. In real battle, you don't get a warning," he shrugged, rushing forward. I quickly blocked an attack from the side, so he didn't hit my head. I twisted my hand, moving my weapon so his blade was directed towards the ground, and I pressed down until the wood smacked into the dirt. Damien swung his sword to the side, trying to hit my legs. I jumped, stepping to the side as I landed, shoving my shoulder into Damien's back. He stumbled, looking back at me in surprise.

"You underestimate me," I taunted, feeling confident in my abilities.

"And you forget—I'm going easy," Damien retorted, sliding to the left and swinging his sword, the blade aiming for the middle of my face. I used my weapon to hit the side of his, thinking that he would lose his grip and it would go flying, but he used the momentum to spin around, stabbing me in the chest. It didn't hurt anything other than my ego, but it was a shock. "Don't let your guard down," he reminded me.

I nodded, re-adjusting my grip on the wooden sword, going for the offensive this time. I sliced at his side, and he simply stepped backwards, out of my reach. I jumped towards him, stabbing at his stomach, but he batted my weapon away, continuing to walk away. I tried to assess his style, but it didn't do much. I obviously had a lot to learn, but I needed to be quick and witty right now, figuring out a weak spot in his defense.

"Well… I'd say we're evenly matched, wouldn't you?" I huffed as I continued to advance, trying to hit at every angle.

"Honestly, I'm surprised I'm not on the ground by now!" He smiled, always having a comeback, just like with this battle. But this time, when I swung, his block faltered. He couldn't resist the banter, but that made him distracted. I tried not to let the revelation show in my eyes, keeping up with what seemed like a hopeless attack. Figuring out what to say wasn't an easy task either, though.

"What're the rules with this? Three strikes, you're out?" I asked, steadying my breath.

"Nothing was set, so let's go with that," he chuckled, his eyes closing for a second as he laughed. I dug my shoes into the sand, slipping behind him as he lost focus. I tapped his back with the flat of my blade, trying to keep behind him as he turned in confusion. He turned his arm awkwardly, but the sword hit me in the nose. I ignored the slight tinge of pain and poked his side, then pushed his shoulder to the side so he spun, now facing me. I held my sword to his throat, gently pressing down.

"Three strikes. You're out," I said, my heart racing. I honestly did not think that could work. Damien looked impressed, and I heard a muted, polite applause from outside. The sound was dulled by the walls, but I felt proud.

"You're a fast learner, that's good. You need that type of speed on the field." Damien dropped his sword, holding his hands in the air. I pulled away, looking up at him. He still held that cocky expression, but it wasn't overly proud. He wasn't a sore loser, but instead took the loss as an opportunity to be humbled. I could tell that he didn't go all out, however. His speed, technique, and strength would make me nervous if we were in a real battle. All of that also made me wonder how he'd been raised. What had happened here? He wasn't that old, so how was he already so skilled?

All of my questions went unanswered as he stepped away, walking over to the General, who was still standing in the middle of the arena. I couldn't tell if he had been there the entire time, or if he kept disappearing and coming back. He patted Damien's back, beckoning for him to lean down so the General could whisper something to him. I couldn't tell what they were saying, but Damien kept nodding, not saying anything. They both stood, and I glanced around, wondering if I had done something wrong.

"Due to the results of the duel, Damien and I both agree that it would be best to move ahead of single battles, and test your abilities to work together as a team. First, you will fight with two other people against three people, and then you will all band together against a monster," the General said, turning to me. "Good luck." As soon as he finished, the doors around the arena creaked open, five other people filtering in. Damien came to stand by my side, as well as J, the guy from before. He walked up to us with a wave, and I smiled, nodding in acknowledgement.

"I'm joining your team as a friend, but the others are really good so I'm honestly a little afraid," J whispered.

"Thank you for your sacrifice," Damien teased, and I smirked.

"We'll be fine! But there's… not a chance they'll go easy, right?" I tapped my chin, examining the other team. There were two girls and one guy, but they were all very fit. Their skin was a deep charcoal that shone with sweat, like they had come right from the gym. It was really intimidating.

"Don't count on it. We'll have to beat them in speed and skill, but that's also gonna be hard. Let's just hope the General calls for—" Damien started, but was interrupted by the General. His cane thumped against the ground, drawing attention.

"There are two rules—no killing, and no magic. Be careful, children," he announced, his form fizzling and disappearing once again. Damien clenched his fists, smiling.

"Yes! We have a good chance if they can't use magic," he bent down, picking up the wooden sword he dropped. "They coordinate really well, so stay together. Oh, and watch your step." I looked down and stumbled back, shrieking as the floor started to tremble. Small structures and walls made of various types of wood rose out of the ground, too high and sleek to climb up, but I could see a few towers and stairs that we could use to our advantage.

"This looks so cool," I whispered, spinning around. "It's like a laser tag arena!"

"A what?" J and Damien both said at the same time, glancing at me.

"Uh… I'll explain later. But I'm also really bad at laser tag, so this might be a problem." A dark cloud seemed to sweep over the arena, so I looked up, realizing it was actually the sun setting. "Isn't that also a—" before I could even finish, the sun started to reverse, slowly climbing back into the middle of the sky. I stood there for a moment, shocked, unable to process what just happened.

"Careful, the game started. They're on the hunt now." Damien tapped my shoulder, taking my arm and leading me into what seemed to be a maze. My eyes still wide, I looked down, wondering how everyone could ignore that.

"Step lightly. The other team isn't exactly what you'd call… quiet, so they can't sneak up on us if we're not making much noise," J said, beckoning for us to follow. He crouched down, sliding against the walls. I almost felt jealous, everyone here knew each other so well, they had already examined each other's weaknesses and strengths. I was at a serious disadvantage in that area; I knew nothing about anyone, or even the world I was now stranded in. But I had already made friends, and that kept me hopeful.

We all snuck around, keeping our heads low and stopping if we ever thought we heard a sound. We kept our swords in our hands, and finally stopped when we reached a tower. There wasn't a door, but there was a frame, so we passed through and quickly jogged up the stairs, glancing out the windows.

"I see them!" Damien said, pointing. J and I crowded around him, all glancing to the ground. The three seemed to be in the same spot as before, sitting in a circle and waiting.

"They want us to come to them. Bad idea, right?" I asked, glancing around.

"Of course, it's obviously a trap. But if we time out, we lose. We don't have much of a choice," Damien cursed under his breath, tapping his chin in a thoughtful gesture. "They trapped us. All we can do now is hope to overpower them. We'll need to be quick."

"We can't climb the walls, so we can't attack from above. But… would they expect us to come in without hiding? If we surprise them by doing what they don't expect, we might have a better chance." I put my back against the wall, sliding down so I was sitting.

"That might not be a bad idea, actually," J said, contemplating our options. "All we have to do is get them on the ground. They're already sitting, so if we distract them, all we have to do is push them over."

"What if we… I don't know, throw a rock where we aren't and then sneak up?" I suggested, thinking of scenes in movies. I didn't know if that would work, but it didn't seem impossible.

"I guess we won't know until we try," Damien shrugged, standing and offering a hand to both of us. "It's go time."

The maze ended up being a slight problem, but we headed in the general direction of where we knew the other team was. It wasn't long before we stumbled upon the three—or, I did. Damien had to pull me back before I crashed into their camp, not watching where I was going.

"I have a rock, but what's the entire plan?" J asked, lifting a sizeable rock that fit in his palm.

"If you throw that at the opposite wall, they'll be distracted and look at where the noise is coming from. Damien and I will then jump in, pushing them down and holding them there. You'll have to come in too, because we can't hold down three people," I whispered, glancing around the wall. Everyone was still sitting. Both the boys nodded at me, and J lifted his arm, chucking the rock at one of the walls. Either the wall was too brittle or his throw too strong, but it busted a hole in the center of the wood. He winced in embarrassment.

"Let's go!" I whispered. "If that didn't distract them, I don't know what will." I ran forward, sword raised, but needless to say, it didn't exactly go as planned. I simply whacked the first person I came across on the head, and they stumbled sideways. I grabbed their shoulders and pushed them down, holding them on the floor. Damien jumped over me, but not before his target could stand up, and he ended up landing on one of the guys, but not entirely knocking him down. He swung himself around the guy's neck, pulling him down from behind. J started to try to pull out the other one's leg from beneath him, but the arena shook, making him fall over.

"Hey! The General said no magic!" J huffed, his arms crossed.

"That wasn't us!" the girl in front of me cried, struggling in my arms. "Let go! Something's wrong!" I pulled back my arms, a little flustered, but the girl didn't seem to care. She stood, trying to glance over the walls as another tremor rocked the floor.

"You don't think—" Damien didn't even get to finish his sentence. A deep roar echoed through the sky, and screams came from outside. A scaly, brown leg with thick, sharp claws emerged over one of the walls, completely crushing the wood. Maybe it was just brittle.

"Game over! Time to slay the dragon!" one of the boys yelled, the weapon in his hand suddenly becoming real, the silver gleam of steel taking over the blade. I looked at my sword in shock, but nothing happened.

"That's his power, not the swords being magic," J said, helping me up. "He can re-equip anything in his hand into a weapon that's the same size. So a butter knife might turn into a dagger, but it's easy with the fake weapons."

"Can we help?" I asked, ducking away from the battle scene. As soon as I saw the creature, all confidence fled. The face of the monster appeared, and a shock went through me as I realized it looked like a dragon. It had mottled brown, shimmery skin, and a long, pointed nose, with two curled horns jutting out the top of its head. Two of its fangs poked out of its mouth, and steam curled out of its small nostrils. But… it didn't have any wings, so it simply crawled across the arena, its long body slithering back and forth like a snake with legs. I felt a shriek building up in my throat, and I couldn't even move, especially not when it turned its beady red eyes on me.

"Amber!" I just vaguely saw Damien reaching for me out of the corner of my eye, but my limbs froze, my heart racing and my brain overloading. I couldn't process anything until it shrieked, raising its tail that looked like it had a fin on the end, and using that as a weapon to smack me down.

I sat up, my head buzzing. I didn't know how much time had passed or what had happened, except for the pain. All I remembered was the moment before, one blow and I was out, the world spinning around me. Everything was blurry, the side of my head flaring with pain. I could hear faint yelling, and a door closing. I felt a hand on my arm, gently pulling me up, the spinning stopping and my vision slightly cleared. My head still hurt and I was in pain, but at least everything was stable again. I looked up into the concerned eyes of Damien.

"I'm sorry... I—I totally freaked out..." I said groggily, holding my head.

"No, you're fine. I wouldn't expect you to suddenly have the courage to fight something like that. It took a team of us to get it subdued," he reassured me. I looked back towards him in surprise.

"Wait, what? How was anyone supposed to fight it then?" I shook my head worriedly.

"We… underestimated it, to say the least. And someone accidentally made it angry, and it escaped, so it wouldn't have been as bad if that were planned."

"This doesn't happen a lot, does it?"

"Oh, no! This is actually pretty rare. We usually have it under control here, I promise." Damien smiled weakly, and I looked up, realizing I was in what seemed to be the infirmary.

"I… I feel bad. I could have helped, but I totally froze," I sighed, feeling weak. My head really hurt as well.

"That's why we have this training. You'll get better. You'll learn how to use what you have, and be able to fight things like that with no second thoughts. I know you'll be a great General. You're obviously really powerful- you took out a Zanzagar without even knowing what that was! You just don't quite have a handle on everything yet, but I promise we'll work on that," Damien said with a light smile. I couldn't see him very well, but I could tell by his expression that he was being genuine. It seemed like he actually cared. "But for now, relax. B will handle you for now. After the demon and now that, you might not be in very good shape."

I looked around again, trying to take it all in. I was in one of the two hospital rooms, no front desk or anything, just two rooms separated by a curtain. I was laying down on a bed, Damien in a chair next to me. Two people walked in, one woman who had pale skin and pointed ears, and a man standing next to her, both in white coats. The woman checked a chart she had in her hand, then glanced up at me.

"Hello! You must be Amber!" The woman said cheerily. She looked so happy, it almost seemed fake, like she was hiding a frown under a mask of a bubbly personality. "First of all, welcome. I'm the camp's resident doctor, B, and this is L, my nurse!" She gestured to the man sitting next to her. He had dark skin and dark eyes, but a kind, soft smile.

"He's a Druid, and she's an elf," Damien whispered to me. I nodded, a little surprised. All this magic stuff was forced onto me so quickly that I became numb to most of it. I just had to accept this existed, but it was still very confusing, shocking, and slightly terrifying. B asked me to close my eyes, and I heard a deep hum. It felt like my brain started vibrating in my head, and my heart raced for a moment, the strange feeling very disturbing. I felt a sense of warmth, and numbness, then all the pain was suddenly gone. As I opened my eyes, the world around me finally stood still, and my vision was much clearer.

"You'll be fine, just a minor injury to the head. We've treated it, but make sure to avoid fighting for at least a day. Be careful out there you two!" They all but pushed us out. I laughed, looking back at the small hut.

"That was quick," I commented as we walked through camp.

"Yeah, they're fast. They don't like wasting time or sitting around to talk. We don't exactly know why, but it helps us a lot. And they use magic instead of regular tools, so that makes it go a lot quicker as well. But, anyway, you're probably done with training for today. The General won't make you do more if something intense like that happens. Want to see something cool?" He smiled a mysterious, child-like grin. I nodded, a bit confused but excited nonetheless. He jogged in front of me, and I quickened my pace to catch up. We went to the far side of camp, behind the castle. Giant stables were hidden behind the stone walls, and I thought it was for horses before we walked in. As we entered, I saw giant dogs standing in the stalls, some asleep, and some awake and prancing around. I gasped, stumbling back. Ten heads looked at me. I strangely recognized the dark coloring and the size from myths. Was this a stable for… Hellhounds?

"Don't worry! They're just babies," Damien took my arm, chuckling.

"They're huge! No way they're that young!" I was very wary going further into the stable. They all looked kind, and were mostly calm, but I was terrified of dogs. Giant ones were even worse. Nothing against dogs of course, but they always scared me. Damien went up to the stall and reached out to pet one. The dog's giant tongue reached out to lick him, and I laughed as Damien stumbled back, covered in slobber.

"This one is... very friendly," he said as he shook the spit off of his clothes. "His name is Diablo, which is funny. Sarcasm aside, he is actually very sweet. But he's big and powerful. We're training all of them to be warhounds, but he's been learning the quickest. He's almost ready to start learning how to take commands so we can ride him."

I choked on my own laughter. "You ride these guys?" I said, looking around at the dogs.

"Yeah, ride them into battle, ride them above the enemy while they crush the monsters under their giant paws..." Damien smirked as I went pale. "They won't hurt us. Humans are completely safe."

"Wait, if you shape-shifted, does that mean you're still human?" I didn't know if what I said could be offensive in any way, but I was really curious.

"Yeah, people with powers are still human. You're not any less human if you have elemental powers. And, heck, you might have something beyond that. We don't know yet. But since you're from the outside world, you're definitely human."

"Oh, okay. So, about the hounds... can you ride them before they know commands?" I slowly crept up next to Damien, reaching up and petting Diablo's silky nose.

"Well, you're not supposed to until they're about a year old. Their back muscles aren't strong enough when they're younger than that, so a human's weight could literally break their backs. And they don't understand commands so it would most likely just be you flailing around like you're on an angry bull." That last part sparked a question.

"Wait, you guys have bulls here?" I inquired, dodging a lick.

"Yeah. Why wouldn't we?"

"Well, I thought you only had magical creatures here. I haven't really seen any animals from the... place I came from."

"We probably have most of the animals you do, and more. At least, that's what I would guess. The actual Earth doesn't seem much different," he said with a shrug.

"Ugh, so I still have to worry about bugs?" I sighed, disappointed. "Mosquitoes are the worst in the summer."

"Uh… I'm not entirely sure what that is, so let's just assume that's one of the things we don't have," he laughed and gestured to the door. "We should probably get going. You're probably gonna have a lot more experience with these guys later, so I thought I'd introduce you now, but we don't want the General catching us sneaking in here without permission."

"Well, apparently I'm gonna be the General soon, so just wait, like, a week and it will be totally forgotten," I winked, and we laughed, going further into camp. "So, what do you guys do for fun here?"

"Well, we're usually training a lot. Evil never sleeps, so we have to be ready at all times. This camp is protected, so they can't easily get in here, but going outside is always dangerous, even in the daytime. Night crusades are very rare and widely frowned upon. Our scouts have to be careful when they leave." He looked down with a sullen look in his eyes. "My family was a part of a crusade group that took the chance of going out when the sun was going down. But… they weren't careful. They got trapped in the darkness, and… all of them were completely destroyed. We still don't know by what, or even exactly where, because everyone we've found has been scattered in a different place. They… they still don't know where my mom is."

"Oh… I'm sorry. That must've been horrible," I put my hand on his shoulder in a feeble attempt to cheer him up.

"It's okay. It drives me to do my job, try to avenge them, even if I don't entirely know what I'm looking for. And the others are like my family now. I'm closer to them than ever, and it helps me work with them as a team." He looked back at me, a slight smile on his face. "I hope it doesn't take someone dying for you to trust the people here."

"No, they all seem really cool. I hope I do get to work with them." I gazed up to the sky, watching the sun slowly move through all the clouds. "The only thing I'm worried about is... the real world. I've never had the best relationship with my family; I could live without them. But my friends? There're so many people I'd at least want to say goodbye to, or even bring them here. I know I'll miss them, a lot more than I do now. I was supposed to go see them today, but... I was brought here. Somehow."

"Hey, it's okay. You'll get to see them again. Remember how I told you that time doesn't pass correctly here? We're completely separate from the outside world. We don't have specific times of day, really. We have the hours, but the sun goes up and down as it pleases. If it works so weirdly here, I doubt that much time would actually pass in your world. You can probably be here almost all your life before people start to worry." He laughed. "Or, until you have to leave."

"Yeah, then I can definitely be here for a while," I joined in his laughter. That made me feel a lot better. I wanted to stay here, at least for a while. This was like a strange dream come true, even if it was scary, I was excited to be here and actually use magic. The entire concept was incredible to me, something I never thought could be possible.

Loud screams echoed through the camp, rustling, clanking of metal, and people yelling jolted me out of my daydreams. Yelling came from the middle of camp as a crowd assembled, weapons at the ready. I stood up quickly.

"What's happening?" I asked, shocked and quite scared.

"Oh, no! There might be an attack!" Damien rushed off, not even waiting for me to catch up. I sprinted after him, panic starting to take effect. My hands shook, and my breath was shaky, and by the time I got there, I lost Damien in the crowd, but decided to stay where I was and try to see what was attacking us. As I looked up, my question was answered.

A giant black cloud slowly rolled over the camp, dark lighting crackling inside it and a deep thunder booming. The thick mass of dark, soupy fluff was slowly corrupting the sky, leaving a trail of gray in its destructive path. Wind shook the camp. It was so strong, it almost knocked me over.

"What is *that*?" I cried out over the noise.

"Everyone get to cover if you cannot fight! We need the mages, and B!" the General stumbled through camp, shouting orders. I ran over to him, stabilizing him before the wind could sweep him off the ground. "Thank you," he said softly, patting my arm, then going back to giving commands. I stuck by his side, unsure of what to do. Strong gusts continued to fight against us.

"What is that thing?" I yelled. I wasn't even positive that my voice could be heard now, but somehow the General seemed to understand me.

"A mass of darkness and evil. It must have built up over a few years. We'll be okay, don't worry," he smiled up at me. I admired how calm he could stay in the midst of all of this. I nodded, then another burst of violent wind completely knocked me over. Before I hit the ground, I began to float. Not just hovering, but ascending higher and higher into the sky. All I could do was scream, completely weightless.

"Maybe worry now!" I heard the General yell. So much for his positive attitude. Soon, I could see the entire camp, including a few people pointing up in surprise. I didn't know what was happening, but I almost reached the giant cloud when I stopped. The wind below me died down, but I was still suspended in the air. The black mass spread in a line towards me, almost like it was growing a hand. The thing grabbed me, fluff surrounding me.

"So *this* is the one…?" a deep, garbled voice spoke, projecting from the cloud. What was happening? "A pathetic human, with no real powers. How far will this camp fall? This prophecy predicted not a savior, but the final straw that will bring this world to its knees. Oh, well. I'll help this universe in a way no one else will dare try." The thing spoke slowly, a rolling boom that sent chills down my spine. I was lifted up, nearly to the cloud. "Goodbye, mortal. Your chaotic future will never come to pass," it hissed, and swung its hand forward, viciously throwing me. I flew through the air, once again powerless to save myself. I felt so weak, defeated by everything that came my way. I couldn't even beat a cloud. That deathly grip held tight, but now I was rocketing towards earth. There was no way I could survive.

CHAPTER THREE

At least, I thought. I looked down, tears in my eyes as the wind ripped past me, and I saw a small figure sprinting across the ground. As I fell further, I could tell it was Damien. I wanted to shout, object in any way to what I knew he was planning, but my voice was gone, every word I tried to speak was torn away by the breeze. I could see him jumping, briefly growing wings and soaring through the sky, until he reached me. I felt myself slamming into him, pushing both of us back. His arms wrapped around me before pushing away, trying to slow the fall while also using himself to soften the landing. My momentum was totally disturbed, and I hovered in the air, falling softly as I heard a crash beneath me. I landed on the ground, squealing with pain as my back slammed against the floor, but I didn't have it as bad as Damien.

His body was nearly buried under a mountain of dirt. There was a long path of destroyed earth showing where and how he landed, and I almost cried. I wasn't in much pain, but I looked down to see Damien's lifeless body, practically covered. My body was sore and tears blurred my vision, but I desperately tried to dig him out. Everything was bent the wrong way. He didn't look like he was breathing. His eyes were glazed over and his body was completely limp. Scratches and bruises completely covered his body, bleeding everywhere, small pieces of roots and rocks embedded in his skin. Just trying to pull him out covered me in blood. I cried out as B and the General, as well as half the camp, came rushing to our side. The elf quickly but gently took him out of my arms and rushed off into camp, speaking softly to L, who joined her side.

I tried to stand, run after them and make sure he was okay, but my legs withered underneath me. I felt numb, and broken. I could barely control my own limbs and fell to the side as the General pulled me down, laying me on the bloodstained ground. The ringing in my ears was deafening. I saw everyone talking, but I couldn't hear it. I couldn't understand it. My heart was beating out of my chest and I wanted to rip my hair out. Despair and rage crashed over me, slowly taking effect as my breathing became rapid. I felt hands on my shoulder and saw kind faces, but no words would come out. I slowly laid my head down, tears still pouring out of my eyes, and I sobbed for my friend, my closest and almost only friend in this strange, cruel world I had come to. One thought kept running through my head—why for me?

That day seemed to end quicker than the rest, the sun setting when I felt like it shouldn't have. All I could think about was Damien, if he was okay, and why he would do such a stupid thing to save a person he didn't know. I kept trying to ask B about his condition, but she wouldn't give me an answer. I ended up sitting at a booth in the Waffle House, picking at some eggs while J and H sat in front of me. They were both wearing casual clothes, simple cotton pants for H and jeans for J, and matching sweaters, mottled with a maroon red, pearly white and dark green, like they had tie-dyed them together.

No one smiled. Silence hung over us. The clinking of the fork against the plate and the oven whirring were the only sounds. I could barely focus. Eating made me feel sick. I was wrapped in countless bandages, still having taken damage from the fall.

"He'll be okay," H said, as if he knew what I was thinking.

"How can you know that? He was basically dead when we reached the ground. That type of impact… I'm not sure anyone could survive that," I said sullenly, my voice quivering.

"Damien isn't a normal person. He's powerful, and he'll pull through. I can't exactly say how but... I can see that he'll make it." I looked up at H, a kind, soft smile on his face. Where the white streak went through his hair, his eye on that side was clouded and gray. I never noticed that before, but it wasn't a regular gray. More like... he was half blind.

"I—uh—" Questions ran through my head, too many that I thought would be rude. I couldn't think straight with all these thoughts crowding my head. He must have seen me staring, because he chuckled and nodded.

"Yes, I'm blind in this eye. Not as inconvenient as you may think. In fact, it almost helps," That puzzled me. J nodded, smiling fondly at H.

"Wait, what? How?" Curiosity took over, making me forget my sorrow for a moment.

"I guess he didn't tell you. I basically traded an eye for an eye, as much as D likes to warn people with that saying. I made a deal with a powerful sorceress once, one revered as a god. Or, my parents did when my mom found out she was pregnant with me. She was mortal in this world, no special powers, and she wanted more for me, so I could fit in. She asked what she could do to make my life better. The god at first offered to make me completely blind in trade for full power, but she decided on one eye for half of that, so now I'm a seer. I can partially glimpse into the future, a short distance. It's a bit hazy the further it goes, but I can see Damien with us. He will be okay. I promise," H reached across the table and put his hand on mine in a comforting gesture. I smiled, a bit overwhelmed with emotion. A tear fell down my cheek.

"Thank you," I said, my voice a bit hoarse. I was learning a lot about these people, their powers and my own, and their pasts. It made me feel a lot closer to them, and gave me hope for the future. "I hope you don't mind me asking," I said, a bit anxious to ask, but I was very curious now. "But do you have powers?" I turned to J, and he shyly smirked.

"Well, I—" he didn't get to finish before L rushed in, the little bell on the door alerting us that someone was coming in. I stood up, worried that he carried bad news, but he only nodded towards the shack they used as a hospital.

"You can see him now," L huffed, out of breath. I looked at H, who smiled, and started to get out of the booth, J right beside him. We all rushed over, and I resisted the urge to burst right in as I knocked. The door creaked open and I saw Damien, lying almost lifelessly on the bed, B at his side. She gently touched his shoulder and his eyes fluttered open. I smiled, excited and overwhelmed with joy. B held her finger to her lips in a sign for quiet. I nodded, and went over. H and J stood in the doorway, and I noticed they were holding hands. I was a bit surprised, and outright gestures of romance sometimes made me uncomfortable, but this was simply… sweet. It was a small gesture of comfort and love, one that I didn't mind. I looked back to Damien, his face severely bruised and scratched. Bandages covered his entire body.

"Damien?" I said softly, almost afraid to speak. My voice cracked, a whisper I didn't even know if he could hear. One of his eyes twitched, and with great difficulty, opened. A grin spread across my face like wildfire in a dry forest. "You're okay," I muttered, feeling like I was about to cry. His mouth slightly moved into a smirk, before his eye closed and he went still. It would take him some time to heal, I knew that. But it looked like he would be okay. I stood up, nodding at B and mouthing *thank you* before walking out towards H and J. I backed up, waiting for them to go inside and say hi to Damien, but they just followed me.

"Didn't you guys want to say... something?"

"Oh, we should let him rest. Besides," J pointed behind me. "I think it's training time."

I looked back to see the General slowly approaching. I waved to him, wiping a tear off my cheek.

"Sad, it is," he grumbled. "Time waits for no man, woman, or anything in between. If you're going to face things like that again, you need to work. But today won't be fighting. We're going to the books!" he raised his hand excitedly, and started off. I looked at the two guys with a questioning look, quickly wiping another stray tear off the side of my face.

"Are you two gonna come?"

"Hey, we might as well give you some company," H wrapped his arm around J, smirking. I was really grateful to have them with me, and hopefully take this chance to get to know them more. H was still quiet, but he was more confident and comfortable with J around, so I knew it would probably be fun. I waved my hand, and we jogged after the General. He was walking down the stone path, towards the castle.

"We're studying in there?" I asked.

"Yes, these are where the archives are. And the General's headquarters, so you'll live upstairs if you want to. Whenever the General isn't overseeing something, he's working in there." J replied. That was surprising, and something I definitely was not aware of. We opened the heavy wooden door, and entered a brightly lit, medieval-style castle. The walls were stone and a dark red carpet lined with gold rested beneath a large, circular wooden table. A chandelier hung from the ceiling. Bookcases lined the walls, and some doorways lead to spiral staircases up into the castle. The General went to a bookshelf closest to the door, and picked out three books.

"You'll read, going from level one to level ten today. Then, you can test each other for every level advancement." He put the books on the table and gestured to the chairs. We all sat down, and the General nodded. "I have some business outside the walls to attend to. Try to get this done, but no rush. Good luck, children!" He walked out, the door slamming behind him.

"Wait, if he's leaving us alone, couldn't we just... cheat?" I suggested, looking around the room. I wouldn't normally cheat, but was his trust so solid that he would just leave?

"We shouldn't, that's not fair. He's trusting us to follow the rules, and cheating will break that, and won't help us learn anything." J opened the book, its leather-bound cover soft to the touch.

"Are we all studying? Or are you guys basically just quizzing me?" I asked, glancing over the letters on the yellow, brittle paper in front of me.

"I think we're all doing it. We don't know much about monsters, so it would be best," H commented. J and I nodded in unison. I looked down, tracing my finger across the page underneath the words to keep myself on track.

The Raspin

A catlike animal that moves slowly and is very weak. Hunt and live together as a pack. Strongest during the summer. Can spit poison when extremely intimidated.

The Zombie

I examined the page, surprised to see it didn't have a strange name, and was practically the same monster as I knew.

Slow, but strong. Humanlike, not very intelligent and moves impulsively. No special powers recorded. Easy to kill.

I read through every single monster I'd faced, all the way up to the dragon.

The Dragon

Strong, fast, and smart. Can think almost like a human. Flies, and usually can breathe fire or spit acid. Their scales act as armor, so the only way to defeat them is a blast down their throat. Soaking them with water will temporarily disable their magic.

I flipped the page, and discovered tier two on the next page. I must be done. So, that means... there are different levels in tiers of monsters. A dragon was level ten, tier one. I wondered if every type of monster was hidden in these pages.

"Guys, is it okay if I flip to the end really quickly? I finished the tier." I looked up, and saw J and H still buried in their books.

"Probably. We're not done yet, so go ahead," J muttered, distracted. H simply nodded in agreement. I looked down, slowly flipping through tiers before coming to the very last page.

The Cloud of Chaos

The very culmination of evil and darkness, the Cloud is a monster that should not be engaged. Its body is made up of mostly water, so attacks phase right through it. It can solidify so the entirety of it acts as armor, or it can disperse within seconds. The wind it conjures is so strong, it can pull trees right out of the ground. It has no observed weaknesses, and it's very resilient.

Do not engage, avoid at all costs. This rare creature spawns every ten years to wreak havoc it believes is justified.

Well, I guess I didn't quite have a choice on engaging or not. Now my friend was really hurt, and this thing just left for another ten years. I noticed how the book changed as it got older. The first few pages were crudely written, yellowed over time, and wrinkled. The last few ones were new, flat and white, and eloquently written, with much more detail. The handwriting switched from print to cursive multiple times. This had obviously been recorded over generations. J slammed his book closed, and I jumped. "Done! He exclaimed. H laughed, and nodded.

"Me too. Should we take the test now?" He looked up at me curiously. I nodded, my mind still clouded over and my thoughts distracted.

"We can, if you guys want to," I squeaked. They smiled politely and J re-opened his book.

"Question one. What monster breathes fire?"

"A dragon." I replied, wondering if the questions would get

more difficult as this went on, or if it would stay like this.

"Question two. What monster is considered the weakest?"

"The... Respin? Raspin? I think it's Raspin."

"Three, what monsters can be defeated with water?"

"The Dragon and the... Mongrer?" I said, stumbling on the name. The Mongrer was a snake-like animal, quite like a Dragon but smaller, and didn't have any wings. Its feet were tiny and its claws were poisonous barbs. It kills by wrapping around the victim's neck and suffocating them while slowly poisoning them. This went on until question fifty. I assumed we were getting all of this correct. We all took turns answering, and I felt like I learned a lot. I went back and studied the small drawings of all the monsters that were included in the book.

The images varied from crudely-drawn to extremely realistic and beautifully detailed. This had been really fun so far, a lot more enjoyable than most studying had ever been for me. I continued dragging my finger across the page, tracing the words. The hypnotic motion, back and forth, made my sight blurry and my eyes droop. Suddenly, my head felt heavy, slamming against the table. That simple motion seemed to completely knocking me out, the world going black around me. Or, so I thought. I never really slept. My eyes stayed open, but what I saw completely flipped. I was in a wide, flat plain. The sky was blue and cloudless. But not... wordless? Small scribbles of ink floated around above my head. J and H materialized next to me.

"What is going on?" I asked, spinning around, trying to see across the flatlands, but it stretched far beyond the horizon. The grass waved below me, swayed by a gentle breeze. Two words appeared in the sky, bold and bigger than all of us. It was so in my face, I could barely read it, but I somehow managed. It said *Tier Two*.

CHAPTER FOUR

I looked at the two boys in alarm. They had the same expression.

"Does that mean…?" J's question was answered in a second as a malformed zombie came waltzing in. It wasn't like the normal zombie. Its face was stitched together, gruesome blood and brains spilling out of its crudely sewn-together head. It looked like it was made of different people's faces. Its clothes were covered in blood and it was much faster than the regular zombie. Words appeared over its head.

Tier Two Zombie

Fast and intelligent. Usually carries a sword. Hunts alone at night. After it kills its victims, it takes a part of their body and sews it on. Most commonly, their face.

Reading that, I almost threw up. That was the most revolting thing I'd ever read, and the thing in front of me didn't help, the grotesque creature making me feel queasy. But I forced myself to focus on defeating it.

"Do we have any weapons?" I yelled to J and H. As soon as I did, a sword appeared in front of me. It was made of smooth steel, not a single scrape. I grabbed it out of the air and poised to fight, my heart starting to beat faster. H grabbed a bow and some arrows, and J got a whip. They looked at each other and quickly switched weapons. I smirked in amusement before turning back to the zombie. While I was distracted, it decided to attempt to strike. It rushed at me, and I barely had time to deflect a claw aimed right at my face. I swung upwards and sliced its hand off from the wrist, and the severed hand flew backwards, hitting H in the face. I would have laughed if it wasn't so repulsive.

Blood slowly trickled out of the wound, and I backed up, sword at the ready. The zombie didn't seem affected by the missing hand that had flown across the landscape (and hit my friend in the face) and kept on moving. I backed up, sliding up right next to the two guys, and dove behind them just as they attacked, H using his whip to hold back the zombie and J quickly drawing his bow, shooting at the thing with incredible speed. It was almost like the arrows floated out of the quiver and into his hand. Soon, it looked like nothing more than a pincushion. I ran forward, jumping as high as I could before coming down hard on the zombie's head. It exploded into dust that slowly settled to the ground. I turned around and held up my hand, high-fiving both of them.

"That worked surprisingly well for our first time fighting together," I laughed, a little proud of myself and them. It felt good to accomplish something like that.

"It looks like it isn't over yet, though." H pointed behind me. A swarm of what looked like angry bees was flying towards us at full speed. I couldn't even read the words above their head, they were going so fast.

"How do we defend ourselves against *that*?" I exclaimed, ducking and weaving to avoid the vicious stings of these strange creatures.

"My bow won't work against them!" J cried out, being struck multiple times before he ran to the side, flailing his bow in the air, the wood smacking down some of the little bugs.

"I'm not exactly sure how a whip will either!" H wildly flung around his weapon, knocking a few out of the air every time he swung. I picked up my sword, angling the flat of the blade to where I could swipe down, and hopefully hit a few. Like a giant, less-effective fly swatter. Somehow, a large chunk of... bees were taken out. I noticed they stuck together, a bit loosely but they would fly in a certain formation, close enough to be able to strike them.

"Guys!" I yelled, swinging my sword sideways, taking out another group. "The bow and whip won't do much. Get somewhere safe, I'll handle this!"

"Are you sure?" H yelped, swatting at the bees.

"Yeah, I'll be fine!" I said, not even believing my own words. I had an idea, but I wasn't certain it was safe.

I spun in a circle, knocking a few more onto the ground. The floor around me was covered in dead bees. H and J made a run for it, and I started screaming, trying to get the monsters to focus on me. The loud noise worked, and they all charged. I sliced through one attack, but then dropped my sword, my arms shaking with the idea of doing something like this. I raised my hands as the creatures turned around, heading back for me. I had no clue how to work with magic, and I only had inspiration from the books and movies from my world. A common theme seemed to be channeling your energy into power, but how would you even begin to do that?

I tried to imagine it like veins. A source of magic flowing through me, coursing below my skin, in my blood. I felt my palms start to warm up, but I wasn't sure if that was some sort of flame or just me being nervous. I tried to focus on the former, increasing the heat and letting it flow out. I felt an almost painful burst of heat where my heart was, and I almost fell over, being pushed back by the rough torrent of fire suddenly appearing in the air, coating the entire swarm of bees. The sizzling sound was a little disturbing, but I quickly overlooked that, panicked by the fact that the blaze wasn't stopping. I cried out, my arms encased in the red light, and it felt like I was overpowering myself. The warmth inside me kept growing, and I shrieked, my eyesight blurring as I desperately tried to cut off the power flow. I was so numb, I barely even felt myself fall to the ground.

I didn't know how much time had passed, but I eventually woke up, J and H hovering over me worriedly.

"You're awake!" H said with a smile, taking my arm and helping me up. We were back in the normal world, but I was for some reason lying on the floor. My head still hurt and I was a bit dizzy, but other than that, I felt fine.

"What happened?" I mumbled, almost afraid to speak.

"We're still not entirely sure. You practically turned into a living flame before you collapsed, but you demolished all of those things. Then we fought a dragon, with you still on the ground, and… appeared back here. What's with all the dragons anyway? There are, like… ten different kinds," H said, throwing his hands in the air exhaustedly. J smiled softly, putting his hand on H's shoulder.

"Really? That's weird… I'm glad I didn't get stomped on or something," I smiled in a feeble attempt to make a joke. The only reaction seemed like a pity laugh. "Anyway… H—"

"Harlequinn."

"What?" J looked surprised, as if he has just told me a secret no one could know about. I wasn't even aware that they had actual names, though. I thought the initials were all they had.

"My name's Harlequinn. After doing all of that for us, I think I can trust you with a name. You can call me Harley as well." He smiled nonchalantly, but J looked like he was going to explode.

"Why would—they—I don't—what? Why would you do that?"

"It's not that big of a deal," Harlequinn laughed. "Besides, I trust them now. They helped us, and almost risked their health for us. They don't seem to have much experience with magic, and almost died after making sure we were out of the way." He smiled and patted me on the shoulder. I nodded in recognition as J took a deep breath and crossed his arms.

"Alright. But don't go around asking people their 'real' names. It's private and really a trust thing, which needs to be earned," J said with a pointed look.

"Trust me, I know how that feels," I chuckled, wincing slightly. That comment hit a little too close to home. "Wait, how long were we in there?"

Just as I finished, the door flew open, and the General stood behind it.

"Oops! Didn't mean to slam it," he smiled kindly, hobbling in. The sun was still high in the sky. "How have you all been doing?"

"I think a bit better than we were supposed to. We kind of…

went into the book?" I didn't know exactly how to explain it, but he seemed to get it.

"Ah, I accidentally gave you those books. You all must have activated the Scape. It's a magical realm only accessible by books like these. It helps you learn about the monsters while also learning how to defeat them. In the Scape, it seems to take a toll on your body, but once you get back into reality, you'll be fine."

"That's really cool," I looked at the book, baffled by how amazing magic could be, making ordinary items absolutely extraordinary.

"Indeed. Well, now that you're not occupied—you might want to visit your friend," the General said with a sullen look, which immediately made me nervous. A scream echoed through camp just as he finished, and we all looked up, worried. I gently pushed past the General, my legs still feeling like they'd turned into jelly and then been left out all day, but I pushed forward to see what the problem was.

I ran, worry taking over my mind. I almost slammed the door to the infirmary open, which warranted a harsh look from B, who was standing right next to Damien, her hand on his back. He was sitting up, his eyes wild, like he'd been attacked.

"Are you alright?" I asked, stepping forward. Damien looked up, his movements stiff.

"I—yeah." His voice was hoarse, and it seemed painful for him to talk, but him sitting up and talking must've meant he was getting better.

"What happened?" I whispered.

"Nightmares," B replied. "They're... a lot worse when you've been hurt or your body is damaged. Sometimes, more realistic. And if you get hurt, sometimes you can actually feel pain."

"What?" I exclaimed, shocked by how horrible that sounded. In the real world, I had constant nightmares, so I wondered what that would do to me here. "That's awful!"

"Agreed, but we can't find anything to stop it. And for some people, it can be predictions."

"Do you think his were predictions?"

"I'm right here you know," Damien croaked, his voice rough.

"Sorry, I didn't wanna make you talk," I laughed nervously, and sat down next to him on the hospital bed. "Do you think it was?" He shook his head, staring at the floor.

"I think we should let him rest. He still has to heal, and probably eat. You should go finish training," B suggested, looking at the door. I glanced back to Damien, who smiled kindly, and I nodded.

"Get well soon," I whispered, jumping back to my feet. I walked out, quietly closing the door behind me.

"How is he?" Harlequinn asked, jogging up to the infirmary.

"It seems like he's better, but B said he was having nightmares," I said, looking back at the wall. "I didn't get to see him for long."

"Poor guy," J said quietly, looking worried. "I get nightmares whenever I'm sick, and they are not great to deal with."

"With B watching over him, they'll be gone in no time. We should leave him to heal." Harlequinn advised, turning his head as the light sound of shoes padding against the soft grass approached us. The General had apparently tagged along, an ever-present grin on his face.

"Oh, you all need to cheer up! Trust me when I say, Damien has gone through worse," he said ominously, but jumped right back on track before anyone could ask questions. "Let me help you take your mind off of this. I have a mission for you three!"

"A mission?" I asked, puzzled.

"Yes. You three get to go on a special, low level mission, as a part of your training. We've gotten word that a village, a few miles south, has been attacked. You are not to use magic. It could put the villagers in danger, and I got a little rundown of what happened in the Scape. Amber, I don't want you hurting yourself, so please don't meddle with those types of forces before we cover it in training," the General patted my arm, and I felt my face flush in embarrassment. "And not to mention, you need to learn to survive without it," he said with a pointed look at J.

"What? Magic is fun!" He pointed to the ground, right at a leaf, and it started to gently float, climbing up and resting in the palm of J's hand.

"So, that's your power! And probably why you use a bow..." I nodded, realizing that fit very well with his weapon of choice.

"Yeah, I was going to tell you that earlier, but we didn't have time. So, anyway, the mission? Do we leave now?" J said, turning back to the General.

"Yes, before it gets dark, you should leave. The sun is acting strange, but you should have some time before it sets. And since it's a long journey, you can take a hellhound."

"We're supposed to ride one of those things?" I squeaked. If the ones Damien showed me were just babies, I couldn't imagine how big the full grown ones would be...

"They're very gentle, unless you're an enemy. Then they would rip your head off. But you're the General-To-Be! You'll be fine!" Harlequinn joked, placing a hand on my shoulder and smiling. I knew he meant well, and that he was trying to encourage me, but that just made me even more worried. What if they didn't know I was one of them? What if they mistook me for an enemy? I knew, deep down, it would be okay, but that didn't stop my brain from thinking up every single way I could die in this situation.

The two boys jogged off, obviously very excited to ride a hellhound again. I was extremely anxious, but I couldn't blame them. In any other circumstance, I would probably wish to be in this situation right now. On the other side of the castle, opposite of the young hellhounds' stable, was a much taller stable, obviously for the older ones. I walked in, and looked up, giant black dog heads looming over me, their big heads hovering about ten feet in the air. My eyes widened and I almost screamed as a reflex. These dogs were much bigger, stronger, more regal, and they didn't have as much energy. They stood still, unlike the younger ones who bounced around at every chance. These gentle, beautiful beasts were somehow much less threatening, but equally as terrifying at the same time. They held their heads high, proud creatures that were determined to prove how amazing they could be. My worry dissipated slightly at the sight of their calm nature. Harlequinn walked forward, towards the first stall. He had to reach up to unlatch the metal lock, struggling for a moment before it popped open. The giant dog took a small step, as to not shake the building or the world around it.

"Get the ladder, please," Harlequinn said to J.

"You need a ladder to get on these?" I exclaimed. "What about in the middle of battle?" Harlequinn perked up at that, a sly smile spreading across his face.

"I'll show you," he grabbed the... leash? Reigns? Whatever that was wrapped around the hellhound's face and neck, and started jogging towards the exit of camp. Any passerby quickly jumped out of the way, as J and I tailed behind Harlequinn, my jaw hanging open at the magnificence of this amazing, yet painfully simple moment. J, however, was completely unamused, his hands in his pockets, a bored expression on his face as we sprinted to catch up. At least it was a nice day, with a slight breeze, and I was always up for a run. We passed through the gates, Harlequinn jumping as much as an excited baby hellhound as we walked further into the woods.

"Okay, here!" He stopped the dog, tossing the reigns to J, and ran backwards a few feet. He planted himself, his stance wide, boots digging into the dirt. He whistled, and the hellhound jumped to attention, staring at Harlequinn. He then ran forward, jumped into the air, twisted, and started to fall. The dog caught his shirt, and swung him upwards, high enough to land softly on the back of the hound. I heard a distant whoop of excitement from above, and laughed.

"Now... how do you get down?" I yelled up. Even from that distance, I could see Harlequinn blanche, and J burst into laughter.

"We... uh, we usually do that once we get back to the stables... I guess I'm riding the hound!" He reached around the dog's thick neck and grabbed the edge of the reigns, pulling them up so he could take control.

"Can't we all ride?" I asked J. Surely a dog as big as that would be able to take more than one person.

"Oh, yeah. Fully grown, these hounds can take an entire army, including heavy armor and weapons, and still run like the wind. He just likes to show off. That's the fancy, almost... dressage way to get up, but in real battle, this is how we do it." J ran, no whistle, no planting. He just ran and jumped, grabbing onto the dogs fur, climbing up until he was able to flip himself backwards onto its back.

"I can't do that!" I crossed my arms, a bit upset I probably wouldn't be riding this.

"J said I'm just a showoff, but that's the expert way of getting up. The easy way, well... anyone can do it!" Harlequinn clicked his tongue, and the dogs ears went back as it basically collapsed, its legs falling in, and it sprawled down on the ground. I climbed up on the exposed paw, gently as to not hurt it, and I jumped, grabbing its fur right before the center of its back and hauling myself up. Even lying down, it was really high up. But then, it started to move. The wind rushed by as we rose even further into the air, the tops of the trees almost within reach. They weren't the tallest trees, but tall enough to be scarily high. The sudden acceleration made me feel sick.

"You okay?" J asked, obviously holding back laughter.

"Yeah, but I think I left my stomach down there," I covered my mouth, letting myself settle down for a moment. "Okay, I'm good. Now, where's the other camp?"

"A few miles south he said, right? We'll start that way."
Harlequinn gently flicked the reigns, and the dog started slowly
to the south.

"Didn't J say this thing could run like the wind?" I questioned.
We were going pretty slowly.

"I mean, we could, so if you want to destroy the camp and
everything around it with massive earthquakes, we can go top
speed," Harlequinn smirked.

"On second thought... I'm good," I croaked, blushing. This
entire experience was breathtakingly wonderful, so I didn't mind
going slow. I could feel the muscles underneath the dog's back,
slowly rumbling across the earth. I was so high up, I could see
the village. It seemed to be in ruins, houses collapsed in on
themselves, vines growing out of all the structures. I couldn't
quite tell, but from here... they didn't look like cabins. They
looked like modern houses. Wires spiked out from a few,
sparking every now and then.

"Wait, why does your camp look so different from this? I
thought you guys didn't really have access to electricity or
anything like that?" I asked, shouting up to J and Harlequinn.

"We don't. We barely managed to scrape together enough
supplies to work the Waffle House. That's why it's the only
'modern' building in the camp." Harlequinn's voice sounded
bitter.

"Why... why not?" I was almost scared to ask. He seemed so
upset so suddenly.

"The other people around us keep it from us. They do
whatever they can to make sure we don't get what we need.
They're obsessed with power, so they take away our basic rights.
It took the original founders years to even get one building up.
They sabotage our camp, steal our supplies, and make
everything a struggle. Magic here is illegal, but for only one
reason. To target people like us," J responded. His voice
quivered. These poor kids were forced to endure all of that just
because of their powers...? Or was it another, underlying

reason?

"So, no one else has powers outside the camp?"

"If they do, they hide it. They don't have a choice. They either suppress it or join us and struggle through even getting shelter. What would you pick?" he asked, a pointed look at me.

"Suppressing it, probably. But why did this all start? It can't just be your powers, right?"

"What else would there be?" Both Harlequinn and J looked back at me, confusion blatant on their faces.

"You guys really are separated from everything else. There has to be something else, one thing… most of you have in common," I mumbled. They turned to look at each other, then back at me. "You don't get it?"

"No, can't say we do."

"I'm going to sound terrible, but… something that you have in common that separates you from them. Skin color."

"You—you think that's the reason?" Harlequinn almost dropped the reigns.

"Think about it. If you're all diverse and they're not... that leaves a path open to oppress and separate you with that. Maybe we shouldn't help these people..." I looked down to the village, angry at the thought.

"Harlequinn… Think about it. Black magic," J whispered, leaning his head on Harlequinn's shoulder.

"No matter their opinions, we have to save them. We can't let them die because of how they think," he protested, shaking his head.

"They're letting you guys die!" I said, exasperatedly. I didn't want to fight, but this… it seemed too despicable to be true, but looking at my own world, I feared it wasn't much different here.

"We're not like them. We have to show them that we're better than them, that we don't deserve what they're doing to us. We have to prove a point." We sat in silence the rest of the way. What everyone else was doing to them—it was horrible. But these people still wanted to help. I knew then I wanted to stay with them. These people were caring and didn't ever put themselves first. Honestly, I could learn a thing or two.

The hound stopped, and we all slid off. Looking around, it seemed as if this place had been abandoned long ago. I picked up a fallen bamboo staff on the ground, brandishing it like a sword. If I couldn't use magic, at least I'd have something to protect me. We slowly walked through the camp, examining houses and looking for any sign of life.

"These look like they haven't been used in years," Harlequinn muttered, examining a wire in his hand. "I don't know much about electricity, but these are covered in dirt and rust. No way would these work."

"So, why were we sent here?" J spun slowly, eyeing the surrounding area.

"I'm not sure. The General wouldn't make us go on a wild goose chase. Would he?"

"Maybe it's another one of his pranks."

"He hasn't done anything like this in years!"

"Wait, the General pulls pranks?" I questioned, giggling at the thought.

"Oh yeah, he's a master. One time, he made J think he was invisible. And once, Damien thought he'd let out ALL of the hellhounds. He uses illusions and well timed special effects to create amazing tricks." Harlequinn's eyes lit up just talking about it.

"You know... I don't think that's an illusion," J said, and we turned to see a shadow monster looming over us. It had curled horns, beady red eyes, and a dark body. It snarled, revealing razor-sharp teeth. Its hands were clawed, and it seemed to have goat legs.

"A... Satyr?" I suggested, confused as to what we were even fighting.

"I think it's corrupted," J whispered, barely moving. "Stand still. I'm pretty sure they have bad eyesight."

That, however, was wrong. Enraged by... J's statement,

probably, it roared and reached out to grab us. I shoved my bamboo stick into its hand, pushing hard enough to draw blood, but I was pushed back by its strength. It whined, stumbling backwards, hooves clicking on the rock. I felt the earth move, and the hellhound bounded in front of us, growling and biting.

"Down, boy! Down!" Harlequinn called, grabbing the reins.

"Don't we want his help?" I yelled over all the noise.

"No! He'll destroy this camp and hurt himself in the process!"

"Oh!" I dodged another swipe, jumping backwards, and skidding across the dirt ground. "I know we're not supposed to use magic but... J!" I tossed my bamboo stick up in the air. J seemed to understand what I was doing, thankfully. He closed his eyes and the stick hovered for a moment before shooting forward and impaling the monster where its heart should have been. It roared, and the hellhound bounded away while it was distracted. The bamboo shattered and fell to the ground, bits of it still stuck inside the creature.

"Guys!" Harlequinn sighed exasperatedly.

"Sorry?" I heard gunfire, and suddenly my body stiffened. Pain spread through me, and I knew I was badly hurt. I couldn't quite pinpoint where the pain started from, but I knew it was there. It seemed to happen in slow motion. I fell, hitting the ground hard. All I could do was lie there, motionless. I heard someone call my name, the shout echoing through my head. I tried to open my eyes, and I saw Harlequinn, standing over me, screaming, his expression pained and desperate.

"J!" I heard him shout. "Walls!" From the rubble and debris surrounding us, J pulled broken logs and trees from the ground to form a little fort around us. Harlequinn pulled out a first aid kit, or what seemed like one, and put something on my side. I screeched, the pain almost unbearable. "Calm down, calm down. We gotta get this under control, stop the bleeding."

"What happened?" J yelled. A giant boom shook the earth as more gunshots were fired. The giant shadow creature had fallen.

"They were shot. But I have a feeling the people with the guns weren't going for Amber..." I could feel the shaking of Harlequinn's hands.

"We come to save them, and this is the welcome we get. Maybe Amber was right. They can obviously deal with this stuff on their own. And they don't seem to want visitors..."

"We had to try. I can't believe they have guns! How did they even manage to get their hands on those?"

"Focus on getting the bullet out! You're going to make them bleed more!"

Wait, I was bleeding? The pain had slowly been dissolving. I heard more gunshots, and something pinged against the walls.

"I don't think we have enough time or cover. We need to get them back." Harlequinn took my arm, speaking softly now, a determined look in his eyes. He looked up, letting out a loud, piercing whistle. The dog bounded towards us, tearing down the walls and grabbing all of us gently in his mouth. He flung us into the air, catching us all on his back. The dog whimpered, bullets peppering his backside.

"We can't go this slow if we wanna get out of here alive. Full speed bud!"

"Maybe just half!" Jay screamed in panic.

"Ugh, fine, half!" Harlequinn whooped as the dog sped up, creating mild tremors in the village below, causing everyone to drop their guns and stare in awe as the giant hound leapt over the landscape. J muttered curses as he held onto Harlequinn's waist. Woozy with pain, I tightly clutched the dog's thick fur. I kept slipping, almost falling unconscious. I could barely keep my eyes open long enough to slide down the dog's side, then pass out on the ground.

CHAPTER FIVE

I woke up, facing the low light of the infirmary, unsure of how much time had passed. The dim lanterns made the room glow with a dusty gold. I sat up groggily, noticing the stiff bandages covering my side. The white was slightly soaked with blood, but I was able to get up without any pain. I brushed away the soft brown blanket draped over my legs and tried to stand. Just as I was regaining my balance, B walked in.

"Amber! Are you feeling any better?" She said with a soft smile, stepping forward and basically patting me down, assessing my injuries.

"Yeah, I am. What... what happened? Why did they attack us back there? We came to help." I held my head in my hands, still confused as to why they would try to hurt us and not the monster rampaging around. B sighed, turning around and sitting down on the bed, patting the side in a gesture for me to sit with her.

"Please, sit. We don't want to risk making your condition worse. I'll tell you what I know, but... it's not much."

"I'll take anything I can get at this point. No one has really given me much information so far." I sighed, gingerly lowering myself back onto the bed.

"That's because they don't know enough to be able to tell you. To be honest, I doubt even I do. But I was a part of the outside world once, which is a privilege that not many people in this camp can say they had, but that means I can provide something that others might not be able to."

"You didn't start out in the camp?"

"Well, no, but almost everyone else did. If you look around, you'd see that most of them are still kids, born in the middle of the war. This has been the only safe place for a while, and I ended up having to come here when everything started going south. I tried to help people there, but my talents were reduced to… being just a medic." She got a sad, longing look in her eyes.

"Are you saying you didn't want to be a doctor?"

"Well... I always wanted to be in the army. I was devoted and loyal, but out there... the military denied my application because of my family. The stigma against magic had just started gaining popularity, thanks to the King, and I had no clue until I was attacked for being an elf. I had to seek shelter here after they told me I could serve the King's health or leave, and I still had to be a doctor because of my powers. They didn't force it on me, but they needed me. People died every day before I arrived. Now, it's rare that even one sees their end. It's not what I wanted to do, but... I'm beyond happy to help save people."

"That's horrible... so, it's not just humans affected?"

"No, anyone with magic is a target. They take our opportunities away; force us into little boxes we don't fit in at all. They make it to where we have to resume the positions we would have had in the Outside. They keep us captive, never letting us fall out of line even when we're beyond their reaches."

"It seems like the real world is really similar to this place..." I crossed my arms, staring at the tiled floor. "People are born with expectations. Wear this, wear that, play with this, play with that, be like this, be like that. It's always two boxes, black and white. Anyone who dares venture outside is ridiculed. There aren't many people who can live in peace. These boxes are forced onto us literally the second we're born, sometimes before. I thought this place was more of a utopia at first. You guys have family, friends, and magic. But our worlds... aren't so different."

"I think I've heard of the place you come from before. It was portrayed in a better light as well. We were taught that everything had its place, and no one fell out of it. But I guess the people that did... were forgotten. Shunned and erased. Their history and their fight... useless." I glanced to the side, looking at B closer than I had before. Tears fell down her rosy cheeks, her gaze falling, now holding her own hand like she was trying to comfort herself. Her blonde hair delicately curved in slight waves, her ears just barely poking out from underneath. She looked young, probably around eighteen. She was like a doll, if they could cry.

"So I guess we were all fooled."

"I guess so... but anyway. You're looking better; the bullet wound is healing well." She stood up, plastering a cheerful smile on her face once again. "Damien left before you arrived, he's doing much better. He should be waiting outside for you."

"Really?" I practically fell off of the bed. "Thank you so much. I really appreciate it." We nodded at each other, and I could still see the lasting sadness in her gaze. I felt strangely protective of her, even though I could barely protect myself.

Despite the events, I left with a smile, closing the door gently behind me and looking around for Damien. I saw him at the wall to my left, leaning backwards, unsteadily balancing on crutches.

"Damien!"

"Hey, Amber! I'm glad you're okay; the guys told me what happened."

"I'm glad you're alright, too. Coming back from something like that... that's amazing, dude!" We both chuckled, glad to finally be able to talk again. "I would hug you, but I think that would be painful for both of us."

"Yeah," he chuckled, smiling to the sky. His eyes lit up with life once again, no longer glazed over, but a brilliant, crystal green. "I'm sorry about what happened out there. I probably should have told you about the outside, and what those people do to us. It's awf—" he trailed off, the smiling quickly fading off his face. A deep rumbling sound filled the sky, a dark shadow falling across the buildings. I looked up, seeing what seemed to be the hull of a giant ship floating in the sky, right towards us.

Screams arose from around camp.

"Get to cover!" I heard someone shout. The ground rumbled, almost throwing me off of my feet. Damien clumsily grabbed my arm, trying to drag me while holding onto the crutches. I rushed forward and grabbed one of the sticks when it fell away from him, shoving it under his arm and continuing to run. Damien pushed me through the door of a nearby cabin, even though that seemed like it definitely wouldn't protect us. A few other people hid inside, crouched against the bed in the corner, hiding in the closet. Everyone was bracing themselves, obviously waiting for doom and destruction to rain down from the sky.

"What's going on?" I whispered, almost afraid to speak. A loud sound echoed across the camp as, once again, a tremor passed through, shaking the ground. Any loose objects in the cabin rattled, falling to the ground with a crash. Damien looked up and cursed.

"A sky ship. Not again! Everyone, get out of the open!" he yelled into the camp, shouting through a window.

"What's a sky ship?" I yelled above the noise.

"Magic ships that float on air. The military sends them to sabotage and bomb our camp," he scowled into the sky.

"I thought magic was illegal?"

"You know how humans work. They can get past what's legal and what's not as long as you work in the right place."

"So, that's the same here too?" I winced, wishing our worlds weren't so similar.

"Yup. I guess humans never change, even in different dimensions." I backed away, further from the door as another shadow passed over the camp, covering the sun and eliminating the light filtering through the cabin. There was a whoosh of air, then an explosion, a loud boom that seemed to surround us. Smoke and dust clouded the windows as three people rushed to close up every opening in the house, and small bits of shrapnel and debris were flung at the walls, clinking against the wood.

"Why would anyone think of doing this? Especially with how much you help people..." I looked out into the camp, squinting. I could just barely see the others through the smoke, but I could make out figures crouching under buildings. It seemed everyone was safe. Another blast of air, and I backed up just before an explosion rocked the camp. "Something has to be done about this," I snarled. My mind was clouded with anger, the unjust notion of it all infuriating me. Acting without thinking, I rushed out, pushing through the door and the screen of smoke that hit my face as soon as I exited.

Above me, gliding slowly through the air, was a wooden ship, and all I could see was the bottom of it. Two faces peeked out behind the boards, giddy smiles on their faces. They pushed a small black bomb off the deck of the ship, right towards me. Fear and rage working together to guide my every move, I closed my eyes and held my hand to the sky. I basically left my body on autopilot, despite knowing what had happened before. I raised my palm, warmth flooded through me, and a blast of blue fire snaked through the sky, shattering the bomb in midair, and burning a hole right through the deck of the ship.

I guess it didn't matter that I didn't know what I was doing. From where I was, I could feel a blistering heat, my face burning even as I looked down, my hands tensing up and aching, the blaze hovering just above my arm. The destruction was unrelenting, fire slowly spreading through the sky, breaking the entire ship in half. It fell, riding on the breeze, gently tipping over and careening off to the side.

I looked up in awe at the damage I had created, but my head was suddenly aching. I felt dizzy, and drained. My throat was dry and my limbs were weak. This terrible sensation took over in an instant, and I crumpled, falling to the floor.

"Amber!" My eyes fluttered open to see Damien standing over me. The campers were racing to collect the people from the ship that had dived onto the ground before they went up in flames, making sure they were okay and tying them up. "Amber, are you alright?" I nodded, holding my head, then tried to sit up.

"What... ugh—what was that?" I could barely even talk. My voice was scratchy and my throat felt like it was on fire. "Why am I—"

"That amount of magic you expelled seems to have taken a toll on you. Without proper control or weapons, that can happen. Blue flames... that's even hotter than red, right? So it must have used up too much of your mana too fast. That was incredible though... you're lucky to be alive, especially if you've never wielded magic before. It's difficult to take sky ships down, because of protection spells. You either broke through them, or they didn't have time to put them up. You really did us a favor," he held out his hand, a faint smile on his face. He pulled me up, and looked over to the invaders.

"Mana? What—what is that?" I groaned.

"The magic energy that helps all of us use our powers. It's nearly unlimited when you use it in controlled bursts. Expelling too much at once drains it really quickly, though." Suddenly, his smile dropped. "They—they're all kids." I glanced behind my shoulder and sure enough, they looked to be around our age. The guilt on their face was blatant, replacing those childish smiles with pain.

"Who would recruit children to do that?" I said in shock, my own expression dropping. "Can… Can I go talk to them?"

"What?" He looked at me, confused. "What are you planning?"

"I'm... not entirely sure. But I think it's worth a shot, right? I might be able to get something from them, something you guys wouldn't think of asking. Also, I'm very intimidating," I looked towards him with a straight face, which quickly dissolved into laughter from both of us.

"You'll have to ask the General, but since you're a new face they'll probably be nicer to you. We're all on the 'wanted' list- you just got here, so you won't be considered a threat yet," he chuckled to himself. "Once they do find you though, you'll probably be on the top. With your elemental powers..." he turned to look at me, a smile on his face that quickly turned into a frown as he saw my wide-eyed, terrified look. "I mean, they probably—I don't think—General!" He started speed-walking towards the old man, talking with two people I hadn't seen before. They wore cloaks even inside the camp, and they were very tall. I could barely see their faces, but they had their arms crossed and symbols floating above their heads. Weird, squiggly lines I didn't recognize. They looked up to see us approach, their eyes glowing red. I stopped in my tracks, frozen with fear. Their horrifying gaze seemed to stare right into me. "General! Can Amber talk to the kids that were on the ship?"

I sauntered over, my arms crossed, smirking. "He thinks it's a good idea because I'm not on their watch list yet," I said, directing a pointed glance at Damien.

"I mean... that's a good thing! Right?" He helplessly looked towards the General for assistance.

"It is actually helpful. They don't know you, so they'll be less violent."

"That's what I said!"

"Well then, I give you permission. Zander, Diego, escort Amber to the prisoners." My eyes widened, looking up at the guards, their faces veiled in darkness. They nodded in unison, and turned, walking to the castle. Damien and I followed warily behind.

"These guys are from the Council. The General only calls them in for emergencies. The sky ships usually don't get much attention, since they're so common, but I guess you really made a mark when you took it down," he whispered to me. I smiled, a little honored. The guards opened the door for us, and we went inside to the library we were in before, but instead of picking up a book, they went up one of the spiral staircases on the side. The hallway was a bit cramped, but at the top was a metal door. The guards opened it, and then stepped aside. I went in, examining the large room.

Three lanterns hung from the ceiling, lighting the entire place in a slightly ominous dim glow. A kid, who looked a little bit older than me, sat in a chair, his hands tied behind him with rope. Another rope was wrapped around his waist. An oak table sat in front of him, with a chair at the opposite side as well. His head hung over the table, red hair falling over his eyes. He had loose, baggy clothing that was torn. I hoped we didn't have a part in ruining his outfit. I sat down quietly, his head still hanging. I didn't exactly have much experience interrogating people, or doing whatever it was that I was doing. I wasn't sure if I should speak or let him do his own thing. Hoping that the very few crime shows I'd watched would guide me, but still going against what was probably my better judgment, I decided to speak.

"Hey," I said, placing my folded hands on the table. He just barely looked up, glaring at me from behind the curtain of bangs. Then his eyes widened, and he sat up.

"Who are you?" he asked, seeming genuinely confused.

"That's not important. What's important is... what happened."I stumbled, wishing I could have been briefed or something before I went in. But maybe it was a better idea to just talk to him like he was another human.

"What about it?" he retorted, seeming to stutter on his own wording.

"I guess I'm having trouble understanding your motive. Maybe if you explained, we could clear things up." I spread my hands out in what I hoped was a sort of retreating gesture.

"I don't want to clear anything up, I want to leave. You're no better than the Kingdom if you lock me up like this!" he hissed, struggling against the rope.

"What are you talking about? You know the Kingdom is bad?" I still wasn't entirely sure what the Kingdom actually was, but I could connect the dots.

"Who doesn't? Are you really so dense that you can't see how unhappy everyone is? You're in a secluded little paradise, away

76

from the demon that controls us. You're spoiled!" I was taken aback by that comment. Even after bombing us, this kid thought that we were living our best lives?

"I don't know what you're on about, but we just need to figure out—"

"Why do you care? What are you doing with these people? You weren't here before, it shouldn't matter to you!" he seethed, struggling against the rope tying him to the chair. "You're not like them, these... these barbarians. So why are you here? What did they do to you?"

"Calm down, they didn't do anything to me. These people are much kinder than most of the people from where I come from," I muttered, rolling my eyes at the ceiling. "How am I different from them? We're all human. We all have powers. We all keep to ourselves and don't bomb people," I glared at him, a pointed look which he withered under, shame in his eyes.

"We didn't want to do this," he whispered, his gaze turned to the table between us. "But we have a job. They told us that we have to keep you in fear or else you'll take over. You're supposed to be bloodthirsty monsters who have it all but want more," he grumbled, and I shook my head in confusion.

"Who are 'they'?"

"The military! The royal family! The people who always tell us what to do!" He started to choke up, obviously upset. "No matter what we want, if they don't like it, our opinion doesn't matter. They rule with an iron fist. Obey them... or die."

"They punish you with death?" I gasped, absolutely amazed to hear how awful the outside really was.

"You're lucky if they do. Sometimes, it's worse. Absolute torture. But I—that doesn't matter! You guys are the ones forcing us into this!" Now he was turning red. I took a deep breath, and sat back in the chair.

"First things first, I need to know your name. Then I'll explain more."

"Why would I want to tell you my name?" He scoffed.

"I'll tell you mine," I offered, smiling. He turned his head to look at me, obviously intrigued.

"I—I shouldn't do that," his eyes once again turned to the table. Luckily, I had a plan.

"Fine then, I'm just gonna have to call you Bob. Or Robert. Or David. I could go on." I flicked my hair behind my shoulder, waiting for his reaction. Somehow, he stayed completely straight-faced. "Fine, Bob. Let me tell you something. The people here never wanted war. They just wanted supplies to keep themselves alive. They wanted to be able to provide for themselves, build their own shelters, and farm their own food. But for whatever reason, the military didn't like that. They've been sending people to sabotage and steal these people's plans, food, and buildings. In fact, we've been trying to help. Not long ago, I was sent on a mission with my friends to defend one of your villages. We defeated a monster, protected and saved the people, but were met with violence. I got shot, and so did our hellhound. We saved them and they tried to kill us." As I was talking, I could see his interest peaking, getting more and more involved in the story.

"That—that can't be true. We were told that the hellhound attacked the village. There was no other monster," he protested.

"Oh come on, David, who is telling you this? They're feeding you lies. Have any of you ever for a *second* considered that possibility?" I slammed my fist onto the table, making him jump. He leaned back against his chair, and sighed.

"It doesn't matter if we did or not. If we say anything, we're threatened. They can hurt us. They can take our families away and—ugh! I shouldn't even be saying this!" He closed his eyes. "They didn't want to send me because they knew I wouldn't hold up if we were caught. They knew I would do this." He attempted to blink back tears.

"You're a kid. They can't expect that much from you." I stood up, pacing around the empty room. "It's a lot better here. No one is forced into anything. No one is hurt unnecessarily. People are fair and kind. Why don't you stay with us?" I turned to face him, and I could see how surprised he was at the offer.

"Why would you want me here? I helped bomb you guys!"

"It's called a second chance. I guess where you're from, you've never heard of that. But I'm sure we'd be willing to help you. All we need is some information from you." I walked behind his chair and untied the rope. "I think whatever options you have here are much better than going back to the military reporting a failed mission. Am I right?" I slid back into my chair, and he pushed his bangs back.

"I guess so... but now, aren't they gonna be more hostile towards me?"

"Not if we explain. Here, the people are actually forgiving," I chuckled.

"Must be nice..." he mumbled, still staring at the table. "I'm Alexander, by the way."

"Amber. Nice to meet you." I held out my hand, but he didn't notice. I awkwardly let my hand back down at my side.

"Listen... I'm sorry about what we did. We shouldn't have—it wasn't right. The people outside, in the Kingdom—they're cruel, and unforgiving. Everyone shares their beliefs because they have to. The reason I wanted to get on that ship was to get away. But I just caused more damage."

"Well, now you have a chance to make things right. Maybe you can even help me talk to the others?" I suggested, once again holding out my hand. He looked up, hope sparkling in his eyes, and took my hand, shaking it as he stood. He was a lot taller than me, I practically had to look up to look into his eyes, but he was lanky and thin. With how much he was slouching before, I never noticed.

"I'll try to help in any way I can. I—" the door burst open, Damien standing there with a bewildered look on his face.

"Amber! Hallway, please?" I nodded, letting go of Alexander's hand and walking down to the stairs. The door silently closed behind me.

"I don't doubt your decisions, but are you sure this is a good idea? He's from the Kingdom. He was on the ship that bombed us. I'm worried that he could be trying to trick us." Damien looked serious, his hand gripping my arm.

"We don't have to tell him any secrets or whatever. We can just keep them here until we know for a fact we can trust them. Besides, you really think they'd want to go back? Reporting a failed mission, where they got captured and held for weeks or months? They wouldn't be safe in the kingdom." I moved towards the door, but Damien pulled me back.

"Don't you think they could use their information to escape punishment? A failed mission is nothing if they used it to get what they need to know to attack us again. I want to trust them, but I think it's too risky. You have to learn to question everything. This could be our demise. We have to be careful with this," he clenched his jaw, obviously getting worked up.

"You're right. We have to be cautious. We'll make sure we can trust them before telling them anything. I have to talk to the others, though. How many more were on the ship?"

"Five, I think. Your friend in there was the first one to surrender. We're still having... problems, with two of them. They're stubborn and violent. They won't give in no matter what we do or threaten to do."

"You're threatening them?"

"Not—well, kinda. We aren't actually going to hurt them. But no one can—"

"Let me talk to them. I'll bring Alexander. They'll trust him." Damien sighed, letting go of my arm and stepping back. I nodded to him, and stepped back through the door. Alexander was sitting in his chair once again, but leapt up when he saw me.

"What—what did they say?"

"Apparently, they're having 'problems' with the others. You'll come with me to try to calm them down and get them settled so we can see what we'll do with them. Is that alright?" He nodded, the corners of his mouth slowly forming a smile.

"I can do that. Just show me where they are."

We stepped outside, the sun high in the sky, the warm rays a nice change from the chilly breeze inside the small castle. We immediately heard shouting, coming from the side of the castle, near the hellhound stables. Damien, Alexander and I all rushed over to see what was happening. A girl with long, blonde hair and piercing blue eyes growled in the grip of two people I had never met. She was screaming and even biting people. I ran in, trying to help hold her back as she spat and shrieked. Out of the corner of my eye, I saw Alexander steadily creeping forward.

"Alex? What are you doing?"

"Calm down! Stop fighting them, I'll explain everything but we have to get inside," Alexander said calmly, waving his hands like he was trying to settle down a horse. I was surprised at his cool attitude in the midst of all this chaos.

"You—I can't believe—AH!" She screamed again, and a blast of cold wind threw all of us backwards.

"No! Stop!" Alexander's skin seemed to bubble, a layer of pitch black growing over him, and he threw himself at the girl, wrestling her to the ground. Frost crawled over her skin, and her eyes turned completely white.

"Amber, stand back," Damien commanded, and I almost fell over myself trying to scramble away. "Lumae Shieldum!" A semi-transparent bubble encased the area where the two fought. Dark shadows wrapped around the girl as they both jumped around, trying to avoid the others attacks.

"I thought people in the kingdom didn't have magic?" I gasped, still in shock from the sudden explosion.

"Some do, but they're forced to hide it. I can't believe the chances that we got two of them..."

"Speaking of magic... how did you do that?" I said, standing up and brushing the dirt off of my clothes.

"The shield? You can do some magic with spells, as well as what powers you're born with. We haven't gotten to that yet, but it's dangerous to do without a tool to channel the energy, like a sword or an amulet. This was an emergency, so I had to make do." He turned at the sound of footsteps approaching. The General, eyes wide with shock, slowly hobbled over.

"What's going on?" he croaked, looking pale.

"The people on the sky ship turned out to have powers. Amber ended up talking to one of them, and got him on our side, but when we tried to approach the girl, she literally exploded. It looks like he has control over shadows and darkness, and she has ice powers," Damien reported. Another explosion shook the earth. The sides of the shield were coated in ice, stained black. We could barely see inside. The General sighed in disappointment, and nodded.

"Lower the shield," he commanded.

"What? Why?" Damien exclaimed, taken aback.

"Do it!" the General snapped, looking at Damien sternly. He clenched his jaw and nodded, pointing at the shield. Damien closed his eyes and it started glowing blue, shattering, sending ice and thick, goopy shadows crashing to the ground.

"Mutatio Animosa, mice!" the General yelled, and the two fighting stiffened, slowly shrinking, their noses, arms, and legs shortening, their skin overcome with fur, and long tails growing until the only thing left was two small mice, jumping around and still trying to bite each other. The General calmly walked over, grabbing them both by the tail. "That should hold them," he chuckled. "Everyone, back to your assignments. The situation has been handled. We'll keep these until further notice," the General declared.

"That's it?" I questioned, watching everyone disperse. "That's all?"

"Did you want a fight?" Damien laughed, turning towards me.

"I mean, that would have been cool," I joked, nudging his arm. "But I thought there would be more to that. Not just... suddenly, we're done."

"Like I said, the General moves on his own time. He likes to keep things going." Damien shrugged and started to wander off. I couldn't shake off the feeling of unease, though. Something about this unsettled me. But we had other things to do.

Later that day, while the sun was still high in the sky, we were all called to the stadium. Quiet swept across the gathered crowd as the General stepped into the middle of the arena.

"Something that has become very apparent in the past few days is our need for defense, both inside the camp and inside you all," the General announced, his voice carrying over the field. "Today, we will train you to use your magic as a defense. No matter what it is, there's some way you can defend yourself. We'll hone your skills with magic as well as teach you proper care and handling of your extraordinary powers." The crowd started whispering excitedly. The unease from before was still with me, but I tried to put it aside to focus on the task at hand.

Damien and three others entered the arena, standing beside the General. "Today we will focus on defense and fighting. Amber, J, H. You three have seemed to be in the midst of all of this chaos, so we'll train you first." I heard Harlequinn chuckle next to me as both of them got up from the stands, and headed towards the door. I quickly followed, a bit confused and worried about what would happen next. We stepped into the sand, examining the few others that were already in the arena, and then stood across from them. The two boys were next to me, each of us facing who I assumed were our opponents.

J was paired with Damien, Harlequinn, and I with the other two I didn't recognize. The General nodded, and a thought popped into my head. Why are these matches public? Wouldn't it be better to have them in private?

"First, you will take turns attacking each other and defending yourselves. Amber, J, H, you will defend first." The General quickly walked out of the arena. I turned to my opponent, a girl with curly red hair and dark green eyes. She was tall, but muscular. The look in her eyes was determination, a fire set on winning. I widened my stance, ready for an attack. She smirked, raising her hands. The sky above us turned black as clouds piled in, and it started to rain. Just a drizzle at first, a light, cool shower. So little that I could ignore it, but it slowly turned into a downpour. Drops of water pelted me, soaking my clothes. I tried hopping around, but the rain followed me. How do I defend myself in this case? I couldn't just use my hands. I had to fight fire with fire. Or, rain with fire.

My hands trembling, I focused, feeling that warmth once again flood my veins. My blood was fire. I was made of heat. I channeled my hope, my drive, my desire to win, and fire exploded on my palm. I held my hand to the sky, and the fire grew, creating a small shield around me. The air filled with a sizzling noise, and steam rose up above the arena. I looked over to see the girl nodding. This wasn't over in the least. We'd barely gotten started. She quickly moved her hand down, and the clouds above me crackled with streaks of light. A rumble, and then a blast of lightning struck right in front of me, throwing me back, my clothes smoking. I was barely able to catch myself, looking up to see her... grabbing the lightning? She harnessed the brilliant light, making it swirl around her body. She held it in her hand like a whip, a deathly glare pointed towards me. I tried to think of something to do, and remembered that my powers weren't limited to fire. Like her, I also had control over the elements. Trying not to take my eyes off of her, I reached towards one of the puddles on the ground. I touched the cold water, and a shock went through me.

The arena shook, and water seeped out from the sand and wrapped around the girl. The lightning thrashed in the water, obviously electrocuting her as she screamed. I took my hand out of the water, horrified at the sight of this poor girl trapped in her own attack. But the water continued to lash out around the arena, smacking people off of their feet. I saw the water slice across Damien's arm, and he yelped in surprise as blood started oozing out of the wound. I heard gasps and screams as everyone scrambled to avoid the water. Adrenaline pumping through my body, my heart and mind racing at the same pace, the cold shock getting warmer and warmer. I didn't know what to do. I looked at the girl, still trapped, her eyes filled with absolute horror.

"Stop!" I yelled, my voice hoarse as I screeched at my own power. The water fell; she stood shakily for a couple seconds, then she fell over, her eyes rolling into the back of her head. I gasped, covering my mouth with my hand. I wanted to call out to her, ask if she was okay, anything, but my voice wouldn't work. That piercing scream echoed in my head, filling me with guilt. B rushed onto the scene, carrying the girl away. I looked over to see everyone else staring in shock. Tears welling up in my eyes, I couldn't handle the stares, and the growing pain plaguing my arms and head. I ran, not thinking of anything else except escape, trying to push that image from my mind.

CHAPTER SIX

I reached the gate, hearing concerned yelling behind me. I didn't care to check what that was for. I sprinted out of the gate, my eyes set on the woods. That was always my safe place, and I wanted to go there now, too. I ran until my legs couldn't hold out anymore, collapsing on myself deep into the woods. Pain shot up my leg as a sharp stick dug into my skin, drawing a ragged line of thick, crimson blood. Attempting to control my emotions was pointless; hot tears fell down my face as I sobbed, that little streak of pain throwing me over the edge. And now I wasn't just worried about the girl, as horrible as that was. It was the onlookers. Most of the camp witnessed me practically killing a girl. My friends, the only people I had to lean on here, all probably thought I was a monster, a beast just like those Zanzagars. I thought this world was so perfect when I first arrived. But now, I found it so much different. The outside was anything but a haven. These strange powers I'd acquired made me basically a death machine. The people closest to me now would never look at me the same. Maybe I was overreacting, but I was too panicked, emotion overwhelming my mind, and I couldn't think straight.

I tried to get up, wiping the water from my cheeks. I didn't mean to hurt her. I just wanted to prove I could use this magic, and I did the complete opposite. I wasn't even sure what I wanted to do with the water; it just took control, jumped out and never looked back. I groaned as I sat down on a rock, a burning sensation washing over me. This wasn't the warm, barely painful heat like when I used my powers, but a sickening bonfire of guilt. I sighed, looking around at the still-changing forest. The soft moss underneath my feet slowly morphed into dead grass, and I heard footsteps behind me, crushing the newly grown shrubbery. I turned to see Damien, his hands in his pockets.

"Hey," he said nonchalantly. "Man, I thought I could sneak up. These woods are out to get me."

"Hi," I looked down, embarrassed, my voice breaking, not willing to joke back.

"It wasn't *that* bad, you know," he said with a sigh, kneeling beside me.

"I don't know. Even if the damage wasn't bad, what kind of leader would that make me? I could put everyone in danger. Maybe the General was wrong. Maybe the prophecy really was about someone from the Kingdom. I don't see how I could be the savior of anything." I put my head in my hands, my skin still wet from the rain.

"Yeah, that's probably it. Your incredible powers could never be used for good, especially not if you can learn to control them. Come on, it's gonna be okay. You're new to this whole magic thing. It got out of control. But I know you'll be a great General." He put his hand on my shoulder. "Everyone loves you. You're a good person; you didn't mean to do what you did. Harlequinn is a really good judge of character, and he loves you already. I bet he'd tell you the same thing."

"Well, he's a seer, he can basically see people's personalities," I shrugged, looking at the floor.

"He told you about that?" Damien said, genuinely surprised.

"Yeah, a while ago, actually. After that cloud thing attacked, he was trying to cheer me up and told me that he knew it would be okay." I sighed, still feeling guilty.

"Listen, you're gonna be alright. You might not feel ready for this type of responsibility, but we all have faith in you."

"I just... I feel like I'm not ready for any of this. Becoming General?" I crossed my arms. "And... And I hurt you. I hurt everyone." He glanced at his arm, blood soaking through a white bandage.

"Emotional scars are much more painful than those from wounds," he said humbly, placing his hand on my shoulder.

"But how can anyone trust me now? They won't feel safe near

me. What can I do about that? What do I even do about my powers? I couldn't even think in that situation. I just reached out, and it was…" I couldn't even finish my sentence, my voice cracking, tears once again welling up and falling down my cheeks.

"Come on, the first few days you got here you were already taking command. You fought demons, you blew up a sky ship, you helped capture and interrogate the people on the ship. You knew what had to be done, and you did it while listening to other people. You've proved over and over that you're one of us. They know they can trust you. *I* know you can lead. You already have been." Damien stood up, offering his hand. "Let's go back. And this training is for a reason, you know. I don't think the General would trust anyone with his camp before he assessed them. You don't have a lot of experience, but that's okay. It'll change."

I couldn't help it; I smiled, taking his hand and standing up. "Yeah, we should get going. Thanks." I nodded to him and smiled as we headed back to camp. I was really grateful I found a friend here. I was worried at first that I'd be alone, but Damien had never failed to stick by my side. He immediately made me feel better about this horrible situation. I was worried about the reactions I'd get when I got back, but it gave me comfort knowing that at least he didn't feel any different towards me. I'd caused him and all the people around him pain, but he was still there for me. That didn't seem entirely healthy, but I guess he saw the good in things and understood I didn't mean to hurt people. I heard the crunching of leaves behind me, and turned, expecting to see someone else traipsing through the woods in an attempt to give me a pep-talk, but I didn't see anything at first. I started to turn back around, but then I spotted a gleam in the forest. I saw the end of a cloak—no, it was more fitted to their body, a coat—disappear beneath the trees. The feeling from before returned, the sickening, gut-twisting worry that something was about to go horribly wrong.

"Damien?" I whispered, touching his shoulder. He looked back at me, curious. "I think we're being followed," I said, pointing into the woods. "I saw some weird gleam and then a coat... I think."

"That's... strange. Stay here for a minute. I'll be back soon," Damien said quickly, glaring into the forest. He turned, his arms morphing into feathered wings, nose elongating into a beak, his hair melting into fluffy white feathers, as he swiftly turned into a dove. My breath caught in my throat before I remembered his power. He took off, soaring into the sky and over the woods.

What? Where are you—oh!" I realized he probably was going up to see if he could spot who was in the woods from above. I heard another rustling and turned, examining the forest, peering through the thick clumps of trees. Just as before, the first minute I arrived, I felt eyes everywhere. This time, I was sure it wasn't paranoia. Something was in the woods.

My hands trembling, forcing myself to not let out more than a tiny flame, I let a small fire dance on my palm, illuminating my face as the sun started the set, the light fading from the trees.

The sun...

"Damien!" I yelled, wide-eyed at the sight of the sun disappearing behind the horizon. With the fall of night, the demons started to spawn. Hissing filled the woods, and from every direction came the piercing glares of hungry monsters. I spun, my heart pounding, the flame in my hand flickering. As if sensing my fear, the beasts circling around me closed in. I felt a sudden weight from behind, as claws gripped onto my shirt, cutting through my skin and tracing down my back. I screamed, pain overcoming me as I felt the blood pour down my back. The scent of torn flesh hung in the air, my painful shrieks echoing through the forest, encouraging an attack. A green creature leapt out of the trees, landing on my neck and opening its tiny mouth to take a bite...

A sense of peace fell over me. My pain disappeared and, for a moment, I thought I was dead, something that seemed to happen too often here. I closed my eyes, letting go of what I thought was the tiny bit of life I was clinging on to... I breathed a sigh of relief, but what came out was not air. The woods around me lit up, fire spewing out of my mouth, my body encased in flames. Horrific screaming was all I heard as the monsters attacking fled. They were gone as soon as they came. Terror once again enveloped me before I realized—the flames were controlled. Surrounding my body was a blazing bonfire, white fire circling high into the sky, but not touching any trees. It didn't lash out or try to take control. We lived together in the same space, barely even touching, calm, and a little bit surprised. That warmth I felt before was gone, it wasn't flowing through my veins, and it simply... stood next to me, holding my hand in guidance.

"You were just scared?" I turned to see Damien, staring at the fire.

"What?" I asked, stuttering. I stood up on my own, my legs quivering, the fire slowly flickering out; the light it created retreated into the shadows.

"You were just afraid of the powers taking control. Once you let go and came to terms with... something, it held itself back." He didn't look angry, or disappointed like I thought he would, but a small smile was creeping up on his cheeks. "Your full power is immense, unfathomable and uncontrollable energy, and because of that, you were scared. But then you accepted it, didn't try to obsessively control it, and it died down."

"I—I guess? I don't know. Before... yeah, I was scared. I didn't want to hurt anyone. But no matter how much I tried to contain it, it always got out of my control. I thought I was dead, or dying, so I didn't care. Why did that help, though?"

"Think of it as a baby. When you yell and get angry or controlling, the kid doesn't want to do what you're telling them to, right? But when you calm down and talk to them, they're more understanding and helpful. Your power doesn't want to be controlled; it's already bottled up inside you constantly. With how wild it is, all it wants to do is escape. So when you let it out—it does what it wants." Damien looked at his hands. "I had to learn that the hard way too."

"Wait, you're saying my powers are... sentient?" At that, he chuckled.

"Not exactly, but it's good you've kinda unlocked a different control of your powers. We should get back, everyone's probably worried." He smiled, walking ahead as I nodded. Fear controlled my steps as we hobbled through the gates of the camp, but I was surprised at the greeting- grateful sighs and loving hugs instead of disgraceful glares and punishment. Here, life was what mattered. Family was the most important, and as long as no one got hurt severely, we were okay. Through what I learned since I was here, with the outside world constantly against these people, they somehow still found a way to be kind, loving and forgiving. That amazed me. My embarrassment didn't make it through the gate. I was just glad to see so many smiling faces, and the girl, whose name (or letter) I learned was T, turned out to be completely fine.

"A few bruises, but who doesn't get those, am I right?" She laughed, playfully punching my shoulder. "Besides, with B taking care of me, I knew I would be fine. She practically brought Damien back from the dead!" She was much more energetic and cheerful than in the arena, where she seemed like a different person. That devilish glare still stuck in my mind. She must have been really focused on winning.

I went to sleep with a clean conscience, delighted to be welcomed back with open arms. I couldn't stop thinking of that person in the woods, however. That still puzzled me. But what could I do?

I didn't have a very restful sleep, tossing and turning until I jolted awake, feeling like I couldn't go back to bed now. I rose, glancing around the cabin I'd been stationed in. The twin bed in the corner was comfortable, but I still couldn't settle down. I got up, glancing outside, where I saw the sun was just barely rising. Maybe a quick walk would be good for me.

I changed quickly, stepping outside into the crisp air, still cold from the night. No one was around, no lights were on. The silence made the place slightly eerie as I crept through the quiet town, not a soul to be seen. It was beautiful in a way as well, the serenity settled over the place. I heard a crackling around me, like TV static, which shocked me so much I almost yelped. I turned, not able to pinpoint the sound but trying to find the source. It kept going, and I heard a small voice.

"Amber! Amber!" It repeated, still filled with static. I held my hands to my temples, wondering if I was going mad or if this was normal here,

"Hello?" I whispered, now getting concerned.

"You can hear me?"

"Uh... yes? Who are you? More importantly, *where* are you?"

"I'm... not close enough. I'm sorry if the static is loud, I can't get any closer."

"Why not? What do you mean? Who are you?" I spun, worried I somehow was imagining all of this.

"It's too difficult here. Go outside, to the west. You'll know me when you see me."

"What? How do I know I can trust you?" The static stopped. I growled, stomping in frustration.

"Amber?" Damien opened his cabin door, rubbing his eyes. He almost stumbled down the steps and into the camp. "What's going on?"

"I—uh... someone was talking in my head."

"Excuse me?"

"I heard this weird static, then someone started talking. They knew my name. They told me to go west until I found them." I looked down, digging my heels into the dirt, waiting for him to laugh or something.

"Seriously? That's awesome!" He said, excited instead. "But... to the west is the Kingdom. Are you sure it's not a trap?"

"Wait—why is this awesome?" This whole ordeal confused me to no end.

"Telepathic powers are extremely rare and super powerful. If they're used correctly, they can control people. I think you should go, but I'm coming with you." He stood up straighter, looking determined. "With your training situation... it's dangerous to go alone. But I think I know something that can help." He dove back into his cabin and emerged a minute later, holding a sword. The blade was made of thin steel, and the hilt bound with leather. The leather looked worn down, but the blade was sharp and about the length of my arm. I took it from Damien's hand, and it felt light.

"What's this for?" I asked, examining my reflection in the steel. My hair was a mess, looking like a curly lion's mane.

"Weapons can sometimes help direct your power. It significantly weakens it, though. If someone has powers and isn't using a weapon or amulet to direct them, chances are, their power isn't very strong in the first place, so they can't use something like this. For you, it will work perfectly. The sword is enchanted, so it will attune itself to you and your mana, and since it's something you hold, you can send the power flowing from your hand into the steel. Try directing a small line of fire with it." He looked excited as I brandished the sword in front of me. I glanced at him with a worried look, and he nodded encouragingly, then stepped back a few feet. He obviously trusted me with this.

I took a deep breath, trying not to get into my head and simply focused on the fire and what I wanted it to do. Power flowing through me, I willed it into the sword, which started to glow and catch fire. It spewed out of the sword, glowing white and almost burning my hands. I didn't let go, determined to get it right this time. I pictured in my mind the flames dying down to a peaceful red, barely coming off of the blade. The fire slowly copied what I imagined.

"Wow. What happened when you were sleeping?" Damien joked. "Good job. You're a quick learner." I shut off the rest of the flow to the sword and smiled.

"Before we go, you should probably get dressed," I said, and he looked down at his pajamas, striped blue pants and a white t-shirt that looked like it had some sort of band symbol on it.

"Uh... yeah. I'll be right back," he said sheepishly, rushing back inside. I heard a rattling sound and a yelp from inside and held back a laugh, brushing my hands through my tangled hair. He came out with hair more disheveled than mine and wearing a short-sleeved black shirt with a flannel over it, along with jeans and tennis shoes. "Alright! Let's go!" He started down the stairs and immediately tripped, landing face-first on the ground.

"Are you alright?" I said, laughing as I helped him up.

"Yeah, I'm okay. I don't know what's wrong with me today," he said, holding his head. "Anyway, do you have any idea who this person could be?"

"None at all. But I'm curious. There was something familiar about their voice... I guess all we can do is go and see," I looked around, examining the other cabins. "Hopefully we can get back before everyone wakes up."

"We'll make it! Don't worry. Just a quick visit and back. Well, that kinda depends on how far it is... but we'll be fine." We walked together through the looming gates, quickly heading west. We walked until the camp couldn't even be seen anymore.

"I feel like we should have met them by now... right? I mean, I—" I paused, amazed at the wonder before me. A huge city stretched out in front of us, tall buildings and lights shimmering in hundreds of different colors. People biked past on concrete roads, some were sitting and talking at a café, and I could see shadows milling about in apartment buildings and houses. A giant stone castle sat in the middle, towers stretching into the sky as red flags waved above. Damien grabbed my arm and we ducked behind a building.

"This is the Kingdom. We have to leave, now." He looked serious, a glare on his face.

"But we didn't find—"

"I don't care. If they see us, they'll kill us."

"You're right. We should hide," another voice chimed in. I jumped, looking at a figure behind us. They had a thick black jacket on, the hood hiding their face.

"What is up with people in this world and hiding their faces with hoods?" I exclaimed, throwing my hands in the air.

"More importantly, why is he here? I talked to you, not him," I couldn't see their expression underneath the coat, but they sounded a bit angry.

"You didn't say come alone or anything. He wanted to help. Now, even more importantly, who are you?" I grumbled, having to ask for the third time.

"I—I can't tell you with people around. In fact, it's dangerous even being around you. I just needed to tell you one thing. They're after you. They have spies, and now they know who you are and what you are. They're planning a massive attack, an assault to end this battle before it gets out of their control. Stay alert, and always be prepared to fight. You might need to speed up your training. And your hair looks fine."

"Thanks, but I fixed it before—wait, how did you know my hair was a mess?" I inquired, a bit shocked.

"I can read thoughts, remember? Telepathy? That doesn't just let me communicate. That's irrelevant, though. I didn't mean for you to go so far, but I saw him, and got worried. You need to leave. Be careful on your way back. Don't tell *anyone* about this." They shuffled off, leaving the two of us more confused than before.

"That was... strange, for lack of a better word. But they're right, we should go. Being this close to those monsters... I don't feel safe even standing outside," Damien said, looking at the ground, a scowl still prominent on his face.

"Did something—ah, never mind. Let's go," I started off, leaving the gleaming lights and the beautiful appeal of the gorgeous city behind. It wasn't fair that the kindest people suffered the most, while the cruel ones sat up in their towers, laughing, surrounded by money and power. Those greedy cowards were taking everything from us.

Right then, I promised myself I wouldn't let anyone hurt these people, my family. I would fight until nothing was left. I would protect them.

No matter the cost.

CHAPTER SEVEN

We were almost back to camp when we heard something akin to barking. The path we took was close to the woods, but not inside it, so I assumed it was a wolf or coyote, some animal of that type. I just dismissed the noise, stepping a bit away from the leaves that vaguely marked where the woods started. The gates were a few yards in front of us, but something stumbled out of the forest, stopping us in our tracks. It looked like a dog, silver and white fur matted to its thin figure. Red marks trailed down its face and stomach. The poor thing could barely stand, whimpering and attempting to growl, biting at our ankles weakly, and watching the trees, like something was following it.

"Man, this day has been random," I muttered, leaning closer to the ground. The dog was huge, but severely malnourished. Its bones were sticking prominently through its thin skin and fur. Its ears had chunks taken out of them, and it was panting when it didn't lash out at us. "Hey… buddy? Oh God, what happened to you?"

"What do we do with it?" Damien whispered, trying to put his hand on its head. The dog snapped, barely missing his wrist.

"It seems to be trying to... eat us?" I giggled despite the severity of the situation.

"It must be really hungry," Damien stepped away after the dog continued trying to take off his hand. "It can barely get up. If we can make it fall asleep, or lure it into camp... then maybe B can help us. She's also worked as a vet. Wait, that gives me an idea! I'll be right back, don't leave its side." Damien stood, scurrying around the dog, and running towards camp. I looked down, the dog's eyes showing fear and vulnerability.

"This day has been really strange. First, a voice starts talking in my head. Then we almost run straight into the Kingdom to meet someone who apparently knows me, and then you just... hop out of the woods. I wish this could have happened to me in my world, though. That would have been cool. I hope we can get you healed up... you poor thing. What happened to you?" As I talked, the dog seemed to settle down, listening to me as I rambled. Not thinking of what I was saying, just going on as if I was talking to myself. Before I knew it, I was reaching out to pet it, and it didn't seem to mind, calming down as we sat together.

"Hey," Damien said. I jumped, pausing mid-story. He was holding a plate with a giant slab of meat on it, and the dog nearly tackled him to get it. "Ah!"

"Down! Down! Calm down!" I reached forward, grabbing the dog and pulling it back. I could feel its ribs, which made me wince. Damien placed the plate on the ground and watched as the dog went at it, gulping down the food.

"How did you get it so calm?" Damien whispered to me.

"I just talked to it. Where did you get that?" I asked back.

"Oh, this tiger guy was eating it, but he gave it to me."

"A what?" I asked, astounded at how he could say that so casually.

"He's an Elite. A group of fighters that is more skilled or experienced than anyone else. A lot of them are half human, half animal. I know one dude that's almost entirely a crocodile. They're pretty cool," Damien smiled, taking his eyes away from the dog.

"That sounds... slightly terrifying. We should probably get back soon, though. Can we take the dog?" I looked hopefully at Damien.

"I mean, it'll probably die if we don't, so it would be best. We can get it to B, and she can help." We both leaned down, and on the count of three, we both lifted the dog, which was a lot heavier than it looked. We hauled it through the gates and gently set it down.

"I'll go get B," I said, turning and nearly running into someone. I looked up into a harsh gaze, and almost fell backwards in shock. This person in front of me looked mostly normal, dark brown hair and pretty much pitch-black skin, wearing a coat over an orange t-shirt and jeans. One eye was a menacing gold, the other so bright it almost gleamed with silver hues, but half of his body was covered in fur. Orange and yellow stripes went down half of his entire body, which was startling, to say the least. He loomed over me, a judging look on his face before he offered his hand to help me up. I noticed he had black claws instead of regular nails as I accepted his... paw, and lifted myself off the ground.

"You're a new face," he purred, still looking me up and down, like he was assessing me.

"Uh, yeah. I'm Amber," I said, nodding, already feeling like I wanted to leave.

"So, the new General. Nice. I'm Tigre," he said his name with a thick, very fake French accent.

"Hah, I get it. Tigre is tiger in French. Clever," I remarked sarcastically.

"I try." His mouth twitched, and he leaned in. "So, what's this?" He asked, pointing to the dog behind me.

"What does it look like?" I said, pushing him backwards. He was much too close for comfort.

"A wolf?" Tigre raised his eyebrows. "That type is a very rare breed around here. Usually native to the other side of the world. I can't imagine how it got here..." he hovered over the dog, or wolf, I guessed, examining its frail body. The wolf snarled at him, but I placed my hand on its head and it stopped. Tigre's eyes widened, a mysterious gleam within his gaze.

"Well, I should get going then. I'll see you later," he winked at me and I visibly cringed, honestly disgusted by his flirtatious manner.

"Amber! Damien! Where were you two this morning?" The General stormed towards us, rage evident on his face.

"We... went for a walk. We both woke up early. I'm sorry, General." Damien looked towards the floor.

"Your mistakes could cost us greatly," he growled. "The mice have escaped. We don't know what they heard, saw, or have

99

taken. Damien, if I recall correctly, you were on watch today."

"What?" I exclaimed, shocked to hear the slightly terrifying news. They had escaped... so Alexander might have been lying to me to get information.

"They won't get far, as they're still currently mice, but the further they go, the weaker the spell gets. That's why I called in the Elites. Those children are powerful, and they're not trained, so if they use their powers... the damage could be catastrophic. We have quite a few people guarding the outside, but sadly... we'll have to somehow get to the Kingdom." With that, he turned to me. I stiffened, knowing exactly what he would say, but still scared to hear it. "We're going to have to accelerate your training, and this time we can't delay. I understand it can be a lot of pressure, but no running away. We have to get you ready, in case things like this happen again," he said gravely. I sighed, but simply nodded in reply. I had to do this for them, and for myself. It was time to get serious.

I once again entered the arena, more determined than ever to train. The wolf, still following me around and still unnamed, sat obediently in the corner.

"We've decided to ditch the crowd," Damien said, sauntering towards me. "The General thought it was for the best, since it seemed to make you anxious. It's just you and me now, okay?" He put his hand on my shoulder and looked into my eyes. It was a reassuring glance, and I did feel more confident without all of the judgmental gazes from the crowd.

"Yeah, alright. I can deal with that." He nodded and backed away, raising his sword. I did the same. "Is the General coaching, or just you?"

"Well, he thought I could handle this by myself. For now, at least." We started to circle, each preparing a plan for what to do.

"Interesting. Are we using magic?" I inquired, teasingly stepping forwards and slashing to make him flinch.

"No, this is just more combat. In some places, you can't use magic. It's against the law and there's a specific type of stone, and while it's a very rare substance found deep within the earth, it can make it to where all the mana drains from our bodies, rendering our powers completely useless. We don't know exactly what it is, but we know it exists, and it's dangerous." He sliced diagonally and I blocked, holding the sword for a moment before pushing away. He nodded approvingly.

"So, who has it? Do we know?" I charged forward, and Damien blocked my sword. He twisted the blade, nearly making me drop it, but I tossed it into the air instead, then grabbed it with my opposite hand and hit him with the flat of the blade, right on top of his head. He stumbled backwards, looking slightly impressed.

"That was... an interesting move. We have a guess as to who has it—somebody from the Kingdom. Some scouts have come back reporting that their powers malfunctioned or just stopped working the closer they got to the castle. That seems like a pretty obvious sign."

It was hard to talk while focusing on defense, but it obviously wasn't easy for him either. We went back and forth, dodging and blocking, striking and slashing, stabbing and pushing. It was never clear who had the upper hand, but I had a hunch he was probably going easy. Every stroke we blocked, every attack we dodged. In my world, I had experience with sword fighting, but I guessed that this would be the only time I had the experience or advantage in training.

"You're good at this," Damien commented, almost like he read my thoughts. Which, apparently, people can do here.

"I've taken classes." I lunged at his stomach, but he swiftly batted my sword away with his.

"In your world?" I nodded, trying to focus. "What's that place like?"

"Well, it's not that different. We just don't have magic. There are some places that punish people just for existing, or even have laws against it. It's horrible; we're all in a desperate state. The world, the earth... it's dying. We've ruined the only place we have, and continue to destroy it. Some people spend money on making sure that it doesn't get saved, and it's a lot of money. Billions of dollars, wasted. Just because we're greedy. It's all about money there! People kill for it, die for it, and destroy for it. Pieces of paper or metal, that's all they are, yet they're worth everything to some people." Explaining the horrific truth of our world got me worked up. As I went on, I got faster, hit stronger, barely focusing on blocking. "No one cares for anything else, and they'll do whatever they can to make sure they get their way. No matter the cost!" I pushed the flat of my blade against Damien's so hard that he fell down. I spun my sword so that the point was on his chest. I didn't press down, but I did smile smugly.

"You win," he croaked, grinning. I put down my sword and offered my hand, hoisting him up. "Not the award for best universe, though. No offense, but that sounds awful." I laughed, shrugging.

"I agree, man. It sucks, seeing the world around you dying, and not being able to do anything about it because you don't have billions to spend on fixing others' mistakes." I jokingly raised my sword, bouncing back and forth on the balls of my feet. "Want to go again?"

"Well, since you already know how to do this, we can get back to it. Now, we're focusing on magic." I winced, not liking where this was going.

"I was gonna say I'm horrible at that as an excuse, but I guess that's why we're training. Let's do it," I sighed, giving in.

"That's not exactly the spirit, but I'll take it. You can still use the sword for this. Like I said before, magic can be contained in items. Metal works the best with most types of mana. The one thing that doesn't work at all with it is stone. If you're using stone, it will spark and can possibly burn your hands. Some different types of magic that don't match your own can be contained and used. In the woods, I used this to hit the Zanzagar." Damien pulled a small amulet out of his pocket. It was made of smooth, carved wood, with an eye in the middle and symbols around it. "This amulet contains light mana, one of the easiest types of mana to contain and transfer. This can even be created."

"Whoa, that's so cool. So, people can use different types of magic with stuff like this?" I asked, running my hand over the pendant, examining all the grooves and the detail on the eye.

"Correct. Right now, since you're so good at using a sword, that's probably the best weapon for you to carry. But you also need to practice using different things in emergency situations." He bent down to pick up a small stick that was on the ground. "Say you lost your weapon, and your way. You're trapped in the forest, no way out, enemies on all sides... the only way to win is to keep your powers under control. You can't explode and hurt yourself and the forest. So, you grab a stick from the ground, and...?" He tossed the branch to me, and I caught it. It was thin and still had a leaf attached to it. I gripped it, turning the end towards Damien, and focused. I imagined the energy flowing forth, enveloping the stick and reaching out, surrounding Damien...

My powers complied. I let go, opened the doors in my mind and got rid of my fear, trusting myself and the fire to do what it needed. Flames poured forth, a little more vicious than I intended, but they did what I wanted them to and trapped Damien, a circle of fire surrounding him.

"I'm assuming you'd like me to hold off on the killing or hurting part," I joked, watching his eyes widen with fear as he nodded.

"That would be best, I think," he squeaked, and I put down the stick. The flames dissipated at my command. "I'm impressed. That scare in the woods did wonders for you! You're learning to trust yourself and your instincts more. Opening up to magic and accepting it. Very good!" Damien smiled encouragingly, putting his hand on my shoulder. I nodded, ecstatic to finally be getting control over this. "Okay, let's try with the sword now. We'll move on from fire afterwards."

"Wait, what? What do you mean, move on from fire?" I nearly dropped my sword again.

"Well, obviously you can use other elements. We need to expand on that. Don't worry, not right now. We'll focus mainly on fire, and getting control over it." Damien stepped backwards, a smile still on his face. "I called in a little favor for a friend. This is Mirage, they're an Elite." The door to the arena opened with a puff of smoke, and a person stepped out. They had long, silver hair that curled at the bottom. They were tall and lithe, a mask covering their pale face, framing beautiful golden eyes. They wore a dress woven with little jewels, and heels that made them look even taller. They smiled at me, holding a large cane.

"Hello, Amber." Their voice was like silk, smooth and deep. I was mesmerized by their grace and poise. "It's an honor to be able to help a future General with their training. I truly hope my powers aid you in your progress," and with that, they bowed. I nodded in thanks.

"Mirage, like their name suggests, can create illusions. We're gonna step back and let you unleash your powers on fake monsters. They can't hurt you, but it will look like they can. Good luck, and try to remember—it's not real." Damien rushed through the door, and Mirage waved their cane. The world around me melted. Damien's words echoed in my head. It's not real.

Darkness surrounded me, covering me like a blanket. It was almost suffocating. I extended my arm, setting fire to my sword like a torch. The light didn't reach far, but from what I could see, I was in the forest. Leaves brushed against the back of my neck, and the cool breeze whisked around me. It was peaceful, and I didn't see any monsters.

"Uh... hello?" I called out, hearing nothing but the swish of the wind. This really did seem real, I could feel everything. Even the eyes on my back. I didn't know what the darkness was hiding, and I could feel my heartbeat start to speed up. I heard the small crunch of leaves and turned, coming face to face with a scaled figure. A forked tongue slithered out of its mouth, baring fangs. Out of instinct, I stabbed forward, my blade still ablaze, right where its heart should have been. The body was human-like, but still covered in scales. The thing collapsed, and I once again was alone. It was eerie; the pauses were too long, the serene night too dark. It was agonizing, waiting for something to attack. I took a deep breath and tried to stop the shaking of my hands. How could I speed this up?

I could always seek out the fight.

If I didn't think it through, I was bound to end up making a mistake. As slowly and as silently as I could, I crept through the dark woods. The trees lit up around me with the pale glow of moonlight, basking everything in a glimmering silver. I brushed my hair out of my face, keeping a lookout for any monsters. The one place I didn't have eyes on was behind me. I felt a sudden weight on my back as I fell to the floor, nearly stabbing myself. I wasn't aware that illusions could have weight, or even touch you. Mirage was good. I twisted as much as I could and shoved my sword into a zombie's throat, nearly slicing its head clean off. It melted into goo that slid off of my clothes and into the floor. I shuddered at the disgusting feeling of the weird gunk sliding down my body. I got up, wondering how that could possibly be an illusion. The silence was still ominous, and I couldn't wait any longer. Even walking forward, the monsters barely appeared. It was time for me to smoke them out, quite literally.

I took a deep breath and closed my eyes, raising my sword above my head. I willed the flames to rise, seek out any shadows, and destroy them. The fire roared in fury as it spread, snaking through the forest, every twist and turn lit up by the raging bonfire. Monsters were revealed, sneaking up, staying behind, and waiting in the trees. Disgusting slobber dripped from their mouths, which were decorated with sharp teeth. Fur-covered animals snarled, hissing birds snuck through the leaves far above. There were thousands of them, all eyes on their target. Me.

I didn't think; I just took action. I jumped forward, bending the fire towards me. It swept towards the monsters surrounding me, reducing them to ash. I danced around within the flames, a dress made of the colors of the sunset, gliding gracefully across the floor as it demolished everything in its path. Fire was not a toy. Here, it was a weapon. Its only purpose to burn down, to destroy. The beauty that came with it was nothing compared to the destruction it left in its path. Fear bowed to me as I inflicted pain and death with one swipe of my sword. I couldn't imagine the power I would have if I left my weapons behind. This was chaos, but without the control?

I lost my train of thought as the world around me glitched. It faded back into the arena and I stood up straight, breathing hard from all the movement, dropping my sword as my arms protested the weight. Damien and Mirage stood side by side, shock and disbelief on each of their faces. Even the wolf looked surprised.

"Hey, I wasn't done!" I joked, wiping sweat off of my forehead. The one light bulb in the entire arena flickered above us, suddenly shutting off. "Uh... power outage or do we need to replace that?"

"I—uh—probably a power outage. We get those a lot. But it's always hilarious because the Kingdom is almost entirely fueled by electricity, and we have, like, one house that runs on it," Damien giggled to himself. "So, in their hatred they accidentally made it worse for themselves. But can we talk about how quickly your powers advanced?"

"I agree, that is definitely a topic of discussion we should be getting to. Somehow, you were able to take out all of my images so quickly, it affected my powers. That isn't a small feat." Mirage looked at me with mixed emotions, looking impressed, confused, and upset at the same time.

"I—I don't know what happened. I just went with my instincts. I knew I had to pass; I needed to get rid of these things. So I used the fire already surrounding them to kill them."

"You said you worked with swords before, yes?" I nodded towards Mirage. "That makes sense. Your technique shows your experience, and you've learned to think quickly in stressful situations. Now that that's covered, we should go see what the outage is about." I nodded, turning to the wolf that was still obediently sitting in the corner.

"Uh... stay," I commanded, before we stepped outside. Raging wind batted at us from every direction, tree branches were flung at us from every angle, multiple doors swung open and shut, and a lantern was torn from its place on a wall. A large creak echoed throughout the camp as a tree broke in half and started to fall right in front of the gates. The wooden doors, moving slightly from the wind, were completely blocked off. We had no way out.

Damien, Mirage and I all struggled into the closest building, which happened to be the infirmary. B was focusing on something near the sink, her back turned on us as the walls rattled around us. Lanterns lit up the room.

"Where did this wind storm come from?" I groaned, trying to fix my hair before giving up. The usually tangled mess was impossible to even slightly undo.

"I'm not sure, that was really sudden. It can't have been the alarm, that doesn't affect inside here. This is just nature getting back at us, I guess." Damien sat down in a chair next to the door, up against the wall. B still didn't turn around, like she hadn't even noticed us.

"Hi, B." I smiled slightly, but she didn't react. "Hey, B?" I called, but again, there was no response. "B?" I said again. She was still at the sink, examining a bottle of weird green liquid, her back turned to me. I got up, and tapped her shoulder. "B!" She jumped, almost spilling the green stuff. She chuckled nervously, setting the bottle down.

"I'm sorry Amber, I was... distracted. What's wrong?"

"Are you alright? I called your name, or... letter, like, three times." I was genuinely worried about her. What had happened?

"So, the roles are reversed now, huh? At least now you finally walk in here by yourself." She chuckled nervously, shifting her hair slightly to cover her ears.

"Yeah, I guess that is better than magically appearing here. Now, I'm conscious!" I couldn't resist a joke.

"Glad to hear you're alright, and don't worry, I'm fine. Oh, hello Mirage. Nice to see you again." Mirage smiled, nodding in recognition.

"Same to you, B," They said sweetly. My eyes flitted between the two before I shrugged.

"Anyway, I hope its okay we're here. There's a giant storm outside, it doesn't look safe. I saw an entire tree collapse in front of the gate," I explained.

"Oh, no! The wind is that bad? I thought we had protections against fierce stuff like that... something must be wrong." B scrunched up her face, looking very concerned.

"I thought so, too. The General usually handles this stuff." Damien looked to the floor, before abruptly standing and gasping. "A person's magic starts to weaken and spells break when they're hurt or... close to death." It was my turn to gasp.

"So, does this mean the General is in danger? We have to go find him!" I reached for the door, trying to pull it open, but the wind pushed back, and the door forcefully slammed shut. "Oh, come on!" I groaned.

"It's dangerous for us, too. We basically live in a forest. You said yourself that a tree was uprooted and tossed over. We don't know what could be in the air, flying around. Debris from recent battles, bricks and stones from buildings being constructed... a person could have even been whisked off of the ground. We have to think of a different way to get to him." Damien put his hand on my shoulder, and I stifled a laugh thinking of an entire person flying through the air, flailing as they were tossed around.

"Wait... remember, I said walking in is better than magically appearing here? Is there any way to actually teleport?" As soon as I asked, all three of them gasped.

"No! Well, yes, but it's way too dangerous! The last time someone tried it, they were literally pulled apart by the vortex the spell created. We don't know if they did it wrong, or that's just the spell's effect. Either way, we can't risk it. We'd be safer in the storm." Damien crossed his arms, still seated in the corner.

"Well then, let's go," I stated, attempting to open the door again. This time, the wind offered no resistance, and the wood moved in front of me. The storm seemed to have halted, only a few gusts of wind desperately trying to push stuff around. Mirage peered over my shoulder, a thoughtful look on their face.

"The wind will pick back up soon. Why it stopped could be one of two reasons: nature decided to stop tormenting us for a while, or the General is safe. Let's hope it's the latter." I timidly stepped outside, Damien behind me. I looked back to see Mirage hesitating.

"I... I think I'll stay here. I'm probably not much help in this situation. Besides, B and I have some catching up to do." They smiled reassuringly.

"Oh... well, okay then. It was nice meeting you." I smiled back, and offered a quick wave to B as the two of us sprinted across the camp, into the castle at the edge of the wall before the wind decided to sweep us off of our feet. Damien strained for a minute against the heavy door, before opening it for me. I nodded in thanks before rushing inside, keeping a hand on the edge of the door so Damien could come in. Inside, there was silence. Nothing moved, but the quiet was unsettling.

"General?" Damien called, glancing around the room.

"Maybe he's upstairs," I commented, turning to the staircase. "Shall we?" I joked, but he didn't smile. "Uh... never mind." We both rushed up the stairs, into the interrogation room I met Alexander in. That memory was still bitter. We tentatively opened the door only to see the General, lying face down, his cane on the other side of the room. He was sprawled on the floor, not moving.

"General!" Damien skidded across the floor, kneeling down next to the old man. He gently turned the General over on his back. Our leader looked weak and frail, like he would break if someone sneezed too hard. He groaned, taking in a deep breath.

"I don't have enough time. The training... we were too slow. Too many obstacles. I—I don't have—don't have enough—"

"Shh, it's okay. You have time. Amber's a quick learner; they'll get what they need. Besides, I'm here. I can help them. You have my word on that." Damien spoke softly, and I kneeled beside him. The General and I made eye contact. He smiled at me.

"I—I see. I trust you, both of you. But it—it's time to—time to get serious. We can't have anything get in the way. No running. You need to push—need to—need to push yourself to your—your limits. Please, promise me that, Amber." His voice sounded as weak as he looked. My eyes teared up, realizing he meant the end of his life was coming closer and closer every day. Soon, he would be gone.

"Of course! I promise, I'll do what I can. I'm so sorry I didn't—I didn't take it seriously before." I hung my head, disappointed in myself. I let fear take over and made rash, stupid decisions that were now backfiring on me. Damien put his hand on my shoulder in a comforting gesture.

"Let's get you to bed. I'll work on training with Amber." Damien barely spoke over a whisper, trying to hold back tears. I helped him carry the General down the stairs, and then we went up the opposite staircase on the right. The door on this side was wooden and opened to a small bedroom. A big bed took up most of the room, with a desk on one side and a bookshelf on the other. We laid the old man down on the bed.

"Thank you. Now... let me be. I'll be okay." Damien nodded. I had questions, but I felt it was best to leave it be. The two of us exited, walking in silence. I opened the main door just a little, examining the camp and trying to figure out if the wind was still there. My question was answered by a swift breeze whisking the door out of my hands, slamming shut.

"Well, the wind's picked back up. I guess we can't leave," I sighed. I looked over at Damien, who was sitting at a table, head down and eyes closed. I exhaled, silently walking over and sitting beside him. I was at a loss for words this time. "He'll be okay," I offered. "I mean, he's survived over four hundred years, right? He's had to have gone through stuff worse than this."

"You don't get it," he whispered, and my face flushed. I was worried I'd said the wrong thing. "Everyone dies. It doesn't matter what he's gone through, or what he's going through now. He's old. Heck, I don't even think people usually live to four hundred where you're from." I suppressed a chuckle.

"Yeah, we only get to around seventy or eighty." Damien looked at me with shock on his face.

"*What*? You die that young?"

"Young?" I choked. "I guess here it's considered young, but... that's pretty old with us." Damien laughed a little.

"Either way, I'm worried about him. He's like my dad now, or… grandfather, I guess. I don't want to disappoint him... I want you to be ready to take on leadership. I want him to know this camp is in good hands." His smile faded, and he sighed.

"That's on me, too. I've made so many mistakes here — running away when I needed to face what was coming. I've been weak. I need to take this seriously. I've been shoved into this life, and if I don't accept it... everyone and everything around me could suffer for that." My voice broke. I didn't want to let them down. I didn't want to disappoint anyone either. "I wish we could get to training right now, but the wind..."

"You can still train." A deep, rough voice echoed through the walls. Damien and I both looked up, a little spooked. The shadows around us moved, converging in one spot and solidifying off of the wall. A human-like figure made out of darkness emerged. His body was entirely made of smoke, and his eyes emanated a deep red from under the curtain of shadows he was engulfed in.

"Who are you?" I cried, trying to back up.

"I'm Shadow. I'm one of the Elites." He nodded, closing his eyes for a second. I noticed the slight tinge of a British accent, though I didn't know what that could be considered here.

"You guys have really original names," I said under my breath, but somehow they both heard me. Damien looked almost scared, and Shadow looked slightly offended. "What? Come on! Tigre literally just means tiger, and he's half of a tiger. Mirage can create mirages, and Shadow is made out of shadows. That's really obvious." The Elite paused, pondering my statement. I was worried he would be mad, but... he chuckled, the soft laugh evolving into a rolling bellow, until he was cackling hysterically. Damien glanced at me questioningly.

"You have a good point. Our names are... quite redundant. It would be silly to change now, though. We've lived thousands of millennia, and not once have our names changed." Shadow started to walk, but it didn't look like walking. He basically rolled, the shadows underneath him creating a path on which he floated across. "Do you recall when I said that you can still train? Here, this is a place for learning. You train your mind." He tapped his temple in reference.

"The Elites are a mysterious force, old as time itself. We were created with the universe, hybrids of humans and animals or matter. We were born with special powers, unique at the time. We were held in high regard, but also fear. The beings that existed—some of which are now extinct—didn't understand. And since humans are incapable of accepting things they didn't understand, we were all but exiled, forced to live in secret and evolve on our own. Time has expanded our minds and our skills. We were not aided by others. We are the original founders of this camp, forged from a friendship made of tears. Pain brought us together, and we used that fear and suffering to create something amazing. Generations of families have thrived here under our careful watch, and we became dormant, powerful beings sleeping beneath the Earth, only awoken by major threats.

An inexperienced leader, spies that have taken information and escaped, oppression from those on top, and panic spreading. We are here to make sure that what brought us together does not divide us now." He bowed, having successfully delivered his monologue. I couldn't see the rest of his face, but his eyes glowed with pride.

"Wow. So, basically you're here because of me?" My face flushed in shame.

"Not entirely. There are other factors to this. The point is, we are not called for no reason. We are ancient beings, capable of things no human mind could ever hope to comprehend. Some things you see will make so little sense, you'll go mad if you think for too long about it. No matter what you've learned on Earth, don't question everything. Be open minded, but don't try to expand your mind beyond your capabilities." I sighed, trying to take in all that information.

"Wait, what I learned on Earth? Isn't *this* Earth?" I questioned, confused.

"Some form of it. Merely a... shadow, practically an alternate reality. Somehow, you drew magic into your world, moved the Earth in such a way that it allowed you to pass through your shell of existence. Reality is a construct. With the right power, and the right mindset, you can change what you thought you knew. You can discover or even create new universes at will. You harnessed what little power your Earth has to get where you are right now. Science is a form of magic, so your world is already aware of the possibilities. That awareness creates the power. Knowledge is a generator. Feelings and emotions amplify that. All humans have magic within them. The right use of it can create unlimited possibilities."

I was about to argue, say that didn't make any sense. But then I realized, no, not to me. I'd been stuck in what I thought I knew, trapped in what I imagined as reality. But reality didn't exist, not the way I thought of it. If it did, there are endless realities, varying from person to person, planet to planet, universe to universe. Every living being has a different reality. This was confusing, but only because I refused to understand what I didn't know about. I was no better than the Kingdom in that way, unaccepting of challenges to their mindset. What I knew, what everyone knows is both a lie and the truth. Things that seem like they don't fit together actually connect in the most unlikely ways possible. What's confusing, what's impossible, the things our minds aren't able to understand are always in some way true, and in others, false. It's random, but when you think about it... it actually all makes sense.

Shadow must have seen the look on my face, because he chuckled.

"You understand now, at least to some extent. You know that you aren't able to truly know. Nothing is definite. Things are always changing. The truth and the lies evolve with that. Nothing is set in stone, and everything isn't understandable."

"So... not even the Elites understand everything?" I remarked, curious about that.

"In some ways, we are just as in the dark as you humans are. Us being old doesn't prove or disprove anything. There will always be things out of our grasp, galaxies we can't reach, information we can't obtain, even if that information is the knowledge that it's unattainable. This won't ever make sense, to anyone. But that's because we're always changing, shifting, adapting. Our language is made of symbols that we mush together to somehow make sense. You can understand what I'm saying, but... how? How did this come to be? How did you learn this? How do you understand that pitch in a sentence determines if it's a question, statement, or anything otherwise? How did this all come to be? We will never truly understand the workings of the Earth, or its multiple realities. Shadows are created from light, so there must be some dimension that feeds off of light, correct? But how do we get there? How have we not discovered this already?"

My head started to hurt. Processing all of this was taking a toll on my body. I put my hand to my head, and Shadow looked at me pointedly. "Even pain is fake. Generated by the brain as a reaction. We can never know everything. We can never know the extent of our future or our past. What happened before? Was there something there that we never learned about? Did other planets have life? Was it just wiped out like we could be? What happened? How did we truly get here? Our knowledge of the past is not complete, and can never be. As the future and the present change, so does the past, in a way. Some things become lies. Some become truths. Time isn't even real. Our days, our months, even minutes and seconds are just the imagination of humans trying to comprehend passing. We compress infinite things like time into small numbers so that we understand them. Now, that's enough. I don't want to destroy your brain. None of this will make sense, not to you, so I'm done with my ranting. I've taught you something you needed to know, though. It will help you advance your powers to learn this. Good luck in your training. Now, I have faith you will do well."

Once again, Shadow nodded, and then faded into nothingness. My jaw went slack, my eyes unfocused. That information nearly sent me into shock. I couldn't even begin to describe what was racing through my mind, but the feeling was like someone just tried to open my third eye. It was strange, but I remembered Shadow saying to not overthink, or there would be consequences. I looked over to Damien, who was seemingly unaffected.

"Are you okay?" I asked, hoping he wasn't so stunned that he just stopped working.

"Yeah, I'm alright. The General... he explained some of that to me a while ago, even though it can't fully be explained. All the leaders know this, or grasp the concept. Shadow told you this because he knows what's coming in the near future. He told you so you'd be ready to be the General, and lead us to where no one else could."

I smiled, more confident in what I could do now.

"How are you gonna use that?" He inquired, grinning towards me. I closed my eyes, took a deep breath, and willed myself to do something. Nothing specific, but what I needed to happen. I let the universe decide on this one.

I felt heat, and opened my eyes to see flames spreading around the table and into the entire room, crawling over the walls but not burning anything. This was fire that didn't need physical fuel, which was already a feat in itself. But to conjure a destructive force and harness it to not do what it's supposed to is another miracle. I felt almost enlightened, but I knew it wouldn't last. It was a temporary feeling of bliss, one I could probably tap into when I needed it most.

"Even after all of that, I bet ninety percent of what I say is gonna sound stupid," I joked, and Damien chuckled.

"I doubt it. Come on, you didn't sound like that before."

"Well, some—" I stopped, noticing a small squeak coming from the room around me. "What was that?" I asked, looking around.

"It sounded like... a mouse!" Damien rose from his seat, suddenly excited. We scoured the room, looking under tables and shelves and carpets, even examining the walls for any holes, but we came up empty. After we exhausted all our options, I listened instead, letting my sense of sound guide me. I opened the door a little, straining against the wind, thinking that the noise was coming from out there. There was another squeak as two small white figures flew into the castle, and I stepped back, the door closing by itself. The mice were sprawled on the floor, somehow still fighting. I could tell which one was the girl by her constant screaming.

"You found them!" Damien exclaimed, grabbing them both. He placed the girl into a glass cage on top of a bookshelf, and set Alexander back on the ground. "Uh... I don't remember the spell, hold on..." I giggled to myself as he ran around, looking for a book. I glanced down at Alexander, who waved at me. I smiled and returned the gesture. "Here it is! Mutatio... Hominem? Mutatio Hominem!"

Nothing happened. Alexander's ears perked up, and the scratching from the cage behind us stopped. We looked over, pure terror engulfing the girl mouse's face. Even Alexander started to squeak, pointing at the door.

"Uh... what happened?" I asked, confused. Damien shrugged, picking up the small mouse.

"What's wrong?" Alexander jumped up and out of his palm, right next to the door, pointing and practically screeching.

"Something must be out there," I remarked, a bit worried. "Be ready to fight. I'm gonna open the door." Damien nodded in acknowledgement. I took a deep breath, and slowly reached for the door, pushing it open against the wind. "How is this still going on?" I muttered, forcing the door open. The building shook, and I fell through the doorway, onto the ground and nearly hitting my head.

"Amber!" Damien rushed forward, keeping the heavy door open so it wouldn't crush me.

"I'm okay! But... what was that?" I stood, trying to examine the camp but my hair was whipping around my face, impairing my vision.

"I'm not... never mind, I'm sure!" Damien pointed up, but with his short hair, he could see perfectly. I, however, couldn't tame my mane enough to clearly see.

"Is it another sky ship?" I questioned.

"No, look up---oh. Never mind again. It's a giant machine! It looks like... a rhino?"

Another quake shook the earth. I glanced at what I could, but all I saw was a hunk of metal. I reached up and parted my hair, holding it back. What was in front of me did indeed look like a rhino. Large, but stubby legs and a curved horn. It was even gray, built with metal. However, even with danger sitting right in front of us... I couldn't help but laugh. It looked quite stupid, fumbling over itself to get to the camp. I heard Damien sigh, but that made me laugh even more.

"I'm sorry, it—I just—you know—oh, come on, look at it!" I chuckled. He suppressed a smile. I jokingly poked his arm, and he turned away, trying not to laugh or smile. "You gotta admit, it looks weird."

"Okay, maybe. But it's also attacking our camp, so we should probably get going and kill it." I nodded, but paused before I started off.

"This wind might end up killing me, if I can't get my hair in check." I mumbled, pushing the curly locks behind my ears and sprinting forward.

CHAPTER EIGHT

We rushed to the edge of camp, watching the robot approach. There were three mages on top of the camp wall, each adorned in a green cloak, putting up shields and blasting the rhino. Not many people were out due to the wind, which made this a perfect time to strike.

"They must have planned this," I cursed under my breath. "They knew people wouldn't be out in a storm. They took this as an opening to attack!"

"You're right. Those monsters," Damien growled. "We should get on top of the wall. Come with—" He held his hand out, but I shook my head.

"We don't want to attack from above. The legs are a weak spot. You see how it's kinda fumbling over itself? And the magic attacks from above are doing nothing. It's more armored at the top. They probably don't have much or any defense at the bottom."

"Quick thinking. That's good, and as close to a plan as we've got." We both ran out of the gates, some sticks and roots flying through the air, but the giant log now gone, and into the forest where the robot was coming from. We heard shouts behind us, but they were faint, carried away by the whipping wind. Damien and I vaulted over fallen logs, weaved between tree trunks, and dashed across the landscape until we reached the feet of the giant animal, slowly making its way through the forest. I reached down to grab my sword before remembering that I didn't have it. I left it in the arena... with the wolf!

"Oh, no... I left, like, everything in the camp," I grumbled. Damien looked at me in surprise.

"Remember your training," he commented before sprinting towards the rhino, dashing underneath its stomach, looking for a weak spot.

"What does that mean?" I crossed my arms, trying to think,

looking at the ground. He sounded like he would be the ghost of my long lost father, attempting to contact me from beyond the grave in my time of need. My eyes skimmed over all the debris, fallen leaves, sticks, and... wait, sticks! That's what he meant; even simple things like loose twigs can help control power. Anything can be a vessel. I turned, looking for a stick about the size of a sword. I found one quickly, lying next to a small tree. The wood was thick and it wasn't brittle, so it wouldn't break easily. I could use this. I carried it in one hand, and then followed Damien.

"They haven't noticed us yet, or else they would have stopped. We need to figure out a way in or a way to make this thing fall," Damien commented quietly, watching me slip beneath the metal of the monster's stomach. I pondered the possibilities as we hunched down, walking with the machine.

"I could go out and distract it, try to lure some people out or stop the machine. A giant blast of fire will probably attract attention."

"You can try it, but be careful. We don't want to burn the woods down, and you don't have a lot of experience. Don't hurt yourself." I nodded, and rushed forwards, bringing myself to the front of the rhino. I held my hand up, and sent the fire through the stick I was holding and into the sky, creating an explosion. That quick blast sent a jolt down my arm, but it wasn't painful, and the fire was a controlled line of heat.

I heard metal creak as the animal halted, its head going towards me like it was sniffing. I reached out to grab it and hopefully melt the metal, but it moved too quickly. The curved tip of the horn on its face snagged my shirt and sent me flying into the air. I soared above the trees, screaming as I plummeted. I'd almost reached the ground when something shot towards me, a fuzzy material scraping against my back, grabbing me out of the sky and setting me down safely, right in front of the walls of the camp. I looked behind me to see J, his hand in the air, controlling what looked like a carpet. He waved, standing in the door frame of the gates, and I smiled in thanks. I turned towards the monster, trying to formulate a plan.

"Damien! Rhino!" I yelled, dodging another strike from the machine. I didn't fancy taking another trip through the trees.

"I know, I'm under it!"

"No, turn into one!"

"Oh!" The machine was lifted slightly off of the ground as Damien morphed into a real rhino, silver skin gleaming as he pierced through the steel of the creature's stomach. He rocked back and forth, shaking the robot and anything inside it. I leaped as high as I could, nearly slipping down the slick steel but grabbing onto any surface I could find, launching myself off of its nose and landing on its back. I set the stick ablaze, imagining blue flame swirling around the wood, then driving the stake into the rhino's back, slowly melting away a human sized hole. I looked inside to see three terrified faces, liquid metal dripping above them. I smiled before dropping in, landing on one person's head and swinging so I knocked into the other three, throwing them to the ground, unconscious.

I examined the room I was in, trying to keep myself steady as the place moved. Towards the front of the animal was what looked like a control panel, with red and green buttons strewn about and four levers. I assumed the levers were to move the legs, but I wasn't quite sure. I heard footsteps, so I knew I had to act quickly. I pressed one of the red buttons, and the walls started compressing around me, creaking as they closed in. I heard screaming and thuds. The metal closed around me, and I yelped, until it passed through me, like the floor of the ravine had when I got here. I landed on the leaf-covered floor, nearly tipping over. Behind me, the rhino was folding itself into a small box of metal. About five or six men sat beneath the trees, looking stunned. I picked up the box, and chucked it as far as I could through the forest, hearing it clang against a tree. All heads turned to see their weapon just thrown away. Damien morphed back into a human, giggling hysterically and rushing to my side.

"I don't know how you did that, but it was awesome," he snickered, glancing at everyone now sitting on the floor.

"We still have an obstacle, though. Quite a few of them," I said, tilting my head towards the people still lying on the ground. They were beginning to collect themselves, and regroup. J walked up behind us.

"We can deal with them. No use in bringing them to the camp," he said, and I nodded. We stood only a few feet apart from everyone else, but they seemed to be waiting. For what was a mystery, though it was a bit awkward, just assessing each other. Unlike with the sky ship, they were all grown men, so there was some added tension with the adults facing three children.

"I'm guessing it would be bad if we made the first move, or else they would have attacked already. Are there traps or something?" I questioned, looking around.

"Not any that would affect them here. And the wind has stopped, so I'm not sure if that was their doing or not..."

"Right. I think... well, I'm not sure but I might have something that could work," I suggested. "Damien, remember the wolf we found?"

"You found a *what*?" J asked, baffled.

"Yeah, I left it in the arena when we went to go check why the power went out. But if it can get out..." I whistled, even though the thought was farfetched. It wasn't trained, and I left it behind. The best possible scenario was that it caused confusion between the others' ranks. Which, luckily, they were confused. But for a horrifying second, nothing happened. Then I heard a piercing, drawn-out howl, and the wolf jumped into the fray.

It leapt across the space between us, charging at the others from the Kingdom. Snarling and biting, it ran around them, jumping over their heads and causing panic. I laughed, rushing forward, the stick setting fire in my hand. We danced between the people, knocking them down every chance we got. A few times I ended up having to fight off individual people, but after a few minutes, they had all fallen. I was breathing hard, but smiling.

"Is this all the Kingdom has? I'm surprised you guys haven't completely overrun them yet," I joked, pushing a stray hair out of my face.

"We didn't have you before," Damien said, coming over to check the carnage. "But... why were they waiting?"

"They knew they didn't stand a chance without their weapon, I guess?" I remarked, shrugging.

"Maybe it—duck!" I looked behind me, expecting to see the animal, but I was lifted off of my feet. A man, tall with a snarl on his face, took the back of my shirt and lifted me. From what I saw, he was bald, and wore a dog tag with indecipherable writing, and a long, green trench coat. I let out a choking sound, the edge of my shirt pressing against my neck. "Amber! Let them go!" Damien tried running forward, but was held back by two guards. J was in the same position.

"I guess this is what they were waiting for," J muttered, struggling against the grip. "Reinforcements."

"The Kingdom is weak, eh?" The man behind me hissed. "I guess we have to prove our strength." He dropped me, gasping for air, and put his boot on my back, shoving me into the mud. I wanted to do something, but I'd lost my stick and didn't want to risk anything. "You can kill the other two. We only need this one." My eyes widened. My friends' lives-and the camp—were at risk now. I was away from most of the people I wanted safe. If I stayed calm, I might be able to control it.

I was nearly shaking with nerves, but I managed to summon a small flame in my hand. I tilted my palm backwards, to where the man was, and let go. I felt the heat on my back as fire blasted out of my hand, throwing him backwards in surprise, his jacket smoldering. He quickly patted out the burns, yelping. I jumped up, my hands glowing dimly. I looked around for the wolf, but it was gone. I was on my own.

I planted my feet, examining the enemies. We were somehow

surrounded. J and Damien were still in captivity; some of the wounded people that we knocked down had risen to aid their leader.

My friends looked hopeful, though. Knowing they were counting on me didn't entirely help my nerves. I spread my hands, shooting fire around the circle, but it was mostly dodged and blocked. I didn't want to unleash my powers just in case they went out of control. That fear still resided in me, blocking any control I could entirely have, which was another problem. Fear was an obstacle, one that tripping over could mean catastrophe. I tried to remember all I'd been taught, physically and mentally. In times like this, what I needed was to let go.

I took a deep breath, trying to go into that calm, the-entire-universe-makes-sense mode that I got with Shadow. My nerves relaxed, I stopped my shaking. The time to fight was now.

I looked up at the enemies, my blood boiling at their confident sneers and cruel glares. They underestimated me already, but they were still cautious. They would never have any clue what was coming. I raised my hands above my head, almost out of instinct, and let the power flow through me until I was encased in flames like they were armor. Honestly, in that moment, my thought process was slightly inspired by an animation trope — the sudden appearance of armor, summoned by the person's power. I wondered if I could create that same type of gear just with the flames surrounding me, and my magic complied.

Almost unwillingly, wings sprouted from amidst the fire. Everything was ablaze. The sudden surge of power created a panic, and they attacked. I finally learned the answer to an old question everyone asked — what was the enemy doing, just watching the transformation? Yes, but instead of patiently waiting for an end, they rushed forward. I tried to move forward but felt woozy, slipping and falling to the floor. Everyone launched themselves at me, tired of waiting. I smacked away one, turning to grab another's coat and use him as a weapon, pulling him onto the ground. I jumped up, swinging around to land behind them and unleash a torrent of fire from my palm, leaving most of them on the floor.

Still drained, I snarled, running towards who was left, still too many men for my quickly fading energy. It was strange to not see any women or others, but that just added to the list of what was wrong with the Kingdom. I grabbed the first man's shoulders, jumping and twisting to vault over him, using the momentum to swing him over my head and slam him into the dirt. I felt something tug at my ankle, and I looked back to see a fallen soldier trying to sweep me off of my feet. The fire swirling around me that was acting as armor burned his hand. I kicked him away before being tackled from the front. I tried to roll before I hit the ground, away from the person who hit me. I succeeded, and ended up with my elbow pressing into his back while he winced in pain on the ground. I noticed others getting up, hurt but not dead or incapable of fighting.

Some pulled out knives and swords, others what looked like relics. They were literally going to fight fire with fire. I dug my hands into the ground, hoping my idea would work. I sent out shockwaves of fire that uprooted trees, shook the earth, and spread heat throughout the enemies, burning them. It was almost as if the earth amplified my powers, using one element hand in hand with another. Maybe an Elite was around, helping me. Maybe it was just me. I didn't know, but using all of this power made me feel sick, and faint. I tried to keep consciousness, but even that was difficult.

I spotted two men and the leader, the only one that had actually talked yet, dragging away Damien and J. They appeared to be unconscious, and everyone else was heading towards the camp. I jolted in a realization that this was all a diversion. I cursed, sprinting towards the others. They saw, or maybe heard, me coming and started to run, not even looking back. I was afraid that they would get violent, and actually kill my friends. I was fast, but they were faster. At one point, the guy in the back tripped, falling over a root. He was holding Damien, so I punched him, knocking him down and grabbing Damien's limp body, dragging him along with me. I broke through the trees, my fire now flickering to a stop, as I marveled at the destruction before me. Craters surrounded the camp, parts of the wall were falling off, and one of the gate doors were missing. Not only was the attack on me a diversion to escape with the others, it was also a diversion so they could attack.

The wind around me fueled my rage, fanned my flames into a roaring bonfire, until I was wreathed in an uncontrollable smoldering inferno, like a demon walking along the Earth's surface. I charged at the men, feeling like I wasn't even in control of my own limbs, my only focus to save what I could of the camp. I barely paid attention to my moves; I only attacked. Jumping from one person to another, flying through the air with the strength and heat of a volcano, I let my emotion take control, sorrow ripping at my heart to see this place destroyed. I felt so protective, but now I knew that was for a reason. I had the power to protect, and I wouldn't back down. Even if I didn't hurt anyone today, this would send a very loud message:

I am here to protect this place. They wanted to take this from me, they wanted to hurt and kill my friends and family to end a senseless war. Those thoughts sent me into an immediate flurry of rage. My heart beat faster and faster, my vision became blurry as the flames encased me. They couldn't fight, they could barely move at the same speed I was. With the fire surrounding me, I looked and felt like an actual demon. Just like how it started, it was over in seconds. In the time I took to pause, they were all on the ground, their clothes on fire and not moving. I hoped no one was dead, but severely injured. I crept up to the man that had tried to choke me before, as he was still writhing on the ground. He looked up, terror unmistakable in his eyes. I thought he would run, but he only lay there, still spitting and flailing about.

"Is he working for you?" He demanded. I was taken aback by his sudden, very random comment.

"Who?" I asked, and the flames around me dissipated.

"Adam! He told me you were weak, and frail! He told me we could take you! He LIED! He's working for you!"

"First of all, rude. Second of all, I don't know anyone named Adam. Third of all, why do you all have such mediocre, generic names? You would have thought, being from a different dimension or whatever weird shadow world this is, you would all have cooler names." I crossed my arms, my throat aching like it was burnt by the fire, tears welling in my eyes from the heat, but I was satisfied. I felt light, like I could collapse at any second, but I stood before this man, trying to pretend I couldn't be thrown down by someone breathing too hard.

"Okay, *Amber*." I heard Damien mutter behind me. I swung around, shooting a glare at him. He shrugged, trying to look innocent.

"Who cares about his stupid name? *He lied*!" the man roared, and I rolled my eyes, sighing.

"Gotta update your sources, man. A baby lion is probably harmless, but they quickly grow into some really deadly animals, if you mess with them. Also, let it go." I leaned down, swiftly backhanding him, knocking him down once again, his head landing in the dirt. I grabbed J, who was sprawled out a few steps away, hoisting him up onto my arm. I sat him down next to Damien, who was barely conscious, but apparently enough so that he could make a snarky comment.

"What happened to the camp?" J muttered, his eyes fluttering open.

"I... I don't know. It was attacked." I hung my head, disappointed in myself.

"It's not your fault," Damien murmured, trying to stay awake. "You got a lot of them. We weren't aware that some were here." He spoke with slurred words, like he had too much to drink.

"But we left this place practically defenseless. With the wind, and the General's state... the General!" I looked up at the castle. The tower he would have been in was knocked clean off of the building. I ran into the camp, dodging and jumping over fallen stones and bricks. I slid on the mud, but managed to stay balanced and kept going. It was obvious where the tower fell, as the entire room was strewn about, right in front of the stables. The hellhounds were all barking, baring their teeth and getting into a frenzy. I ignored the sound and searched through the rubble of the General's room. There was no body to be found. I couldn't tell if that was good or bad.

I heard a piercing, bloodcurdling scream from across camp. I looked up, deciding to abandon the debris over here and see what was wrong. Across camp, J seemed to be the source of the shriek. He was kneeling over a body, a knife impaled in the person's skin, right where their heart was. My breath caught in my throat at the gruesome sight. Tears streamed down J's face as he stood over the corpse. There was no way they were alive.

"What happened?" I whispered, my own eyes tearing up. Damien could barely look.

"They killed him. That's J's brother. They... they've never gone this far. They've never directly killed someone. But we saw them... they rushed in and just..." he wasn't able to finish. He sniffed, turning away. I looked back down to J, who was tearing at his clothes. I knew the feeling, not being able to cry enough for the amount of pain you were experiencing. I looked at the body. It did resemble J. He had a mop of dark hair, strewn over his face. He wore simple, colorless clothes. His eyes were closed, but I remembered seeing him around camp. He was always helping with one thing or another.

"Where is he?" I said with my teeth clenched.

"Who?"

"The man who killed him. Where is he?" I looked up with anger in my eyes. This was not okay. We could rebuild the camp, but a person couldn't be brought back from the dead.

"We have him in captivity. He wounded four others, including... including H." Damien said softly, but J's head whipped around, his face showing more pain I'd ever seen in a human.

"They hurt H? They killed my brother and they *hurt H*?" he screamed, his voice cracking.

"I'm going to see him right now. I promise, he'll get what he has coming." I put my hand on J's shoulder, hoping it was a comforting gesture.

"What he has coming is death. A slow, painful death for what he's done," J growled, and I pulled my arm back.

"An eye for an eye makes the whole world blind," Damien said, seemingly trying to warn his friend, but it didn't help.

"Your favorite saying. Right, I forgot. Not like you've mentioned it so many times, it's burned into my head. I definitely can't hear it in your voice at this point!" J snapped, glaring at Damien, who stepped back in surprise. I knew in this state, he would only be mad at all of us, no matter what we said or did. I was angry, and upset, but I could never know the pain he was going through. His brother was killed, his friends hurt, his partner injured. His heart couldn't take much more.

"We'll leave you. Once everything calms down, you can help us choose the fate for whoever did this. You'll get a say in what happens." I nodded towards Damien, telling him to follow me. We walked across the camp in near silence.

"Did you see what happened?" I finally asked.

"Not really. Enough to be disturbed. I can't imagine how J feels. At least H will survive." He bit his lip, looking guilty.

"It wasn't your fault," I said, sighing and holding my head. My gut twisted, and every muscle protested my movement. I tried to press forward, ignoring the growing pains. "Like you said, we had no idea what was happening. None of us could have prevented this."

"I wish I could have done something, though. Now he's so upset... I don't know what will happen."

"Yeah... so, I just realized I don't know where I'm going," I said sheepishly. Damien looked up and smiled.

"Right, I never told you. We're holding him in the library." I nodded, and we started off towards the two doors. We had to backtrack, but we reached the library shortly. I had only just put my hand on the door when I heard a shrill scream from inside. I looked back to Damien in confusion. He smacked his palm to his forehead.

"Alexander and the other girl. They're still in there!" he groaned. My eyes widened and I threw open the door. A relatively short man stood in the corner, ginger curly hair cut short. He was pale, but had a fire in his green eyes. He held a knife to human Alexander's throat. I was excited to see him human again, but not as happy to see him being threatened. I jumped in, grabbing the man's shoulders, twisting his arms behind him, knocking the knife out of his hand and forcing him to the floor. He cried out in pain, a high-pitched squeal.

"What is up with this dude?" I muttered.

"I'm not a *dude*!" they spit. I raised my eyebrows. "I'm a girl!"

"Great! Now when do we get to discuss the fact that you've killed someone and threatened my friend?" I said cheerily, a fake smile on my face. She looked surprised, and then her face fell.

"I didn't mean to kill him. I was sent on an intimidation mission. He got in the way, and... I slipped."

My anger took over. "He's dead because of you. Human lives aren't pawns in a game, killing someone can't just be written off with an 'oops'. And you could have killed so many others! Even the fact that one person is dead is... deplorable. I can't believe you're okay with this," I snarled, letting go of her and standing up. "Are you alright?" I asked, turning to Alexander.

"I think so. That spell worked, like, ten minutes after you cast it. Problem is, though..." He winced and pointed to the cage. The glass was shattered.

"We have a lot of problems now," I grumbled, with a pointed glare towards the girl on the floor. "We have to rebuild, find her, and thanks to someone, plan a funeral." She wilted under my gaze.

"We need time for this. I think we need to take a break. I'll take care of her; you've been working a lot. Your mana is probably really drained. Go rest," Damien basically ordered. I knew it was pointless to argue. I nodded, not content with this but it was necessary. I closed the door behind me with a sigh, looking up to see the sun setting. The sky exploded with vibrant hues of orange, red, and yellow—a beautiful end to a horrific day.

I climbed the broken wall at the front of the camp, avoiding crumbling spots to sit atop the stones, watching the sun dip below the horizon as I felt the cold night breeze sweep over me. I heard rocks clanking together behind me, and turned to see Damien also scaling the wall.

"Hey," he grunted, finally making it to where I was.

"Hey," I sighed, wanting to avoid a lecture. "What happened with the girl?"

"She's in custody. I don't entirely know what's gonna happen to her. She says she didn't mean to kill J's brother, but… I'm worried his death marks the real beginning of this war we're stuck in with the Kingdom. They've never been this aggressive, so who knows what will happen now?"

"Oh." I leaned back, looking up at the sky, and seeing stars bloom from beyond the blue blanket of the sky. "I can't help but feel like some of this was started by me."

"Eh, this was inevitable. But now, with you, we have a better chance of winning against the King. I saw what you did in an effort to protect us, and the camp. You had them under your complete control!" Damien smiled at me, and I grinned back, his sparkling eyes blurring as my vision faded, and I felt myself slip backwards. I heard a grunt, and Damien grabbed me before I could fall off the wall. I sat up, holding my head. "Amber, are you okay?"

"I'm just… tired…" I sighed, my head lolling in front of me, like my neck wasn't strong enough to support it. Damien grabbed my shoulder, drawing me into a hug as I sat there, limp.

"You can't be so reckless," he whispered, the world around us falling silent. The crackling of fires still burned in the background, but it seemed like time had stopped. Or maybe I was going deaf. "You just… kept going, after that stunt. You gotta be more careful. Magic isn't harmless, not to others or yourself."

"I know, I—I'm sorry. I'll… sit." I muttered, and he chuckled gently. I could feel his heart beating, and his shoulders shaking as he laughed. "Did you just come up here to give me an update and a hug?" I tried to open my eyes, but it was like my eyelids had turned into lead. Lying down, I felt calmer, and more focused.

"Well, I also had some questions. Like… you didn't seem very shocked when you were introduced to all of this magic. You took control of it and absorbed it, accepting it into your life. Why? Weren't you surprised?" He questioned. I turned my head, thinking.

"I… I guess I've known about this, hoped for it. I'd read about myths and magic, wishing it was real," I swallowed, feeling now like I could talk better, actually form words without stumbling. "I dreamed about things like this, I've always wanted powers, sometimes… to escape. Wandering in the woods, I hoped to find something like this. I thought I saw strange creatures across the creek, or things that seemed like they couldn't be explained, so I always held onto the thought of… this."

"Hmm, that makes sense, I guess. Sorry to also plunge you into all the drama and chaos, though. You're handling it really well. I can tell you were meant to be here." He offered a smile, and I sent one back.

"Thanks. I wish I could do more, though. I feel useless, still. I know we need to do something against the Kingdom. They need to know they're not allowed to bat us around, like we're toys, but... I can't think of anything to do." I raised my hand to my temple, feeling defeated.

"Well... there might be something, actually. You should keep resting here for a bit, but it might be time for you to meet the Council."

I think I fell asleep, but I couldn't be sure with how hazy my brain was. By the time Damien shifted, tapping my shoulder so we could get up, I felt a lot better, my headache dying down and while I was still sore, I felt refreshed. We got down from the wall, walking behind the hellhound stables, and Damien faced the wall. He tapped the stone twice, then three times below where he tapped before. The wall started to glow, then gave way to a staircase, the rock making a low scraping sound as it separated. As we descended into darkness, the sound of voices chattering became louder and louder. We soon reached another door, far underground, the chill down here almost making me shiver.

Damien knocked once, paused, and then knocked twice. A hush fell over the room as the doors swung open, seemingly by themselves. We stepped into a massive room, barely lit, but still evidently beautiful. The floor was engraved with an image of a sleeping woman, stretched out across the room. The walls were smooth, black stone, small niches glowing dimly. Hundreds of cloaked figures stood on floating chunks of what looked like obsidian. I couldn't see anyone's faces, but I could feel their watchful eyes.

"Council, I have brought news, and a friend. The Kingdom has attacked us once again. We also lost one of our members; Amos Avargaurd was murdered, stabbed in the chest by one of the people sent in the attack. She is currently imprisoned. Amber, General-in-training, courageously defeated countless enemies in the woods. They fought with true valor. The Kingdom managed to get to our base and destroyed a huge portion of the front wall, leaving craters outside of it. In all the chaos, we lost track of the current General. We do not know of his location or his status—alive or dead. That is all the news I have." Damien paused, and they all began talking again. No one could speak alone. "Don't worry, they'll calm down in a minute and begin to make sense. It always takes a second for them to agree," he whispered to me, as if reading my thoughts. I nodded.

The voices began to slow, coming to a stop once again.

"This child, they are the General-in-training?" One council member asked.

"Yes, as the prophecy foretold," Damien confirmed. "An outsider from a different world."

"Are they ready to sit in until we learn of the General's status? Are they trained enough to handle the responsibility; are they wise enough to make good decisions when we cannot be summoned; are they strong enough to hold this weight on their shoulders?" another pondered. I felt like I should step in, but I also knew it wasn't my place, no matter how much I wanted to defend myself.

"Enough that, with a little guidance, they will do a lot of good for the camp. If you approve of our request to let them sit in as the General, they'll continue their training."

"It will be intense. We may send the rest of the Elites, whichever ones are able to coexist," one suggested. "This war has stressed them out, spread their forces too thin, but we may be able to summon a few."

"That will also upgrade security, which we need, unless we want to be discovered. The Elites are powerful, and know how to defend this place," yet another said. They didn't seem to be capable of saying more than one or two sentences each.

"That could work," one agreed. "Though I'm not sure Tigre or Melioca are very appropriate for this type of thing. They can get... vulgar. Too powerful, as well."

"We need power!" one argued. "Especially if this one is able to take on the Kingdom's men, they'll know and send their most seasoned veterans to fight. We'll be under a lot of pressure and firepower."

"Damien," a deep voice echoed through the cavern, quieting everyone else's. "Give me an example of their power. Could you compare it to an Elite's?"

"With or without something to channel it through?" he asked, almost awkwardly.

"Without," they responded. I could feel the tension thicken, all air seeming to seep out of the cavern as the Council waited with baited breath.

"From what we know, yes. Their power seems to be very strong, and we haven't seen the half of it yet. They have elemental powers, as does... you know."

"Wise not to say her name so close to her. All elements, or the main four?"

"Unknown, but it seems to be the four."

"I see. You, little General." I felt a cold wind as the shadows seemed to peel off of the ceiling above, forming into a man with a soft face, and a rugged beard. "You will do great things, I suppose. Do not focus on one thing and ignore your other traits and powers. The council acknowledges and accepts your suggestion, Damien. Amber, you are hereby the temporary General. Now, the Elites will be called soon. Go, and meet them." Another breeze, and we appeared at the top of the steps, the door closed in front of us.

"What was that?" I whispered, a bit shaken. "Why didn't I know that was there?"

"Not many people do. The council helps us when we're in dire need of help. They can repair things that are extremely damaged and call backup. They can grant people powers and shift leadership. The guy who came down from the ceiling? That's Hinder, Shadow's son. He's pure darkness, but also pure power. That group can never be found by the Kingdom, or we would be in big trouble. Now, the Elites will be arriving soon. You're not gonna wanna miss this."

Once again, I was in shock and in a haze, but time was running along without me. I had no choice but to blindly follow. I heard shrieks, hopefully of joy or excitement, coming from the front of the camp. Damien and I jogged over to see light coming down from the darkened sky, and I vaguely noted that the bitter smell of smoke was gone, and the wall was now whole, no longer crumbling. I felt a weight on my shoulder and looked back to see Tigre putting his arm on my shoulders, smirking into the sky. He looked down and half smiled, showing his sharp teeth. I rolled my eyes and pointed my gaze to the sky, to see quite a few figures descending. They all reached the ground with their own flare, purple fireworks, bursts of water, sparkles, rainbow glitter, all sorts of overly dramatic entrances. Then, standing before us, was a very diverse group of people. Some were mixed with animals, others made of light or bearing wings, and then what seemed to be a single human. They drew a crowd, milling about with the people who quickly rushed to the scene, greeting everyone like old friends.

I stared in astonishment. One, however, stayed alone, behind the group. She looked like a child, short with a small pout on her face. She had brilliant white wings, folded down on her back, and she wore a gorgeous white gown—flowing, glistening fabric that fell to her ankles. She wore Greek-style sandals and a pearl necklace rested delicately on her chest. Her hair was dirty blonde, cut short, and delicately curled. Her blue eyes scanned the crowd, a serious, almost judgmental look on her face. She caught me staring, and I smiled, waving in greeting, trying to make it seem less awkward. She simply turned away.

"Who's that?" I asked, caught between annoyed and stunned.

"That's Melioca, the one the council members were talking about. She's a dark and light angel mix, and when she fights, you see her true form. It's... horrifying, to say the least. You never want to face her in actual battle. She's very sensitive and picky, and... a sore loser, to say the least," Damien advised. "Don't tell her I said that, but she despises losing."

"Noted," I replied, feeling a bit sick. She didn't look to be much, but I could imagine the terror she inflicted when fighting. "Should I go introduce myself to anyone?" I asked, looking behind me. Damien shrugged in response.

"If you want to, but we should go ahead and get to training. They don't like waiting," he said, a bit sheepishly. I nodded.

"Then, let's go to the arena. I wanna get started, too." We

departed, heading towards the building at the side of the camp. Entering, we saw B, shifting through the sand and mumbling. "B! Are you alright?" I asked, going up to her. Once again, she had her back turned and didn't notice me. "B?" I gently tapped her shoulders, and she jumped.

"Oh! Amber, Damien. I... uh, sorry, I lost something." She smiled.

"What did you lose? We can help find it," I offered. Her eyes widened, and she stammered on an answer.

"I, uh, lost my... Bluetooth headphones!" she gestured, looking proud of her announcement.

"You guys... have Bluetooth here?" I asked, confused.

"No, actually. We've heard about it, but... there's no way you could have gotten it. What's up, B?" Damien looked more than a bit worried. B sighed, defeated.

"I lost my hearing aids," she admitted, looking to the floor.

"Why would you need—oh." Realization dawned on me. She looked back up at me, sadness showing in her eyes. "Why is that such a bad thing, B? You don't have to hide that type of stuff, we can help you," I asked. "Wait... can you hear me?"

"I can read lips, for the most part. I... I didn't wanna tell you, because I was worried you would see me as... less of something. I didn't want you to treat me like a child, or differently at all. I can do everything a hearing person can do except hear. But people still manage to treat me like I can't do anything. You are all good people, but I didn't wanna risk it." She looked almost ashamed. I put my hand on her shoulder.

"I'm sorry you feel that way. You're still you, there's no reason to treat you differently. I just wanna know if there's anything we can do to help make the camp more accessible." I was worried I might say something wrong or offend her in any way, but I also knew I should try to assist her.

"Oh, uh... I hadn't really thought of that. Maybe—" before she could finish, the door to the arena burst open. Melioca stood in the doorway, an ever-present glare on her face.

"I heard I'm supposed to help train someone," she rolled her eyes, so subtly I could barely catch it.

"Yeah, any help would be greatly appreciated. This is Amber, stand-in General until we figure out what happened to the other one." Damien lowered his head, almost in a bow.

"Can we wait a second? We were—" I started, but Melioca cut me off with a suspicious glare.

"It's best if we get this over with. The forces of evil aren't going to wait while you have a tea party," Melioca retorted, and I was taken aback. B simply nodded, looking a bit disappointed, and walked back to the infirmary. I was a bit irked by that, but it wouldn't be wise to start a fight.

"She'll be okay, don't worry. We'll get back to it," Damien whispered, leaning towards me.

"I have two others with me," Melioca sighed, stepping aside. In walked a tall, burly man, with deep brown hair and a thick beard. He held a giant axe, and a thin scar ran across his face. One of his eyes shone a bright golden, the other humbly glowed silver. He almost looked like a lumberjack that was decked out in intricate armor. A woman stood beside him, roughly my height but she had a soft aura to her. She was wearing pants and a flowing shirt, along with combat boots similar to mine. She looked like a normal human unless you looked up. Her black hair was braided with moss and twigs. She had giant antlers sprouting out of her head. Her skin was dark, but cracked. Not wrinkled, though—actual cracks weaved through her face. Her eyes were as blue as the sky on a cloudless day. "This is Ija," Melioca pointed to the man in reference. "And Quartz," looking to the woman.

"And here I was, thinking you all had obvious names," I laughed. "I guess that was coming from meeting Shadow, Tigre and Mirage first. Nevertheless, it's a pleasure to meet you all. We're honored to have you here," I smiled brightly, excited for what was to come. Quartz's reactions were a bit sluggish, as she lifted her head and smiled at what I said, and then slowly nodded.

"Same to you," Ija nodded in agreement. His voice was a lot higher than I thought it would be. I had imagined a gravelly, booming voice. But he had a soft tone, and not exactly a high voice but not a low one, either, with a thick accent. I couldn't quite place it, but it sounded like Scottish, maybe?

"You guys can get started on this. I'm going to go join the search team, to find the General. Good luck, Amber." Damien nodded in farewell, and bounded off. I turned, kind of overwhelmed by the people in front of me. I could feel their power, radiating from here. I took a deep breath, and smiled again.

"Shall we?"

CHAPTER NINE

A lot had happened in the span of a few hours. But it was going to get a lot more intense. At this point, my brain just accepted any strange stuff that happened, numb to the unreal. What went on in that arena constantly tested me, though.

"I'll help first," Quartz offered, stepping forward, and I nodded. "To begin, you must have an understanding of your power. The elements are always around you—the air you breathe, the water you drink, and the earth you live upon. Fire, however, is not a constant. That's good for our health, but not for trying to master the elements. Due to this reason, it's harder to completely understand and grasp fire, because you cannot take it from the world around you. You must draw it from nothing. It is the hardest element to master, so you're lucky you started with that power." Quartz spoke with a slight accent, once again difficult to pinpoint, but her voice was deep and smooth. "First, we will work with air. It is the easiest, because no matter what, it's with you. If it's not... well, you're usually dead by that point." I chuckled, surprised she was making jokes. "You can use the air around you to start off with techniques, and even enhance your other power."

"Wait, what?" I asked. "How… how does that work?"

"Fire can be fueled by air; the two elements feed off of each other. Using two parts of your power together could create a whole host of abilities and options, and it could make your attacks even more powerful. Fire and air are just one, but be careful when using all of your powers at once. That could very well create a catastrophe," Quartz warned.

"Noted," I gulped. If I had gone out of control with my fire, I couldn't imagine what using all the elements together would do.

"We will also work on harnessing your flames, to where you can at least perform basic attacks without losing control. A power such as yours can be difficult, but I have faith you will prevail!" She said cheerily. I nodded again, grinning. She was very calm, but bubbly and happy. Her personality was almost contagious, and I felt motivation flowing through me. At that point, a gust of wind whisked by. "Feel the wind around you. Air is a part of us, we rely on it, we live in peace with it." I took it in, noting the way it curved around my body. I could imagine it, flying past, not a care in the world. What cares would wind have, anyway? I took a deep breath, picturing the air coursing through my lungs. "That's good, notice the air working with you and how you use it. Air, wind, oxygen is vital to our survival. It flows through you; it's a part of all living things. Now, move me." I faltered, opening my eyes in surprise. Quartz's face was dead serious. "Use your wind. Move me from this spot."

"Are you sure? I don't want to hurt you," I stuttered. She chuckled.

"I'm an Elite. I'm not easily taken down. Give me your best," she challenged. I nodded, determined to prove myself. I used what I'd learned with my fire, and tried to harness the wind. It was already inside of me, around me. I needed to harness something invisible, but powerful. Something that's in our everyday lives, but normally uncontrollable and wild. The task at hand seemed much more difficult when putting it like that, but it was true. I held out my arm, trying to think of where the air was coming from. All around me, but I could direct it, right? Channel it towards me, not entirely using it, but asking it for aid, in a way.

I felt myself breathe, the rise and fall of my chest, the air escaping from me. I felt my fingertips start to go numb, but a soft breeze pushed by, coursing around me in small circles. I couldn't see it, but I could feel the push of the wind, tossing my hair and making my arm cold as it swirled around my hand. I felt small pinpricks of pain, like the wind had picked up some broken glass and was throwing it at me. In the shock of that pain, I let go of the little bubble that was holding the air around me. It made a popping sound, the wind flowing forward and lashing at

Quartz. It wasn't very strong, however, so the stream simply broke around her.

"It's a start!" she exclaimed, cheering me on. I glanced past her, looking over at the Elites standing on the sidelines. Ija gave me a thumbs-up, and Melioca sighed dramatically. She couldn't hide the curious gaze she had before I looked over, but she did try to erase it, looking away with a glare. I felt a little proud when I looked back over to Quartz, knowing I peaked her interest. I held out both my arms, determined to turn that emotion into power.

I tried to think. Fire seemed to be influenced most by anger or desperation, which made sense. Pride wasn't exactly an emotion I felt I could connect to the air, so what was? A sweeping sense of calm could help for a light breeze, but I needed something bigger, something that could sweep someone off their feet. How did I feel when that wind storm blew in? What emotion does a large gust of wind conjure?

The fleeting feeling of fear. Maybe not the best feeling to exploit, but it could work. I focused on how I felt, especially while fighting. A harrowing sense of hopelessness, this freezing terror that made my heart miss a beat. I didn't even think about what I was doing, I was so lost in thought that the wind started spiraling without me, my mind trapped in yesterday.

It started swirling around me, causing the sand to shift and sending dust and small rocks into the air. I held my hands out in front of me, wrists connected but palms out, aiming at Quartz. She smiled weakly, and I let a thin stream of wind blast towards her. The beam shot towards her, clashing against her skin, but not making her move even an inch. I had to dig my feet into the sand, throwing out all my fear into the wind, assembling my emotions and using them as fuel.

I felt myself get pushed back, almost stumbling over myself as the air in front of me surged, throwing me around so I couldn't balance. I tried to hold everything together, but it kept going, and I winced from the cold. I yelped, cutting off the power and falling to my knees. Quartz was a few feet away from where she had been previously, holding her arms out in front of her. They seemed to have fused together, becoming like a rock in front of her face. I panted, exhausted from the effort that took, and a little flustered that I almost lost control. Quartz was right; it was significantly easier to use wind, and I was able to stop it. I stood, jogging towards Quartz to check on her.

"Are you alright?" I asked, a bit embarrassed.

"Just fine. You're talented, that was a very quick advancement! I noticed you lost your focus at the end, though, so try to be more careful, and don't use so much mana at the start of a battle. Keep that in mind." I beamed, the compliments filling me with warmth. I glanced over to Ija and Melioca, who looked towards us with surprise.

"You... you moved Quartz!" Ija's shock turned into laughter. His laugh sounded more like what I thought his voice was going to be, loud and bellowing, something that carries over the landscape, no matter where you are. "This one is special. You'll do good things, mini-General." I blushed, laughing a bit myself.

"Thank you," I pushed my hair behind my ear, smiling towards him. I glanced at Melioca, who scowled and turned away.

"You are very gifted. But we have more to do!" Quartz laughed. "You can try to use your powers together, now. Summon some fire in your hand, go for just a tiny spark. When your powers are out of control, aim lower and you'll get higher results." I nodded, and looked down to my hands. Fire burst from my palms, flames dancing around my fingertips. It grew into a small ball of heat, but didn't escape my grasp. I tried to use the wind, willing it to swirl in my hand, but I felt shaky. Using two powers at once was apparently really draining, and my arm gave out before I could connect the two.

"I—I'm sorry, I can't. I think… I overdid it in the battle. I'm drained." I looked up, a little ashamed, but Quartz nodded.

"Then it may be best for you to recover. We'll have to cancel for the day."

"What? I didn't even get to do anything!" Ija threw his hands in the air, seeming like he was joking, but I couldn't tell.

"Amber is still a child, and one that doesn't have any experience. Taking it slow is the best option," Quartz said wisely, and Ija lowered his hands, nodding.

"First things first, please tell me you all hear that?" Melioca asked, looking into the sky. The two other Elites followed, looking up with questioning glances. All I heard was a small rattling, which I thought was the wind, but Melioca spread her wings and took off, spiraling above the arena. The ceiling blocked her way, chain mesh guarding the outside. She snarled, raising her hand. A beam of black light shot through the ceiling, disintegrating part of it. She rose, perched above us like a huge bird. I saw a figure leap up to the same spot she was, right behind her. It raised its hand, looking like it was about to attack.

"Behind you!" I yelled, worried. She turned and screamed in anger, pushing the figure down the building. I ran outside, pushing through the door and running around the arena to see what that was. "Tigre?" I gasped, surprised to see him lying on the ground, groaning in pain.

"Why did you sneak up on me like that?" Melioca snarled, floating down, her wings elegantly spread. "I would've killed you if it wasn't for Amber!"

"Calm down, girl! I was trying to get you all for dinner!" Tigre grunted, glaring at his fellow Elite. "I'm hungry, and there's nothing to eat!"

"Why didn't you go to the Waffle House?" I asked.

"Still no power. I guess it's not that obvious since you all still run on lanterns—"

"Not our fault."

"Still. It's easier to eat together. I asked the cooks and they said that they didn't have any orders from the General. Because, for some reason, your word is more important than mine."

"Because I'm the General. You know, like the person who

leads the camp?"

"I'm an *Elite*!" He scoffed, rolling his eyes. "I've been around much longer than you have, shortie. I defended this camp, willing to give up my life for it, and this is the thanks I get. No food. No respect. Honestly, it's deplorable." Now it was my turn to scoff.

"You'll live," Melioca growled. "If I let you." Tigre held his hands up in defeat.

"Fine, but seriously, I'm hungry. Can you tell them to make something?" He asked, looking to me.

"I guess it wouldn't hurt to get some food. We can get everyone together for dinner, maybe like a picnic. Everyone could help prepare something!" I smiled at the idea.

"I mean, there's a lot of people here, but we can try. I just want *food*." He grumbled, standing up. Melioca slapped him, and he stumbled again. "Hey!"

"That was for scaring me," she glared, and walked away.

"Hmm. She's in a good mood."

"If that's her good mood, I don't wanna see her bad mood," I said, not exactly joking.

"At least she didn't try to kill me this time. Her attacks are hard to avoid," he sighed. "So, food?"

I walked through camp, realizing I didn't actually know where the kitchen was. Tigre pointed me in the right direction. There was a small building, huddled into the side of the wall surrounding the camp. It was right by the doors, so it was hard to see coming in, unless you knew where it was. I walked in, expecting to smell food cooking, but... nothing. The inside had no place to sit, only counters, some pantries, and ice boxes. Two people stood behind the counter in the middle of the room, each reading a book. They looked up when they heard the door open.

"Oh! Amber, hello!" one of them kindly greeted me. She was pretty short, with a bob of black hair, with almond-shaped brown eyes and fair skin. Her partner had eyes that almost glowed, a deep violet color that was really interesting to look at.

They were taller and a bit stockier, with a very androgynous look.

"Hi! Uh, I'm here to see about food. Some people—well, Tigre, mostly—were asking about dinner." They looked at each other, and then back at me.

"Well, the General usually tells us what to make, and with the power out... we don't have many options," the shorter one explained.

"Well, what can we—" the door slammed open, and I turned to see Tigre sauntering in.

"Hey, Amber," he purred, patting my head. I rolled my eyes as he walked past. "What are we making?"

"We were just talking about that," I sighed, trying to keep my temper. "Without power, it might be difficult to prepare anything."

"We usually don't have anything that uses power, but we have acquired a few things that help," the girl said, pondering our options. "We can, however, use fire."

"That's a good idea! Tigre, come with me. We'll get some fires started, and get the food. Can you two get some pots and pans so we can cook stuff?" I asked, turning to the two behind the counter.

"Of course. We'll meet you outside!" I smiled in response, and grabbed Tigre's wrist, dragging him out. He groaned the entire way.

"This is going to take way too long. I'm hungry! Why are you mortals so slow?" He huffed.

"I'm so sorry we can't magically summon food," I said, my words dripping with sarcasm.

"Amber!" Damien ran up to us with a wave. "We have a problem."

"What's wrong?" I asked, worried by his tone.

"The council has summoned us for a meeting. The second one in a day. That's... not good. They're rarely hosted even once a year."

"The council wants to talk to you?" Tigre exclaimed.

"Keep it down! But yes. Specifically to Amber." His eyes looked almost glazed over. They were dull, and he was very obviously tired. All of this stress was taking a massive toll on us. I could feel the effects getting to me, and to everyone else. Our energy wasn't very high, the camp was slowly crumbling, and the General was still missing. But I had a chance to make it right.

"Tigre, get together the fire and food. I'll go with Damien to see the Council." Tigre groaned again, exasperatedly sighing as an addition to his temper tantrum.

"Why do you get all the cool stuff?" he whined.

"How old are you again?" I said with a pointed glare. He opened his mouth to speak before settling back, still muttering angrily. "Please, just do it. Hopefully, I'll be back soon." I nodded as I departed, and headed off with Damien. I examined the camp as we walked, and felt hopeful. Most of the wall was fixed, and only a few cabins retained signs of destruction. We were coming back, though the power was still out. Some wounds, however, would never heal. Even one life lost was a bad sign of what was to come.

We headed back behind the stables, and I was shocked to see two robed figures standing outside the doorway. They bowed in greeting.

"Amber, Damien. Our apologies, we didn't mean to surprise you like this, but it's best to meet out here to discuss current... problems. Inside is a bit hectic at the moment; a disagreement caused chaos," one said, head still bowed.

"I understand. Would you like to go inside the library so it's a bit more quiet?" I suggested. I noticed with the council members and with the Elites I'd met, I almost had a different tone when speaking to higher authority. More professional, I guess. It wasn't a bad thing, but hopefully made a good impression instead of the opposite.

"That's a good idea." I couldn't see his face, but I sensed he was smiling.

"This way, then." I lead them to the doors of the castle. "Be careful. The top is... not in good condition at the moment, because of the attack," I said wearily.

"Noted."

I realized one of the council members wasn't talking at all. That confused me, but I thought it would be best not to ask. We entered, the smell of old books and dust wafting through the air. We sat down at the table in the middle of the room.

"Thank you for having us. We understand it's a bit of a strange setting, but with what's happening down there... it could be dangerous for mortals. But to the task at hand. The attacks by the Kingdom have gone too far. Recently, a life was taken from us. Accident or no, we have to start investigating the attacker and where it started from. So... that warrants us with spying on the Kingdom, its leaders and civilians. We need to do research and see what they're planning next, and how to stop them. We're suggesting sending you two in disguise. You'll need easily hidden weapons, as well. But the problem would be the disguises. We don't know exactly what normal people there wear, or what they act like. We're taking a big risk because you might not blend in. Sticking out is the first step in getting caught."

I tapped my finger on the table, considering the thought. "What if we wore masks? Like superheroes!" I beamed, like a child waking up on Christmas. The council members didn't speak, but I could sense their disappointment. I cleared my throat, trying to stay professional. I turned to Damien, who was sitting idly. "Do we have anything else we can use as disguises?"

"Well, you'll be fine. You're so new, no one will know who you are. But I think we do have a place for... not exactly costumes, but similar." He didn't look very happy about the option, but I assumed from his suggestion it was the only one we had.

"Can you take us there?" The council member asked. Damien

nodded, and stood. We had just opened the door when something flew by, stirring up dirt and sending it splattering across my clothes. Melioca sped past my face, cackling with joy. I growled in frustration, wiping spots of mud from my glasses.

"How old is she?" I muttered, trying to shake off all of the dirt. I was very unsuccessful. "I'll go change, and meet you all... where are we going?" Damien chuckled at my response.

"It's near the infirmary. We'll wait outside for you." I nodded in thanks, and rushed to my cabin. Searching through the drawers in my dresser, I found a new pair of jeans, combat boots, and a short sleeved gray shirt. The material was very thin, so I looked for an undershirt. I found a black tank top, and quickly pulled that on, wiped off my glasses again, and rushed out, eager to join the three. I passed the infirmary, feeling a bit guilty about having to cut off B, but rushing away from the small hospital to nearly behind the arena. It was such a small gap, you wouldn't imagine a building back there. But, sure enough, the camp didn't fail me, and I joined Damien and the Council members right before a small building, that looked like it only had one room—from the outside, at least. Damien reached for the door, and revealed that it was the exact same size as it appeared. Inside, hangers filled with clothes lined the walls. Shields and boots were propped against the sides, and various relics hung from hooks. A small, locked chest sat, collecting dust, on the floor.

"Whoa," I said, marveling at the wonder inside. Everything sparked with a magical energy.

"Pick anything you want. As long as it's not like, two cloaks," Damien joked. I smiled, studying everything laid out before me. I picked up a leather sheath from the floor, and attached it to a belt I'd also found, going across my stomach, above my clothes. It was black with buttons on the sides. It didn't cover the entire sheath, but it managed to obscure at least a few inches above the hilt. I could use this to keep the sword Damien gave me by my side, but now I needed some sort of armor.

"What's this?" I asked, drawn to a piece of fabric that looked like a storm cloud. Intricate, silvery designs wove through the fabric, so light you could barely notice them.

"It's an armored cloak. It looks and feels like regular fabric until it's hit. Then it generates a full body shield. It's kinda hard to use, though, as not every hit activates the shield and you'll need to manually bring the shield up when it doesn't."

"I'll take it. I mean—if I can." He nodded, and I grabbed it off of the hook. The side went over my shoulder and stopped a little above my stomach, but the back was a long cloak that flowed out. The sides were connected by two buttons, and the top of the fabric gripped my neck a bit—not enough to choke me, but I could feel it. The front was a bit too low, and I felt like it might hinder me in battle, but I had an idea. I unbuttoned the top button and pushed it back, behind my neck, so the fabric was higher and more secure. "How do you manually activate it?" I asked, turning to Damien, who was searching through the chest, which was apparently filled with wigs.

"Oh, it's a spell. If I say it too loud, it activates it, but..." he leaned in, whispering the words to me. It was weird, so strange I couldn't even attempt to spell it, but I knew—just barely—how to say it. I nodded in understanding.

"Thank you," I smiled. I still felt like something was missing, however. I looked up, examining the shelf above the hangers. I felt what seemed to be cold fabric, but it was stiffer, like it was infused with metal. I brought them down from the shelf to look at them. Two cylindrical silver gauntlets rested in my hands. The two sides opened, the material flexible so I could fit it around my wrists, and three seemingly decorative buttons clamped to one of the sides, fitting over onto the other side as the gauntlet closed. Little pieces of rust corrupted the otherwise smooth surface and it was covered with symbols and runes. I slid them onto my wrists, clasped together the three buttons, and the gauntlets buzzed for a moment before resting silently. I looked up, happy with my outfit to see, to my surprise, Damien with purple hair and poorly applied makeup. He had blotchy eye shadow, messy lipstick, uneven eyeliner, and his eyebrows—I don't even want to talk about them. His new hairdo fell down to below his shoulders, and he now wore a green cloak. He smiled, pulling daggers out of his sleeves. I giggled in response.

"Interesting choice of... everything," I laughed.

"Hey, at least I won't get caught. You look great, though. I see you found the ancient gauntlets."

"The what?"

"Those gauntlets were forged from the fires of the first volcano, by dwarves. The cloak was woven centuries ago by talented elves, every string hand-sewn, and threaded with special magic. So... powerful stuff."

"So, either the wig is made with real hair, taken from thousands of unicorns to create one wig, or... it's fake hair," I smirked.

He chuckled, patting his own head. "It's... as much as I would love a wig made from unicorn hair, it's fake. So is the makeup. This cloak doesn't have anything entirely special either. Except that when I transform, it will sink into my body, so it will stay on if I'm morphed for long amounts of time. I only have about... thirty minutes before my clothes disintegrate, becoming a part of my form. It gives me more energy, but... needless to say, it's a bit embarrassing in front of people."

"I can imagine," I giggled. "Now, we should start off. The Council members are probably waiting for us, and I still have to get my sword." I brushed back my cloak to reveal the sheath I'd picked up.

"Ah, yeah. The sword I gave you... where is it?" he questioned.

I pondered for a moment, not quite recalling where it was. "Either the arena or my cabin, I think. I'll check before we go. But before we even leave this room..." I giggled, gesturing to his face. "I'm assuming you didn't have a mirror?"

"What? Is it that bad?" He flushed, and, ironically, blush was one of the only things he didn't have on.

"Not... yeah, kinda. Here, I'll help," I offered, still giggling. He held up a pack of makeup wipes and I gently removed all of mess from his face. I hummed a tune as I applied the makeup correctly. I made sure the lipstick actually went on his lips, swapping out the bright red for more of a pinkish, natural color, blended the eye shadow, changing the neon colors to more of a subtle brown and gold, evened out his eyeliner and just added a little bit of product to his eyebrows. I also picked up a brush and brushed out the wig a little bit, making it sit more evenly as well. I sat back, smiling at my finished masterpiece.

"I still don't have a mirror," he joked.

"Well, just trust that you look beautiful," I said, exaggerating my speech when I said beautiful. We laughed together, and I was glad that after all of this heartbreak and mayhem, we were still able to just sit and be friends. Laugh with each other, smile and make jokes. It was a little moment of bliss that I knew I had to cherish. Because the worst of it lay ahead of us.

We stepped out, and saw the council members still waiting patiently. They looked shocked, to say the least, when Damien appeared. I just smiled politely, pretending I didn't notice.

"Well, uh... I suppose we should leave you two now, good— good luck on your mission," one of them choked on his words. I bowed my head in farewell, and we started off. I picked up my sword in the arena, where I must have left it after training with Mirage. That felt like so long ago, even though it wasn't even a week ago. Or... maybe it was. Time was strange here; the sun didn't always set or rise over days. All I knew was I hadn't slept much, but I was still energized. I met Damien at the doors of camp.

"Who's gonna look over everyone while we're gone?" I asked, looking back through camp. A few fires were strewn about the stone path leading to the castle. Tigre was milling about, actually smiling and laughing, helping people carry bags and buckets. It made me smile, seeing him finally getting used to life here and helping everyone.

"I think they'll be okay with the Elites with them. I told Melioca where we're going, so she knows. They're not completely helpless, you know," he joked. I punched his arm playfully. "They all have powers. The camp will be okay. Don't worry," I sighed, nodding in agreement.

"You're right. We should get going." I put my hand on the sword at my waist, comforted by its presence as something a friend gave me, and as something I could use to defend myself. I stepped outside the camp, and started on our way to the Kingdom. I was excited, yet scared. Thrilled to see the wonders of the world so advanced in comparison to the camp, but terrified to be caught. I was angry that they had so much more while constantly throwing us into the mud, then standing on our backs. This, no matter what happened, would definitely be an adventure.

As we were walking along in silence, I heard a howl. I perked up, looking into the woods beside us. Another howl, a lone cry within the forest. Then something came barreling at me. I thought it would be the wolf we had found, but this one was very well fed, had groomed fur, and was huge. If it stood up on its hind legs, it would be much taller than me. I could ride it if it would let me. It jumped up, knocking me over as I yelped. It licked my face, and Damien stood behind me, holding back a laugh. I pushed the mass of fur away from my face, standing up. It sat obediently beside me, almost looking like it was smiling at me. "Is... is this the same wolf from before?" I questioned, looking to Damien. He went forward to pet it, but it snapped at his hand. He pulled back, surprised.

"Seems like it," he replied awkwardly. I turned to the wolf, examining its markings. Silver fur going down its back and mottled on its face, a white blaze on its chest. Hazel eyes stared back at me, and I noticed the holes in its ears.

"This is the wolf," I confirmed, sure of it. I pet its head, smiling.

"Well, I guess it's... bonded to you? Maybe you should name it," Damien said jokingly, but I thought about it for a minute.

"What about... Aster?" The wolf's ears perked up, and it spun in a circle. "Aster then. You wanna come with us, boy?" Aster dipped his head, almost in a nod. I laughed, happy to see him again.

"A wolf might stick out in the Kingdom," Damien warned.

"Well, we can investigate when we get there. If people don't have giant beasts walking next to them... Aster can wait at the border for us." I turned, looking at the wolf to confirm. He panted in response. "Cool." I looked back up at Damien with a smile. He exhaled, motioning for Aster to follow. We trailed behind him like two children. The walk was filled with quiet, though joking glances between us. It was fun hanging out with Damien, but it was quickly over when we reached the looming buildings of the city. The structures made a wall around the Kingdom, similar to ours at camp, but with small gaps in between. I stood behind one, looking through into the busy streets. Countless pedestrians wandered around, and a white car passed by. I heard Damien stifling a shriek.

"What?" I questioned, looking back, expecting to be attacked, but nothing was there.

"What was that thing?" he whispered, frightened.

"Oh, that... that was a car. It's fine, not too dangerous as long as people actually know how to drive. You sit in it and someone uses a wheel and pedals to make it move. It can go pretty fast, so a lot of people use it instead of walking."

"Oh. I thought it was... like, a monster or something." He seemed to relax. I smiled at the thought of a car attacking someone, then turned back to looking through the city. Everyone was dressed... normally. Nothing special or anything that looked out of place. Some people did have dyed hair and cloaks, so I assumed we wouldn't stick out too much. I heard laughing and watched as someone passed by, a tiger on a leash next to them. So, large animals also weren't uncommon.

"This place is so weird," Damien muttered.

"It will probably get weirder. Don't worry, we'll get in and get out." I motioned for him to follow, and I put a hand on Aster's neck, keeping him close. We stepped into the bustling town, glancing around and pacing so we didn't look like we'd never been here. "I just don't know how we're gonna get into the castle. We probably have to if we want any information..."

"I can distract everyone with Aster, and you can sneak in. I'll pretend he's attacking me or something," Damien offered.

I lit up. "That could work! It's our best bet, anyway. Just... be ready to either fight or answer questions. Or both." He nodded, and I glanced around at the busy shops surrounding the border. I pushed Aster towards Damien, and walked forward, across the street, trying to act confident, like I belonged here. The truth was far from that, but I didn't care.

I weaved through the streets and across sidewalks, trying to find the entrance to the castle in the middle of the city. I quickly found it; it was surrounded by tall hedges—a giant stone building that was actually quite small in comparison to what I had expected. It was still a castle, but only a bit bigger than a mansion, just sitting in the center of this city. A dirt path lead up to the metal doors. Two guards stood positioned at the entrance. They wore black suits and badges.

I heard a scream, a piercing shriek that I assumed came from Damien, but hadn't expected him to be able to make. I heard barking, Aster working himself up into a frenzy, pouncing on Damien. The guards perked up, rushing to help with whatever was happening. I flew past, my cloak flowing out behind me. I dashed through the doors, my heart racing with fear, but it didn't seem like anyone saw me. I started walking down the hallways, my heels tapping on the marble floor examining the portraits lining the hallway. It seemed like they were all pictures of past Kings, or people important to the Kingdom. At the end of the wall, I noticed a mural that looked exactly like the General... but he was from the camp. That's impossible... isn't it? I heard footsteps from behind me, and before I could react, I was shoved into the floor, my head slamming into the concrete floor, knocking me out.

CHAPTER TEN

I woke up, my head pounding. I sat up in a soft bed, in a room I thought was a prison cell at first. The walls were gray stone, the floor a similar color concrete. No windows were to be seen. The bed was just as lifeless, a dull brown. It was very comfortable, I could give it that. I groaned, my hand on my head when I looked up... into the face of one of my friends. Aaron. I shrieked, jumping backwards. He stood against the wall, arms crossed, wearing a red cape with golden clasps, holding onto a royal blue jacket. A belt crossed his waist, a leather sheath attached, with the metal hilt of a sword sticking out. He had on brown pants and black combat boots, like his outfit was taken right off of a Disney prince. His blue eyes sparkled with a childish gleam, his wavy blonde hair flowing down to his shoulders. I was in such shock, seeing him here, I could barely say anything, so he took the first word.

"Hey. Are you alright?" he asked, standing up.

"I—uh, yes? No—my head is killing me," I chuckled, my head still in my hands. "What are you doing here? And what are you wearing?"

He looked down at his clothes. "Oh, yeah, this. I got it when I got here. I don't know what happened. I tripped, and suddenly... I'm in this weird world. Everything seems so much more advanced."

"Huh, so I got the short straw," I muttered. Of course I loved it at the camp, all the amazing people that weren't stuck up or overwhelmed with their own privilege. But it wasn't fair that some people were forced to live in the past while everyone else is so far ahead.

"So you *are* from the camp?" He looked surprised. As usual, his voice was still soft and he had a slightly shy aura about him.

"Yeah. It's awesome there, but the people are constantly tormented by the military and the people from—oh." It clicked, and I looked up in surprise. "You live in the Kingdom!"

"I was told those people are barbarians set to destroy the royal family and everything we've worked for out here. What do you mean we're tormenting them?"

"They've done nothing wrong, unless trying to live is somehow a bad thing. The people in here literally send frequent ships to bomb them. They sabotage their work and force them to live in cabins. We barely have working electricity! While you're living in the future, we're stuck in the past. The most modern thing they have is a Waffle House!"

"That can't be true. I was told that they steal and lie and kill. You're saying... we've actually been doing that?" Utter disbelief filled his face, along with confusion and guilt.

"Yeah. You should see the camp. They're in a bad place. We've only recently been able to fight back," I quieted down. Yelling was useless. He didn't know what he had been doing or supporting. It wasn't his fault for all of this.

"I'm so sorry. I... I've been in command of a lot around here, basically taking over the duties of the royal family. I've probably allowed those ships to go and attack innocent people. What— why do they tell us we're in the right?"

"I don't know. They wanna pretend they're better than everyone, I guess. Always higher than the rest of us. Especially when you have power like the Kingdom has... that can easily to go your head." I sighed.

"Yeah, that's true. I can't believe you're actually from there, though. I'm guessing the screaming guy with the wolf is as well. I remember seeing him with you, but that... that was a time I couldn't exactly talk much," he chuckled, a light laugh. I tilted my head to the side in confusion.

"You... what?" I asked, genuinely confused.

"You've seen me before, in this world. We weren't able to talk, though," he said, but without moving his lips. His voice echoed in my mind, and a realization dawned on me.

"Oh!" I yelled. "That was you? I thought I recognized the...

cloaked figure. That sounds weird," I blushed. I remembered him from my world. We went to school together, and he was in a lot of my classes. We'd grown to be very close friends. It was nice, seeing a friendly face in a land that was so foreign and hostile.

"You're fine. So, what are you doing sneaking into the castle? Especially with weapons?" he asked, walking over to sit beside me.

"The Kingdom recently launched multiple attacks on the camp. One of us was actually killed. Almost the entire place was destroyed, and we were worried that more attacks were to come. So, we were sent here to try to find any plans or something that could help us in the war."

He looked to the floor. "It's considered a war now?" He said wearily.

"I mean, what else could it be? It's been going on for years, from what I understand. I don't get why they're getting more violent now, though..." I crossed my arms, upset by the thought of what could happen next.

"I don't entirely understand, but the King knows that something is up. He said he sensed a great power rising." He put his hand on his temple, something I noticed he did frequently when he was nervous.

"So that's why this has all been happening... either way, we need to stop this," I said, determined to do what we came here for. I reached for my sword, to discover it was gone. "What—my sword!" I yelped, examining the room.

"Oh, we had to take that. Couldn't have you... attacking us. We tried to take the cloak and gauntlets too, but they wouldn't come off. It was really weird, but we figured they couldn't do much harm," Aaron shrugged. I looked down at my wrists, examining the metal. Small symbols had been engraved into the edge, ones I could just barely make out. I was reminded of what Damien had said, that these were forged in the fire of the first volcano. Fire, hmm? I looked up at the wall, summoning my flames, this time directing them through the gauntlets. I pointed my arm towards the wall, fists clenched, and a blast of white fire tore through the air, demolishing the stone before me. The metal once again buzzed, creating even more heat and power. I stared at my wrists in shock, the familiar ache still there, but not as bad.

"I did not expect that to work," I whispered, turning to Aaron, whose jaw was slack, and his eyes wide with surprise.

"How—what just—why—what?" He coughed, stumbling on his words. "You have fire powers?" he yelped.

"Yeah, apparently. Elemental, technically, but... you know," I shrugged, cutting off the power surging to the gauntlets. The heat died down, and looked towards the hole in the wall. Splotches of the fading sunlight trickled in, and I saw an identical hole in the wall of a building across from where we were. The part Aaron and I were in was an elevated room, at the back of the castle. Two men painting the outside stone white paused, astonished to see a random blast of fire soaring past. They looked up and I ducked in surprise. Aaron gently touched his forehead to his palm.

"You know, if you're gonna escape, you shouldn't draw too much attention to yourself," he whispered. I smiled, a bit embarrassed.

"Well, at least now you have a window. It was dark in here," I joked, standing up, avoiding the hole as to not get caught. "So, you're gonna help me escape?"

"I'll do what I can, but... that might not be much. I'm supposed to be loyal to the royal family. They trust me." He looked down. I knew he wasn't one to betray others, but in this case, it wasn't ideal. "I've been here for a while, building my reputation. I don't want to destroy all of that."

"I get where you're coming from, but the royals are pretty much evil. You don't want more people to die, do you?"

He looked at me, his eyes sparkling with worry. He was torn between two worlds, and I wasn't making the decision any easier. "Helping at all is gonna put that in danger. Maybe... maybe I can do things behind the scenes. Get you information while still acting like I'm completely devoted to them," he suggested. I nodded with a smile. He was smart, and I had faith in him. I was also glad to have another friend on my side. At this point, we needed everyone we could get.

"That reminds me, I've been meaning to ask. How long *have* you been here? I've been at the camp for quite a while and still can't control my powers very well. You seem like you've already mastered yours," I said, pacing the room idly.

"I've been here for years, now. And mine weren't very hard to get used to. I'm... pretty weak, especially compared to you. Telepathy, while being rare, isn't very strong if you don't use it to its full extent. The difficulty of learning it depends on the power level. With mine, it took me a few months to get it down. Yours could take... years. That blast completely knocked down a stone wall, which is magic resistant. Not proof, but holds up pretty well against magic attacks. And, I'm guessing since you said elements, that's water, fire, earth and air, correct? So that's four different abilities to master. I'm surprised you've gotten this far with fire!" he exclaimed, looking really excited. He knew a lot, which was pretty normal. Like I said, he's smart. He loves to learn and always absorbs information like it's nothing.

"Not to brag, but I've also gotten pretty far with wind," I smirked, reaching out my hand and letting the air swirl around my outstretched arm. He didn't look impressed.

"Can you do what you just did with that wall?" he said blankly.

"Challenge accepted," I said, turning to face the stone. I took a deep breath, and aimed to knock over more stones where the hole already was. I shot a blast of air, and it shifted a lot of the stone, but none fell. "Challenge... failed."

"I mean, you're not bad. But, again, a bit too much attention. We should get you out of here before it's too late," he warned, pushing me towards the door.

"Yeah, you're probably right. But one more thing," I said, putting my hand on his shoulder to stop him. "Downstairs, in the hall with all of the pictures. I noticed one of the General at our camp. What... what's up with that?" Aaron looked confused.

"I don't know why we would have a picture of your General... where was it?"

"At the very end of the hallway, on the right side."

"Oh, that's not your General. That's the King's brother."

"He's—he's *what*?" I gasped, shocked. There was no doubt the man in the picture was the General, but... how could he also be the King's brother? Why would his picture be here if they were fighting? "We need to figure out what's going on. I need to regroup with Damien and get back to the camp, now."

"Okay. I think I know where he is," Aaron opened the door, gesturing for me to go through. I rushed into the hallway, met with three directions I could go. "Oh, yeah, the top part is a bit like a maze. Maybe you should stay behind me instead," Aaron stepped ahead, and I followed. We weaved through corridor after corridor, occasionally passing windows, a small table, or more pictures, but we were overall undisturbed. We went down two flights of stairs before we got to the main level. Before I got off of the last step, we heard voices. Aaron pushed me backwards, behind the wall, and continued forward. Two guards appeared, chatting. They both had full body armor and spears. They stopped in front of Aaron.

"What are you two doing here?" he asked.

"Patrolling, as usual. Now, move. We have a job to do," one of them snapped.

"Didn't anyone tell you? The King summoned everyone in the castle for an emergency meeting downstairs. I was heading there now."

"He—he did?" one of them asked, looking back at the other, who shrugged.

"You should go before he gets angry. You know his temper," Aaron shrugged.

"I—uh... yes, we'll be going now." I heard a small trace of stumbling, the guard's voice shaking, which made me wonder. What had this man done? What kind of ruler was he, using fear to keep control? More like a garden stick than royalty, if you ask me. Certainly not anyone that deserved to have a major role of authority. The two rushed back down the hall from where they came, and Aaron motioned for me to follow outside.

"Quick thinking," I remarked, smiling as we walked through the castle doors.

"You learn that here. You have to be fast, or else... well, bad things can happen." He stopped before exiting, placing his hand on the door. I looked back, confused. "I can't come with you. I can help you from the Kingdom, but... I've already lied. I don't want to dig myself into a deeper hole and lose everyone's trust. We'll stay in touch, but... this is goodbye. For now." The last part, he said using telepathy. I nodded, sad to see that we wouldn't cross paths much. In a sudden, rash decision I launched into a hug. I hadn't seen him in so long, and now... I was losing him again. Tears welled up in my eyes, making it to where my vision blurred as I pulled away.

"I'll miss you," I managed to get out.

"I'll miss you, too. We won't lose contact, don't worry," he smiled kindly, but not worrying was the one thing I couldn't do right now.

"Hey, the King only hosts meetings at night! What are you trying to pull?" one of the guards marched up to Aaron, demanding answers. He saw me and froze. "The—the prisoner! Sound the alarm!" he yelled. Aaron grabbed my wrist, and I expected him to run away, but he turned to me with an evil look in his eyes.

"Got you!" he hissed, but I noticed he was keeping a very loose grip on my arm. He winked, and I pulled away, running before I ever really got to say goodbye. I ran across the castle grounds, my cloak billowing out behind me. I ended up pushing down some bystanders taking pictures of the looming structure.

I hid behind a wall, pausing for a minute to catch my breath and think. Then I whistled. One long, piercing sound before I got up and kept going. I hoped, wished, and prayed to gods I didn't even believe in that this would work.

Surely enough, my prayers were answered. A giant mass of fur bounded beside me, panting with glee. I grabbed Aster's fur, gripping on to the thick locks around his neck. I jumped, swinging my leg over his body and onto his back. I remembered thinking that he was large enough to carry me, and indeed he was.

We raced around the city, tearing through crowds of people, around buildings, and away from screaming guards. I laughed, the wind in my hair and adrenaline pumping through my veins. I saw a white dove overhead, which swooped down to land on my shoulder, its claws gripping into my shirt while it squawked gracelessly, the exact opposite of what you'd think a dove would do. I assumed it was Damien and turned Aster towards the edge of the city, aiming to leave as fast as possible. But the universe really has it out for me, so that's not how it played out.

A swarm of armored guards barricaded any exits. I heard people scream and the frightened pad of footsteps as they sprinted as far away from the giant raging wolf as they could. Aster stopped short right before touching one of the guards, completely out of breath. I glared, reaching for my sword before realizing... I'd never found it. My heart sunk, and I gulped, quite terrified at this point. The gauntlets buzzed on my arms, as if to alert me of their presence. I didn't want to hurt anyone, but that might be the only way out. The guard in front of me suddenly dropped to their knees, their legs crippling underneath them. They gripped their head, screaming in pain. I looked behind me, to see Aaron's head peeking out from behind a building, two fingers on his temple. He must have been somehow doing that to the soldier. He held out his other hand, holding my sword. I nodded in thanks, and took off the other way, everyone else too distracted by the suddenly fallen guard to notice me escaping. I could imagine the look of confusion on Aaron's face, but I had a plan. Once we got far enough from the Kingdom, I gently tugged Aster's fur, nudging him into the forest. We broke through the leaves, gliding across the forest floor until we gracefully came to a stop. I hopped off of his back, and Damien flew to the ground, transforming back into himself. Now, he was suddenly without the wig and makeup.

"I'm glad I guessed that it was you, but also, it would have been strange for a random bird to suddenly latch onto my shoulder and start screaming," I joked, and he rolled his eyes. "I need you to transform again, though. In the Kingdom, a friend has my sword. Can you turn into, like, maybe a bigger bird and go grab it?"

"What friends do we have in the Kingdom?" he scoffed. He had a point.

"This is an old friend, from my world. He helped me escape, twice. From the castle, and he made that guard fall. He's the one who was using telepathy. Trust me on this, please. He's hiding behind the building we were at, he has blonde hair and blue eyes." Damien looked at me skeptically, but sighed in defeat.

"Fine, but if I get caught, you and your giant wolf are coming to save me." I giggled in response, and waved as he morphed into a giant eagle, flying through the canopy above us, leaving a small hole that let in the light of the fading sun. I cursed under my breath as I noticed the bright rays dipping beneath the horizon. This was trouble for us, especially if Damien didn't get back soon. Aster snarled at the approaching shadows, and I felt almost useless, and alone in this forest. I set my hand ablaze in fear, quickly gathering stones, sticks, and leaves to create a small fire on the ground, hopefully warding away the night and any monsters that dared to approach. I shivered against the cold, wrapping the thin fabric of my cloak around me for more warmth.

Honestly, I didn't get the whole 'I huddled closer to the fire' thing. To actually feel the heat, you have to get really close, and by that time, your hand is burning off. So I stuck with the cloak. I heard the flutter of wings above me and looked up to see a giant figure descending upon us, a sword gripped in its talons. I smiled at the sky, but that quickly faded when something shot out of the darkness, grabbing Damien before he had a chance to land. My sword thudded into the dirt before me. I screamed in shock, looking around for any sign of human or bird. Nothing.

I grabbed the blade, shoved it in my sheath and clicked, trying to get Aster to follow me. He jumped up, trotting at my side. I crept through the woods, my heart racing at every noise. I tried to follow the path that Damien was taken in, but I quickly lost my way with the sun setting so fast and darkness overtaking the forest. I grabbed my sword hilt, trying to create some light, and I used the same thing I used with Mirage. I swept my blade across the forest, sending fire into the air. It wasn't the best lighting, but it was better than nothing. I continued forward, until I heard screaming. Aster yelped, and I turned just in time to see a face right behind me, before they smashed a rock into my skull, throwing me to the ground and knocking me unconscious for the second time that day.

I woke up groggily, my eyes barely wanting to open. I was in a prison again, but this time less of a room and more of a cell. The gray walls didn't provide much space, and there were, again, no windows. Not even a bed, just a few pebbles on the floor. In front of me were bars, with no visible door. I tried peering out into the hallway, but I couldn't see anything. It was all... black. The walls weren't painted, there was regular lighting, and there was just a strange haze dwelling in the corridor. I reached for my sword to find it missing, once again. I needed to put a bell on it, or something. Maybe some Velcro.

"Hello?" I called out, knowing that there probably wouldn't be an answer. Much to my surprise, someone appeared out of the fog. A boy, probably older than me but not by too much, stepped forward. He had a very proud face, like a stereotypical, stuck-up rich kid, with dark brown hair, a streak of neon red going through it. He wore regular clothes, a cotton, pastel blue shirt with black pants, and surprisingly tennis shoes instead of combat boots, which were usually what I saw around here. He also had a bit of armor on top of that, metal shoulder and knee pads. His outfit was strange, and he carried no weapon.

"Hi," he said, smiling, attempting to look dashing but honestly, it was just disappointing.

"Uh... can you get me out of here? Why am I here in the first place?" I had a lot more questions, but I was slightly disturbed, so nothing came out like I wanted it to.

"Sorry, I can't do that," he sighed dramatically, blowing a bubble of gum and popping it loudly. Where did he even get gum from?

"Why... why not? What did I do?" I stepped away from the bars as he leaned on them, blinking really quickly.

"You trespassed. Gotta wait for a trial. Oh, and you had two animal slaves working for you. That's illegal here," he said, examining his nails. Well, what he could see of his nails. He had leather gloves on.

"Excuse me?" I sputtered. "First of all, they're not slaves. Second of all, they're not really working for me. Third of all, one of them is human! He shape-shifted!" I crossed my arms, thoroughly annoyed at this strange man. He looked at me curiously.

"Only one of them is a real animal?"

"Yes."

"And all of its actions were voluntary?"

"Yes..."

"And you only had one?"

"I already said yes to that!" I threw my hands in the air, exasperated by all of this. "Where am I? Let me out!" I growled. "I have to get back to my camp. I'm the General of a camp in the woods, not too far from here—I think. We went on a mission into the Kingdom, and... failed. Everyone could be in danger!" My gauntlets buzzed again, as if sending my agitation. The guy perked up, staring at my wrists. I put my hands behind my back.

"Those... I recognize those." He looked at me with a glare. "Where did you get them?"

"I—uh, from the camp. They were in the... armory, thing." I pushed my hair back from my eyes awkwardly. He paused for a moment, seeming almost suspicious.

"Come with me," he said, his tone completely serious now. He tapped the bars, and they dissolved. I stepped through into the hallway. His previous joking, silly demeanor was now completely replaced. His facial expression was stone, hard to read, but his footsteps were very heavy, portraying anger. He'd changed so quickly, it was weird. We walked for a while, much longer than I thought a hallway would warrant. But, after a few minutes, we reached a door. Light oak, engraved with various, seemingly random words. Protection, valor, and youth were some that stuck out to me. It was also weird that, unlike everything else in this world, the writing was in English. Any other engraved items I'd stumbled across only had these strange symbols. The guy in front of me opened the door, and light flooded in.

My eyes took a second to adjust, but once they did, I was at a loss for words. Wood and rope bridges spiraled into the sky, platforms hugged the trunks of trees, and very few people milled about, but the animals were abundant. Monkeys swung from strangely colored vines, rainbow birds fluttered through the air, small cats and bigger ones, specifically a panther, prowled the ground below, and there were even a few horses galloping around. Everything except the prison I'd come out of was elevated, an entire city snuggled into the trees, the thick curtain of leaves shielding this place from the outside. I even saw houses perched on branches, one with smoke coming out of the chimney. I glanced to the side as I heard a bark, and saw Aster trying to get to me. He was pulled back by chains, two people struggling to keep a hold. Aster howled, claws digging into the ground, body held low to maintain balance. Muscles rippled under his fur coat at he made his way forward. I ran towards him, gasping with shock.

"Let him go!" I demanded, glaring daggers at the two gripping the chains. The guy behind me waved, and they let go. Aster jumped into my arms, licking my face. I giggled, patting his head and stroking his ears.

"So, this is your animal, then?" the guy said, pursing his lips skeptically. I really needed to learn his name.

"Not really, he just helps me from time to time. We... not exactly saved him, but fed him when he needed it. He was just skin and bones, and the next thing we know, he comes back out of the woods like this," I said, shrugging. That still made no sense to me, but I assumed the magic of this world helped him.

"That's because we took him in," he beamed. Apparently, I was wrong. "He was hurt after a fight, and came seeking aid. We fed him, groomed him, did a little nature magic, and—"

"Whoa, wait. Nature magic?" I turned, eyebrows raised. He nodded.

"We are a small village here in the Endless Woods. We take in sick or hurt animals, provide them shelter and nurture them. Some stay, some go. We have very few humans here, especially in comparison to animals, but we do what we can. We're all masters of nature magic, in some form. The healers specialize in healing magic, of course. Then there are warriors like me who use earth and air magic to not only defend the camp, but help predatory animals learn how to fight if they've forgotten, so they can survive in the wild. We have one concealer, who hides our camp from any outsiders. Unless we want them to see it, this place is completely invisible and untouchable." It seemed like he was bragging a bit, but it was interesting to hear about this place. It especially showed me how much more I had to learn. An entire civilization hidden in plain sight? It was honestly quite incredible.

"You can do elemental magic?" I asked, curious to learn how to expand my own powers, and if I could do it with them.

"Well... of sorts. I'm not able to do much, while some of my friends can do air magic, but others can do earth. I'm pretty sure it's impossible to have more than one at once," he chuckled. I held up my hands in challenge, swirling wind in one palm and creating a fire in the other. I couldn't keep the trick up for long, but it didn't hurt as much anymore. I guessed my body was finally getting used to the magic of this world. His eyes lit up, by the sudden light and by excitement. "You... hold on, wait right here." He bounced up and ran, into one of the houses on the ground. I heard clattering from inside, and he emerged with a large plank of wood. "Destroy this," he ordered, which I was taken aback by.

"Why?" I asked, confused.

"I want to see what you can do. Don't worry, I won't get hurt. Use your fire to destroy it, with the gauntlets. But don't touch it." I sighed, nodding. I felt like my powers should be put to more use then party tricks, but I had just used my powers to prove him wrong, so I didn't see the harm in it. I held out my open hand, and watched the fire flicker across the gauntlets. I smiled slightly, and let it burst off of my arm, demolishing the piece of wood, sending bits of it flying into the woods, smoking and covered in soot. The guy holding it, however, was unharmed. I felt ecstatic, not aware I could do that with such precision. He started to giggle, building up to laughing hysterically. I thought I'd done something wrong, but he looked up in amazement.

"I haven't seen those gauntlets used in hundreds of years! Princess Andrea of the fire clan, back in the days it ruled over portions of the Earth, was the last to use those. She found them in the possession of a dwarf skeleton, and used them to change the tide of the war currently going on in her kingdom. She harnessed her powers of fire to completely destroy the enemies, leaving no trace of them behind except for dust." He squealed like a child, and I stepped back, eyes wide. Something was off in this guy's head, but also... that sounded a bit like what was happening now. History once again repeats itself. "I'm Rhidian, but my friends call me Red. And I am so happy to have someone who can actually use them in our hideout! It's an honor, really," he smiled, a genuinely happy smile as he reached out to take my hand. We shook, and I bowed my head slightly.

"I'm Amber. Nice to... be here, I guess," I said, chuckling. I heard Aster growl below me, before I shushed him. Apparently, I wasn't allowed to even touch anyone else with him around. I turned back to Red, an idea popping into my head. "Hey, uh, this might be a bit strange because... I barely know you all, but I need help. Where I come from, the camp, we're kind of in a war as well. We need allies, strong people who can help us defeat the Kingdom. Do you think you can assist us?" I smiled hopefully. He thought for a moment, pondering my offer.

"The wearers of the gauntlets are all destined for the same fate, it seems. We'll help, but our numbers are... very low. However, there is a way you can get more people. This place is called the Endless Woods for a reason. It seems almost infinite, stretching across massive expanses of land. There are thousands of tribes dwelling in the woods that are in constant need of aid. If you use your powers to help them, they'll be loyal to you, and you can overtake the Kingdom with ease." He spread his hands, looking at me expectantly.

"That could work. But first, we have to find my friend. Where is he?" I asked, looking around.

"The screaming bird?"

"Yes, sadly."

"Oh, we did not take him. The creatures of the night did. You'll have to get him from them, presuming he isn't already dead." My eyes widened at the thought. He could hold his own, but... I wasn't sure what had happened to him.

"How do we find him?" I pushed aside my worry so that I could attempt to form a plan. Aster sniffed the air loudly, as if announcing his ability. His sense of smell was much better than ours, so he could possibly find Damien. But... didn't they usually need an item the person had touched to be able to sniff the person out? I was about to ask when Aster put his nose to the ground, sniffing away. He started forward, barking to signal us to follow. I looked to Red, who shrugged, and we started off after him. I didn't expect as much of a journey as we would end up having, surrounded by unfamiliar faces and places, but what was to come was certainly an adventure. At the time of departure, I was clueless about this fact, but would come to learn much more about this magical world around me.

CHAPTER ELEVEN

Getting out ended up being a problem. Aster tried to blindly jump through the leaves, only to hit a tree on his way out. We were stopped twice by concerned and suspicious bystanders, and had to fight through thorny branches to leave.

"It's hard to get in, and out?" I muttered, pulling a sharp splinter out of my finger.

"It's better both ways," Red shrugged. "Keeps us safe. So far, no attacks against us have been successful." We finally made our way out of the brush, standing in the middle of the forest. I looked back, and the camp was gone, an empty space like it just disappeared into the trees. I took a step back, moving through the empty area, but I never touched anything. The only leaves barricading anything were high above, shielding the tops of the trees.

"Whoa," I whispered, astonished at their cloaking ability. Aster started moving on, still vigorously sniffing the ground. He looked up, and gazed into the distance. He shook his head, and looked back at me. "What's wrong, boy?" I moved towards his head, but he shuffled, keeping his back to me.

"I think he wants us to get on," Red said, a bit weakly. "That... doesn't seem safe."

"I've done it before! It's fun," I said. I gently grabbed Asters fur at the scruff of his neck and swung on, gesturing for Red to do the same. He stepped forward, a panicked look in his eyes. He cleared his throat, and then jumped, trying to land on Aster's back, but then swiftly fell off, his shoulder slamming into the soft dirt on the other side of the dog. I resisted the urge to giggle, and held out my hand, helping him up. "I'm guessing since Aster wants us to ride, it's gonna be a long trip. Just... climb slowly, then hang on." Red nodded, taking a deep breath, and this time slowly lifting his leg over Aster's back.

He gripped my shoulders, steadying himself. He nodded to

me, and I looked forward, leaning down a bit. Aster took that as permission to go, and shot through the forest, bounding over the vast landscape, weaving around bushes and fallen trees, climbing hills with extreme speed, and sliding through the obstacles with ease. I whooped with joy, excited to feel the wind in my hair, soaring gracefully over the land. Red, however, looked terrified. Every time Aster curved, he screamed, causing the wolf to jump. Then, when we jumped, he yelped in surprise. Needless to say, I made a mental note to walk next time. After what felt like a lifetime but was probably only about half an hour, when I was at my breaking point and about to throw Red off of Aster's back, we came to a sharp stop at the bottom of a cliff. It reached into the sky, the climb completely vertical. Stone and dirt crumbled off of the drop with no provocation, hinting to me that it was very unsafe to climb. It seemed to stretch for a while, though, further then I could see. I got off of Aster, and looked up, pondering solutions.

"Any ideas?" I asked, turning to Red who promptly fell off of the wolf.

"Not... exactly," he mumbled, face pressed against the ground and a mouth full of dirt. I rolled my eyes sarcastically and went back to examining the cliff. There was no way we could get up it ourselves, and climbing a tree wasn't an option. They were too tall, and none were close enough to the cliff face to be safe. I summoned some wind, trying to make it lift me into the air, but I just hovered for a bit before falling back. The attempt hurt my arms, as if I had lifted my entire body weight instead of having the wind do it. I stretched, completely stumped. I heard Red getting up behind me, brushing dirt off of his armor.

"You have elemental powers, right? Why don't you create a stairway or ramp with the earth?" He said, pointing down to the dirt in example.

"I... I don't exactly know how to use that yet. I've only worked on fire and air," I admitted, sighing.

"Try, at least!" he encouraged. "I'm sure it will be fine. It can't hurt, anyway."

"It won't get us very far, but okay," I mumbled, kneeling to the ground. I tried to focus, feeling the dirt beneath my hands, trying to coax it up, trying to make it bend to my will. I heard rattling, and opened my eyes to see a few pebbles shaking.

"You have to remember, your powers are not just weapons. You have to be in touch with yourself and the world around you. This is not just for you to use; the earth is alive—it's a creature that deserves respect. It graces you with power, lends itself to you, so do not disrespect it," Red advised wisely, standing behind me. I nodded, agreeing with what he said. I faced the ground, and closed my eyes again.

"Please. We need help," I pleaded quietly. I felt a rumble, and the dirt moved beneath my fingertips. I pushed my hand up, and the dirt chased it into the air, forming a spike protruding out of the ground. I looked at the cliff, and shoved my hands forward, pleading for the earth to follow my movements. It did, indeed, work—the dirt and stone shifted, creating a smooth, slightly slanted walkway that we could get up with ease. The dirt packed firmly beneath our feet, so there was no chance of it collapsing underneath of us. Red clapped, a smile slowly growing on his face, but my throat felt dry, and I was out of breath.

"You learn quickly," he remarked, before starting forward, walking this time instead of riding on Aster. I nodded towards him, and he padded towards me, climbing up the hill. The dirt crumbled back onto the floor as we passed. It seemed like the power wasn't really mine, but the earth listening to what I needed and helping me. Nothing else was alive like that. The world had a mind of its own, never truly relinquishing its power, even for a second. The others gave into my will, allowing me to tap into their full powers without ever controlling themselves. The earth was much different, it seemed.

We carried on, Aster slowly sniffing the path towards Damien. After walking for a few more minutes, he started spinning in circles, whimpering.

"What's wrong, boy?" I asked, kneeling down next to him.

"This must be a demon nest. I doubt the entrance will show itself when the sun is out because most monsters are injured by light, but your friend is probably underground. I've only heard stories of people being kidnapped to harvest, and not just eaten." Red explained.

"So we have to wait to get down there?" I asked, not thrilled by the thought, but we couldn't exactly force the sun to go down. I wondered if there even was a type of magic that could do that.

"I guess so." Red cleared a spot of leaves and sat down, staring up at the sky with a peaceful look. I did the same, with Aster sitting next to me. "So, your friend that we're looking for. How long have you known him?" I chuckled, thinking of how long it seemed, but the amount of time actually wasn't that much.

"I'm not entirely sure. I haven't been paying attention to days. And besides, time works weirdly here, so it's hard to keep track of that anyway." I shrugged, sighing. Thinking about him worried me, a lot. I didn't want him to get hurt.

"It does?" He looked over at me curiously. "I thought... this was normal."

"Oh, well, for here it is. I'm from... practically a different world." I didn't want to reveal my entire back-story, but I also didn't want to lie to him. Being vague was a nice middle ground. "Everything there works a lot differently. That's why I don't have much control over my powers yet. I haven't had them for long."

"You must be from, like, all the way across the world, then. Or maybe inside it?"

"Inside the Earth?"

"Yeah. I met a girl from there once. Well, not exactly a girl. They don't have the same social structures as we have up here, but she presented herself as a girl."

"Must be nice," I muttered, a little bitterly. He looked at me sideways in confusion, but decided to ignore it.

"How did you guys meet?" he asked, backing up to talking about Damien.

"It's a bit of a strange story," I laughed, thinking back again. "We got attacked by this pig thing—a Zanzagar. He got hurt and I took him back to camp so he could get help. The doctor there is an elf who has healing powers. She's cool," I winced to myself, remembering that I still hadn't talked to her like I was supposed to. Now, I was on a journey for who knows how long? Once I got back, I needed to fix everything.

We sat in silence for a little while, watching the sun slowly drift through the sky. Birds chirped in the trees, leaves rustled as squirrels scuttled around seeking food, but other than that, things were still. It was impossible to tell that we were potentially sitting on a monster nest. I yawned, my adrenaline fading and exhaustion finally taking hold. When things calmed down and I had a moment to rest, I guess my normal human functions finally started working. I had almost laid down to sleep when Red nudged my shoulder, pointing to the sky. The sun was now setting very quickly, the sky barely even having time to show its color before night set in. I jumped up, reaching for my sword to realize it wasn't there. I figured with the amount of times I'd done that, I wouldn't be used to it actually being in the sheath.

I sighed, figuring that I would just have to be careful with my powers, and channel the energy through my gauntlets. Aster growled, backing up slowly. I followed his steps, not wanting to get caught in whatever he was afraid of. My eyes darted around the forest, examining every shadow that I could see, and keeping watch on the area we were just sitting in. I saw a small spot of darkness move right at Red's feet.

"Get down!" I yelled, pushing him backwards before setting my hands ablaze, rushing them forward to grab the thing. The skin was dense, but slimy, a texture that made me want to throw up. It screamed, a shrill yelp that sounded like more than one voice. I pushed further, surrounding myself in fire and wrapping the flames around the monster. From the looks of it, it was the same creature that attacked me when I was with Damien—the thing that had made me hallucinate. Kind of ironic, once I'd thought about it. I leapt backwards, breathing hard from the effort of pushing back such a gargantuan creature.

The monster was huge, much bigger than the one from before. It dangled from the trees, gripping the trunks to hold itself steady, draping over us like a blanket. It looked like it was barely even hurt from my attack, which couldn't mean anything good for us. I saw the circle of dirt we were sitting in start to shift, twisting and turning, bubbling up above the ground. Red and Aster stayed behind me, probably unsure of what to do. I remembered something I did from before, during the last attack the Kingdom sent. I hadn't known what I was doing at the time, but it worked, though the repercussions weren't something I desired. I held my hands above my head, letting fire flow down my arms and surround me like armor.

Flaming wings sprouted from my back, the gauntlets around my wrist buzzed violently and turned white with heat, and the inferno danced around me, filling me with strength and adrenaline. My body once again moved a bit slowly when doing this, but I assumed it was the effect of so much magic being used. My mana was probably already low, and this didn't help. I knew I didn't have much time, so I launched into an attack. My wings took off, seemingly on their own, and shot me into the sky where I hovered over the monster. I stumbled through the air, my throat drying up and my hands shaking. I summoned a fireball, letting it roll around in my palm before chucking it into the creature's back. It shrieked, and looked up, opening its mouth to reveal razor sharp teeth. I dodged a swipe from its... arm-like tentacle things, and dove onto its back, driving my hands into its skin, sinking further and further as I pressed. It squealed in pain and started to shrink to my surprise. I pushed harder, sending out flames where I could.

My armor flickered and the fire dissolved through my hands,

all my pent-up energy releasing into the monsters skin. It let out one last, small shriek before it fell to the floor, half its previous size and smoking. I felt the thump as it landed, still standing on its back, and I stumbled from the shock, nearly collapsing, but Aster shoved me to my feet. Red looked on, his eyes wide, and he was completely frozen. I coughed into my arm, dizzy and discombobulated, but I knew we had to move on. I looked down, glancing around until I saw a swirling portal of dirt, what I assumed was the entrance to the den. The small area that was moving started to solidify, so it seemed the portal was coming to a close. I grabbed Red's arm and threw him into the dirt, and he passed completely through. I jumped after him, landing in a cold cave, the stone still swirling above us. I saw Aster's nose poke through before it disappeared, and the ceiling went still.

"Well, great. Looks like we've lost the fearsome wolf," Red shuddered.

"Luckily for us, we have a fearsome human," I smiled, breathing hard, only half joking. I felt weak, so I assumed my mana was very low, but my gauntlets still glowed dimly and steamed in the crisp air. I looked around, examining what was there. A domed ceiling circled around us, and the walls were covered in black webs. The place reeked, like a thousand dying animals were all shoved into one place for thirty years. I gagged just thinking about it, but I tried to breathe through my mouth. "We have to find Damien now!" I started forward, into the hallway in front of us.

There wasn't much lighting, but where it was bright enough to see, there didn't seem to be any source of the light. We made our way through tunnels, some tightly packed and others extremely wide. Seeing only with touch, we didn't exactly know where we were going, but we pressed on, following the smell mostly. I resisted the urge to throw up every step of the way, knowing we couldn't lose sight of our objective.

Strangely, we were unbothered, though the frequent tapping made me a little nervous, like a spider was dancing on the ceiling. Red and I stepped into a cavern, a deep passageway that opened up quite a bit. Stalactites hung from the ceiling, water dripping ominously off of them. The smell somehow cleared up in here, but the sight in front of us didn't seem to warrant that. Countless people, mostly because of the dark, were trapped in dark webbing, some struggling, others standing still, their faces blank. Damien was at the front, looking like he was asleep, the strange material wrapped around him, up to his shoulders.

"Damien!" I whispered, running forward and trying to pry the webs off of him.

He groggily lifted his head, blinking. "Amber?" he muttered, falling back asleep.

"Red, help me please." He nodded and jogged towards me. Together, we freed Damien, after much struggling, our nails tearing against the fabric. Once he was out of the webs, he yawned, eyes widening at the grotesque picture around him.

"Where are we?" he asked weakly.

"In a monster nest. We have to leave, now. But..." I looked at all the others, some children, some very old adults. I didn't know who they were, but I wanted to save them. "You two go, and run far away. Red, you know the way out, guide Damien while I try to free these people."

"You look—no offense, but you look awful. Your mana is probably low. You can't use your powers, and this will take too long without our help," Damien said, leaning on Red for support.

"You don't look so good either," I remarked. His hair was matted down, face covered in bruises and feathers sticking off of his clothes. "I'll be okay. Trust me on this, alright?" I'd never been good at using a puppy dog face, but I tried here, pouting a bit. He sighed, waving his hand in dismissal.

"Fine. But if you die, I'll kill you." He smiled, despite his injuries.

"Noted. Now, go." I ordered, a stern look on my face. They both shuffled away, and I turned to everyone else. No one seemed to notice me yet, but I heard screeching down the hallway in front of me, opposite of the way Red and Damien disappeared. I didn't have much time before a hoard of creatures came at me. Fire wouldn't work, it might hurt the people inside the cocoons. Air couldn't do much except push them over, and I still hadn't worked on water. That left one element, one I didn't have actual control over. But it seemed like my best bet. If I could get the earth below everyone to separate, it might tear apart the webbing. I went up to the wall, my hand on the stone. I wasn't sure if this would use mana, and how much if any, but seeing all these people, defenseless and waiting to become monster food... I couldn't stand by and let them die. It wasn't right. "I need your help," I whispered to the wall. The earth softened beneath my touch, molding to my fingertips, leaving an imprint on the wall. "Please, free these people. I can't let them sit down here and die. I need to do something to them, but I can't without your help." It did feel strange talking to some stone, but I knew it could hear me. A tremor went through the cavern, and cracks appeared in the floor. I heard a sharp tearing sound, and dust rained from the ceiling. The webbing on everyone was ripped apart at the same time, everyone falling to the floor, everyone a mixture between asleep and awake. Everyone started to panic as the earth settled, and I rushed into the middle of the room.

"Use your power wisely," I heard something whisper. It was weird, but I disregarded it.

"Everyone! If you can, grab as many people as you can hold up and get out. I know the way, follow me!" I grabbed a sleeping child, helped a few people to their feet, and carried a teenager as best I could out the door. A horrible shrieking noise once again echoed down the hall, and I heard the clicking of footsteps. Everyone started to run, following behind me as I tried to remember which way to go. We all successfully made it to the portal, but the ceiling was completely solid. Only now did the thought occur to me that we might need a plan to get out.

I heard that scream again, and more clicking. Down the

hallway, something that looked like a giant ant appeared. The kids shuffled around and started crying, some of the older ones held up their fists, preparing to fight. I looking around frantically, unsure of what to do until I saw the stone above shifting, twisting into an almost invisible vortex.

"Jump!" I yelled, pointing to the ceiling above. People started to disappear through, getting as high as they could to reach the top. I was the last one out, trying to make sure everyone got through. Before I jumped, I looked down the hall, watching the approaching monsters. Behind them, I saw a face. A woman, with long, dark, greasy hair draped over her eye. She had unnaturally pale skin, and eyes that cast a silver gleam down the dark hallway, a dress so black that it would have faded into the background if not for the sparkly lines of what looked like tinsel, or shiny gems. I barely got a look at her before I leapt into the ceiling, the darkness swallowing me, and spitting me above the surface. I immediately collapsed with a gasp, my body failing, shutting down as soon as I stepped foot into the forest. I couldn't move, but I was completely conscious, drifting between the layers of sleep and being awake.

I was trapped, my mind caged in my own body, unable to do a thing except look straight ahead. I could barely even hear, the voices screaming around me just murky echoes of what they actually were. My eyesight blurred, and my throat felt dry. This must have been the effect of too low mana, or possibly it running out. I struggled to breathe, trying to force air through my lungs, to no avail. It was like I locked up, completely frozen while being totally conscious of my current demise. The feeling was not at all pleasant, but the most painful part was the worry that I wouldn't survive. I attempted to form any cognitive thought, but my brain failed me.

The sudden spike of fear sent my heart racing as I laid on the floor, deformed faces hovering above me, distorted voices yelling my name as those who didn't know me dispersed, running away back to their homes. Soon, only Red and Damien remained, the others having fled the scene. Then, everything cleared. I felt Aster's rough tongue scrape against my face, and I giggled lightly as I pushed him away, sitting up at the same time.

"Your... your eyes were shaking," Damien whispered, his voice a mixture of awe, shock, and fear. My head started to hurt, a deep throbbing pounding at the sides of my skull.

"I saw someone down there. She wasn't kidnapped. She walked among the monsters like... an old friend." I struggled to speak, but I couldn't stop picturing the haunting image. "A woman, with long dark hair, wearing a dress." Red and Damien exchanged nervous glances, despite only just meeting.

"I'm not sure who that could have been," Damien said softly, looking towards the rising sun. "Monsters rarely appear as human. It might have been some sort of druid, or—no, not a god." He shook his head in disgust. Red looked impressed.

"You know a lot about all these monsters. We just know to avoid them," he said, and I couldn't tell if he was joking or not. Damien chuckled, and shrugged.

"Well, I've spent a lot of my time researching these things. The camp I come from has a giant library of books explaining the monsters, their power level, and their abilities."

"It's not that big," I muttered. Unless you counted a few tall bookshelves 'big'. "Will you two stop flirting and help me up? I feel sick." They both blushed scarlet, and looked away from each other. Red's face turned as vibrant crimson as his hair. They both took one of my arms, and hoisted me to my feet. The sudden elevation caused my head to hurt even more, but I ignored the pain for a second. There were more important things. "We should get back. I'm glad you're safe, but... that was a lot. I'm still not really used to magic." I groaned, stumbling backwards. Aster nuzzled my hand, and I pet his head.

"Maybe he should carry you back," Damien said, taking my hand and helping me on to the wolf's back. I slouched, feeling absolutely drained, but glad to be back up above the surface. "I don't want to darken the mood, but... I need to talk to you guys about what I saw down there. It was like glimpses of the future. And... I saw the General." He looked to me with a worried glance.

"That's good, isn't it?" I mumbled through Aster's fur as we trotted along.

"Well, sort of. I think he's in trouble, though. I saw a cage, in the middle of a lake. The sides were made of glass between the bars, but there was nothing I could see making it to where he could breathe. Some weird sea animal I've never seen before was circling the cage, and it didn't look friendly." The situation seemed strange, but he wouldn't lie to me, right? I sat up a little bit, still feeling tired.

"Do you know where it could be?" I asked, nearly yawning, my eyelids refusing to stay open all the way.

"There's a very large lake a few miles northwest from the Kingdom. He's probably hidden somewhere there." We walked in silence for a while, everyone lost in thought. The conversation only picked back up again when we stopped, looking forward at where Red's hideout was supposed to be, but there was nothing. We paused, while Damien marched right ahead.

"Hey, you missed it," I called, and he turned around, confused. Red reached through the air and the trees started to shimmer, his hand sinking through a trunk. He smiled, and the rest of him disappeared. Damien looked on in awe, even though I assumed he wouldn't be so surprised, considering he actually was from a world with magic. I sunk through the curtain, and he appeared behind me, marveling at the way it was hidden and the camp inside.

"We should probably get going soon. But first, two things. I need my sword," I said, looking towards Red. I assumed he knew where it was.

"That's only one thing, but okay." He shrugged and walked into the same building he got the board out of, emerging with my sword.

"Thanks," I bowed my head, taking it from him and putting it in my sheath. Hopefully, it would stay for more than a few minutes. "Now, we need to go back to the camp for a little bit. Our camp. I want to let everyone know what's happening, and where we're going." Damien nodded, agreeing.

"Yeah, we probably should. I'm not riding on that thing, though." He laughed, but Aster snarled in response.

"I don't think he'd want you to," I smirked, chuckling before turning to Red. "We'll be back after we rescue the General. I still want to help the people in the woods, gain their alliance to overthrow the Kingdom. If you can, get your people ready." I expected him to nod and run off, but he just stood there, looking a bit sad. "What's wrong?"

"It's—nothing. I'm fine. Go save the General." He faked a smile. I wasn't sure what had happened, but we didn't have much time. And his mood seemed to change so quickly, it was hard to pinpoint how he actually felt. I nudged Aster, and we were off, while Damien flew behind us as a robin. I thought we must've looked like a peculiar team, a bird and a teenager riding a wolf.

We bounced through the woods, the trip much longer than I thought it would be. After some time had passed, we saw the glowing lights of the Kingdom in front of us. I once again was quite astounded by the beauty of such an evil place. We turned once we got out of the woods, rocketing onto the grassy plane that separates the Kingdom from our camp. We bolted towards the gates, suddenly now fixed and upright, and the sight of it made me happy, like the feeling you get when you come back home from a long trip. We heard shouting from inside, then J and Harlequinn appeared in the doorway.

"Harlequinn!" I shouted, overjoyed to see him again. I heard he'd gotten hurt, but I hadn't gone to see him before we left.

"Amber! D—Damien? And... a wolf?" His tone slowly settled into confusion instead of excitement. We skidded to a stop, and Damien morphed back into a human mid-air. He waved in greeting to the couple.

"We're back!" I sheepishly announced.

"Where did you even go? You've been gone for a while, we were worried about you." Harlequinn hugged me, despite the look of fear mixed with anger on his face.

"I'm sorry. We went on a mission to the Kingdom, to try to get information. We ended up getting kidnapped by people from a camp in the woods and monsters."

"That doesn't make me any less worried!" he exclaimed. I sighed, laughing a bit.

"Hey, you scared us, too. I heard you got hurt in the attack." Harlequinn looked over his shoulder to J, who shrugged.

"It wasn't that bad, I'm fine now."

"Liar," I heard J whisper. He looked up with a slight smirk on his face, crossing his arms and leaning against the doorframe. "He almost died. Luckily, B got to him in time."

"That's good. Were there any more casualties, or attacks at all?" I questioned, sliding off of Aster

"No, it's been pretty peaceful. But enough with the chatter. Come inside, you guys probably need to rest. You sound like you've had a big week." Harlequinn moved to the side, gesturing inside.

"We were gone for that long?" I exclaimed, slowly walking in.

"Maybe," J and Harlequinn pushed the large door shut, after Damien came in beside me, and we drifted through the arches above the doors, into the camp. "Everyone missed you. No one knew where you went."

"Yeah, we thought we'd be back a lot quicker," I laughed, a bit nervously. Everyone was acting weird today, even those two seemed a bit off. I heard a scream and turned to see Melioca, anger in her eyes, soaring across the camp, right at me. She tackled me, throwing her entire weight on me so I fell, and started trying to punch me. I blocked her attacks as well as I could, yelping with every blow. It took all three of the guys to pull her off.

"You left me here, *alone*, with Tigre? Do you have any idea how infuriating he is?" She struggled in their grip, almost dragging the three of them with her.

"I'm not that bad!" Tigre sauntered up behind me, tilting his head to the side a bit. He smiled kindly and helped me up, not being overly flirty for once. Something was definitely off. "Besides, I've been helping out around here. I've helped cook dinner three nights in a row, and cleaned up after everyone," he said, looking to me for compliments. I rolled my eyes, smiling.

"I think he's been possessed," I pointed towards Tigre and looked at Melioca. Her snarl faded a bit, and she stopped trying to get me, breathing hard as she stood there.

"I wish," she growled under her breath, and stormed off.

"Is she okay?" I asked, genuinely concerned.

"Everyone's been a little off since you left. We haven't had anyone to really lead... no specific person in charge. It kinda has everyone on edge," Tigre explained, spreading his hands.

"Sadly, we're gonna have to leave soon again. We think we found the General, and we have to go save him," I sighed, looking around the camp. Not much had changed, but they had definitely rebuilt. There were no more holes in the wall, and it looked taller. There were fewer buildings, but the ones that were there were bigger. The hellhound stables had moved from behind the castle to the corner of the wall, and it looked like now there was a mess hall, instead of having to all eat in the Waffle House. "I like what you guys did with the place." Tigre smirked playfully.

"Thanks. We thought it was time for a makeover after the attack. Come on, you arrived just in time for dinner."

Damien nearly ran us over trying to get inside the new building. The smell of food wafted around, delicious, pleasant scents of roasting meat, cooking vegetables, and even some bread, it seemed. All the campers crowded at the tables, chatting and laughing. Chandeliers hung from the ceiling, their candles lighting up the room. The floor was made of dark wood, and the walls lined with stone, contrary to what it seemed to be from the outside. I figured they had two layers, one of wood, one of stone. The ceiling sat high above our heads, and one portion of the Mess Hall on the left was filled with furnaces and open fires, even a counter to serve food on. I was amazed by how quickly they built all of this. We all sat down, eating pork and rice that the two cooks and Tigre whipped up. He basically had to wear a hazmat suit as to not get fur in the food. I giggled to myself, seeing him struggling to move around in a suit that was probably a size too small. Everyone seemed to be in a good mood, the entire hall filled with lively faces and small celebrations. After the festivities ended, I stayed behind to help clean. I was wiping off the last table when I paused, taking a deep breath, feeling the cold night breeze drifting in from the open door. Tigre, now wearing normal clothes, came to sit by me.

"Did you expect a warmer welcome?" he asked, staring out at the stars.

"Well, I didn't think I'd get attacked by a raging angel, but that thought has never really crossed my mind in the first place. I'm just glad to be back, even if it's for a short time."

"When are you leaving?"

"Probably tomorrow. We don't know how much time we have to save the General."

"Once he comes back, you won't be the General anymore, I guess?"

"No, I won't be." I was still a little scared for when I became the actual General. I didn't know if I had been great at it when I was the fake General, with me accidentally leaving for a week.

"General!" I heard people screaming outside. I looked up, already on my feet, rushing towards the noise. For a little while, I forgot my worries and accepted the title, claimed it, or, at least, responded to it. I ran out of the Mess Hall and saw all of the campers huddled by the gate, occasionally screaming in fear. I quickly dashed over, pushing through the crowd and through the doors. I looked on to the forest, which was changing faster and faster. The trees shrunk into the ground, the green land turned brittle and yellow, the grass grew taller, and dead bushes sprouted randomly. The change spread, affecting more and more of the area around it, and quickly making its way towards the camp. How was I supposed to stop the earth? What was even causing this? The changing land reached the edge of my shoes, and... stopped. I could almost feel the earth breathing a sigh of relief as everything settled.

Worry crept up on me. We didn't know what this meant, what this would cause. None of us could have a clue as to what was coming. Well, I had a hunch, the same nagging thought that occurred to me since day one when I saw the change happening. I didn't think it was possible, but then again—what separated reality and the impossible here?

"Everyone, please get back inside. We don't know if this is dangerous." At the mention of potential danger, everyone scattered, fleeing like leaves in the wind. Damien stepped up next to me, examining the dead grass, now turned a sickly yellow.

"This is really weird. No matter how much the forest has changed, it hasn't been affected this quickly yet. It looks like a third of it got transformed!" he exclaimed, throwing his hands in the air.

"This has happened before?" I questioned, examining the ground myself.

"Yeah, but it stays in the forest. Some trees disappear, moss grows, some stuff randomly dies. It's never this big." He crossed his arms, obviously frustrated by this.

"That might be the problem. Maybe magic built up underground, and you guys just swept it under the rug. Now, the rug exploded." I stood, looking into the night sky, wishing for answers I knew would never come on their own.

"Well, it doesn't seem to be harmful to skin. The rug might have exploded, but we probably won't," he said, stepping into the dead grass, testing the waters. The ground squelched beneath his shoes, and his foot sunk a little. "Ew," he stepped back, disgust prominent on his face. I giggled, amused at his misfortune.

"We should sleep. We can't think correctly out here if we're tired. Meet me back here in the morning, okay? We can try to figure this out then." Damien nodded to me, and I headed off. I wasn't sure where to sleep, but the castle seemed like a strange option. I wanted something familiar, whatever I could get in this entirely different world. So, I headed to my cabin, which was surprisingly still there, tucked away in one of the corners of the camp. I collapsed on the bed, curling underneath the covers, enjoying the warm embrace. I remembered to take off my shoes at the door, but my cape and gauntlets still remained. Exhaustion overtook me before I could remember to take them off, and I fell fast asleep.

The dreams I encountered were stranger than usual. I was sitting in a dark room, only a chair visible. A voice spoke overhead, something I couldn't quite make out. As I turned, the scenery changed. I was on a floating dock, in the middle of the sea. Aaron stood in front of me, smiling goofily, except he had blue hair. He held up a cage with a parrot in it, who squawked before talking.

"Beware! Beware! A traitor in your midst!" I was going to question what the bird meant, but I didn't get the chance to say anything before it changed again. I was standing in front of a pool, the water slowly lapping against the tiles, conforming the liquid to a square. I saw my reflection, slightly deformed, before I fell in head first. As soon as I passed through the water, I woke up in a cold sweat, my heart racing, tears dripping down my cheeks, and my body shaking. I wiped my eyes, taking a deep breath. I wasn't sure why, but that was terrifying. Everything happening so fast, spinning me from one situation to another, the birds warning me of a traitor, a reflection that was my own but also wasn't me.

"Are you okay?" I heard a voice echo around the cabin. I figured it must have been Aaron.

"I'll be alright," I thought, only able to hope it reached him. "Bad dream."

"You seemed to get those a lot on Earth." It seemed like he could hear me even if I wasn't actually speaking.

"Yeah, but this was more random. You were there, except with blue hair and birds that warned me of a traitor." I sat back against my bed, sighing. The sun wasn't even up yet, but I had no way to gauge the actual time.

"Interesting. You know, dreams usually mean something. I wonder if that could be your subconscious warning you not to trust someone. Has anyone been acting weird lately?"

"Everyone, honestly. The moment I got back, it seemed like they'd all changed. Even Damien, after we saved him from the monster nest."

"The what?"

"Oh, right, you don't know about that. He got kidnapped by monsters, and we had to save him from their nest. It was gross," I smiled to myself. I could almost imagine Aaron sitting next to me, his voice so clear in my head it was like he was in the room.

"Huh... well, he's probably slightly traumatized from being down there so long. Even a minute would drive me up a wall." A bit of static cut off the last word, but I figured it out from context.

"Yeah, maybe. I'm worried though. The forest started changing, a lot. It looks like the backyard of someone I know. Or, knew, at least. But that can't be it, they couldn't be here, right? And if they are, why did the forest change so much?" I groaned, frustrated at where this journey was headed.

"I mean, I'm here, right? More people could be appearing. They could be the one to betray you. I—I gotta go, guards coming. I'll talk to you later if I find something. Stay safe." The ringing in my ears I hadn't even noticed before started to fade. It was reassuring to hear a familiar voice, someone who would listen and take me seriously. Though, it did spark a bit of worry. He was from the real world, so it would be possible for someone else to be here. But whoever I thought it was, I absolutely despised. The thought of them made me sick. I desperately hoped it wasn't them, before turning back into my bed, lying against the pillow, and once again fading into the darkness of a deep sleep.

I awoke probably a few hours later, the sun now rising high into the sky. I yawned, though I wasn't really tired. I stretched my arms, and hopped out of bed. I accidentally slept in my clothes, and I didn't have any new ones, so I just put on my boots and left. A few people were milling about, waving when they saw me. I waved back, smiling. It seemed like life was finally peaceful, but I knew that would quickly change, evil constantly turning the tide on us. I heard footsteps, and turned to see J jogging up to me.

"Hey, General!"

"No need to be so formal," I laughed, crossing my arms and turning with a slight smirk on my face. "Is there something wrong?" I asked, interested to hear the report.

"There's supposedly been a Zanzagar congregation, out in the woods. We think someone is trapped inside, which could be really dangerous. There are also rarely ever this many Zanzagars in one place, and from what we heard, there's quite a few-"

"Wait, who's out there? We haven't sent anyone out recently, right? Is it not someone from here?" I was completely puzzled. Who could have been attacked?

"No, we have no clue who it is. That's why we think it's another outsider," he looked to me with a worried expression.

"Another one? That's not good!" It seemed my concerns were for a reason. "We need to go find them. No matter who they are, if someone's in danger, we have to help." I might've despised them, but I didn't want them to die.

"Alright. I'll get Damien, then we can go investigate. Be prepared to fight." I nodded, and headed towards the gate to wait for the two. I looked out into the woods, disturbed by how familiar the landscape was. I must've been really lost in my thoughts, because I didn't hear J and Damien approaching, and when J tapped my shoulder, I jumped.

"Oh! Sorry, I was thinking," I awkwardly coughed and re-adjusted my cloak. "So, shall we go?"

"We shall," Damien replied, and we headed off into the woods. Well, now it looked more like grasslands, but still. We walked carefully, trying not to be very loud so we could sneak up on anything we needed to, though it might not have worked very well because we kept giggling. I hid behind a bush and ended up slipping and falling into the leaves, Damien picked up a pebble, turned into a bird and accidentally slammed into a tree as he took flight, and J followed us around, walking with his knees almost at his shoulders. We only stopped goofing off when we heard a deep snort, and heavy footsteps in front of us. We hid behind one of the very few trees to look around, and saw about ten Zanzagars huddled together. They were roaring and snorting, their hot breath steaming in the air. Their eyes all glowed red as they batted around something in the middle of their circle, laughing occasionally, which sounded more like they were throwing up a soccer ball, but I got the gist of it.

"Damien, you turn into a small animal and get behind them. J, go to the side a bit and see if you can pick up a few fallen logs to throw at them." I set my hands ablaze, keeping the fire small so it wouldn't draw attention. "I'll rush in, take them by surprise." The two nodded, and rushed off to do their jobs. I waited a few minutes to assure they were in position. Then, I leapt out from behind the tree and screamed. All eyes turned to me and things froze before devolving into chaos.

They all charged at once, and I rolled to the side before they could get me, throwing a ball of fire at their heads. It bounced off of one and kept going, hitting all of them before dispersing midair. A tree knocked over a few of them, soaring through the air while a mouse ran amidst them, squeaking loudly before transforming into a hellhound, pushing them away from each other. I ran in, brandishing my sword and stabbing one of the creatures, pushing my blade further into its stomach as I set it on fire. The pig screeched, and disintegrated into dust. I turned to see another Zanzagar reaching for me, and I jumped as it shoved its arm into the ground. I landed gracefully on top of its hand — or hoof, and ran up to its head. It screamed, thrashing and running around trying to throw me off. I sunk my sword deep into its neck, and it fell to the floor as a pile of ashes.

I turned to see J wielding two logs, both floating in front of his hands, but he was quickly losing leverage. The element of surprise didn't last long when the enemies had such brute strength. One of the monsters shattered a log, and before J could reach for another one, he was thrown backwards. Damien was running around, barking furiously and clawing at the pigs, but quickly became surrounded. They seemed to multiply, more and more appearing out of the trees. Soon, even I was barely able to fight, suffocated by these disgusting, huge animals. I did the only thing I could think of at the time, remembering a move that, at the very least, could throw these things off-balance.

I leapt into the air, propelling myself with fire at my heels. I landed right in the middle of the biggest hoard of Zanzagars, digging my hands into the soft dirt. A shockwave of heat spread through their ranks, disintegrating one after the other, fire climbing through the earth until all of them were just dust in the wind. Smoke hung over the forest, and I stood up, smiling sheepishly.

"Too much?" I chuckled nervously, my legs wilting beneath me. I caught myself, but my hands shook.

"Just a little bit," Damien replied with a smirk. I turned, looking around for the person who had been attacked. The debris hanging in the air made it hard to see anyone or anything. I could barely make out the silhouettes of bushes, much less a human.

"We need to find the person," I coughed, inhaling a bit of the smoke.

"I—I'm here!" I heard a voice within the fog.

"Here doesn't really help if I can't see you," I muttered, rolling my eyes. I turned to where I thought the voice was coming from, and blindly walked forward, quickly tripping over a bush. I groaned, looking up into the face of an old... friend?

"Amber?"

I was surprised to see another familiar face, but at the same time, I knew it would be him, I knew he was here. I knew who he was and what he had done to me, and my friends. This was the one person I didn't want to see here. So, I panicked.

"Who are you?" I blurted out, immediately regretting the lie. But I didn't want to admit I lied. So, it seemed I would have to stick with not knowing one of the people who ruined my life. Though, I wish I didn't know him.

"I—uh, I'm Seth. Don't you remember me?" he stuttered, looking a bit disgusted. I could barely see his face, but I knew what he looked like. Short, dark hair and small eyes, he could have easily been mistaken for a child despite his actual age because of his size. The dust started to settle, and I got a better look at him. As I thought, he hadn't changed much from when I last saw him, but today he was wearing a leather jacket and a gray shirt, with dark jeans. I wondered why he was so dressed up, well, dressed up for his standards, before dismissing the thought.

"You don't exactly look very pleased to see me, why would you want me to know you?" I huffed, crossing my arms. He glared at me.

"Whatever. What were those things?" he asked, turning to Damien and J. Before either of them could speak, I answered.

"Zanzagars. Pig-like monsters, they're very strong and very dangerous."

"Unless, of course, you're Amber." Damien snickered, and I smiled, remembering the first day I spent here, and my encounter with the same monster. Apparently, the creatures

195

favored new blood, or... this was their nest.

"Yeah, like she could actually defeat those things," I heard Seth mutter. I punched his arm, hard, and growled.

"They," Damien and I corrected at the same time. I smiled gratefully at him.

"And, you literally just saw me kill... all of them," I replied, rolling my eyes. He was already becoming a nuisance, just as I thought. "But fine. If you're so keen on acting like that, we'll leave you be. Good luck surviving against those things again, especially at night," I chuckled, starting to walk away. I was completely intent on leaving him and his ungratefulness in the forest to die, but I felt a hand on my shoulder before we could leave. I turned, looking at Damien's sad attempt at puppy-dog eyes. Needless to say, my emotions were not at all swayed.

"Come on, Amber. You know we can't leave him here. Give him a chance, you said you don't know him. He could be better than you think." It was as if he read my mind, and knew that we were acquaintances, playing on my guilt. Being as stubborn as I was, I didn't want to admit defeat.

"Fine!" I snapped. "But I'm telling you, we don't want him within thirty feet of us."

"Noted," Damien said, putting his hands up. "Wanna bet on it?" I was about to say no, but then I thought of the possibilities.

"Sure," I smirked. "I bet, he'll start tripping us up and messing with important things."

"I bet he'll be perfectly civil and just follow along quietly."

"If I win, you have to turn into a unicorn and prance around the camp."

"If I win, you have to do the worm while on fire." I laughed at the thought, but especially how strange it was that he requested the worm.

"Deal," I said, holding out my hand. We shook, and I was entirely confident I would win, based on my encounters with him. Especially because his hate for me might inspire him to get revenge. "J, we're going. And Seth... you're coming too." He didn't look happy about the thought of traveling with me. "We should probably go straight to the lake." I suggested.

"That might be hard for me," J laughed under his breath at his own joke. I held back a sly smile.

"Do your best. But, in all seriousness, we don't know how long we have. The General could be in danger."

"Who's the General? And where is this place, actually? What's happening? I don't even know how I got here!" I tuned out Seth's senseless complaints, and whistled. Aster immediately dashed towards me, almost appearing out of thin air. He tackled me, and I nearly fell over from his weight and laughing. He licked my face, and settled down. "Is that a *wolf*?"

"Yes, now shut up. J, you can ride with me on Aster. Damien... you might need, like, a vulture or something." I slid onto Aster's back, and J followed suit. When I turned towards Damien, I found... an ostrich. I snorted, covering my mouth and absolutely started cracking up. Suddenly seeing a giant ostrich in front of me was particularly hilarious at this time. Meanwhile, Seth was gaping in awe, having just seen a human transform into a bird.

"What—how—there's no way! What are you guys trying to pull?" He shrieked, backing up and breathing heavily. "He just—no! No way! I—I don't-" His eyes fluttered shut, and he collapsed backwards.

"Well, at least that got him quiet. But Damien... an ostrich?" I giggled. He nodded, squawking.

"It's the biggest bird I could think of! Though, they can't exactly fly... so I guess a horse or something would be better. Whatever," he spun in a circle, morphing into a giant eagle. He hopped over to Seth's unconscious body, grabbed his arms with his talons, and launched into the air, struggling to stay in the sky. Seeing a bird wobbling through the air with a human in its claws was just as funny as the ostrich. I nudged Aster with my foot, and we took off after the unbalanced bird. J nearly fell from the sudden burst of speed, but grabbed my arm to steady himself.

"We're leaving!" I yelled as we passed the camp. Tigre peeked through the door, waving with a smile. We ran, Damien barely keeping up with us as he struggled with Seth. Not long after we started the trek, the Kingdom appeared in front of us. "Through or around?" I asked Aster, leaning towards his ears so he could hear us. He barked in response, and continued on his path, directed towards the middle of the Kingdom. I smiled, and looked back at J, who was surprisingly calm in this.

"I've never ridden a wolf before, but this is fun," he laughed as he noticed my look. "Kinda similar to the hellhounds, but... much smaller, and less destructive."

"I know, right?" I replied, turning my gaze back to the road in front of us. We burst through the alleyways leading into the city, and rocketed through crowds of shocked pedestrians. Screams rose up from the crowd as we passed, weaving through buildings and around people, even jumping over a bench. We passed the castle, and I saw Aaron in the courtyard, holding a bucket full of water. He yelped, but it turned into laughter as he saw me waving. We were playing with fire, but that's something I handled pretty well here. We escaped out the other side, meeting with Damien at the border. I could just barely see the lake in the distance.

"This kid is much heavier than he looks!" I heard the eagle yell, and he started spiraling towards the ground, Seth struggling in his grip. I turned Aster to where they were falling, and before we reached them, I jumped off, rolling to the side so they could land on the wolf's back. J followed my lead, and we ended up covered in dirt a few feet behind Aster, Damien and Seth. The bird changed back into a human, panting while Seth basically whimpered beside him. Aster calmly blinked, unfazed by the landing or the strange circumstances.

"Why did you do that?! What is—whoa, this wolf is huge!" Seth stared wide-eyed at Aster, who barked in acknowledgment.

"Yeah, now let's deal with something actually important. First of all, what is wrong with you? Struggling like that could have gotten you hurt even if Damien was trying to kidnap you. Think before you act! Second of all, you kind of put us in danger with that. J and I had to throw ourselves off of a moving wolf!" I yelled exasperatedly.

"You expect me to see a giant bird carrying me and think, 'oh, let me take a minute to figure out a solution to this problem.' No one does that!"

"I would! Most of the people I know would! Besides, you thought that you needed to get out, while you were in the sky! Ugh!" I grabbed his shoulder and pushed him to the ground, off of Aster. I swung myself on, and nodded to J, gesturing for him to do the same. With an infuriated glare pointed towards Seth, we started moving forward. Aster panted, his tongue hanging out of his mouth as we walked along, much slower than before. He was obviously tired from such a long sprint. Rage boiled up in my chest, a feeling that wasn't exactly pleasant. Every time I saw him, he made me so angry I wanted to explode, or slap him, or both.

"Hey," I heard J say from behind, putting his hand on my shoulder, a comforting gesture I often used. "Take a deep breath. Don't let him affect you, no matter how stupid he's being. You're under a lot of stress, but don't let it jeopardize the mission." I sat up straighter, sighing guiltily. He was right- I wasn't being fair to anyone. This, however, was a new side of J I'd never seen before. He spoke gently, his facial expression calm and with a kind look. His aura of peace reflected on others easily, creating a much tamer mood.

"Thanks," I said, offering a shy smile back towards him. He nodded in recognition. I set my eyes to the lake, making sure to control my breathing and thoughts. The trek now was much slower, so that also helped to bring my temper down. I was grateful to have friends that could keep a calm head, and help me with keeping mine.

We finally approached the edge of the lake, after what felt like was forever. The water flowed calmly into the bank, but I could feel a strangely dark presence, like the serenity was a facade to mask the evil hidden underneath the gentle waves. The lake itself was about the size of a football field, the bottom invisible beneath the water, even though it was relatively clear. On the other side of the lake was what looked like a glass tube, the size of a slide and big enough for a human to fit in. I guessed that was how you got to the bottom. Damien ran up next to us, Seth close behind as we walked towards the tunnel.

"Is this it?" I asked, glancing back at Damien, who nodded, though he seemed skeptical of something.

"Where are we going, exactly?" Seth demanded, crossing his arms. I couldn't help but roll my eyes and look away, and Damien stepped in to explain.

"To find the General. I don't know why he would be down here, but my dream was really specific with locations. This is an old observatory that a few marine biologists and scientists created to understand the workings of this lake. It's supposedly the perfect place to live for most fish, and they attempted to save some endangered species' by relocating them here, but no matter what, anything that has gone in has disappeared. Even some humans who tried to get to the bottom never came back up, but no one ever figured out what was down here. I'm afraid… now we might find out." He put his hand gently on the glass slide, gazing down into the murky water.

"It couldn't be a mermaid or anything, right? Maybe a siren?" I tried to think of some mythical, water-dwelling creature that ate marine life and humans. I hadn't seen anything like that here, but I knew it wasn't out of the question.

"No, mermaids aren't that vicious. They're terrified of humans because of hunting, so they stay away, and usually live out in more open ocean areas. They're a sight to behold, but extremely rare."

"Who comes up with this stuff?" I heard Seth muttering from a few feet away, his back turned, but he was throwing his hands in the air in exasperation.

"Welcome to your new reality. Get used to it," I advised,

calling back to him, which earned an angry glare and a very pouty face. "Okay, I guess we have to get down there... wherever this thing leads," I peered down the tunnel, seeing only darkness at the end. It shuddered for a second, probably hit by something dwelling under the malicious-looking waters. "Shall we?" I asked, turning to the group.

"It's now or never, I suppose," J said, his voice shaking a bit. I nodded with determination, grabbed the edge of the tube, and jumped.

I slid along the glass, bobbing and weaving left to right. It spit me out at the bottom, barely any light other then the few lanterns placed around. The room I was in was circular, and had another tunnel with a door, leading to a cube. I peered outside and saw the General's lifeless form on the ground of the cube.

"General!" I yelled, and I heard a knocking sound behind me. I expected to see the others coming down the slide, but I was face-to-face with a giant monster. Twice the size of a great white shark, though the same appearance, and jellyfish tentacles instead of a tail. I screamed as it bared its giant teeth, smashing its head against the glass. Luckily, it didn't crack, but held resilient against the beasts threatening strength. Seconds after, Damien slid into the room, landing on his stomach.

"What is that?" he asked, brushing himself off and rushing to the side of the room, gazing at the monster swimming gracefully through the water. "I... I've seen that before, it was in my dream! That's what's been hiding down here? How could no one have seen it until now?" He looked shocked, staring out the window. I tapped his shoulder, gesturing to the General, still being held right across from us.

"We may have bigger problems. Look!"

He turned, his eyes widening even further as he rushed to the glass, pressing his hands against the wall. "Oh, no! We have to get him out. The tunnel looks like it only has space for one person at a time, though." I was about to offer to go first when we heard screaming, followed by J and Seth rocketing in, sprawling across the floor as they stumbled out of the tunnel.

"Have you all never been on slides?" I said exasperatedly. "I'll get the General." I squeezed through the narrow passage, swinging open the glass door that blocked off the other part of the tunnel. I barely made it through, but successfully got to the other side. I rushed to the old man, feeling his forehead. His skin was on fire, and his eyes were rolled up to the back of his head, and his hands lay clasped together on his stomach. I looked up to see Seth halfway through the tunnel, and Damien looking concerned and slightly annoyed on the other side. I tried to gently pick up the General, but as I did, he evaporated, smoke rising into the air. I stared in shock at my hands, terrified of what I had done. I heard the sound of glass being hit, and the door slammed behind me. Seth was huddled in the tunnel, staring at the door with his arms out before he turned and ran back, quickly crawling across the glass. Anger boiled up in my chest, an intense feeling of rage and betrayal as I realized what he had done.

I heard a bubbling sound, and the air grew hot in the cube. I looked outside to see the water swirling around me. Water seemed to be more controlled by emotions, for me. The monster drew closer and I was able to see more details of the strange combination of sea creatures. A menacing face, narrow dark eyes and pointed nose, but long, thin tentacles instead of a tail, thrashed around outside. The water grew ever warmer, and the glass around the cube shattered, the circle suddenly devoid of people. They must have run after Seth, that disgusting traitor.

The liquid around me started to flow, filling the empty air and closing around my body, quickly threatening to fill my lungs and drown me as I struggled, fear overcoming my mixed emotions. The monster took this as a chance to lunge, and bared its teeth, swimming quickly towards me. I looked up, letting my anger out into the water. My rage, a burning, everlasting fire of anger mostly. An air pocket cleared above me, and I was able to see the surface. The water gripped my heels and forcefully pushed me upwards, launching me into the sky and back onto the bank of the lake, the three guys standing there in shock. I stumbled, spat back out of the water so violently that I fell over, the water on my clothes sinking into the sand below me. I got up, climbing to my feet so I could run up to Seth, pushing him to the ground.

"What did you do?" I yelled, my breath short, and my wet hair getting in my face.

"I didn't mean to! It was like I was being controlled, something in my head just… making me do that!"

I scoffed, rolling my eyes. "What in the world could have made you do that?" I demanded, my heart racing and adrenaline flowing through my veins.

"I don't know! Get off of me!" He slapped my hand away, and got up as I growled. My limbs ached and I could barely stand as reality set in, and I collapsed, shaking.

"J, take Seth away. I'll stay with Amber," Damien knelt beside me, and I just barely saw J helping Seth stand, and walking away, talking quietly. "Are you okay? We tried to get back in but the door locked, and then the structure started coming loose… I'm sorry we weren't there for you."

"I'm just glad I'm alive," I coughed, my voice shaking. "That creature… that was terrifying. Deep water and sharks really scare… me…" I paused, glancing across the lake. Damien followed my gaze and gasped in shock. We saw the General, his body once again lying almost in reach, on the shore now, a few yards away. Damien helped me up as I scrambled to stand, both of us rushing over, immediately trying to pick him up. He didn't disappear, but coughed, almost coming back to life.

"General!" I said joyfully, resisting the urge to hug him.

"Amber, I… I am no longer the General. That duty rests upon your shoulders. It has since I left," he smiled weakly.

"What… what do you mean?" I asked, quite worried about the answer. Damien kneeled beside me, silent the entire time, but he looked like he was about to break down.

"My... time is up. It has been decided already. You've grown, very much, in very little time. I trust you to protect the camp, and defend against the Kingdom," he coughed again, turning white. "Damien... I assume will be right next to you the entire way. Your right hand man."

"I... yeah. He's the person I trust the most here. If I had to pick someone, he would be the one." I hadn't thought of it much before, but I remembered what the General said to me when I first arrived. "How did you know? I don't understand--we'd barely met. We could have ended up hating each other, or just going separate ways."

"As you... may have noticed, everyone here goes by a letter. J, H, B. It's the first letter of their name they use instead of their full, because here, names can be dangerous, or simply personal. He gave you his full name the moment he met you, showing a bond of trust already established. That made it clear you two would stick by each other's side, and... and help each other." The General turned to the side, reaching out feebly for Damien, who took his hand with a respectful smile on his face. "I have not been able to teach you all I know. I have not been able to tell the truth at all times. But now you have the chance to right my wrongs. Take care of the camp. Do not... let it fall. My crime is, sadly, now yours to fix." He choked, going white. His face seemed to dry and crack, crumbling apart into dust along with the rest of his body. Dirt and sand went everywhere, and when the haze cleared, a small tree was left on the ground. I gasped in surprise, shocked and confused.

"What... what was that?" I whispered, my hands over my mouth.

"Remember when I told you the General moves on his own time?" Damien replied, looking down sadly at the small plant. "That... wasn't quite true. He was cursed, long ago, a punishment for something we never figured out. He had a limited lifespan, much shorter than anyone normally would have. He had to find and train the next General by that time, or else... he would die with no heir, no one to protect the camp. He fulfilled his purpose, and now has been reborn as this tree." He wiped his eyes, tears glistening down his cheek. For how important the General was to him, he was taking his death really well. I put my hand on his shoulder, still looking down.

"I'm sorry," I whispered.

He shrugged. "I've been with him for a long time. I'm glad he survived for so many years, but... I'm also glad he went peacefully. No use crying over it now. Tears... won't bring him back."

"That doesn't matter. You cry because you're sad. Letting out emotions isn't a bad thing, even if it doesn't bring back the dead. That's not why you cry. You don't have to be strong all the time, it's okay to be upset." He turned to me with a frown, his eyes glistening. He sniffed, then leaned forward in a hug. I felt him trembling slightly, his shaky breathing and sniffling no longer held back. I knew the relationship the two had, but I could never imagine the feeling of losing someone like that. A father figure after his actual dad died, someone to offer love and support, train him in his powers. He was absolutely distraught, and still felt like he had to hide it, keep it bottled up and pretend to be fine. I heard footsteps behind me and J knelt down, hugging both of us. We sat there for a moment, just enjoying the comfort of each other's embrace. Damien took a deep breath, and backed away, his eyes red and face damp with tears.

"Thank you," he said with a sad smile, but obviously noticing my own tears, my eyes stinging.

"There's some dirt in my eye," I said, wiping away the liquid.

"Oh, really? Crying is okay, right?" he said pointedly, and I laughed, nodding.

"You're right. My eyes are sweating. Someone's cutting onions. I'm not crying, you're crying." My emotion was honestly getting the best of me. Damien pulled me back into a hug, holding me for a second as I caught my breath.

"It's okay," he muttered. "It's okay to cry." I nodded, and he stood, helping me up. J didn't say a word, but looked down at the tree between us, seemingly understanding what had happened, and patted both of our shoulders. The wind picked up, and the ashes left the ground where the General's tree stood, swirling around me. I tried to move away, but it followed me.

"Uh... what is happening?" I asked, still wiping away tears, trying to dodge the dust, but it persisted.

"I... I think the Generals pass over their power when the predecessor dies, or is unable to continue leading." Damien didn't look very sure about that information, but I stopped trying to move away.

"What was the General's power?" I asked, watching the same swirl over my arms.

"I'm not entirely sure. You probably get his strength, or wisdom, or something you need to lead properly." The ashes settled, sinking into my skin and glowing purple. Then, the light faded.

"I... don't feel different." Except for a newfound sense of responsibility, but that didn't exactly affect me much.

"Well, we'll see soon if your power has improved. I think it's time to keep going forward, and... stop the Kingdom's reign of tyranny. That's what he was working for, wasn't he? We'll continue his legacy and now, Amber, with your power... we can take them down. We need more people, but we can forge alliances with the tribes in the woods." Damien looked to the sky, his eyes glimmering beneath the sun's rays. He clenched his fist, and took a deep breath. "It's time to end this." He started walking towards camp, and J almost followed, but I grabbed his wrist before he could leave.

"J, I need to talk to you." We turned away from Damien, who was hopefully out of hearing distance. "I'm... I'm not sure the General actually was trying to take down the Kingdom. He never attacked, he never really even defended against their advances, from what I've seen and heard. And... I saw something a bit unsettling. Before we got kidnapped in the Kingdom, I saw a picture of the General on the wall. My friend said he was the King's brother." J looked mildly confused, and worried at the same time.

"Okay, first, you got kidnapped? I thought that was only in the woods. Second of all, we don't have any friends in the Kingdom. They were probably lying," he said, shrugging in dismissal.

"No, he was a friend from my world. I'm not sure how he got here, but he's been here for a while. And while trying to find the King's plans, I got knocked out and woke up in a room he was standing in. But that's beside the point! I saw the picture, and the General didn't seem to be doing much to protect the camp. I didn't wanna say this in front of Damien, but... I'm worried. I don't wanna insinuate that he's a traitor, but it seems like he's hiding something." J pursed his lips, looking back at Damien, who was still marching onward. "Before he... died... the General said something about fixing his crime. Maybe that's tied together."

"We'll have to look into this, but not right now. Especially with his mental state... I don't wanna break even possible bad news." I nodded, whistling for Aster. I heard screaming, and looked across the lake to see the wolf dragging Seth by his shirt collar.

"No!" I yelled, rushing towards them. "Aster, let go!" He looked up at me innocently and dropped Seth, who screamed once more dramatically.

"That wolf is huge!" he said quietly, marveling at the size.

"Yeah, and?" I snapped, still mad at Seth for his actions in the real world and here. Every time I looked at him, absolute rage sparked inside me, even the sight of his face just infuriated me. I'd tried to be his friend before, and every time, it ruined me. I wasn't about to make the same mistake again.

"Why are you so angry all the time?" he demanded, standing. Aster snarled in a warning.

"You'd think you, of all people, would know!" I yelled, feeling my hands heat up. I remembered I had to be careful with my words, but hopefully I could pass this off as rage building up from before.

"This is absolutely senseless! You're completely overreacting. I liked you better when you barely talked," he hissed, his eyes narrowing. Aster barked, launching at his leg and clamping down. Seth howled in pain, trying to shake the giant wolf off of him. My hands burst into flames, as my face grew red. He saw the fire and yelped, falling backwards. "How—how did you—*fire*!" He started to hyperventilate, his eyes widening in fear.

"In case you hadn't figured it out, this place isn't our world. Here, magic exists, and I can use it. So maybe it's time *you* quieted down." I raised the heat, creating a bright white inferno sitting in my palm. "I don't even know you, and you're trying to pretend I'm someone who was in your life. And for what? So you can manipulate me? So you can insult me, get under my skin?" Power surged through me, as my mind clouded with anger. I let out emotion from what he'd done before, playing it as if I only knew what would happen. I felt a sharp pain in my neck, and I stumbled, the fire dissipating. I turned to see J, a stern look on his face, standing behind me with his hand raised.

"You need to control your emotions. With power like yours, it can get out of your hands and corrupt you, or hurt your friends. That's happened before, dark forces taking over when someone gives them an outlet." He sighed, lowering his arm. "That's also how you were able to have sudden control over the water, because Seth here sparked that rage. You both need to be careful."

I took a deep breath, glaring at Seth once more before I walked away. He aggravated me to no end, but sadly, he was stuck with us. I didn't want to leave him at camp, or he could ruin everything, so that meant we had to drag him along. The good thing about that was I could show him how much stronger I'd gotten since he last saw me. Here, I had power over him, both in skill and seemingly in magic. He didn't seem to have any powers, at least not anything that had become apparent.

It didn't matter now. We had to press on, because we had a job to do. Recruit those in the woods, and take down the Kingdom.

Easier said than done.

I caught up with Damien, barely any emotion on his face. J, Seth, and Aster lagged behind.

"Where to?" Damien asked, looking to me.

"We'll have to go back to camp, tell everyone the... unfortunate news. Then, we can find Red, he knows more about the woods than we do. To get people on our side, we'll have to earn their loyalty, by helping the people in the woods that need it. This could take a matter of minutes, or years. We'll start small and go onto the bigger stuff as time progresses," I replied, hoping that was a decent plan.

"Alright, I see you're taking charge already," Damien smiled proudly at me. "We're getting close to the Kingdom, a bit too close for comfort. Want me to scout ahead to see if anyone is patrolling?" Damien suggested, a smile lighting up his face as he held up his arms. I giggled, amused by his childish personality.

"That would be great," I smiled as he changed into a hawk, soaring above us with a squawk. I whistled quietly, and Aster ran up beside me, nuzzling my hand. He seemed to be getting taller every day, now his head reached almost to my shoulder when he stood up straight. I scratched behind his ears as he melted under my touch. He looked up, eyes bright with joy, and jumped to lick my face. His scratchy tongue left a trail of drool dripping down my cheek. I laughed, sitting down on the grass as I pet Aster, waiting for Damien. It seemed like so long ago I met the wolf, but then again, I'd been saying things like that a lot lately. You could barely tell they were the same, his previous malnourished, desperate and hostile demeanor completely replaced by a silly, cheerful, and childlike manner. It was impressive to see how much better he was doing, and how he had adjusted to being a companion. His fur was soft, like he had recently been groomed, and I leaned against his stomach, thinking of recent events.

"I thought you were scared of dogs," Seth commented, seeing me playing with the wolf.

"I was," I replied, not even looking his way. I heard a screech, and turned my gaze to the sky to see a brown hawk, circling above. I waved, and it spiraled down, clipping the top of my head with its wings. It rolled across the dirt, coming to a stop a few feet away and turning into a very disheveled Damien. He sat up, dirt covering half of his face and stretched his arms.

"I'm still not very good at flying," he admitted. I helped him up, grabbing his arm and hoisting him to his feet. "The Kingdom is strangely clear. We can go through or around without having a problem, supposedly. It unnerves me, though... why would no one be there?" He put his pointer finger to his lips in a pondering expression.

"It's probably safer to go around, as far as we can," I looked up, towards J and Seth, who were deep in conversation. J looked almost angry, and Seth, quite guilty. "Guys!" They looked towards us as I called out, and I waved to signal we were leaving. J jogged to catch up.

"Hey, are we going home?" He looked hopeful, and smiled even wider when I nodded, obviously excited to go back, maybe because of a certain someone waiting for him.

"We're gonna be away for a while, though. We just need to inform everyone of the plan." I set my sights ahead of me, watching the golden glow of the sun lighting up the sky for one last moment as it set. The clouds slowly shifted, changing into hues of pink, red, and orange.

"Uh... what *is* the plan?" J asked sheepishly. I looked back in surprise, realizing he hadn't heard our conversation. I flushed, crimson rushing to my cheeks.

"Go back to the camp, explain the General situation, and go recruit as many people as we can before attacking the Kingdom, hopefully dismantling the oppressive hierarchy."

"The overall situation or the situation with the General?"

"Uh... both?"

"Got it," he laughed playfully, and I hoped he actually understood rather than just mocking my poor communication skills. I glanced back at Seth, who had his hand on his arm, simply looking at the ground. I sighed, rolling my eyes.

"Come on, Seth. We're not gonna leave you out here, especially not at night." I waved again, gesturing for him to come forward.

"Why not at night?" he asked, tilting his head a bit.

"It's when the monsters start spawning. They feed off of darkness, so the night provides physical food for them. They're weaker in the light, sometimes even hurt by it, so they rarely come out in the day, unless they're a very powerful monster, or one that isn't entirely fueled by dark forces, like a Zanzagar," J explained, stepping in before I could say something. That explanation seemed to make something click, two pieces of a puzzle fit together somewhere deep inside my brain, but it was also unclear what exactly suddenly made sense.

"Well, shall we go?" I suggested. An ear-splitting shriek echoed through my head. I fell to the ground, my legs crippling beneath me. It sounded like someone was screaming, except amplified ten thousand times, the feeling alone making my body freeze, nothing working like it was supposed to. The sound wracked my brain, making it to where I couldn't even move, the pain only subsiding when the noise cut out. I could only think of one source of the sound, as I'd seen this happen to others when we were escaping the Kingdom. "Aaron?" I muttered, nearly out of breath.

"Don't come to the Kingdom! Stay as far away as—ah!" Static, and then silence, everyone else frozen in shock.

"A—are you okay?" Damien said gently, delicately grabbing my arm and pulling me up.

"I think so. Aaron—he was trying to warn us. He might be in trouble..." Worry started creeping into my mind. Why was his telepathy cut off? Why shouldn't we go towards the Kingdom? Did he get kidnapped? A thousand questions raced through my mind, the answers to all of them I feared. But fear held no place in my heart when it came to my friends. "He said to not go to the

Kingdom. It was cut off, but I'm afraid he's in trouble."

"Wait, Aaron from school? Also, he isn't here. How could you hear him?" Seth scoffed and rolled his eyes. I shot a glare at him, trying to physically manifest daggers with my eyes, but I didn't have that power.

"As I've explained multiple times before, this world has magic. He gained powers when coming here, and so did I," I said, setting my hand ablaze, once again, in reference. He squeaked, staring at the fire in my hand, total shock enveloping his face, like he still wasn't used to seeing that. "He has telepathy now, and he's talked to me before with it. This time... it was panicked. He was yelling, really loudly. That's what made me fall, he's done that to a guard before when they were blocking our way," I remarked, fed up with Seth's obvious stubborn nature. I was literally holding a flame in my hand, and he couldn't accept magic here? It was baffling.

"There... there's no way. This must be a prank or something. Did I hit my head when I fell?" he muttered. Point proven.

"I swear, maybe we *should* leave him here," I rolled my eyes, and looked up to see Damien and J staring at me with a disappointed glance, like they were my dads and I'd gotten an F on my report card. "Oh, come on! Listen to him! He won't survive with us or without us," I scoffed, crossing my arms.

"So your solution is to just leave him?"

"Better than him messing us up!" I did feel a bit guilty, but we put the mission at risk if we brought him, as well as his life. If we left him, it would only be his life at risk.

"I... kinda get what you're saying, but we can't leave him. We don't even know if we should go to the Kingdom. We don't know what's there, or what we could run into. We need to get back to camp, and tell everyone the plan. You're the General, now. You have people to lead." I felt my eyes start to water, but I blinked away the tears.

"If my friend is in danger, I need to save him," I hissed. "You guys can go back. Aaron might need me, and I have to help him. I care about him too much to let him even possibly get hurt," I snapped, and Aster trotted to my side. I leapt on, looking back to Damien and J one more time. "If you want to go back, you can. I'll join you as soon as I'm able to. But... he's my friend. You understand that, don't you?" I pleaded, and Damien's expression softened.

"Yeah, I do. You can go, but be careful. We'll get back to the camp as soon as we can." I nodded, a thankful smile growing on my face. He gave me a sad wave, and they started off. I sighed, regretting the tension and bad note we ended on, but knowing it was time to press forward. I nudged Aster, and we raced off, sprinting into the Kingdom.

When we got there, it was empty. Streets devoid of people, barely any lights on, all the stores cleared of items. It was like walking through a ghost town, the darkness not making it any less ominous. I decided not to dwell on the outside, but head to the Castle. As expected, the guards in front were missing. The doors were unlocked, and I walked into the quiet hallway unopposed, ordering Aster to wait outside. I spent a bit more time lingering, examining the artwork on the wall. It was really quite beautiful, every tiny brush stroke perfect. As I got to the end of the hall, I looked to the right, and sure enough, it was there. The picture of the General, looking a bit younger than before, but it was unmistakably him.

What did this mean? What secrets did he take to his grave? I turned, examining the picture on the opposite side of the hallway. This one was peculiar, a figure of a human, but covered in shadows. You could just barely make out a curly brown beard, and a regal stance. The shadows were blended not to be just pure black, but fold over the shape of everything. It was still strange to see a painting almost entirely covered in black, why would you even have a portrait if you're not really gonna be in it? I dismissed it after a second, and continued into the area I was in before, the open lobby I had stopped at with Aaron. No lights were on, and the silence was almost scary. What had happened here?

There were two ways I could go. Upstairs, where Aaron said it was like a maze, and down another hallway I'd never been. I heard voices and slunk to the side, hiding in the ever-present darkness. As I moved forward, the voices got clearer, until I arrived at two normal sized doors.

"I say we execute him. Giving private information to outsiders, from that forsaken camp, meddling with confidential papers, and harming a guard to aid in an escape. We have the proof! Get rid of him!"

"What we do sends a specific message to the people of the Kingdom. Using our resources, using our time, tells them that these people... are a threat. Which means the other humans from that wretched camp could also be a threat. We have to be careful what our course of action is, because no matter what, it will be public."

"Why don't we just use him as a lesson? Tell everyone that this is what happens when you make the mistake of going against us. You get killed."

"You have a point there. My King, we've reached a crossroads. What do you say? Death, or let him live?" I peered through the crack in the door, following what little light came from inside. I saw a large room, tables on every wall with people sitting at them. A large red carpet was laid out in a path towards two large thrones. Only one was occupied, but you could only see the man's shoes, gold boots with a silver tie. He raised his head, pondering his decision.

"I rule... death." I gasped, covering my mouth, but it was too late. The sound drew all heads towards the doors, which swung open as I backed away. I saw Aaron inside the room, bound with chains and a cloth in his mouth. Rage took over my sense of fear or shock, and my hands blazed with newfound strength. I growled, awaiting the approaching crowd. All held swords, daggers, or some sort of blade, and all had cruel sneers drawn across their faces. There were about twenty, all old men, so I knew I could probably take them. They rushed forward, and I smiled, excited to prove I was not someone to be messed with.

I grabbed one man's shoulders, pushing him back violently into the crowd, which mostly parted, so I shoved him onto the floor. He groaned, hitting his head on the concrete. I drew my sword, using the air around me to fan the flames, creating an inferno in my hand. My gauntlets once again buzzed, and I held my hand out, a torrent of flames unleashing from my palms. I kicked out my leg, toppling two men and slicing at others, the flaming sword creating an ark of heat soaring through the air. I leapt, coming down and sliding away from the remaining few standing. I shut the door with a burst of wind, and slammed the lock closed. I rushed towards Aaron, melting the chains so they dropped to the floor and pulling the cloth out of his mouth. Then I turned, not wanting my back to be towards a killing machine such as the thing in the room. The King leered from his throne, and even though I couldn't see much, I could feel his gaze cutting into me like a knife. He wore a long red cape, and had brown hair, and a long, curly beard. A crown sat atop his head, shining in the dim light.

"You. You're the King, I presume," I said, my breath short.

"I see you brought a barbarian," the man scoffed, his voice deep and rough. "Destroy it, before it gets in my way."

"What? Sir, I can't do that. This is my friend," Aaron protested, rising to his feet.

"You're friends with one of those pathetic wretches? Ha! I never would have believed it. You'll be doing yourself a favor by eliminating the scum. Go on, prove your loyalty and maybe you won't die." He waved his hand, leaning back in his chair, seeping further into the shadows.

"You want a fight?" I laughed. "I'll give you one. But I'm not fighting him." I felt anger surge through me as my hand caught fire. I launched forward, using my emotion to fuel the fire as white flames spewed from my hands, completely demolishing the thrones. I could hear a scream, but I knew I didn't hit him as I stood back, admiring the wreckage. I turned to see Aaron, his mouth open, staring in disbelief at the blazing sight.

"You've... progressed quite a bit."

"That's not all I've got," I growled, looking to the ceiling. I noticed a chandelier, candles adorning it. The King seemed to have an aversion to light. Making the entire room light up might force him out of the corner. I leapt, using a combination of wind and fire to jump a few feet further, and grabbed on to the chain in the middle, the thing that held everything up and attached it to the ceiling. I summoned a small blaze and was about to light the wicks, but then I felt a force push my back. I screamed, rolling across the ground, somehow landing in an upright position. I looked up, seeing nothing amidst the shadows. I snarled, letting flames flow over me like a blanket, encasing me in the fire armor I'd summoned before, wings sprouting from my back. The darkness seemed to swallow any light, but mine persevered, probably on the sheer determination and now anger. I heard Aaron let out a strangled yelp, probably terrified of my... outfit? I flew up, stumbling as I got to the top of the room. Damien was right, flying was difficult, and I felt myself faltering as my mana drained. I swung my hands across the candles, lighting them all in one fell swoop.

"No!" I heard, a figure coming out of the darkness. It looked like the King, but... his face was deformed. Red lines crept across rotting, black skin, a festering corpse come to life. His right eye was bloodshot and nearly coming out of his head, but his left eye wasn't affected by the grotesque infection that only covered half of his face. Worried blue eyes revealed fear and panic. I could barely move, frightened by the horrible picture of this dead thing launching at me. My flames flickered, and I felt myself slipping, losing control.

The ground and walls shuddered as he knocked me off of the chandelier, shoving me to the floor. Fire spewed out in front of me as I hit the ground, shooting across the room as I could only stare. I heard the door slam shut, and I hoped Aaron had run. Spikes of dirt and stone pushed through the floor, metal popped, burst, and melted as boiling water rushed through the walls, the wind started to rage inside the room. My powers... they were acting on their own. The fire, combined with everything else, swirled together to make a horrible demon-like tempest, a hurricane of death swirling around me. I lay still, not daring to move as the King shrieked, bending any shadows he could find to become a shield in front of him. I was afraid, terrified of my own powers, and the King only seemed inconvenienced, fighting away the destruction with a roar.

He shoved through the wind, approaching me with a snarl. I could barely force myself to get up, gripping my sword to defend myself. He held a knife, a curvy blade formed of darkness, a thick, soupy substance. He rushed towards me, stabbing at my arm. I felt like there were sandbags on my shoulders, making it extremely difficult for me to move, but I somehow made it out of the way. The King turned swiftly, stabbing at my chest. I tried to block with my sword, but he nicked my arm. I stepped back, ignoring the pain and the blood, holding out my sword and trying to direct the storm around us. He ignored my movements and closed in, slashing across my neck, spinning behind me and stabbing me in the back.

The metal sunk into my skin, and I wailed, curling in on myself from the agony that I was in, but he was still behind me. I could almost sense him going in for another blow as I collapsed, focusing all my energy on directing the storm.

My tornado swung towards him, hitting the monster with its full force. He yelled angrily, almost like a battle cry as the storm raged on, throwing him away from me. I felt the building creak and heard things breaking, the walls started to peel away and everything burned, a singing, bitter smell filling the air. I felt like I could only watch as everything got destroyed because of me...

No.

That wasn't true. I had control, I always did. These were my powers, and they were nothing without me.

I reached out, harnessed everything, and grabbed the tail of the tornado. It stopped swirling, all the material sinking into my palms, filling me with newfound energy and spirit. I looked up to see the King, his eyes wide, but an enraged look on his face. I felt calm, collected, and entirely in control. Nothing would escape me ever again; nothing would go out of control.

"Foolish child," he hissed from above. "You'll die with the rest of your pathetic little camp. They're already gone, I bet. You won't survive another day."

"Wrong." I projected my voice to echo around the ruined chamber, standing weakly. "I'll live to the end of this. All my friends will. But you and your dictatorship—that is what will fall. Let me leave you with a warning, as well as a few words of advice. Mess with us again... and you won't even have time to say I'm sorry." I held out my hands, and the ground started shaking. I lifted my arms, and I felt the castle uproot itself. I swung, and the room turned upside down. I floated through the door, the King's lasting screams haunting my ears.

Outside, I saw the damage. The castle was almost on its side, walls ripped out, pipes burst, and wires sparking. Aster and Aaron stood in front of the wreckage, both gaping in surprise.

"Remind me never to get in a fight with you," Aaron squeaked. I chuckled, feeling oddly at peace in that moment. I felt more centered, like something inside me had aligned that I didn't know was out of place.

"We should get going. From something the King said, I think the camp is under attack," I said worriedly, looking out into the dark night sky. I tried to ignore my wounds, but I couldn't help limping.

"What happened in there? You're bleeding-" Aaron started, but I waved him away.

"I'm fine," I said weakly. "We need to get back."

"Amber, you can't keep ignoring things like this. I understand the urgency, but your health is more-"

"It's not more important than the camp, or my friends' lives. I'll be okay... They might not be." I glanced at him, begging with just a stare. He gave in, sighing.

"We should go then," Aaron said, and I nodded, hopping onto Aster, almost stumbling before Aaron helped me back up. My back ached, and it felt like something was embedded in my spine, but I sat up straight, the position easing the pain slightly.

"I'm guessing you're not gonna stick around here anymore?" I smirked, holding out my hand to help him into the giant wolf.

"It's not exactly the best place to be right now," he grunted, pulling himself up and sitting behind me, placing his hand on my shoulder to steady himself. I winced at the touch, pain flaring through my neck.

"I'm sorry about that. I put you into a bad position," I admitted, nudging Aster forward. We started at a walk and built into a canter as we went along, if you can describe a wolf's gait as that.

"I probably shouldn't have tried to stay anyway. Those people are murderers, but working with them... might have made me one as well." We rode the rest of the way in silence, both of us with a lot on our mind at that moment.

As we neared the camp, the menacing scent of smoke filled the air. The sky in front of us had been colored black, and screams still echoed throughout the landscape. My eyes widened in fear, and I pushed Aster to go faster. We raced through the gates to see the world around us in flames. Everything inside was broken, smashed to pieces, cabins either just piles of rubble or entirely burnt to ash. The wall just barely stood, crumbling rocks falling off from time to time, and grass was singed, bodies lying on the floor.

People were gathered around the fallen buildings, on their knees and crying, helping people out of the debris, and tending to others' wounds. All air left my lungs and I felt tears welling up in my eyes, hot water pouring down my cheeks.

Limp bodies littered the ground, lifeless faces with blank expressions. My heart ached, seeing these people suffering and dying. I wasn't close to many, but they were still all my family. I saw J, kneeling over someone, his face covered in tears and his expression pained, his back arched as he looked like he was struggling to breathe. As I got closer, I could only see one thing, but that told me exactly who it was.

Black wavy hair, with a white streak going through it, all the way to the back of his head.

CHAPTER TWELVE

"What happened?" I gasped, my jaw trembling as I struggled to stand, the sight of Harlequinn lying on the floor, eyes rolled into the back of his head, and a stain of blood seeping through his shirt was enough to nearly make me fall over. J said nothing, only held out his shaking hand, pointing to someone huddled by the wall, his hand covering his mouth as he trembled with fear.

"Seth...?" I knew there was no way he could have killed even one person, but J pointed right towards him. "What... what did you do?"

"It wasn't my fault!" he yelled, his voice breaking. "I... I don't know what happened. These monsters, they rushed in and—and they went right for me. He pushed me out of the way, and..." Seth gulped, tears flowing down his face in a steady stream. I looked back, seeing the horror-filled expression on Aaron's face. B rushed by, L suddenly by her side again. The two zipped through camp, tending to serious wounds, removing people from rubble, and making sure everyone was alright. I didn't see Damien anywhere, and that immediately worried me. I looked around, trying to spot him, but... nothing. Smoke still hung in the air, making it hard to breathe. Almost everyone was hurt, even if it was nothing serious. The camp had fallen into decay. I was too late, distracted by my own selfish desires to protect everyone.

"This wasn't your fault," I heard Aaron say behind me, as he put his hand on my shoulder. "I know what you're thinking, and not because I'm using telepathy. You wanted to help someone; you didn't know this would happen. Besides, I could've died if you hadn't come to save me..." he looked down, blushing, his blue eyes glossed over.

"So, there was no way this could end well," I muttered, still shaking, the terror barely even setting in and I was still having this reaction. I glanced over towards where the castle would have stood if it wasn't completely gone, not a trace of it left, and saw the hellhound stables demolished. Only one hound remained, slinking across the ground with its head held low. Damien appeared from behind it, whispering and stroking its head gently. My eyes widened and my heart stopped beating so fast, I started to relax as some of the worry faded. He looked up and I waved him over, brushing the tears from my face. He jogged over, gasping in surprise as he saw Harlequinn lying on the ground.

"What—I—is... is he alive?" He kneeled next to J, who almost hadn't moved since I arrived.

"He's barely breathing," he managed to choke out, his words caught in his throat. "We can't do anything now."

"That can't be true. I'm sure bigger miracles have happened," I put my hand on J's shoulder, feeling a similar sense of terror, despite my words. Glancing around, no one else seemed to be on the brink of death, the grass was only littered with people we really couldn't save. "What if we ask B-"

"She isn't an option. She's powerful, but she's already drained, and I'm not sure she could help anyway," Damien knelt beside us, picking up a piece of ripped fabric off the ground, pressing it against Harlequinn's stomach, where the blood seemed to be mostly coming from. "He's losing too much blood. There's a lot of shrapnel and debris still stuck in his skin… I'm not even sure how this could have happened- did he get hit by the wall?"

"Everything was so fast—I don't know what happened. I should have been right there with him, I should have protected him as soon as I heard the commotion." J's voice broke, and he took Harlequinn's limp hand, holding it close to his chest.

"Isn't there somewhere we can go at least to escape all the chaos? See what we can do, if anything?" I suggested, doubting a place like that existed. What we needed most right now was the eye of the storm.

"There—there is a place that offers advanced healing…" J lifted his head, and I could see that he'd taken a few hits as well. Lengthy scratches wound their way up his arms, small puncture marks dotted his face, and his lip was busted open. A dark bruise was already forming, on the bridge of his nose and migrating towards his eye, which was swollen. "How could I have forgotten? We need to leave now! Take him to the fairies!" He looked over at Damien with a pleading stare, his broken heart showing through his gaze.

"What? I don't know if we'd be allowed in their realm anymore. It's been almost a decade since anyone from this camp saw them."

"It's worth a try, isn't it? We... we have to. I can't lose him." He looked back down to his partner, pushing stray hairs away from his face and gently kissing his forehead, lingering for a moment before rising, gazing sadly at Harlequinn's face, his dull, nearly closed eyes and blank expression.

"Damien, we have to do what we can, right? It's not like they'll kill us for trying to come in... will they?" I winced as I leaned down, glancing over doubtingly, and he shook his head.

"If we're denied access, they won't touch us. But it's far enough away that if H isn't dead by the time we get there, he will be before we get back. If we go, there's no turning around, no second option. We could stay here and try to have B help him, but... She may only be able to stabilize him, keep him in a coma. But we wouldn't know if he would wake up," he shrugged. "If we don't move quickly, but also evaluate our options... this could go very badly." Harlequinn made a strangled sound, and coughed, his eyes fluttering for a moment before he sunk back to the ground. J looked back up at Damien with a pointed glance. He sighed, throwing up his hands.

"Amber, get Aster. We're gonna need him to carry H." J's face lit up, and he gasped with happiness, his eyes tearing up again. I nodded, whistling sharply for a second, and Aster crawled up next to me, examining Harlequinn. He quickly licked his face, and I pulled the wolf back gently. I saw Harlequinn's breathing steady a bit, as he took a deep breath and seemed to settle.

"Help me lift him, please," I whispered to J. I placed my hands on Harlequinn's shoulders, expecting J to kneel down and start lifting, but he stood, holding out his hand. Harlequinn started to float, though J's grip was shaky, and I had to lead his body over to the wolf, setting him down on the soft fur. My arms burned and I could tell my wounds were noticed, just ignored as I pretended the pain wasn't there. I climbed on behind him, holding his shoulders to keep him steady.

"I can turn into a bird and carry J so it's not as many people on Aster." Damien offered.

"Alright. But we better hurry," J agreed, and Damien swiftly changed into an eagle, fluttering up onto J's arms.

"Wait! I'm... I'm guessing I can't come?" Aaron called out from behind us, looking disappointed.

"I'm sorry, we need to go and there's no other transportation. But... you have an important job now, too. Help everyone calm down, give them medical attention, and clear the debris. Please?" I raised my eyebrows and he nodded, looking satisfied. "Thank you. Also, watch Seth. We don't want him causing more trouble." I turned my eyes towards the gate, Aster sprinting right at it. Damien and J launched into the sky, smoke swirling around them as they soared through the still-dark sky. I followed what I could see of them, skirting around the woods for a while before diving inside the cover of trees. Damien flew lower, making J almost kick my head accidentally. I focused on keeping Harlequinn's lifeless body on the wolf, worry eating away at me the entire way. I felt my hands shake uncontrollably, trying to keep an eye on his breathing as he kept almost falling off of Aster. After a few agonizing minutes, not just because of the wait, we slid to a stop deep within the woods.

A hush fell over everything, the only sound the crinkling of dead leaves at our feet. All animals had fled the area, not a single creature to be seen. The trees surrounding us were almost barren, casting ominous shadows across the ground. Thorned branches littered the ground and circled around tree trunks. J fell from the sky, crashing through the branches and rolling before he hit the ground, landing gracefully. I raised my eyebrows, impressed. Damien quickly followed, spiraling down as a bird and flipping mid-air, changing just as he landed.

"You two are so dramatic," I giggled. "But... are you sure we're in the right place? This doesn't look like a gateway to a fairy realm," I commented, looking around at the desolate area.

"Exactly. They don't want this place to be found, for obvious reasons. We better hurry, though." J went over to Aster, picking up Harlequinn bridal-style. I saw the stain of blood on his shirt, steadily growing, and pushed down the ball of worry climbing up my throat.

Damien knelt, pressing his hand firmly on the ground. He muttered something I couldn't hear, and the ground started to glow. A spiral of light spread across the ground, searing a symbol into the dirt before it faded. The trees around us shimmered, and everything went black for a split second. I felt dizzy, a sudden sharp pain on my back, and I hoped this was the effect of whatever Damien had done, and not me dying.

I stumbled through the darkness, suddenly bumping into a wall. I traced my hand against the hallway, feeling the walls made of wood, and seeing a weird light approaching. I burst through the tunnel, a bit confused but anxious to find my friends, and I nearly fell into gorgeous forest. I looked around, gaping in awe at the majestic sight. Trees stretched into the sky, shimmering gold and silver leaves adorning the branches. Small glimmering specs floated through the air, and large patches of land did the same. Everything was floating above a pitch black void, one I couldn't see the bottom of. I glanced over my shoulder, trying to take it all in when I noticed a dark purple, shimmering... something on my shoulder. I yelped, backing up, but it followed me, fluttering like... wings. I looked over my other shoulder, and sure enough, the same thing followed me there.

"What's happening?" I squeaked, letting go of my shock at the whimsical land around me. I heard sweet, melodic music in the distance, and I quietly took note of the soft, pastel purple grass beneath my shoes.

"Oh, that's what entering the fairy realm does to you. If you hadn't stumbled in first, you would have seen us get them." I turned to see big gray wings protruding out of Damien's back.

Harlequinn, still lying in J's arms, had rainbow wings, and J had a gradient of blue, pink, and purple. "The portal is enchanted to give us temporary wings so we can get around easier. Didn't you feel the little sting on your back when you fell through? That was the wings forming."

"Oh," I commented, glad to see that the pain wasn't my wounds getting worse. "Is there a mirror around?"

Damien smirked and pointed to one at the side of the glowing portal. "They have these specifically for newcomers who want to study their wings. The wings are supposed to reflect something about you, especially when it's able to be expressed through color." I turned around, looking into the mirror as best I could. My wings were the same shape as a butterfly's, with splotches of black, gray, white, and purple. On the inside, a little bit of green and yellow. It didn't look bad, and it wasn't exactly rainbow, but I could figure out just what the colors meant.

"This is incredible," I smiled, spinning a bit, a bit shocked, but pleasantly surprised, though the wings seemed to be struggling to appear with my cloak in the way. The air was humid, and I was a bit hot so I decided to take it off, unbuttoning the two sides and leaving it below the mirror. I heard chattering and looked up to see a woman flying around the trees, talking to the specs. She had short blue hair, and a sweet face, with a sharp jaw. Her hair was in the style of a pixie cut, and she wore a uniform with a similar color to her hair. A long sleeved navy jacket, with a white undershirt. A belt was tied across her waist, which held a small sheath for a sword. She wore black flats as well, and she had a cheery laugh. She noticed us and glided over, smiling kindly.

"Hello! Welcome to the fairy realm! How may we help you today? Do you need a meeting set up? Flying lessons? Therapy?" I raised my eyebrows, a bit confused.

"We need healing. We're from the camp, and we got attacked. My—H. He's dying." J held out his arms, gesturing to the fallen. The fairy flew above Harlequinn, examining his wounds.

"Oh dear. Our hospital is quite full- right now only two extra people can fit in the rooms. And, we're low on defense. If the ones who attacked him try to hunt him down... well, we need protections."

"I'll go with you. And... Amber, you helped me get him this far. You can come if you want to." I looked back to Damien, and he nodded his approval.

"I can wait out here and guard the entrance. And, miss, if you have time, check out Amber's wounds too," Damien noted, and I winced. "Yeah, don't think I didn't notice. Your back is stained with blood—and your neck? That's hard not to notice."

"Point taken," I said sheepishly, my face flushing. "Is that okay?" I asked, looking back up.

"Sure! We'll try to assist you in any way we can," the fairy beamed, waving her hands over Harlequinn. He floated up, and a blue sheen encased him. J fluttered into the air, and I realized I had no idea how to fly.

"Uh... help?" I said sheepishly. The fairy looked down to me, and giggled.

"Here," she said, flying down and taking my hands. Her hands were cold, but delicate, like porcelain. She helped me up, and I felt myself lift into the air, my wings gently lifting me into the air, but I was focused on the fairy's eyes. They were like two little galaxies, deep blue with spots of white, gold, pink, and red. Before I knew it, she let go, and I was flying by myself, the wind picking up at my back and letting me breeze through the brisk air. It was easy, I barely even had to think, just lean and I glided that way.

We soared above the floating islands, stars dotting the pastel skies above us. Everything here was incredible, even down to the sound. It was like there was a constant band, playing medieval-style music, sweet, pristine, and calm. My heart kept racing faster as we flew, something I never thought I'd experience, the wind in my hair, taking in the landscape below me.

We passed a sparkling waterfall, the flowing liquid suddenly a mint green. Flowering bushes lined the lake, and a few fairies splashed in the water, one of them going right up to the flowing fall and bringing out a cup to hold the water. I glanced over to J, who I thought would be entirely encased with glee like I was, but his worried gaze was held fast on the body of his partner. I felt my own smile fade, realizing the weight of the situation as the horror once again settled on my shoulders.

After passing a few islands, all entirely breathtaking and colorful, we reached our destination. A large hut stood on a lone patch of grass, surrounded by tall, silver trees. The leaves hung down, like weeping willows, their soft branches gently scraping the ground. The fairy touched down gracefully, as did J, but I stumbled on the edge of the island, tumbling over my own legs as I attempted to settle. The two in front of me ignored me, which I didn't complain about, but I felt myself blush as we all headed inside.

A few beds lined the walls, wooden barriers separating each little room. The beds were white, almost every one filled with a hurt or ailing fairy, all equipped with a nurse and a small desk that seemed to hold some useful tools, gauze, casts, and anything else you would need to treat the sick. Two smaller fairies drifted in as the one that led us set Harlequinn down on an empty bed, and immediately got to work. They pulled up his shirt, revealing a wound that seemed really deep. His stomach was covered in blood, and he didn't look like he was breathing. The two grabbed a bottle from the table, spreading a pastel blue liquid over him, that quickly paled and sunk into his skin. They wrapped his stomach in gauze, and then laid down something that looked like an ice pack. All J and I could do was sit on two green chairs that looked like they magically appeared, waiting on their verdict.

"Are you okay?" I whispered, putting my hand gently on his shoulder. He sighed, leaned over in his chair.

"I'm... worried. I don't want him to die, I don't want to... to lose him..." he brushed away tears, beginning to choke up.

"J, I—"

"Jay."

"What?"

"My... my name is Jay."

"That's—that's what I said... wasn't it?"

"Well, yeah, I mean J-A-Y. It's not that different, but... you've helped me a lot. You've been courageous and kind the entire time you've been here, and you're sticking by my side now. You at least deserve to know my real name." He looked up at me gratefully. I remembered how, in the library, he freaked out when Harlequinn gave me his real name. Jay obviously thought they were special, almost sacred, so it meant a lot that he was trusting me with this.

"Thank you, dude. I'm glad you trusted me enough to tell me that. But, listen, he's gonna be okay. You're here for him, and he's in good hands. I'm sure things will be okay, one way or another." I smiled, and he returned the expression.

"You're right. I couldn't protect him before, but I'm here for him now. The fairies have really advanced medicine as well, so… yeah. Things will be okay." He sat back with a sigh, but I couldn't tell if it was relieved or worried. I couldn't hold back my own stress, so I was surprised he was keeping himself together so well. Harlequinn didn't even look like he was alive anymore, and Jay had a much deeper connection with him, so I couldn't imagine what he was thinking. All we could do now was wait, and stay by each other, sharing our scarce flickers of hope.

Silence fell over us, and I stared at the ceiling, listening to the soft coughs and moans of the fairies around us. I wondered how Damien was doing, or the camp, and I almost felt bad for leaving them in a crisis like this. I wanted to support my friend, but was my morale boost more needed back at home?

I almost shocked myself with my own wording. The camp really was home to me now, and I guess that attachment was strengthened with the recent attack. That also meant my people, my family, had been torn apart in so many different ways. A bitter taste filled my mouth just thinking about it, but I got so lost in my own memories, I didn't realize when they turned into dreams as I drifted off into sleep.

I awoke to explosions. The building we were in shook as chunks of land fell off, and smoke once again rose into the peaceful air. I jolted up, dizzy and discombobulated. Jay was leaning over Harlequinn in a protective stance, debris and rubble hitting his back. He winced, looking back at me with a desperate expression. The building shook again, screams echoing as parts of the walls peeled off, revealing the outside. Harlequinn's eyes opened as the tremors continued, sitting up and almost bumping into Jay. Both his eyes were pure white before he gasped, breathing in sharply. His eyes returned to normal, and he looked up at Jay.

"Harley!" Jay cried, throwing his arms around Harlequinn, who laughed, probably a bit confused.

"Sorry to interrupt, but we should probably leave!" I yelled as another blast rocked the floating island we were on. The wings on both of the guy's backs flickered, and disappeared. "Your—your wings!" Jay looked back and cursed.

"The Queen's Quarters must have been attacked!" Jay cursed, lifting Harlequinn up and off the bed. I looked towards both of them, confused. "All fairies get their power from the generator in her room, and the guests get their wings from it as well," he quickly explained.

"We're in the fairy realm?" Harlequinn exclaimed.

"Long story. We have to get you out of here, now. I don't want you getting hurt again!" Jay looked sullenly into his eyes, one hand on his cheek.

"I—okay. But we also need to help these people. We can't just wreck the place and leave," Harlequinn laughed. Jay nodded in agreement, holding his partner's hand as we rushed to a door. I noticed Harlequinn limping, but other than that, he seemed to be fine. Distracted by my thoughts, I almost raced out of the building, but I would have plummeted to my death if Jay hadn't caught me, grabbing my shirt before I slipped off the edge.

"Hey! The islands are falling, and we don't have wings. We can't get anywhere like this!" Jay sighed in defeat, glancing outside.

"Well, how are we supposed to get down?" I questioned, peering out the door. The ground was hundreds of feet below, and the only thing I could reach from the crumbling island was a vine, wrapped around a branch of a tree. Explosions, battle cries, and desperate screams came from every direction, so much noise that it was almost overwhelming. I tried to come up with a plan, wracking my brain for ideas, but I realized I didn't have time as I noticed a flaming ball of rock, hurtling towards the cabin we were in. "Bad news!" I yelled back into the house.

"Not again!" Jay muttered. "What's wrong now?" I yelped, jumping back into the building as the bomb made contact with our island, the impact causing the floor to shake, collapsing beneath us. Wood and dirt slowly fell into the void, the hole getting larger.

"That!" I pointed towards the missing chunk of ground. Harlequinn looked out the window, and pointed to the vines.

"We don't have many choices right now, but I've seen some people use the vines to get around when their wings aren't working or they're hurt!" he said, hobbling towards the door, Jay still helping him stand.

"With your condition, how is that safe?" Jay shrieked in panic, avoiding some of the withering structure.

"What other option do we have?" I remembered the fire armor that gave me wings, allowing me to fly, or at least hover. It took away a lot of my mana, so I might not even be able to carry two people, but I could try. I attempted to summon a flame, but... nothing happened. I focused, wondering if it was simply fear getting in my way, but I felt nothing. The lack of magic was almost like ice in my veins, a lack of warmth where there should be something. "My powers aren't working!" I cried, desperately trying to conjure fire.

"No one told you? The fairy realm had to find a way to disable outside sources of magic, so that visitors wouldn't accidentally become fairies. If you use any unknown source of mana, the wings you get soak it up, and entirely drain you. Too many people were forced to stay in this realm, and overpopulation became a problem, so now we can't use anything," Jay explained, having to yell over the sounds. "It was supposed to help protect from attacks like this, but that obviously didn't go as planned." I glanced once more out the door, and spotted another rock, twice the size, making its way towards us.

"More bombs. We have to leave, now!" I leapt through the empty doorframe, holding on to the side of the house, keeping an eye on the object that was weaving its way towards us. In the forest, trees were falling, branches snapping, and people were screaming. It hurt to know I couldn't do anything.

Harlequinn and Jay scrambled up next to me, and I reached out to grab the vine. My arm wasn't long enough, and my fingertips barely reached it. I stretched, trying not to fall off of the island before I finally grabbed it, jumping off of the crumbling land and swinging through the trees. I screamed, unable to control where I was going and barely able to hold on. I saw a vine in front of me that I was nearing very quickly, so I went with my gut and jumped, grabbing on and swinging once more. I plummeted for a second as my hands slipped, my heart going down faster than I was, the leafy material of the vine scratching at my fingers. I managed to regain my balance and hang on, the vine twisting around a tree in a circle.

I yelped, sliding towards the ground and rolling away from the spot it dropped me, almost tumbling off the small island I had found a bit of safety on. I looked forward, trying to find a path on the falling islands, dirt and rock slowly crumbling, making even the safest path into a treacherous obstacle course. I heard screams behind me, Jay and Harlequinn landing by my side, flying through the air and groaning as they slammed into the trunk of the tree.

"Nice landing," I commented, turning back. I could see some vines, and all the islands were theoretically close enough to jump to. Now the only problem was actually surviving the debris. "I think I have a plan. Luckily, we aren't that far from the portal—all we have to do is cross over. Follow me!" I leapt forward, almost missing one of the vines I needed to swing on. I grabbed the end, my legs dangling over the pitch black void beneath us, but I ignored the terror as I swung from the trees.

Quickly flying towards another island, I used the momentum from the fall to launch myself forward, leaping onto the chunk of dirt in front of me. I dodged a thin tree, grabbing onto a vine from one of its branches and catapulting myself to another patch. I barely wanted to look back to check on the boys, but I knew that worry and guilt would eat away at me, so I glanced back as I leapt towards an island, and saw the two, hand in hand, falling onto a tree. Jay yelped, but they seemed to be fine.

I kept running, knowing if I stopped, I risked losing my balance and falling into whatever resided below this checkerboard of islands. I jumped once more, to some land that was slightly higher than the others, grabbing the edge and pulling myself up. My arms strained, and I nearly lost my grip. Breath short, adrenaline, mind, and heart all racing at once, I got myself onto the dirt and continued my terrifying trek. I didn't see any more places to jump until I looked down, staring at a tiny piece of crumbling land far below. A path led up from there, a little staircase of rock that seemed to go right up to the glowing portal, but it was too far to jump directly to. I approached the edge of the island nervously, wondering if I could even land on a patch that small.

I didn't have much of a choice, it was either waiting down here to be rescued and possibly crash into the depths below, or take my chances and get out. Needless to say, I was leaning a bit more towards the latter.

I backed up a bit before running full speed, leaping off the edge of the island. My hair flew out behind me and I reached for the dirt, my heart stopping as I realized there was more distance than expected, and I just barely was able to grab the corner of the small patch. The dirt, soft and crumbly, gave way underneath my sudden weight, and I plummeted into the abyss below the fairy realm.

CHAPTER THIRTEEN

I screamed until my throat was dry. I was trapped in darkness, like a thick blanket I couldn't seem to find my way out of. It was warm, but I couldn't see a thing. Sometimes I could barely tell if my eyes were open or closed. The wind created a breeze around me, so I knew I was falling, but to where? And why for so long? Was I just stuck in an eternal limbo, never to see the light of day or another soul for the rest of my pitiful, suffering days? I crossed my arms, wondering when or if this excruciatingly long fall was going to end. I tried to turn, see what was around me, but I accidentally started spinning. I didn't have the voice to scream or yelp, but if I did, I would definitely have been making a ruckus.

A blurry glimpse of light started to shine from below me. I couldn't see what the source was because I was doing barrel rolls, but it filled me with hope. Until, of course, pieces of trash and debris got in the way of my peaceful plummet, which surprised and alarmed me. I could barely make out the figures of planks of wood, some broken bricks, a lot of dirt, and what seemed to be an entire roof, stuck to a tree. All the trash and demolished buildings from the fairy realm fell down here... and immediately became a danger to me as I smacked into a brick, falling at such a speed that I was completely knocked out.

I awoke in a dream. Well, I wasn't really awake, but I was conscious of my surroundings. I was back in the fairy realm, standing next to the mirror. Damien leaned over the edge of the island, screaming. Harlequinn and Jay stood next to him, pulling him back, making sure he didn't fall like I did. They ended up dragging him towards the portal and he sat against the wall, his head buried in his hands. The fairy from before fluttered over, looking ashamed.

"Where did they go?" Damien demanded, not even looking up.

"What?" The fairy asked in confusion, tilting her head a bit to the side.

"Where did Amber go? Where does that lead? What's down there?" he yelled exasperatedly.

"We don't know, no one does. I'm sorry, but we haven't done much research into the void—it's too dangerous for us to go down there. We lose our wings, and all powers we may have," she calmly explained, wisely keeping her distance. Damien gulped, his face showing absolute despair.

"So they could be anywhere. Trapped in an eternal darkness, in another dimension, or dead for all we know," he scoffed. "H, you can see at least a bit into the future. What do you see?"

"Uh, not—not much. Everything's blurry right now, which means nothing is set in stone. But from what I see... I don't think Amber's there," Harlequinn said sadly, his hand on his arm.

"I... we need to leave." Damien put his hand on his forehead, and then stood, glaring at the fairy.

"They just might not be in the near future. We can still look-" Jay started.

"No!" Damien yelled, waving in dismissal. "We could get hurt, we could die, or we could end up in a different place than them. It's too risky," he sighed, looking to the floor. Before storming out, I could hear him whisper one last thing. "Everyone's going to be heartbroken."

I actually woke up after that. A jolt went through my spine, and I felt goose bumps forming on my arms, as well as a piercing pain in my head. I had stopped spinning, which was good, but I looked down, and the worry didn't stop, but I was shocked. The sight below me took away my breath faster than the whipping breeze and sudden drop did.

Rolling hills circled a flourishing valley. No trees, but colorful bushes, seemingly covered in flowers and berries. A thin stream ran peacefully through the middle of everything, bubbling joyously as it flowed. Nothing moved except for plants and leaves, swaying in the wind. A sunset erupted above the valley, changing the sky to match the hues of the land below. Everything had a sense of ethereal beauty, the normal colors of everything warped and switched. The mountains were different shades of red and orange, the grass a pale, cool blue. All the bushes shifted between gradients of purple, and the water had a slight tint of green. I took everything in as I fell, marveling at the strange but gorgeous utopia. I realized too late I was plummeting to the ground, about to be crushed on the very ground I was staring at in amazement. I felt like I couldn't do anything but brace myself for the inevitable death, not too disappointed to be dying in a place as beautiful as this.

The second before I reached the ground, I heard the air rush beside me. A mass of deep, shimmering purple grabbed me, soaring through the sky at a more even and controlled pace. I resisted the urge to scream, knowing it would only hurt me. I turned, trying to examine the beast that was now carrying me. Almond shaped, catlike yellow eyes stared at the skyline in front of us. Sharp teeth sunk through my belt, hoisting me above the colorful dirt. Massive black horns curled up out of its head, and three hooked talons lined the edge of its giant, bat-like wings. It held its clawed feet up to its stomach as we flew, scales shining in the sun's dying rays. The underside of its wings were pitch black, leathery and flexible, but everything else was covering in slick scales.

This was definitely a dragon. I yelped to myself, both scared and surprised to see something like this here, dwelling beneath the darkness of the abyss, but what terrified me the most was the height of this thing. One of its legs was the size of me.

We circled through the sky for a minute, the beast never even glancing at me. I heard a guttural growl building up as it sneered, seeming like it was running from something. I figured out what when a much bigger dragon pulled up beside us.

The creature was twice the size of the one carrying me, and a mixture of blue and green. Sharp fangs poked out of its closed mouth, but it didn't have as big or elegant horns. Lengthy, pale scars covered its long, nimble legs as it roared, its forked tongue tasting the air. The purple dragon carrying me seemed to sigh, and curved to the side, dropping me on the ground before landing softly. I stood between the two beasts, amazed. They exchanged a series of growls and roars, then turned to me expectantly.

"Uh... hello." I smiled sheepishly, waving. The green dragon rolled its eyes, turning back to its... friend? I didn't even know dragons could roll their eyes, and I especially didn't expect it to be directed towards me. It wasn't my fault I couldn't speak dragon. I wasn't even aware dragons existed until now, though I suppose it shouldn't surprise me anymore. They once again started to bicker, the bigger dragon growling loudly and stomping his foot, his thick white claws digging into the soft dirt. The purple dragon looked nearly offended, stepping back with a short snarl. The green one gestured to me, narrowed his eyes, twitched his nose and took flight, the force of his giant wings almost knocking me to the ground.

His long tail spiraled close to his body as he flew into the distance. I glanced back to the purple one, who seemed to be glaring into the sky. He sighed, shaking his head as he turned and walked along the stream I'd noticed before. The grass on each side seemed to have a different hue, on this side it was darker, and the other... shinier, a bright almost neon instead of pastel. The air was filled with a gentle breeze, which almost smelled sweet. It was like I got trapped in Candy Land, except with dragons.

I continued to follow the purple dragon, curious as to where it was leading me. I wondered how many dragons actually lived here, as I'd only seen two so far and it seemed impossible that any more could hide in this vast expanse of mostly flat land. Unless the rest were all babies, hiding in the bushes. That still seemed unlikely. I sped up a bit, walking alongside the marvelous creature.

"Thank you for saving me," I quickly called out, feeling like I had to say something. "What is this place?" I asked, not sure of what answer I was expecting. It glanced to me, then turned its gaze back in front of us. "I'm guessing that means you can't talk." It snarled, snapping the air in front of me. I took that as a no, though I found it strange that it could understand me.

Once again, the trek was taken in silence. There wasn't much to see, the area wasn't much different from what you'd normally see except for the colors, so I quickly got used to it, not able to absorb anything new. Of course, the dragons were extremely interesting and amazing but as for landscape? Majestic, but humble in a way. Quiet, toned down, like the calm within the storm.

Funnily enough, I got distracted thinking of how mundane the scenery seemed after a while, and bumped into the dragon once it stopped. It looked back with a sharp growl, but calmed down with a sigh, turning its head up. We'd come to a cliff edge, the drop a hundred feet or more straight down. A small cavern sunk into the wall about fifteen feet up the wall, and I saw light illuminating the walls. The beast in front of me spread his wings, shooting into the sky with ease. He gently touched down inside the cavern, the opening big enough to hold his massive size, and eagerly waited for me to come up. How did he think I was going to, though? He saw me fall all the way down here- if I could fly I would have done that before I was even close to hitting the ground.

Well… maybe I could fly. Perhaps my armor worked down here, since I was away from the fairy realm. It was worth a shot, I figured, there weren't many options anyway. I held out my arm, expecting fire to crawl up and encase me, but nothing worked. I tried once more, with the same result. I looked up to the dragon, shrugging.

"My powers don't work here either!" I yelled up. I doubted I could climb the wall, with how steep it was. There was nothing to hold on to, and I definitely couldn't jump that far. I started to question if the dragon was even aware I could fly at all… He continued to stare at me, snorting. The hot breath made steam dance in the air in front of him. "I don't know what you want from me!" I threw my hands into the air, a little bitter that I didn't get to fully appreciate the majesty of the dragon that was now judging me, or even the land around me. This experience had definitely soured the sweet taste.

The dragon cooed above me, licking the air. His horns tapped the ceiling as he threw his head back, roaring in an almost melodic tone that seemed to mimic laughter. I raised my eyebrows, shocked that he was mocking me.

"Oh, what, you think I can't get up there?" I jogged forward, trying to grab onto the wall. I noticed it was slightly slanted, maybe enough to actually be able to climb. There were a few little niches I could grab, but it wouldn't be easy. "Who needs wings?" I grumbled, lifting my leg and trying to hang tightly onto the wall. I started my ascent, my arms straining as I pretty much defied the laws of gravity. After climbing a few feet up, maybe halfway to the cavern, the rock below me started to loosen. "Okay, maybe I DO need wings." I struggled to go faster, grabbing the edge of the cave floor, seeing the dragon hovering above me.

He didn't help much, just stood there as I flailed, desperately hanging onto the side of a mountain. I almost reached out to grab one of his claws, but I figured that might just get me flung across the island, or off of it, so I decided against that. I scraped at the rock, bringing my forearms over the edge, so I could actually scramble into the large space. I fell over on the floor, breathing hard, not used to having to climb up such a sheer mountain face — in fact, I usually didn't climb mountains at all. The dragon, however, seemed quite pleased.

"Having fun, there?" I huffed, entirely unamused. Ignoring my spiteful comments, he lifted his head, directing my gaze down further into the cavern. There was a long hallway that slowly thinned as it went along, closing in so that it seemed only a human could get through. The dragon nudged me into the cave, his deep purple scales shimmering in the fading light. "You… want me to go down there? This isn't a trap, is it?" I asked, looking back. The beast narrowed his eyes, snarling in what seemed to be offense. My own expression dropped, and I shrugged, begrudgingly standing up, and walking forward.

A few torch sconces lined the hall, but most of them had burnt out, crumbling ash and soot tumbling onto the already dirty floor. I couldn't see much, but when there was light, gemstones revealed themselves along the walls, shimmering veins of gold and iron, chunks of what looked to be sapphires and diamonds embedded in the ceiling. Looking around, there seemed to be more ore than actual dirt, making the cave really beautiful when you could actually see three feet in front of you.

The walkway started to get really thin, the walls pressing against my arms. I almost had to walk sideways to continue forward. I vaguely saw an opening, and I quickly slid into a much bigger room, one that I couldn't see anything in. I wondered the purpose of me being here, before I heard a roar down the hallway.

Glancing behind me, I shrieked, seeing a blaze of fire rocketing through the tunnel, the flames hugging the walls. I moved out of the doorway, my back pressed against the frame, watching as the entire room lit up. A few torches mottled around caught fire, lighting up the walls as the other blaze faded.

"What was *that* for?" I demanded, yelling down the hallway. I was only met with a satisfied gargle, a guttural, content roar. I knew I wasn't going to get an actual answer, but I was still pretty peeved that he had done that.

Turning back to the room around me, I realized why. Everything in the cavern was shimmering, reflecting the light in colorful hues across the room. Rare gems, a lot of which I didn't recognize, made up the entire structure of the room. Though there was one disturbing feature. In the corner, a human skeleton sat, holding a piece of paper. The bones were bleached an almost unnatural white, and the figure slumped against the wall, everywhere a trace of the person touched was entirely devoid of the majestic jewels that adorned... pretty much everywhere else. I cautiously stepped towards the body, almost scared that it would jump up and start talking, maybe do a little dance. I had figured out that you never really knew in a place like this.

Luckily, nothing like that happened. I carefully pried the withered paper out of the skeleton's hands, holding it up to the light so I could read the yellow page.

"If you've found me, you're already lost," I muttered, confused. The print was almost hard to read, sketched out with a material that obviously crumbled a lot, some of the words drooping or the letters difficult to make out, but I figured it out. "What? Why was I sent here for… this?" I wondered if this was the dragon's way of telling me that I was never getting out.

I placed the paper back down, not wanting to take it with me, and hoping that if anyone else stumbled across this, it would be of more use to them. I sauntered back down the hallway, the words running through my brain, distracting me so much that I didn't see the dragon in the low light. I bumped into a scaly stomach, wincing as I stumbled back, looking up to see him snarling, his mouth open and a light glowing between his teeth.

"Sorry," I muttered, holding up my hands in defeat. "I don't get it. Why did you want me to see that? Are you saying I should give up? I don't even know what I would be giving up!" It was hard to tell his expression, but he looked like he was marveling at how I missed the elephant in the room. I returned his glare with my own, shaking my head.

He snorted, nodding towards the entrance of the cavern, glancing down at the world below. The sun was hovering below the horizon, casting colorful rays across the land, creating even more of a rainbow than before. As I was admiring the beauty, I felt a sharp pressure on my back, and I stumbled forward, falling out of the cave and down the cliff. I screamed, tumbling to the ground much faster than before since it was a smaller drop. Just before I landed, I leaned into a spin, and I rolled across the grass, touching down with a bit of pain, but I'd experienced worse. I groaned, sitting upright in the grass, my adrenaline rushing as I looked up to the dragon, who was gliding down to stand next to me.

"What are you doing? You can't just push people off of cliffs!" I reminded the arrogant dragon, the ground trembling as he dropped, stepping towards me. He reached down to gently sniff my face, the slight touch tickling my cheek, his slick scales scraping softly on my skin, almost the same coarse feeling as a cat's whiskers. I giggled, pushing his head away from mine. He took that as his cue to leave, lumbering off towards some bushes, carefully plucking the ripe berries off of the vines and branches. I watched him pad around the island, devouring berries from every plant in sight. I would have figured that dragons were carnivores, but I was surprised once again.

The dragon sat in front of the empty bush, his eyes narrowing towards the ground. I titled my head, turning over on my side so I could see him better. He seemed to be curiously waiting for more berries to grow, his focus entirely taken off of me.

"So... do you have a name?" I asked, but was ultimately ignored. "I guess you wouldn't—it doesn't seem like you get many visitors down here. Unless you name yourselves, or other dragons name you. Like that green one from before... I don't suppose you can explain that, can you?" The dragon snorted, slowly stretching, and lying down. His tail tapped against his stomach, making a melodic clinking sound. "Can *I* name you? Or at least give you a nickname... I wouldn't just want to call you dragon. You like the berries a lot, so why not... Blueberry? I could call you Berry, for short," I absentmindedly suggested, barely even thinking of what I was saying. I expected him to growl, or snap at me, but this time he perked up. That was a first.

Blueberry it was. I wouldn't normally name something, especially a dragon, such a childish or unoriginal name, but he seemed to like it. I guess his love for blueberries transcended any of his hate for a name. I stood up, slowly walking over to the bush he was lying down at.

"What now?" I asked, glancing expectantly at him. He looked up with a bored glare, dark blueberry stains coating his mouth. I giggled at the sight, that image reminding me of when a baby tries to eat. He growled, rolling his eyes again as he gulped, swallowing anything in his mouth, and quickly licking his lips, spraying spit at me. He stretched again, this time half standing up, kneeling towards me in a gesture that almost seemed to say... get on? My eyes widened, my heart racing at the thought of riding a dragon. That was the dream of probably any kid that knew they existed, even in fantasy. I tentatively stepped forward, trying to make sure I knew what he wanted me to do.

I placed my hand gently on his side and looked to him for confirmation. With a swift nod from Berry, I hoisted myself up, swinging my legs over his back. It was a bit hard to get on with his size, but less difficult than the hellhound. What seemed to be his spine just barely poked up from underneath the skin, creating a line of ridges. I sat between two at the base of his neck, barely having time to settle down before he snorted, suddenly taking off, not even bothering to properly stand up. I screamed, grabbing on to his short neck as we flew through the air, his wings beating and the wind whipping through my hair. My legs shook, I felt so jittery I was afraid I would fall right off, but after a few minutes, I caught my breath.

I could feel the warmth radiating from around me. I let myself open my eyes, and I was able to see the land below us once again. As soon as I focused, letting go of my tight grip and relaxing, Berry took that as a sign to dive right into the murky void below.

CHAPTER FOURTEEN

"Do you not like the name?" I screeched, the wind lashing at me as we plummeted, spiraling down below the floating island. Stone formed into a giant cone beneath everything, holding caves filled with dragons. Nests and what seemed like homes were burrowed into the bottom of everything, completely hidden and inaccessible unless you were flying. The sight once again managed to take my breath away, marveling at all of the beasts swarming. Hundreds upon thousands of dragons, old and young, hid here, protected by the mass of land above them.

We flew around the cone, dodging small dragons floating around and spikes of obsidian protruding out of the formation. I heard some growls and some coos as we passed, floating with the slight breeze that was down there, accompanying us on our adventure. We pulled up, doing a flip over the edge of the island and standing on solid grass once again. I practically fell off Berry's side, my heart and adrenaline racing.

"That was so cool!" I gasped, a smile prominent on my face. "You really could have warned me, though." Berry made a sound almost like a purr in acknowledgment. I wanted to see it again, but leaning into the void didn't seem like a great idea, and the dragons were too far below to see.

I heard a soft cracking sound, and looked over at the dragon, who was stretching his neck backwards, towards his spine. I raised my eyebrow, a little concerned and slightly freaked out, but I dismissed it with a shrug. The rush I felt earlier had quickly worn off, and I yawned, the exhaustion of the past few days now catching up with me. I strangely hadn't felt tired before, and I took a small nap in the fairy realm, but I was suddenly falling asleep. I felt my eyes droop, and I let myself lean back, the aqua grass surprisingly comfortable beneath me. It was more like a bed of moss than grass.

My eyes fluttered open after I'd closed them for a bit, the ground shaking beneath me. I sat up, just in time to see Berry taking flight. He spread his wings and launched into the air, spinning like he was doing a trick before diving below the surface of the island, snorting as he fell.

"Wait!" I yelled, much more awake now. I stumbled to my feet, but I couldn't catch him. I raced to the edge, gripping the side of the island, but the void was blank. I could hear some roars, a chorus of celebration and angry protest alike, but I had no clue what was happening. And that led me to wonder why none of the dragons came up here, except Berry—everyone stayed down below.

I sighed in disappointment, assuming that I was on my own for a bit. I looked around, trying to see what I could do to pass the time. Gathering berries didn't seem to be an option, thanks to the dragon, but I wasn't exactly hungry anyway. I couldn't build a hut in case the sun ever set; there weren't any trees and the bushes wouldn't do. Once I got past the shock of falling into another dimension and meeting a dragon, this all seemed… quite boring.

I decided to get up and walk around. I was now on the other side of the stream, where everything seemed to be brighter. Here, it was vibrant, as opposed to muted, soft colors. I wasn't quite sure why it was different, but it was interesting. I stepped towards the water, watching the bubbling creek flow, and I noticed a small fish trying to swim upstream. It was bright purple, a color so neon it was definitely unnatural, and I had to wonder how it got that way. I gently submerged part of my hand in the stream, watching the fish swim around my fingers.

As if in reaction to my meddling, I felt the ground rumble beneath me, a shaking similar to an earthquake. I nearly fell over as a giant dragon, bigger than any I'd seen since I got here, emerged from beneath the island. It soared over the edge, and I noticed countless tears and scratches in its weathered, dark silver wings. It seemed to lock eyes with me, flying upside-down as it scanned the area, assessing me and growling. It turned around, landing roughly next to me, the force making me stumble back as the ground shook.

I stared up into a black mouth, sharp teeth that had a similar dark color bared in a threatening gesture. It roared violently, ears held back against its head, large droplets of spit landing next to me and on my face.

This one had no horns, and wide, large white eyes. Its tongue was forked like a snake's, and it had a large body held up by four long, slender legs. A tail covered in spiky scales whipped behind it, and it folded its wings close to its body, looming over me like it was judging if I deserved to live or not. Giant claws protruded out of its feet as it prowled towards me, sleek scales seemingly absorbing all light. Unlike the others, the scales didn't reflect, so it didn't have the shimmering, slick shine.

I crawled back, nearly paralyzed in fear as it approached, the growl carrying on. I tried to flick my hand, summon a burst of fire, or any other element to help me, but nothing happened. I felt useless, hopeless without my powers, now missing the uncontrollable inferno of power. The dragon snapped, lunging towards me as I quickly rolled away, stifling a scream. It turned with me, striking out with its paws and trying to crush me underneath its weight. I dove forward, grabbing my sword from its sheath, then stabbed upwards. I felt bad for trying to harm the dragon, but I doubted it felt any remorse for attempting to hurt me. The blade bounced off of its thick scales, and I had to roll away before it crushed me and bent the metal with the weight of its paw. A claw nicked my side, and I winced, a burning feeling spreading through my stomach. I was already breathing hard, so I knew this would be a fight I couldn't win, ignoring the fact that I should have given up at the first sight of this monstrous dragon. With that thought in mind, I tried to do the obvious—run away.

I hopped to my feet, and quickly sprinted the other direction. I heard wind rushing behind me and a clap as the dragon took to the skies, easily floating on the wind, despite its wings being torn. It landed in front of me and I slashed my sword, digging it into the black dragon's forehead. It roared, not in pain but in annoyance, and whipped its head up, ripping the blade out of my hand. It stuck in the dragon's head, almost like a strange unicorn horn. Despite the severity of the situation, I held back a laugh, before remembering that the 'unicorn' was trying to kill me. I fell sideways, its claws raking against my side, drawing blood in ragged, uneven lines. I screamed, clutching my side. I felt the liquid seeping onto my hands and through my clothes.

I winced, looking down at the crimson cut, almost getting woozy at the sight of it and of the ground beneath me stained red. I crawled to my feet, my vision blurry and hands slippery. I was entirely prepared to fight until my last breath, but thankfully, I didn't have to.

The black dragon bared its teeth, but then got tackled to the side. Berry hissed, standing on top of the dragon, claws sinking into its skin. I scrambled behind a bush, watching the fight from afar. It was almost magical to see these majestic beasts dueling. The black dragon swiped towards Berry, clawing his face. He snarled in return and bit the other dragon's wing. I winced as it screeched, its cries echoing throughout the valley. Surprisingly, no fire or powers at all were exchanged in the scuffle, even though through all the violence I entirely expected something like that to happen. Berry emerged victorious as he pushed the other dragon's head into the ground with a large crack, and it tore itself out of his grip, roaring as it stumbled back over the edge, spreading its bleeding wings to return to its home. I stayed beneath the leaves of the bush, eyes wide and heart still racing. Berry turned right towards me, sniffing the shrub and cooing, a gentle look in his eyes. I tentatively stood, and he held his head towards me. I giggled, stroking his scales.

"That was intense," I remarked weakly, and he nodded. I knew he could probably understand me, but seeing that type of a gesture coming from a dragon was a bit shocking, to say the least. It seemed strange, and out of place almost. He looked down at my side, brushing across the wounds, and I winced, putting my hand on his head in a sign to stay back. He sniffed the air, his eyes widened, his pupils turning into slivers, and I felt my heart stop. I pushed myself away, afraid he was going to attack, but he turned away, hunched low to the ground. He growled loudly, tilting his head and scanning the skies. I backed away, further into the bushes, still worried that the scent of blood had triggered an attack reflex or something, but he didn't seem focused on me.

A shrill scream echoed through the void as a body fell from the dismal darkness above. Unlike what I had done, it soared straight through the abyss and just barely missed the island, plummeting through the air. Excited shrieks rang from below, as three different dragons racing to grab the person, and I assumed it wasn't to help. I looked to Berry, who immediately took off, the sharp burst of wind throwing me backwards. I yelped, crippling pain striking my side as I landed against the mountain, sharp rocks digging into my skin. I scrambled away from the cliff, not only to get away from the danger, but also to get to the edge of the island, to try to see what was happening.

I watched in fear as the dragons below all tried to grasp the human, who looked like a small toy in their giant claws. They pulled and yelped, clawing at each other in anticipation to eat their next meal. Luckily, the three seemed to be either smaller dragons or babies, so when Berry appeared, a mass of rage, they fled, dropping the person down into the void. I was curious as to why Berry seemed to be the only dragon willing to be friendly towards humans, instead of viewing them as enemies or food.

Nevertheless, both of us had Berry to thank for still having our lives, and bodies, intact. I saw him gently glide over the mountains, the person's limp body gently clutched in his claws. He dropped them in front of me, and I kneeled down to examine the damage. Their outfit seemed familiar, but their back was turned towards me so I didn't think much of it. A few rips made their way across the fabric of their pants, blood slowly seeping through. One of their shoes was missing, and there was a gash on their back. The dragons did a lot of damage in very little time. I decided to turn them over to see if there was anything else, and as I gently lifted them up, I nearly dropped them again in shock.

Seth laid before me, eyes closed and breathing a bit labored. I turned to Berry with a glare.

"You couldn't have let him fall?" I scoffed. He growled softly in protest, and I sighed. "You're right. No matter who he is, he's hurt. He's annoying, but he doesn't deserve to die. We gotta bandage him or something," I practically said under my breath, not wanting this to be entirely audible, though the dragon seemed to understand. He reached for a leaf, and offered me that. I giggled, taking it with a thank you and putting it over one of his wounds. The gesture was a joke, just to make sure Berry didn't get upset, but the leaf latched onto Seth's skin, the color seeping out of it as it seemingly dried up and fell off. I blinked in shock, not expecting that to work, but I grabbed a leaf and held it to my own side. The pain lessened, a small pulling feeling underneath the veins of the foliage.

I looked back down, focusing on Seth now that I felt a bit better. My clothes were still red, but the actual wounds were healing. Where the leaf had been placed, Seth's skin was stained a bit, but the cuts entirely disappeared, the only remnant a couple spots of dried blood. I glanced sideways in awe to Berry, who looked at me pointedly. I held my hand out, asking for more leaves. He complied, and after a few minutes, the only evidence he'd been hurt were the rips in his clothes. Just after I took off the last leaf, he groaned, opening his eyes and sitting up.

"Where—what happened?" he mumbled, very obviously groggy and not actually seeing who he was talking to.

"Shut up, you're dreaming," I muttered in a feeble attempt to convince him to go back to sleep. It was a lot nicer here when he wasn't running his mouth. "Nothing important is happening. Just lay back."

"Why do I need to—Amber?" He looked at me with an incredulous look. I rolled my eyes again, sighing dejectedly.

"I told you, you're dreaming. Lay down." I pushed against his shoulder, forcing him to the ground. He grunted, holding his head with a pained look.

"I don't think you can feel pain in dreams," he pointed out, a bored pout on his face.

"You never know," I shrugged, standing up. My job here was done, but sadly the annoyance didn't end there. "Berry, look what you've done." He turned to me, food staining his mouth, and gave me a surprised, slightly offended glare. I heard a sound like a goat being strangled behind me, and I turned to see Seth's eyes widened, him shaking in fear as he slowly backed away.

"D—d—dragon!" he yelped, barely able to move. I smirked, patting Berry's head.

"He's friendly, don't worry. He saved you, actually. You fell into the void and he decided it wasn't quite your time," I turned back to the dragon. "Much to some people's dismay," I muttered.

"Fine, I get the message. I'll leave," he scoffed, a trace of fear still lingering in his dark eyes. He walked to the edge, examining the mountains surrounding us. He picked the smallest peak, and scaled the rock, just to scream when he reached the top, and fall back to the ground below. "Or... not. What is this place?"

"I'm not entirely sure about that, but I think this is the place where the universe was created. You can't exactly leave very easily," I shrugged, not able to confidently provide answers for questions I was asking myself.

"So... what's up with the..." he gestured to Berry, who snorted, the noise making Seth jump.

"He lives here. I named him Berry, because he seems to really like blueberries, or... whatever is growing on these plants."

"You named him *Berry*? How old are you?" Seth crossed his arms, one eyebrow raised.

"It's the only name he likes," I said with a shrug. "And I don't think you could do any better."

"I totally could," Seth protested, crossing his arms. "It's a dragon! You have to name it something cool, like… Doomsday or Death Bringer!" Berry snarled, snapping at the air. Seth shrieked, flinging himself backwards.

"I'll stick with Berry," I hissed, rolling my eyes. "And obviously, he's not violent. He saved you, remember?"

"That was five minutes ago, how could I forget?"

"You don't seem to be the most observant."

"That doesn't mean I'd forget getting attacked by a swarm of literal *dragons*!" He threw his hands into the air, scoffing. "What is your problem? You act like you know me, with how much you hate me already, but you say you have no memory of me. What are you doing?"

"I'm not doing anything! I know what I've seen here, I already know that you're not trustworthy. The others might be willing to give you a chance, but you've already gotten three strikes in my book," I said with a cold glare, leaning against Berry.

"Fine. Whatever, I get the message. How about... I stay on one side of this creek, and you stay on the other." I glanced to him, his face stuck in a stubborn sneer, so I shrugged carelessly, planning to just let him be and see how long it took for him to realize his mistake of going alone. He stomped across the small strip of the stream, and sat down with a huff. Berry looked at me, his gaze communicating an emotion you could barely put into words, but one I felt every time I was around Seth. A sort of groggy, done with everything feeling. A pure emotional exhaustion, mixed with anger and frustration. But I decided to let sleeping dogs lie and move on, promising myself unless I had to, I wouldn't even touch the other side. I giggled to myself at his immaturity, knowing that he would probably soon come crawling back for help. He had no clue what this world held, above or below. He could barely accept magic being real, how was he supposed to survive a night in a place like this?

The night... did demons spawn here as they did above? Would we have to fight instead of sleeping, or was this a small haven, an oasis, a safe place? If it wasn't, how would I protect myself? Did I even need sleep? Questions ran through my head, none of them I had answers to. However, I did have one solution I at least needed to work on, and that was shelter. I scanned my surroundings, looking for large logs, vines, leaves, anything that could help me pull together a good shelter to last. I didn't know how extreme the weather was here, so I needed to be prepared. Sadly, the landscape was almost barren, devoid of real trees that could give me any sizable logs. The only thing was bushes, and I didn't think you could make anything out of twigs. I sighed in disappointment, turning to Berry, who was snarling at Seth from across the creek. I patted his head, right between his ears, and he seemed to calm down.

"Hey, Berry. We need to find some stuff for shelter, okay? I don't want to be stuck here without something like that, but I need logs, vines, big leaves, stuff like that. Do you think you could help me?" I smiled kindly, trying to win him over with a friendly face. He snorted diligently, and took off into the air, wings stretched out as he dove into the void, darkness swallowing his form. "Note to self," I whispered. "You go too far, you disappear into the abyss." I didn't know what exactly he was doing or how long it would take, so I looked around for anything I could start with.

I used a stick to carve a small plot in the dirt, to mark where the hut should be and how big. I dug up the grass on the inside, creating a smooth dirt floor. Just as I finished, I heard the sound of wings and looked up to see Berry, about ten large sticks between his talons. He dropped them, the heavy wood landing beside me with a thud. I scrambled backwards, yelping as it hit, almost crushing my leg. I was grateful for the help, but not so ecstatic about almost breaking my bones. He flew away once again, I assumed to go get more wood or something else to help, so I decided to get started.

I rounded up all of the sticks in a line, trying to figure out how I was going to get them to stay up. I dug a hole in the ground, probably around two feet deep, and lifted up one of the bigger pieces of wood. I hoisted it over my shoulder, managing to get it over to the hole and drop it in, holding it upright as I covered the pit with dirt. The soil seemed to solidify, becoming more like hardened clay than actual dirt. I smirked, glad that seemed to work. For the next hour or two, it went on like that. Me, digging spaces for the logs to sit right next to each other, Berry occasionally dropping off more supplies, until I had a border in a large square, with one opening for the door. The logs weren't totally airtight, some holes and bends in the walls, but it seemed like a good start. It wasn't foolproof, but it was better than just the open sky. Once I was done, caked in mud and thoroughly exhausted, a long line of vines dropped at my feet. I looked up to see Berry, hovering in the sky, what seemed to be a goofy smile plastered on his face. I smiled gratefully, picking up the green, leafy vines. I could either wrap them around the logs to help them stay together, or shove them in between like some sort of insulation. I decided on the latter, and got to work, shoving the greens between the wood. I felt eyes on my back the entire time, but decided to ignore the keen stare from Seth. I didn't understand what he was doing, but I honestly didn't care at this point. He could be creepy on his side of the creek, not mine.

After what seemed like a lifetime, I finally finished. The house was mostly set up, with the walls and floor all done. But I still didn't have a door or roof. Berry hadn't gotten up since he dropped off the vines, and he was curled up in a corner, cooing peacefully as he slept. I sank to the floor, watching his stomach go up and down as he breathed. I leaned against the wood, surprised and excited that it didn't move. Once again, in the stillness, I felt my eyes droop, drowsiness taking over as I slipped into unconsciousness.

My dreams in the real world were never normal. Sometimes, they did seem to predict stuff. But what I envisioned here... it was more like I was watching it in real time, like I was there instead of fiction, my brain creating a strange, twisted environment. My vision was foggy, especially at the sides, but I could see clear enough in front of me. Still draped in shadows, standing away from a window, was the King. The room he was in was barren, with barely any light. I heard him chuckle, gazing over his Kingdom, watching the blinking lights below.

"Oh, dear brother, the champion you've left is strong," he said,

252

sounding like he was reading off of a poem. "But a child is no match for my pawns. Amber… you know this, don't you?" I could barely see his face, but I could tell he was smiling, a type of sadistic joy seeping into his voice. He turned in my general direction, and my blood went cold, chills racing up and down my spine. I then wondered if he was really talking about me… his brother's champion?

Everything halted, slowly coming to a stop, and my dream faded into blue. The sky shimmered above me, clouds filling in some spots. Then, it panned down to the camp as if I were filming. Damien and Harlequinn sat at a table set up outside, near the gates. The buildings looked new and repaired, which was good, but their faces both showed worry.

"I don't know what to do," Damien groaned hopelessly, slamming his head down on the table. Harlequinn frowned, putting his hand on his friend's shoulder.

"I'm sorry, I don't either. No one has been down there, and the fairies have no clue of what could await us. Only two reports regarding the abyss exist from what we know. One fairy, a few years ago, said they heard a giant roar that shook the islands. It was so strong, some people fainted and buildings fell. The other… well, he went in and never came back out. We just have to wait," he sighed.

"You can't see them at all with your vision?" Damien begged, a pleading look on his face.

"No. It only really reaches at most, a month. Only time will tell what the future holds…" Harlequinn sighed dejectedly. Jay walked in, holding a platter with cups, steam dancing through the air above them. Harlequinn's face lit up the second he walked in, and he gazed lovingly at his partner as he walked across the camp to them, placing the tray on the table. "Thank you, Jay." He smiled and nodded before sitting down, moving his chair just a bit closer to Harlequinn.

"So, what's going on? Did we find anything?" Jay inquired, grabbing a mug and sipping whatever liquid was inside.

"No, not really. All we know is they won't be back in a month," Harlequinn said, half joking. "I can't see them with my visions. There's this strange sense, though, an energy or aura that reminds me of them. It's only happened twice, but... I sense them." Damien looked up in surprise.

"So, they could still be alive?" he asked, looking more hopeful now.

"Possibly. I just... don't know, though. The feeling is strange, and very faint. I don't know what it is." Harlequinn shrugged in response.

"Have you tried talking to Aaron about this? He has telepathy, so he could help by trying to find them or... their brain, I guess, whenever the feeling comes around again." Jay set his drink down, the cup empty.

"I didn't think about that, but... we might have to wait a while. He's not in a good state," Harlequinn seemed to wince just thinking about it. That more than worried me. "Say, has anyone seen Seth recently? He's also disappeared."

"I haven't, but it's been a lot quieter around here without him. Don't tell Amber, but I agree that he could be trouble," Damien admitted with a sigh. "I'm worried, but also slightly grateful."

"I guess you have to prance around the camp as a unicorn, now," Jay said with a snicker. Harlequinn shot him a confused glance. The sound started to fade, blurring into background noise. I felt an overwhelming sense of sadness, so strong I could barely breathe. I could barely make out the three boys as everything turned to... static.

"Amber?" I heard a small whisper, the voice weak and broken. "Amber!"

"I'm here!" I yelled, trying to reach out for the source. I spun, the world turning dark and encasing me. "I'm okay! What's happening?" I screamed as something rose out of the abyss, a woman's face with two silver eyes. It approached slowly, hissing and bubbling.

I woke with a start, feeling a pressure on my arm, and yelping.

Sweat beaded my forehead, and I was out of breath. My stomach ached, the cut from before completely scabbed over but still stinging. I gripped my side, groaning in pain. Aside from that, my biggest problem was my clothes now being in tatters, the thin fabric ripped and covered in dried, dark blood. The wind around me whipped my hair into my face, and I spit it out, frustrated. Seth stood over me, looking panicked.

"What are you doing?" I huffed, wiping my head.

"You were talking in your sleep, and… screaming. The dragon looked worried," Seth explained, pointing to Berry, who poked his head around the wall, looking curious and slightly worried. I patted his head and stood, sighing.

"Sorry, buddy. I don't know if I woke you up or something?" He shook his head, and I smiled. "I had a really strange dream. I think I saw my friends, and... the King. I guess they've noticed that you're gone, too," I commented, turning to Seth.

"Good to know I'm appreciated," he sighed, standing up. "Unlike over here." I rolled my eyes as he sauntered out, turning back to Berry.

"You know… I'm worried about what's going on up there, but I have no way to reach them. Is there a way out of here?" I scratched his chin and he almost purred. He looked up, then turned back to me with a stern gaze. Looking into his eyes, it was almost like he was trying to tell me something really specific, something only able to be communicated in words. That made me think, though—was there a reason I was here? The intensity of his stare told me that there was *something*... maybe this was some big cosmic scheme, to help or hinder me, I didn't know. Berry did, but I couldn't communicate with him. I sighed in defeat, and sunk back down to the floor, the soft grass scratching against my legs, through my jeans. Berry growled softly, nudging my shoulder. I reached out to pat his nose, my skin sliding across his scales.

"I don't know what to do," I whispered. "Am I supposed to be here? And… why? I should be up there, actually acting as a General. That's my job now. I just got here, I've been pushed to the literal edge of the earth, I've been tested and… maybe I failed. Maybe the prophecy really was talking about someone else. I don't see how I could be a leader." I held my head in my hands, my mind racing and vision blurring as tears started to flow. I looked back to the dragon with a pleading stare, but he turned away. I wasn't getting any help from him, it seemed.

I looked back, across the creek to see Seth... hiding in a bush. He was crouched beneath the thin branches, inside the shrub. I scoffed, confused and curious. I walked to the cliff wall, placing my back on the stone and creeping along the edge. Berry snorted curiously, but I put my finger to my lips in a quieting gesture, and he sat like a dog. I smiled and continued sneaking, and I noticed Seth wasn't moving. I was still annoyed, but it genuinely worried me. I held myself low, creeping across the ground silently.

As I got closer, he seemed to be asleep, his head on top of his knees as he was breathing peacefully, eyes closed. I raised my eyebrows, wondering why he was in a bush, and what he was watching before he fell asleep. Berry hobbled over, joyously picking at the various fruit on the branches, pressing the leaves down onto Seth. A thorn must have embedded itself in his skin, because he jumped up, howling in pain.

"I—wha—huh?" He looked around, at both me and the dragon, his face blanching as he stared down Berry, who seemed to be upset that he interrupted his meal. Berry snarled, and Seth jumped back, yelping. "What are you two doing?"

"I could ask you the same," I commented, poking at the bush. "Why were you asleep... here?" I gestured to the flora, and he winced.

"I don't exactly have the access to a house, little miss—" he stopped as I shot him a glare, my hand on my sword. Berry must have sensed my annoyance, and reflected it, snarling at Seth.

"Watch it," I snapped, watching terror slowly take over his expression. It felt good to finally intimidate him, but I also felt slightly guilty. "Go back to sleep," I hissed, turning away. I didn't want to cause any more of a scene, but I also didn't want to talk any more. Berry flicked out his wing, smacking Seth in the head and sending him tumbling back into the bush. The one with thorns.

"Ow!" he yelped, scrambling out of the branches. Berry snorted in reply.

"He says oops," I vaguely translated, sauntering back over to my side of the creek. "Speaking of shelter… I need a roof." I looked up at the half finished shack. It wasn't much and it was kind of shabby, but I did what I could.

"Could you get me one, while you're at it?" Seth yelled.

"Find your own!" I called back, dismissing him with a wave. He started mumbling under his breath, no doubt coming up with some colorful insults. "What do we do now, bud?" I asked, turning to Berry. He looked down, staring at his paw. I followed his gaze, but nothing was out of the ordinary. I glanced back up, but the dragon didn't move. "What?"

"Is he ignoring you now? Cold!"

"Oh, shut it!" I scowled, not even wanting to turn around. I preferred Seth when he was asleep. "What do you want me to do, Berry?" He glanced up at me sadly, leaning down, but not in a gesture to get on. He scrambled over to the mountain, pawing up at the cavern. "You want me to go in there?" I asked skeptically. He nodded, pushing me with his tail. He had climbed halfway up the mountain, in a position that I figured I could use him to get up. I gently stepped on his paw, muttering apologies before scaling his back, tumbling into the cave.

Berry huffed, nodding towards the tunnel. I looked back at him, confused, but he simply let go of the floor, dropping back down to the grass below. I sighed, once again making my way through the narrow hallway. Barely any light filtered in from the outside, and this time I didn't have the aid of a dragon's fire.

I looked around, trying to spot anything new. Staring at the ceiling, I noticed a small stream of dirt that I didn't think was there before. It started at the doorway I was standing in, weaving its way over to right above the skeleton's head, the soil shimmering with a strange glimmer. I curiously stepped forward, trying to avoid crushing any bones. I tentatively touched the wall, and a small portion of stone dissolved into dust upon contact. This world never ceased to amaze me, especially with the element of surprise. I pressed my hand further, feeling the soil evaporate underneath me. A small hole in the wall was carved out, and a wooden chest sat serenely on the floor. I reached out to touch the side, and thousands of bugs exploded out of the wood, and the dirt. I screamed, flying backwards in shock as they all collected themselves and dug back into the wall, a flurry of legs scuttling into the deepest, darkest corners.

I had to catch my breath, completely thrown off by the sudden infestation. I guessed that bugs did exist here after all, even if it was just in this strange void. I sat for a moment, trying to calm my heart when I felt a warm breeze on my back and turned to see Berry, standing outside with a questioning glance, his face pressed into the stone, trying to see through the hallway. I waved, and stepped forward to grab the chest.

It was large, and slightly heavy, but nothing I couldn't hold. I brought it to the edge of the cavern, and the dragon seemed to get excited, backing up and raising his wings in confirmation. He gently grabbed the chest in his mouth and brought it to the ground, as I slid down the mountain side. A sharp pain rocketed through my sides; I realized dropping down such a steep, rock cliff wasn't a good idea. I just barely managed to roll to avoid extreme damage, but the back of my shirt was shredded and I had small cuts seeping blood.

I winced but shrugged off the pinpricks of pain, eager to see what this was. I saw Seth out of the corner of my eye, now very much awake and curiously looking at the chest. I opened it slowly, gazing inside to see different planks, what looked like a harness, marbles, three short metal poles, and a variety of other strange items that didn't seem to have a purpose. I looked up at Berry curiously, and he nudged the side of the box.

I reached in and grabbed one of the poles, and once I took it out it expanded into a long staff. I jumped back, taken by surprise at the sudden change. I laughed, glancing towards Berry with a smile. He seemed distracted, directing a glare at Seth. The dragon started to slowly prowl towards him, and I saw Seth's face morph into a horrified look. He scrambled backwards, towards the mountains, eyes wide and hands shaking. I tilted my head, confused as to what was going on and why.

It seemed like Berry suddenly had a dramatic change of heart. He lunged, his teeth sinking into the front of Seth's shirt, who screamed. Not in pain, but in surprise and fear. Berry pranced back towards me, throwing his limp body against the chest.

"Berry! What's gotten into you?" I inquired with a stern look. I didn't reach to help Seth, because I knew he would be fine, but the dragon's actions didn't make any sense. He sniffed the air, shoving his snout into the chest in a gesture I didn't understand. "You're gonna need to be more specific." My nonchalant manner earned a frustrated snort from Berry, and I saw Seth wince as soon as he made the loud noise. The dragon nudged my staff, then looked to the person cowering on the floor. I was a bit taken aback by what I thought. "You want me to fight Seth?" He nodded excitedly, but Seth didn't seem too happy.

"Excuse me?" he exclaimed, looking surprised. He then gently stood, trying to not make any sudden movements. "I'm not fighting anyone."

"Oh, come on! It will be fun. Besides, you get a chance to beat me," I grabbed the pole out of the chest and tossed it to him, watching it expand in midair. Seth clumsily caught it, nearly falling backwards. "However small that chance may be."

"Hey!" he scoffed, glaring. "I could take you down with ease. You're not as great as you think you are."

"At least I'm better than you," I smirked, threateningly wielding my staff. "How about we settle this?"

"I... fine. This will at least knock you off of your high horse." He held the staff out in front of him like a really long sword. I held it more in the middle, so I had more balance and could control both ends. He would be off, the length and weight probably making it to where his movements were slow and clumsy. This was off to a good start for me.

He swung first, a long stroke down. I jumped to the side, jabbing forward while ducking under his arms and sliding to the other side. I hit his stomach, and he folded on himself, groaning. I stood quickly, rolling my eyes.

"Yes, I'm in so much danger. I obviously cannot beat your superior skills," I said, my voice dripping with sarcasm. "I'm so scared."

"This isn't over yet!" he complained, swinging at me again. I deflected the blow, sweeping the pole above my head and onto the other side of my body, lifting up my staff and stabbing his hand with the end, making him drop his weapon. I ran forward and pressed the pole to his neck, shoving him to the ground.

"Now it's over!" I said cheerily, smiling. "If you knew me, you'd probably know I've been taking sword fighting and self defense classes for years, and being here has definitely helped me," I laughed, picking up my staff and looking to Berry, who nodded approvingly.

"I wasn't... prepared! I didn't know you were so good." He cleared his throat, rising to his feet. "I'm sure I can get you if we do that again."

"I can't waste time training you like this. I have to prepare myself for... something!" I tossed my hands into the air, accidentally dropping the staff.

"For what, exactly?" He questioned, mimicking me by throwing his hands up in exasperation.

"I'm not entirely sure. War, I guess." I sunk to the floor, sitting against the chest.

"Whoa, what? War? You're a kid, why do you have to worry about that? It's not like you can be drafted," Seth replied, sitting down next to me.

"You don't get it. I was basically drafted the moment I stepped foot in this world… I'm supposed to fulfill a prophecy, become the General of the camp, and lead them into prosperity. Or something like that."

"Who even is the war against? What's happening? Do you have *any* information?" Seth looked at me, almost alarmed.

"We're fighting the Kingdom—or, more accurately, the King. It seems like we're going against an entire army… he's powerful, and influential. But other than that… I don't know a lot. I'm a little lost, but I have to do what I can. Maybe the gods sent me down here to train, keep some peace of mind while honing my powers, but they don't even work down here!" I held my hands in front of me, feeling a little hopeless.

"You really don't know what you're getting into, do you?" I scowled, not wanting a lecture. "You know nothing about this place or the people, and whatever is happening with this weird magic system, but you're running into a war for them. You don't make very good decisions."

"Come on, I have friends here. If anything, I'm fighting to protect them."

"Like they protected you from falling into an abyss?"

"They couldn't do anything! And you're down here, too!" I punched his shoulder, and he fell forward, groaning.

"Yeah, unlike you, I don't have friends here," he mumbled, and I felt my face flush, feeling a bit guilty.

"Whatever. I'm the General of this camp now! I have to protect my friends and my people. And I'm… I'm finally powerful. I have a purpose, and one that I can do something about. I'm not just sitting around, hoping that destiny will meet me in the middle."

"You weren't one to believe in destiny. Why now?"

"I speak metaphorically. Keep up, dude."

"Fine," Seth said sarcastically, scoffing. "So, what are these… destiny-fulfilling powers, anyway?"

"Elemental stuff, I guess. You've seen it, but I don't know the limit of it. I'm afraid I'm gonna hurt someone… I have already. Everyone else has practiced with their powers their entire lives, and I'm just… brought into this." I held out my hand, trying to summon some fire, but not even a spark appeared. "It doesn't work here, but I'm not sure why. Maybe I have to practice more? I don't have very much control over my powers, so I think I have to gain full control before being able to use them in the void."

"Magic is strange. It makes no sense," Seth rolled his eyes, glaring at the sky. "Nothing does here. We're entirely cut off from reality! I'm so confused and lost, it's... completely different than back home."

"Yeah, you'd think the transition would take a while if you don't already have your head in the clouds, trapped in a fictional world while also being in your own reality." I sighed, thinking of my life before. I barely existed within the real world, always coming up with fantastical stories, my mind wishing and wanting the myths to be something less than fantasy.

"You always did seem distracted. I remember you wrote a lot, about magic, powers, and mythical creatures. I guess your stories came true, huh? I'm also guessing that means you didn't have a very hard time wrapping your head around all of this."

"It wasn't hard. I was shocked, but I'd basically already thought of stuff like this. You, however, it seemed to affect ... a lot more."

"Well, I'm always using logic. We're on two completely different levels. And now... I never thought I would be here, hanging out with a dragon! In an abyss with floating islands, as well. It's... almost incredible, but unbelievable," he closed his eyes, looking like he was falling asleep. "I can't tell anyone about this. No one will believe me, and I'll just become a joke. I mean, come on! How do I explain having fallen into a different dimension twice?" He huffed. I nodded, understanding the worry.

"I doubt anyone would believe me, either. They'd probably think it's a plot for a story, or something." I sighed, biting the inside of my cheek. I did that when worried or nervous.

"You always have insane people surrounding you, I doubt those nut-jobs would call you out." I nearly gasped, my eyes widening.

"I... what?" I blinked, taken aback. Of course, he had to ruin the one pleasant conversation we have had in a long time.

"Oh, come on. Your friends aren't exactly mentally stable," he sneered. I rose, glaring as I grabbed his shirt.

"You have no right to insult my friends like that. Go back to your side before I put this pole through your head!" I growled, shoving him to the floor. He looked surprised, but what did he expect when he had said that? Did he think I would agree?

"What's your problem?" he asked, stumbling to his feet.

"I would think you're smart enough to figure that out, but I guess I held you to too high a standard." I turned away, not wanting to even see his face. I heard Berry stir and loud, quick footsteps as Seth jogged back to his side of the creek. I shook my head at the ground, honestly hurt I trusted him to even sit next to me, and disgusted at myself that I made the same mistake once again. I looked over to the dragon beside me, who had his mouth curled up in a disgusted look. I sighed, patting his head. "Let's move on, bud. With him or without." I smiled, completely willing and ready to leave Seth in the dust when a scream rang out from behind me.

I turned to see another dragon grabbing at Seth, its short claws ripping into his shirt. It shrieked, and I noticed it was smaller than usual. Its wings were mottled brown and green, but its eyes were a piercing silver. Its head was flat, no ears or horns, and its wings were tiny and almost frail-looking. Its tail was about as long as its legs, so it was kind of strange, but it was attacking Seth. I grabbed the expanding staff from the ground and raced forward, leaping over the stream swiftly. I stabbed up, sending the pole directly into the dragon's chin. It yelped as it flew backwards, obviously startled and hurt.

"Why do they always go for me?" Seth whined, lying on the ground.

"Maybe they can tell how annoying you are," I snapped, trying to reach the dragon again. It was hovering right above the staff, in just the right place where I couldn't get it. I had an idea, one so preposterous I didn't think it would work in the slightest—so of course, I tried it anyway. I stabbed the pole into the side of the mountain, running and jumping up, letting the staff expand beneath me, sending me gliding into the air... and right past the dragon. I yelped, falling into the void as I slipped, the staff flying from my hands. I heard a loud grunt and the sound of two beasts colliding.

I once again felt the air flow behind my back as I plummeted, passing the few islands that were hovering in the abyss. Darkness swallowed me and the vague silhouettes vanished into the sky, like stars snuffed out as I descended. But unlike the last time, this journey ended quickly. Figures started to emerge from the darkness, but I quickly realized they were all too familiar… I saw Seth and Berry, the dragon hovering in the void, right next to the island I had just been on. I couldn't reach the edge so I shot by, screaming. Each pair of eyes sent a very confused glare, including some shocked looks from the dragons below the island, but they quickly vanished as I fell. I waved at the dragons huddled together in the nest, and then quickly repeated the ordeal from before. I fell for quite a bit longer, until I once again appeared over the landscape. What was happening?

"Help!" I shrieked, flailing as I dove through the abyss, but Berry, seemingly the only dragon who didn't want to eat me, was a bit busy fighting off a dragon that wanted to eat the only other person here. Seth cowered in the corner, barely even looking at me. I scoffed, crossing my arms and waiting for the same thing to happen. Sure enough, as I passed through the void, I reappeared above. I tried to think, though the rapid falling was messing with my head. Through the fog, I noticed the small islands floating around the main one. If I could somehow get over to one... I could stop falling. But I wasn't quite sure how to move like this.

I laid myself out flat, my back facing the sky and my arms spread out. I slightly angled myself down, and I felt the wind change ever so slightly, pushing me to the side instead of straight down. I knew I was slowly inching forward, but I needed to do what I could before I started to gain momentum. If I hit an island at that sort of speed, I would probably just die on impact. I sped through the air, aiming for one of the closest islands. It was pretty small, but the best thing I could do right now.

I reached the small patch of grass, and grabbed on to the edge. I flung myself onto the dirt, my arm digging into the ground. I groaned, piercing pain spreading over the side of my body. I gingerly brushed the dirt off of my face, small droplets of crimson blood attaching to my fingers. I laid back, relieved to have stopped falling but also confused, discombobulated, and tired. My arm ached, a dull throb serving as a constant reminder of the pain. I heard faint yelling, but the ringing in my ears muted all other sounds, a shriek from inside my head. I could hear my own breath, a symphony of bells ringing in the background, but less melodic and more like screaming. My vision blurred, and I felt myself sink into my own thoughts.

Sometimes this happened in the real world, where I would just get lost in my mind, my emotion swirling into an unrecognizable puddle. I couldn't tell what I was feeling- I wasn't able to understand my own self. I was trapped, inside my own brain, my own head, an inescapable pit of darkness blacker and deeper then the abyss I was physically in. My chin trembled, a sudden wave of fatigue and sadness washing over me, making it to where I couldn't move, my limbs not responding to me. I tried to crawl back to the surface, back to whatever light filtered into this ditch, but I had already fallen. I didn't want to think, I wanted to scream and get rid of everything in my head, but that was impossible. I was stuck, my own mind betraying me. A heavy feeling filled my chest, horrible negative thought swarming my mind. I closed my eyes, sinking into the ground, my feet dangling off of the patch of land, and I slowly drifted into sleep.

I seemed to be able to sleep here very easily, which was strange, but I was also grateful because it gave me insight as to what was happening above. I saw Damien and Aaron, standing together at the gate of camp.

"They'll come back," Damien whispered reassuringly. Aaron looked lost, gazing into the woods. "Someday."

"It's been over two months. I'm worried they're... they're dead. I know they have power, and they can use it, but what if something down there is too strong? What happens if it overpowers them?" he yelped, sighing. "I'm so worried. They're... they're one of my best friends, and I thought I wasn't going to be able to contact anyone here. Seeing them in the Kingdom... made me so happy, knowing I wasn't really alone."

"Trust me, they're tougher than... well, maybe you do know. But they're strong, capable, and smart. They'll come back to us." Damien put his hand on Aaron's shoulder, and offered a shy smile. Aaron returned the gesture, and my dream faded, bringing me into the woods. Red emerged from the hideout, and it made me happy to see his quirky, energetic smile. He held a bow in his hands, gently gripping the wood. A quiver filled with arrows rested on his back, and his outfit was completely changed into a slightly questionable fashion choice. He had on a leather jacket, but it only covered his arms and part of his shoulders. A red striped shirt rested underneath that, and steel armor pants were tucked over black tennis shoes. He had on fingerless gloves and had two pink pins holding his frizzy hair back. About a dozen people filed in behind him, all holding various weapons. They had a variety of strange outfits, similar to Red's, but more determined looks, contrary to his goofy beam and small bounce in his step. They grouped into a circle, crouching low to the ground, wielding whatever they had with them. One in the back seemed to be holding a small canon. The trees around them rustled, certain spots shimmering and then exploding, sending people flying out of trees.

Every weapon was aimed for above as both sides attacked, small explosions rocketing the trees at specific times as soldiers from the Kingdom activated what seemed to be bombs. I watched as an arrow pierced someone's skin, driving through their chest into their heart. They went limp, falling with a thud, eyes glazing over and their sword landing next to them. The sound of a muted explosion blasted through the air, and a small cannonball soared through the sky, leaving a trail of confetti. It was sent right into the temple of the soldier that shot the person with an arrow. Death rained upon the forest in just a few minutes, lives being taken left and right, from both sides. I could barely watch the fight rage on, praying that Red and his friends stayed safe.

In the end, the victor was Red. He stood over everything, only three people left on his side, the fight ending as quickly as it started but claiming too many lives in too short a time. I saw him breathing heavily, his quiver already empty, and his hands stained with pale, dried blood. His own or someone else's, I wasn't sure. The scene faded as he turned to his comrades, and my mind returned to my body as I sat up, still alone on the small bit of land. That experience was strange, to say the least, especially the burst of emotion that lead me into it. I'd never felt something that strong, that quickly. I buried my head in my hands, groaning. It's been over two months? Does time also work differently here? I needed to get through this quicker, and get back as soon as I could. I stood, examining any possible ways back to the main island. I noticed some islands vaguely formed a path, similar to what happened in the fairy realm, but I didn't know if that was too dangerous. Well, now I knew that I would just keep falling in the same place, so it's not dangerous or life threatening... I hoped.

"Don't do anything that could get you hurt," I heard someone say, their voice murky and filled with static.

"Aaron?" I said aloud, looking around. Even the static started fading, the connection extremely weak. Hearing his voice was comforting, no matter how distorted it was.

"Are you close to us? This is the only time I've been able to sense your presence, or been able to talk to you," he asked, and I looked up to the sky. The island I was on was higher up, so that might have been the reason he could use his powers.

"No. I'm still... very far away, but I'm safe. Don't worry about me. I'm... I'll be back as soon as I can."

"Hurry, please. Things are starting to—" the static disappeared, and I groaned, disappointed and now concerned. I started a bigger battle, and now I wasn't there to help stop it. That... made my heart ache.

I looked over to the islands, a rugged path that would be hard to get past, but I needed to try. I had to get back to Berry, figure out what to do and what I needed to do in order to get out. I stepped backwards, preparing myself for a big leap, and launching myself just as I reached the edge of the land. I flew through the air, crashing down on the next patch, little pebbles digging into my arm as I hoisted myself up. There weren't many islands, and not a lot of space, just little floating platforms. I made good progress towards the bigger island, but my entire body ached, the effect of landing so harshly. Everything was spaced out, and resting at various heights.

I heard a loud roar echo through the abyss, and I saw the attacking dragon fall into the void. Berry glanced to me as I tumbled onto the next, much bigger island. He gently flew over, hovering above me as I panted. This was a lot harder than I thought it would be. Berry touched down, balancing at the edge so I had space. He took a deep breath, making a strange gesture I didn't quite understand. He growled, placing his head on my shoulder and forcing me down. I sat, confused but trusting. He inhaled, blowing out a small wave of fire. It danced through the air, and as he bobbed his head, he seemed to control it. It made figures and shapes, like shadow puppetry… with flames.

I watched, curious as to where this was going, but entertained seeing it all prance around my head. The blaze all gathered in front of me, spelling the word FOCUS in big, messy letters, scrawled out into the air. I wasn't aware he knew how to spell, at least not in English. Was he trying to say I could use my powers down here?

I glanced at my palms, trying to tap into some hidden power source. I felt nothing stirring inside me, no revelation or… enlightenment. That, however, reminded me of my conversation with Shadow, and the feeling I had afterwards. I tried to remember that, delving into the universe and the possibilities, trying to deepen a never-ending pit of knowledge. If magic was possible at all, it would be possible for me to use it here.

I felt like I was basically ignoring reality, but I knew I could do it.

Berry did, even though he was a dragon. A small spark popped up on my fingertips, the tiny flame flickering dangerously, like it could go out if someone breathed in my general direction. Even that little burst sent a thrill through me, and I smiled, looking up at the beast towering above me. He looked proud, as proud as a dragon could, or what I assumed he could.

The heat made me smile, but also sparked a realization. I don't know if Berry knew I was struggling with controlling my powers, but he seemed to have some sense of awareness. I guessed that down here, your powers were blocked, so you had to basically override the system. Could that be why he didn't take me back up? He was trying to… help me?

I glanced to the islands, once again calculating the path back. Berry lowered himself to the ground, offering a ride, but his look told me it was my choice. I stretched, pain shooting through my shoulder. I assumed it would be better for my health to accept Berry's help, seeing as continuing like this could injure me permanently. I begrudgingly climbed onto his back, and we gently drifted towards the main island, Seth waving at us as we approached. I didn't return the gesture. We touched down beside the creek and I slid off, almost landing in the water. I stumbled backwards, giggling.

"Thanks, bud," I said with a smile, but he simply sat down. I raised my eyebrow in confusion, and he dipped his head towards the ground, seemingly once again gesturing for me to sit. I sank down with a sigh, right in front of the stream. I held out my hands again, knowing what he wanted me to do, or I thought I did. Instead of me conjuring my own flames, he blew a small fire towards me, and I practically caught it with my hands. The heat spread through my palms, starting to burn quickly. I winced, holding it out in front of me a bit further away, trying to keep the blaze alive. A tremor went through me, my arms shaking like I was holding weights, and I struggled to keep it in the air. I didn't understand how fire could be so heavy, but my strength wasn't enough. I dropped the flame into the creek, my hands warm and breathing hard. "What was that?" I gasped, thoroughly surprised. Berry looked like he tried to shrug, but it was a bit awkward, like he didn't actually know what he was doing or how to shrug. He bobbed his head down, slightly raising his shoulders. I giggled, sitting back on the grass.

I looked up into the blank sky, wondering how long I had been here. It seemed like only a day or so passed, but that obviously wasn't the case. Was time here even more messed up? Could you even estimate that? Every second here seemed to make new questions arise. But no one seemed to be interested in answering.

I stood, really tired of waiting around for someone to give me what I needed. Now, I was gonna actively search for it. I turned to Berry, and held out my hands. He perked up, standing slowly. He opened his mouth slightly, and spit out a small flame, much smaller than before. I caught it, the blaze was still slightly heavy, but not as much as before, and it would fit snugly in my palm if I held it fully. I passed it from hand to hand, being careful to not drop it. I assumed as time went on, we'd go to bigger and bigger flames. As I played with the heat, something occurred to me.

"Hey, if you've been able to use fire this entire time, why haven't you fought with it?" I asked, keeping my eyes on the blaze. He cooed, bobbing his head, not in a shrugging gesture, but like he was trying to explain something. However, I couldn't understand because I didn't speak dragon, or I wasn't able to understand their body language. I stared at him with a blank look as he flailed around, making different sounds I assumed was him speaking. He saw my face and stopped, sighing dramatically. I giggled, tossing the ball of fire to him. Thankfully, it had progressively gotten much lighter. He reached up and swallowed it, gulping it down and he stayed still for a moment. I opened my mouth, prepared to speak when he threw another flame at me. It took me by surprise, but I caught it, this one slightly larger than before, about the size of my hand. The process was boring and repetitive, but I quickly advanced as the weight faded, adding on every time just to disappear.

By the time Berry tossed me a ball the size of my head, my arms were tired and I was breathing heavily. I was so tired, I missed catching it, and it rolled towards a bush. I lazily turned around to go get it, but Berry shrieked and shielded me with his body.

An explosion rocked the earth, and I felt the heat from behind the dragon. I winced, suddenly wide awake. He let out a sigh of relief and moved out of my way, so I could see a massive crater in the ground, ashes raining down in the area, the grass burnt and any nearby bushes turned to charcoal. I gaped, marveling at the destruction caused by a small blaze.

"I guess... that's why you don't fight with fire," I said sheepishly, slightly scared of his power now. "We probably shouldn't do that again." Berry nodded vigorously.

"What just happened?" Seth said, approaching. He stumbled over himself in an attempt to get closer while also being in shock from the damage and probably the shockwave. I pointed to Berry, who grunted. Seth's jaw dropped as he looked back and forth from the crater to Berry. "H—how? What?"

"He's a dragon. Duh," I said, glaring. "Now, if you'll excuse us..." I gestured for him to go.

"Wow, you really want me to leave, huh?" he asked, crossing his arms defensively.

"Oh really, Sherlock? I wonder why." I tapped my pointer finger to my chin in a dramatic, sarcastic motion. He scoffed, rolling his eyes and sauntering back in the direction he came. I heard a shaky sigh as he sat down, but brushed it off. Berry snorted, smoke curling into the air as he breathed. I looked to the dragon, biting my lips nervously. "We need to get a move on. This can't take much longer. My friends... I'm worried. And I'm not exactly excited to spend any more time here with... him," I said, rolling my eyes. Berry looked at me sternly, as if he was saying… not yet. Now wasn't the time. But when would the time be?

I spread my hands out in front of me, gesturing cluelessly. He looked down at the creek, examining the little waving plants and fish that were still scrambling up the stream. He stuck his nose into the water, cooing as he swished around, looking like he was playing around more than trying to help me. He opened his eyes for a second, looking at me pointedly.

I pressed my hands down on the dirt, feeling the moisture from the stream. I felt very peaceful, despite the worry eating away at me. The flowing of the water, the gentle bubbling noise it made, the fish swimming cheerfully—it was almost hypnotic. I felt myself slowly getting lost in the rhythm of nature. My hands took in the water, and I felt a chill, as if something clicked in the back of my mind. I lifted my hands, barely thinking of what I was doing, but the water came with me.

The whole creek rose as I pushed the water into the sky, feeling a pain on my back. The little animals within the stream came with it as it started to float. I looked to Berry in a panic, but he nodded, throwing his head in a circle. I guessed he wanted me to mimic him, and so I started making a circular motion with my hands, focusing on not letting the water splash back down onto me.

The stream changed directions, going from a straight line to an oval around me. It followed me, swishing with every turn, and I felt completely in sync with this, like using magic was natural. I felt at home with my powers, all the uncertainty gone.

I slowly leveled out the water, laying it back on its intended course. I looked back at Berry, who gently blew fire into the sky, creating a halo around him. I reached out before it could dissipate, drawing the flames towards me, the same natural feeling coursing through me. I also felt giddy, entirely overjoyed at the progress I had made.

"What now?" I asked, my voice raspy and hoarse. I wasn't sure why. Berry looked at me, then glanced into the void, letting out a loud roar. He held it for a second, and when he stopped, I could hear the vast echo.

Something returned his call, a deep, guttural shout that sent chills up my spine, and a force that almost knocked me over. I turned to Berry in a panic, who now looked serious, like the games were over.

"What was that?" Seth yelled over the noise, rushing up to me. "And… why are you wet?" I looked down at my shirt, seeing the water marks, and sighing.

"I don't know, and long story. But I guess I'm about to find out what made that sound… Aren't I?" I said weakly, and the dragon nodded sullenly, confirming my fears. "Alright, let's get this over with."

"Whoa, you can't be serious," Seth scorned, and I looked at him with my eyebrow raised, questioning his suspicion. "That was… terrifying. Just imagining what that could come from scares me. What are you gonna do if you have to fight it? It didn't exactly sound like it was willing to sit around, drink tea, and discuss a peace treaty." I wasn't sure if he was making a jab at my diplomatic skills, but I didn't have time to assess his insult.

"Whatever is out there, I think I'm supposed to meet it. I don't get it, I don't expect you to, but I'm going. This seems like a stepping stone to finally get out of here, and I need to get back." I flicked my hair behind my shoulder, and placed my hand on Berry's shoulder. He purred, brushing against me.

"You're an absolute mystery, Amber," Seth muttered. "You're right. I don't get it, I don't get any of this, and I still don't get what you aim to do."

"You know what? Maybe you don't need to know. This is my battle, and it's your choice if you want to dive into the fight or not, but you can't stop me from helping." Berry crouched down, anticipating the end of my speech. I jumped on his back, sliding over his spine, and he took off. I wasn't entirely sitting down, so I almost slipped, but I righted myself quickly, grabbing the dragon's neck. I hoped Seth didn't see that; it would have been a bad end to my already bad enough monologue. I gripped Berry's slick scales, holding myself low to his neck. We glided for a few minutes, long after the silhouette of the main island had disappeared behind us.

We traveled deeper into the abyss, unable to see a thing. I felt a chill, creeping up on my back, and I wasn't sure if it was fear or the temperature rapidly dropping. The darkness seemed to waver, spinning around us, whispers following us from the cover of night, an absolute nothingness that held the secrets of the world within its grasp.

"Where are we going, bud?" I questioned, leaning closer to Berry's back. His annoyed growl answered my question. I rolled my eyes, sitting up and looking for any sign of life, getting creeped out by the strange whispers. The air around us grew thin and cold, so much so that I started to shiver. Silver steam rolled off of Berry's body as we flew, my jaw trembling the entire way. A light shone in front of us, so far away it was barely distinguishable, but as we got closer I was horrified at the image.

Gone were the rolling hills, grassy valleys, small bushes and streams. It seemed like we entered a war zone, the ground marred with deep craters, many bubbling with lava. The floor was pitch black, and a dark cloud hung above the giant island. Rock crumbled beneath the floating land, and I heard guttural growls and yelps coming from every direction. Berry shook, his eyes fluttering as he snapped at the air, his irises turning a bright red before pooling into black. His movement stopped, his wings folding and the wind rushing in front of me as we suddenly dove, and I screeched in panic as we hit the ground with a thud. I was thrown off of the dragon's back, onto the warm ground, and sprawling across the rock. Ash stuck to my fingers when I removed my hand from the stone. I started coughing as a bitter taste filled my mouth, the air tasting toxic. I stood shakily, my legs barely working beneath me. I looked up to see Berry approaching, a trill rising in his throat, a vengeful, malicious sound as he prowled towards me. My heart sped up and I clenched my teeth, my hand resting on my sword handle.

"Berry? What happened to you?" I whispered, rapidly looking around for any way out. He roared, forcefully hitting his head on the sharp ground. I shrieked, my hand flying to my mouth. He looked shocked, his eyes clearing for a moment instead of being pure black. He glanced around with a glassy gaze before launching backwards, falling into the void. I ran to the edge of the platform, watching his body be consumed by the darkness. "No!" I yelled, nearly throwing myself into the pit. I didn't know if he was dead or alive, but I couldn't think for too long.

I shivered, feeling a cold breath going down my neck. Not entirely wanting to face whatever was lurking, I slowly turned, examining a strange monster that has snuck up on me. It almost looked like a dragon, but not quite. It had no front legs or wings, so it stood, but only half of my height. It had three eyes, and large black fangs sticking out of its slobbery mouth. It had an elongated snout like a dragon, but fuzz covered its body. It screamed, a high pitched wail that hurt my ears. I grabbed my sword, clumsily pulling it out of its sheath before stabbing the creature through where I expected a heart to be.

It fell, eyes quickly closing, letting out one last whimper. Smoke rose into the air as it caught fire, accidentally having landed in a small lava pit. Its fur quickly burst into flames, and I scrambled back, the heat stinging my face and hands. I stood, my clothes covered in soot and my skin dusted with ash. I breathed a sigh of relief, presuming the worst was over.

My heart stopped as another cry rang out from the abyss. I jumped back, further into the island, so I wouldn't be thrown off the edge as the ground shook, the rocky land crumbling as I raised my palms, stumbling over myself. A giant mess of shadows rushed past me, the wind throwing me back with a vengeance.

A massive dragon flew over the side and landed delicately in front of me, its talons grasping the dead body of the other monster. It swallowed the poor thing in one gulp, its long neck pulsating as it ate. I stared up at the giant mass, which was glittering slightly, its skin a shimmering silver. It was ten times the size of me, towering over my form as I cowered on the land below. Its body was that of a snake with legs, broad wings curled up at its side. It stood with a limp, one leg withering beneath its weight. Two small horns stretched up out of its head as it hissed, baring surprisingly dull teeth. I propped myself up, one arm on the ground as I gazed into the sky at its head. Its jaw was square, and its eyes were seemingly cycling through different dark colors. All of that combined gave me shivers as I waited silently, hoping it didn't notice me below.

I felt a small tug on my arm, and I suddenly fell back as something yanked my elbow out from underneath me, making me lose my balance and crash into the rock floor. I heard a little pitter of laughter as a small creature ran out of my sight. I silently cursed at the little demon, keeping still on the floor as the dragon sniffed the air around it.

With the way it was hunting, I would guess that this thing was blind, but that didn't make it any less dangerous. As it became occupied with whatever scent was haunting the air, I tried to slowly crawl away, barely moving one inch at a time. My plan was foiled as the floor beneath me started to heat up, and I winced at the searing pain coursing over any exposed skin, my clothes smoldering. I looked down to see small holes opening in the ground, the rock almost melting to show bubbling flames rising from the earth. I rolled away, jumping to my feet just before a geyser of lava shot into the air where I was sitting. The stream splashed the burning liquid over the giant monster's face, getting into its eyes. It shrieked, thrashing around in pain.

"I guess that's a good distraction," I muttered, quickly sprinting in the opposite direction. A roar rung out behind me, echoing through the void, such an angry emotion conveyed with one sound that I immediately recognized it from before. Despite the heat, I felt cold, fear coursing through me.

Trying to ignore the sound, I pressed on, running from the enraged monster. I passed a large lake, filled to the brim with melted magma. Junk littered the ground around me, the most noticeable ones being a smoldering tire, a broken trash can, and a purple stool, completely intact but decorated with bright blue stars and the name Amanda carved into the wood. I wondered where it came from, and who Amanda could be, but I didn't have time to stop and ponder the origin of a stool. I heard crashing footsteps as the floor rumbled, and I looked over my shoulder to see the dragon, barreling at me. It leaned down to the floor so it wasn't as tall, but a monster like that running towards you is still a terrifying sight. I shrieked, knowing I couldn't outrun that beast, so I had to form a plan. I glanced at the trash, and an idea popped into my head.

I leaned down, grabbing the tire. The rubber was very hot, but hopefully not enough to burn me. I jogged around the lava, trying to make it seem like I was still scared or running, to keep my distance but also continue the chase. It followed my movements, slithering across the sharp stone ground, occasionally hissing or biting the air. I took it in a few loops, still hauling along the heavy tire. My arms felt like lead and my legs couldn't carry me much longer, so I turned, determined to succeed. It saw my pause as an opening, bolting like I'd hoped. I held the rubber at my waist, waiting for the right time to strike.

I could feel its breath, it was so close. I saw the detail on its shining skin, every scar and bump, and I knew I dodged a bullet at the last second. Before it could swallow me whole, I shoved the tire onto its snout and dove out of the way. I heard a confused grumble as the monster attempted to pry off the nuisance on its nose, to no avail. The dense material was thoroughly stuck, causing the creature to thrash in rage and panic. Its dark eyes locked on to me for a second, and it tried to roar before giving up, the only sound coming out a muffled squeak. My eyes widened as it once again charged, spitting mad now. I yelped, hopping to the side in fear. I felt my heart speed up, and worry crept over me. I hadn't gotten this far into the plan.

I once again examined all the trash. I doubted dragons or things like what I was fighting could handle the intense heat of the lava, so that could be my weapon. I picked up a glass beer bottle, the top of which was shattered, and wielded it like a sword. I had a real blade by my side, but that might bring me too close. With the bottle, all I had to do was aim, and throw. I stepped back, waiting for the dragon to glance back at me, so its back would be facing the pool. There was a short pause before it did, its black eyes staring into my soul. I nearly froze, my blood turning to ice before I snapped out of my stupor and chucked the bottle right between its eyes, where I knew was a sore spot.

I barely thought about the small roar of anguish that came from the poor creature, but it was trying to kill me. I couldn't exactly muster a lot of pity. I ran, using all my strength and weight to push the thing backwards, trying to throw its body into the massive magma pit. I should have known that I wasn't strong enough to move a dragon, but the thought didn't cross my mind until it turned to me, snarling, watching me press against its leg.

I backed up, glancing around me once again. It tried to snap at me, still being held by the tire, so it resorted to using claws. It used its good leg, swiping out at me, but almost falling over, having put the weight on a leg that couldn't hold it. As I rolled backwards, that gave me an idea, puzzle pieces clicking together in my head.

This lake was filled with human trash. I didn't know why, and I doubt anyone could explain, but that meant I could rely on people's litter to help me—something I never thought I would ever say. I ran around the lava, trying to find what I needed, but I was alarmed at how quickly it flew my way. A plastic bag floated through the air, and I jumped up to grab it, landing on some fishing nets. The dragon examined my movements, slowly approaching me as it struggled with the tire, hissing and snarling in warning. The lake was big enough that it couldn't just hop over, and it seemed a bit wary of flying, so I figured I was safe as long as I kept my distance.

My time ran out quickly. I heard the loud snap coming from the dragon. Burning rubber fell to pieces around its snout, now covered in lava. It looked like it had quickly dipped into the lake, letting the magma tear apart the rubber. I picked up my trash, holding piles of bags and rope in my arms, knotted together to make a giant rope, one I really hoped would work. The dragon let out a deep roar, grunting in anger and pain as it ran towards me, shaking the ground with its thunderous steps. I fell backwards, my shoe getting stuck in a hole as the ground started to open again, warning me of another geyser.

I pulled away, the residual spray hitting my back. I sunk to the floor, trying to put out the flames eating at my clothes, rolling around to snuff them out. The dragon seemed to stop, maybe confused at my strange actions as I panicked on the ground. I stood up, now covered in ash with my back burning, wearily holding the rope I had made. The monster roared, stomping forward, snapping at me. I slowly dodged, my movement fatigued and my arms sore, but I wrapped the end of the rope around its bad leg as it passed by. It huffed, turning swiftly and smacking me backwards.

I grunted in pain, holding tight to the rope. The bags started to rip, and I cursed, pulling harder. The dragon stumbled, and I yanked the rope to the side, hearing a snap as the line went limp in my hands. It seemed to be enough momentum, the dragon gurgling in confusion as it stumbled face-first into the lava pit, falling over with a thud that made the lake overflow, magma flying all different directions.

I tried to catch my breath, my lungs burning as much as my muscles and skin. I wiped sweat off of my forehead, trying to see through the sheen of fog that had built up on my glasses. The haze impaired my vision, but I could make out my general surroundings, at least preventing me from falling into the lava. I heard a bubble, and slowly approached the pulsing lava pit. My jaw fell open as the monster rose, the magma sliding off of its skin as it broke above the surface. I groaned in frustration and fear, unsure of how to take this down without using my surroundings, since that obviously didn't work.

Being resourceful wasn't the aim here—I assumed harnessing and using my magic was. Sometimes, just being clever doesn't work, you need power on your side, and my physical strength would do nothing. I took a deep breath, stepping back from the monster still struggling to get out of the pit. I had time, but not much, so I shouldn't waste any. I put my hands together, trying to calm myself down as I attempted to summon a flame, focusing my mind and energy towards bringing out something that was buried deep inside me, somehow forced back by exiting the realm I was previously in. I tried to remember what training I had gotten, the advice from Shadow, the battling with Quartz. I could use my powers together to strengthen what little magic I have here.

I heard a growl, and looked up to see the thing had fully emerged, and its sights were set on me. Heat rose in my palm, and before I knew it, a blaze encased my arm. I giggled in joy, jumping into battle with a determined mindset and holding on to the hope that I could win. I dodged its first attack, a simple bite that nearly took off my leg. I held my hand to its face and released a wave of flames, white hot fire exploding over its nose. It screeched, rearing its head in anger, and I took its distraction as an opening. I ran at its good leg, attempting to dig under its thick scales and get to skin so it would do more damage. I managed to pry off a large slab, and I directed my fire to the exposed part, unleashing a torrent of what I could muster, trying to use the hot wind in the air to aid my attacks.

The inferno caused the creature's skin to rupture, bubbling and burning unnaturally. I stepped back in disgust as the scale snapped back into place, digging in to the blistered, swollen skin. The yelping from above assured me that what I had done hurt, a lot. The thing tried to walk forwards, but its legs gave out beneath it, the burns rendering the limb useless.

I held my hands out, attempting to conjure the fire armor again, even though I knew it quickly drained my mana. Nothing happened, the air standing still as pained cries rang out through the island. I scoffed, not knowing what I was expecting, but the monster noticed I was preoccupied. A tail, something I hadn't noticed before, unfurled and smacked me across the island, sending me flying towards the lava. I screamed, falling backwards into the magma as a searing sensation overtook my body.

Pain from all sides, I felt as if my skin was dissolving beneath the liquid. I screamed in shock, thrusting my hands towards the sky, and... everything stopped. It was such a dramatic halt that I thought I was dead before I felt the hot molten rock recede, and my body temperature slowly declined. I couldn't have been engulfed for even a second, but it felt like a lifetime. The lava parted, and I kept my hands outstretched as I laid on the rock floor, the floor still warm beneath me. I moved my arms slightly, and the magma shifted with my motions. I wasn't entirely sure how, but I was in control for at least a moment. I stood slowly, as it was difficult to rise without using your arms, but I managed. The creature stared at me curiously, growling as it weighed its options. I didn't let it think long, as I shot it off of the island, carried in a wave of bubbling heat. As the substance left my sight, falling into the void along with the monster, I fell to my knees, out of breath as I collapsed in the dome shaped dent in the ground. My eyes fluttered shut, and I drifted into slumber.

I was surprised to see that this night my dreams held no visions, simply a black fog clouding my sight for who knows how long. It dissipated not long after it appeared, and I partially awoke, my body still limp. I heard footsteps, soft clicks as someone traveled lightly across the stone floor.

"Amber? Amber! Come now, get up," I heard a voice in front of me say with a soothing, coaxing tone. I didn't recognize the voice, but it felt familiar.

"I'm not moving for three years," I groaned, my arms aching and legs weak, barely able to catch my breath. My voice was raspy, and I felt like I had spent a few hours in boiling water. "Maybe more."

"Don't exaggerate," the voice hummed, giggling. "The world needs you. Your camp needs you. It's time to move, and get out of this place." I sat up, my head hurting and eyes barely able to open. I glanced in front of me, seeing no one there. Did I fall back asleep? Or maybe that was a dream. I wasn't quite sure, but I kept myself conscious anyway. After a minute, I saw Berry gliding over the island, hopefully searching for me. I held my hand to the sky and he turned towards me, quickly scooping me up in his talons and taking off before I had a chance to say anything or even greet him.

"Nice to see you, too," I huffed, turning my head as the wind whipped my hair behind me. The air tore at the various cuts and burns I had, seeping through my torn and bloodied clothes, creating a lot of pain. We glided through the abyss, and I'd never been happier to fly through endless nothingness, even though every inch somehow inflicted agony. We approached the island I had been stuck on before, and I saw Seth waiting expectantly. Berry dropped me in front of him, and then sat down next to us. I groaned, laying down on the grass.

"You've been gone for a while," Seth remarked slyly.

"Sorry, I've actually been doing something productive," I said, my face in the grass. "Seems like you've just been sitting on this island."

"Not exactly much else I can do," he hissed back, scoffing. "You're the one who has magic, but you seem to just be using it as an excuse to disappear."

"That doesn't even make any sense. Maybe you should learn some magic, actually make yourself useful for once."

"As useful as you've been? If that's the case, I'm doing better than you by just standing here."

"Sorry, who has a house built?" I looked up, glaring at him, still spread on the ground.

"Who launched themself into the void while trying to prove a point?" Seth rolled his eyes, pouting.

"Don't poke the bear," I glared, and Berry snarled behind me.

"Is the bear you or the dragon?" Seth muttered, crossing his arms.

"Don't poke either of the bears." I slowly rolled over, putting my hand in the air. Berry reached out, putting his snout in my palm. "I'm guessing, since I now have more control over my powers... it's time to go?" The beast nodded, and I sighed in relief.

"Finally." I heard Seth mumble, and I could imagine his eye roll, but I ignored him.

"I'm gonna miss you, but my friends need me. My camp needs me. We need to leave." I pressed my forehead to Berry's, and heard him coo. "The only problem is... how do we get out of this void?"

"We can't just, like, jump in and hope, can we?" Seth questioned, looking over the edge of the island. Berry perked up, suddenly grabbing his shirt and flinging him upwards, with all the strength he could seemingly muster on the ground. Seth went spiraling into the abyss above, screaming every second of the way as his figure disappeared into the black sky. Berry then turned to me, a light in his eyes.

"I'll... pass, thanks. You can just fly me up," I giggled nervously. The dragon looked almost disappointed, but lowered himself so I could climb onto his back. I stood weakly, my limbs screaming out in pain, but I slowly lifted myself up. "It's gonna be good to be home." I hugged Berry's neck as we ascended, flying swiftly through the void. A surge of adrenaline coursed through me, an ecstatic smile spreading across my face. Hopefully I'd make it in time to help the others.

We sped through the sky, and I felt the air becoming warmer, more humid. I kept my gaze turned to the sky, but we only flew for a few minutes before I saw light. I gasped excitedly, then I felt myself rising off of Berry's back. I looked down to see I was floating, and the dragon was spiraling back down into the pit. I only had the chance to sullenly wave goodbye as I was shot back into the fairy realm. I ascended quickly, yelping as I picked up speed, but gently landed on the small island with the mirror and portal I had gone through so long ago. My cloak was no longer on the ground, and I assume Damien probably took it back to camp. I glanced around, seeing the fairy world was, luckily, back in order.

The islands looked as if they hadn't gone through a war, the trees almost glowed, and I saw a few fairies swirling around. I offered a small smile, not to anyone in particular, but a gesture to myself almost. I turned, looking down the hallway I had to go through to get to the real world, a bit nervous for reasons I couldn't explain, but I charged through nonetheless.

CHAPTER FIFTEEN

I blinked away the darkness, looking around, trying to find any sign of life or someone to help me get back. Trying to recognize the area, I realized that I was somewhere else from the original portal. The trees all looked the same, the paths weren't anything I could follow, I was very lost and I couldn't see the end of the forest.

I slowly started walking around, brushing my hand against the trunks of the trees surrounding me. Arrows littered the ground, as well as confetti and small pieces of stone or iron. I examined the strange plethora of items, confused as to why any of this would be here. I heard a soft rustle and my hand instinctively flew to my sword, eyes wide and ears alert. The tree in front of my shimmered, and Red stepped out, wearing the same outfit as he was in my vision. He turned to wave at someone, not yet noticing me until he fully stepped out of the cloak. The look of shock on his face was honestly quite funny.

"Amber?" he gasped. "Amber!" A wide grin covered his face as he launched into a hug, almost knocking me over, as I was kneeling on the ground. I giggled, wrapping my arms around him and returning the hug. It was nice to see him and his goofy, childish personality again.

"Hey, Red! Sorry I… disappeared. I didn't exactly mean to," I explained with a short, nervous chuckle. He stepped back, rolling his eyes playfully.

"You can tell me later. I'm glad you're here now! Everyone missed you, a lot. But… What happened to you?" he asked, looking down at my torn and bloodied clothes.

"Oh, uh… that's also a story for later. I should probably get to camp. I wanna say hi to everyone and let them know I'm back." I stood, offering my hand and pulling him up alongside me.

"Well, if you want to talk to Damien, Jay, and Harlequinn, that might be a problem," Red said nonchalantly.

"What? Why? Did something happen to them? Ugh!" I slapped

my forehead, worry creeping up on me.

"No, everyone is fine! They started some missions while you were gone, trying to recruit people in the woods. We've got some good allies now, but they went to the Pyramid," he said like I was supposed to know what that was. I stared at him for a moment, but he simply smiled.

"They went where?" I finally asked, and he lit up with realization.

"Oh It's an old structure, basically a storage unit that used to belong to your camp. The Kingdom took it over, hoarding the weapons inside, but the Pyramid is laced with traps. The whole thing will collapse if the Kingdom isn't careful—which they won't be. That, and retrieving the magical items is why they left."

"Can you take me?" I asked, anxious to see them especially. Besides, even though I'd just come back from one, a little adventure was something I wouldn't turn down.

"Of course! I found it in the first place. I know the trail by heart," he chuckled, lightly punching my arm. "Hey, where's that little kid? I thought he disappeared when you did, or that's what the camp said."

"Seth?" I asked, giggling at the fact that Red called him a kid. "I... don't know, actually. He got back before me, and I guess I lost track of him." In my mind, it wasn't a severe loss.

"Maybe he's already at the Pyramid," Red joked. "Did you two go to the same—"

"We should get going! I really wanna see them again." I forced an awkward smile, not knowing if I should tell people about my encounter yet.

"If you say so," he shrugged, gesturing for me to follow. "This way, General."

"Not you, too," I groaned, thinking back to when Damien did that, though it was when we first met. "No need to be formal, Red." That title seemed like something that I couldn't claim yet—and it was so uptight. These were my friends, I wouldn't want them to feel like they had to call me their General. I wondered if I would ever feel like I really fit in that space.

I followed along behind Red. It was a small trek, probably only ten or so minutes before we reached the Pyramid. A large stone triangle reached up to the tops of the trees, but not going past them. Crumbling sandstone lined the outside, and a small opening was visible, a square of darkness leading in.

"We have to be careful. Wait here, I'll either bring them out or signal when you can come in," Red whispered, approaching the Pyramid with a crouched stance, barely making any noise on the leaf-covered floor, which was quite impressive. He disappeared into the shadows, and I leaned against a tree, waiting. I quickly realized I didn't know what the signal was supposed to be, but I kept a lookout for anything out of the ordinary. I scanned the outside of the building, looking for any sign of life, but it seemed to be abandoned. Curiosity got the best of me as I followed Red's path, sneaking up to the structure. I heard a faint, shrill scream from inside, and my eyes widened. I unsheathed my sword, pausing for a moment to weigh my options, but I decided if someone was in trouble, I needed to help. I knew it was stupid, but I rushed in against my better judgment.

The hallway went two ways, left and right, with no lighting down either side. I could barely see, but I charged down the path to the right, because that's where the most noise seemed to be coming from. I walked along blindly, stumbling through the darkness. My outstretched hands hit something—a stone wall. I pressed myself up against it, trying to find a door—or an opening at all—but there was nothing. Did I go the wrong way? I continued examining the wall, and found that there was another path, which curved to the side. I sighed in relief and followed the wall into a vast room filled with light. Torches decorated the walls, and a gold slab rested in the middle of the square room.

I approached tentatively, holding my sword up so I could defend myself if I needed. I skirted around the edge of the strange, shimmering gold, trying not to touch it. I made my way around it, turned with a suspicious glare, then quickly exited the room from the door on the other side of the slab. I assumed if you touched it or tried to take it, it would activate a trap of some sort. As I had nothing to do with some gold, I left it alone. I put my sword back into my sheath, then continued down another hallway, passing a few door frames and large arches. In some rooms, the stone seemed unstable or the room was crumbling, which made me anxious to get out. At least now the walls were lit up.

I heard voices up ahead, coming from a room right in front of me, and sunk slowly into the shadowy parts of the hallway, sliding along the stone walls of the pyramid, slowly approaching the noise in case it wasn't someone friendly. As I peered further into the lit room, I saw Damien, Jay, and Harlequinn standing next to Red. I smiled widely, extremely excited to see them again. I noticed their conversation was clearer now, so I paused.

"It's like a game of chess, the King keeps getting away. We can't corner him, he's always one step ahead!" Harlequinn groaned, his hand on his temple.

"We're outnumbered now, he has all the weapons. Amber had a plan, but... they're not here. No one can find or talk to them, not even Aaron, who had the most luck," Damien crossed his arms, biting his lip nervously. "What do we do now?"

"We put our final pawn into play," I announced loudly, stepping through the doorway. I smiled, a hand on my hip. Everyone turned, eyes wide and Damien gasped. Red smiled joyously.

"Oh, yeah! That's the surprise. Amber's back!" he said cheerfully. Everyone paused, mixed emotions showing on their faces.

"I never was very good at chess," Damien said weakly, breaking the silence. I laughed, and they all slowly jogged towards me, looking like they didn't believe I was real. They examined me for a moment, Damien even poking my arm, confirming that I was, indeed, standing there. "You… you're back!" he exclaimed, scooping me up in a hug. I laughed, though I was slowly being crushed in his arms.

"Calm down! I just got back, you don't want to break me

already," I joked. "Seriously though, I'm so glad to be here again. I missed you guys a lot."

"What happened to you? And your... your clothes? Are you hurt? Is that blood old?" Damien asked, pulling away. His fingertips were slightly stained red, and I winced. I once again glanced down to my shirt, which had the most damage done to it.

"Don't worry about me, I'm okay. But what about you guys? What's happened?" Damien looked back at the other two, who sighed.

"It's been months. A lot has gone down," Harlequinn offered quietly. "We've held our own, but the Kingdom has always been ruthless. Something else must have happened, because this is more daring than we've ever seen them."

"We can barely go outside anymore. Even with safety in numbers, a lot of the camp is... down. We're fine inside thanks to the Elites, but things are getting risky," Damien crossed his arms, looking glum. "I don't even understand it. It's like a switch flipped... they're suddenly uncaring, apathetic, totally hate-driven monsters."

"And the worst part is... Amber, I think you were right. If a group goes out, it seems like anyone with darker skin is more likely to get attacked, and killed. This isn't unbiased," Jay chimed in, and I felt guilty, the warm sensation of shame passing through me.

"The Kingdom hasn't exactly been... a safe place, for black people. For years, they've forced them out, using slurs and criminalizing magic by saying black people are more likely to be born with it, and if magic is bad... obviously the people who wield it must be, too," Harlequinn commented sadly. Damien looked ashamed, flushed with crimson, and Jay looked uncomfortable. Red glanced between us, obviously sensing the tension.

"So, Amber, what happened on your end?" Red asked, trying to change the subject.

"Uh... That might be a story better told with the whole camp," I said, trying to stall for time. I didn't want to spill the news about a realm where dragons existed, especially if they've been living in peace without humans bothering them. I didn't want to infect their safe haven with a disease probably worse than the plague, even though it seemed that our trash had already touched their land, corrupting anything that touched the island. But that was even more of a reason to not let anyone know.

"Alright, but we're talking soon. Hey... where's Seth? He disappeared with you, right?" Damien said, glancing around.

"Oh, he's—" I gasped, my hand flying up to my mouth. "I don't know. But is it really that big of a deal?"

"Amber..." Damien said with a stern glare.

"Ugh, fine, let's go find him." I turned, and a scream rung out through the halls. I sighed, swinging my head to where the noise seemed to be coming from. "You know, I have a hunch he might be in this building."

"Was he not with you when you got back?" Harlequinn inquired, looking confused.

"No, I... lost him, actually. I guess it's technically lucky he's here," I said with a shrug.

"We should go get him. He probably touched something he shouldn't have... even though everything is gone, the traps are still there. Even touching parts of the floor can kill you. This place is rigged with arrows, poison gas, and even enchanted stones that will suffocate you. I'm surprised anyone from the Kingdom survived while coming here." Damien crossed his arms, starting to head out.

"This place seems fun," I muttered, following. Red, Harlequinn, and Jay all hung behind us. "The screaming has stopped. Do you think something happened?" I said in a hushed tone.

"I'm not sure," Damien replied. "He doesn't exactly know how to fight, unless some major stuff happened while you two were gone, so he's probably in danger."

"Something major did happen, Damien," Jay said, almost seeming like he was prompting a conversation. Damien winced in return, slowly halting.

"I wasn't going to bring that up until we got back to camp," he said, jaw clenched, but smiling, talking through his teeth. That didn't seem good.

"Why wait? I know a lot has happened, but they probably need to know." Jay crossed his arms and Harlequinn nodded. Red looked around, confused.

"Can you just tell me instead of beating around the bush? Don't be vague," I scoffed, rolling my eyes. "Jay's right, though. Tell me."

"Well... you're not gonna be happy. The woods have started changing again." I gasped slightly, looking at Damien in shock and dismay. I groaned, putting my hand to my temple.

"Not again. Just one more thing I have to deal with now," I sighed, straightening my back. "No, we'll be fine. We just have to get through this, and then we'll see how much trouble we're in."

"A lot has happened to you, too," Damien chuckled. "This is gonna be an interesting story once we get back."

"Focus on the now!" I yelped. "Let's go find Seth." I hurried off, not wanting to get into another conversation about where I had disappeared to, as I didn't really want to give answers. I could picture the concerned looks on all of their faces, but I didn't turn back.

Everywhere we looked was empty. We scoured the building, being careful to not touch anything we didn't have to. No traps were activated, and there were no remnants to indicate any had been triggered. After what was probably about an hour of searching, we all met back in the room I found everyone in.

"We got nothing," Harlequinn said dejectedly, holding Jay's hand. "There isn't more than one floor, is there?"

"Not that we know of," Red huffed.

"I've been here a few times, and there's never seemed to be anything. I was never able to get weapons, but I discovered a lot of the secret areas that are open now. No other floors, though." Damien folded his arms, looking frustrated.

"What do we do?" I said quietly. I had no problem leaving, but I didn't want Seth to get hurt or die. He was horrible, but didn't deserve death.

"Seth?" Damien called out, cupping his hands around his mouth to try to make his voice louder. "Seth!"

"Won't that get us caught along with him?" I asked, my hand drifting to my sword hilt.

"It's the best option we have," Damien said, shrugging. "Seth!" I sighed, joining in on the calls. We all wandered a bit, shouting his name continuously, pausing in between. After a minute, another shriek rang through the halls.

"Seth!" I yelled, slowly heading towards the noise. However... the screaming seemed to be coming towards me faster than I was going to the source. I peered down the hall, waiting. The boys stood behind me, and all of us were still for a moment. We watched helplessly as Seth sped past, shrieking as four guards, all carrying long spears and decked out with full suits of armor, chased him down the hall. I put my head in my hands with an exasperated sigh, then quickly drew my sword and followed.

"Careful! The guards are automated. They're extremely strong and nearly invincible with their armor on!" Damien yelled before turning into a hawk, a trick that made me strangely happy to see again. He raced to the front, waiting for Seth to pass before he turned back into a human, blocking the threatening guards from passing. Harlequinn stayed at the wall as Red, Jay and I charged forward. I set my sword ablaze, driving it into one of the robot's arms, right where the metal left a little bit of exposed skin. Except, what was underneath the armor didn't seem to be skin, but dark matter. I twisted my sword, prying off a metal plate and watching as the guard collapsed, black, sparkly liquid oozing out of its arm.

I stared in disgust as everyone else attacked the remaining robots, unfazed by this. I looked up to see Jay, levitating some fallen rocks and smashing two together into the guards head, crushing its helmet. He then took some stone from the floor and threw it into the air, smashing the armor into the ceiling. The metal cracked and more black liquid flowed out where its body should be. I thought Red was fighting with a sword or knife at first, as he was bouncing around, hollering and stabbing at the armor, but as I moved closer I saw that he actually had an arrow in his hand, one with a metal shaft instead of wooden. It was a bit alarming, but he seemed to be having fun without getting hurt, so I turned to Damien to see if he needed help.

Seth hid behind him, and Damien smirked. He made a small motion with his hand, seeming to urge me to come to them. I snuck around all the fighting, and made my way over to Seth, who I dragged a little further backwards. I examined the guard in front of us, and noticed something was different. This one had thicker armor, and more plates guarding weak spots. It had a bigger spear, and actual eyes glowing beneath the helmet as opposed to the others blank faces.

"Be careful," I whispered, unsure if the machines could hear or not. I saw Damien nod, the back of his head bouncing slightly. However, he seemed to be stalling, simply standing with his arms out in a protective stance. All the other attackers were down, and everyone was standing still expectantly. Everything was silent, no one moving a muscle, until the guard menacingly swung his spear, jabbing at Damien's chest. He dodged, turning into a small bird and flying up the length of the weapon, turning back into a human as he got to the face, catapulting himself towards the creature, kicking his leg into its helmet. Then he shrieked, his skin colliding with the metal, creating a painful cracking noise. "Damien!" I yelled, almost rushing forward before I saw a blanket float through the air, wrap around Damien before he hit the ground, and whisked him towards Jay.

"I got him!" He yelled with a smile. I nodded, the guard not wasting any time with the boys and turning back to me, glaring specifically at Seth.

"What did you touch?" I groaned.

"What? Nothing!" he yelled, exasperated, but obviously lying. He looked down, biting his lip nervously. I rolled my eyes, not wanting to argue. I examined the armor, thinking that it should be heavier than the others, therefore slower or less agile. But I was quickly proved wrong as I charged, and it flipped over me, ignoring my attacks and going right for Seth.

"Hey!" I yelped, throwing a fireball at its back. The armor absorbed the heat, not even melting, so fire wasn't an option. I pointed my hand towards the guard's legs, and summoned a large blast of wind that nearly knocked it off of its feet, but it held its ground. I scoffed in surprise, knowing I had to get between it and Seth. I sprinted forward, throwing my weight against the armor, attempting to push it to the ground, but it stood, flinging me off. I winced, my arms scraping across the stone floor. I heard a small rumble and the ground beneath us ruptured, splitting apart and throwing all of us backwards. I looked behind me to see Jay, hands spread out in front of him as Harlequinn supported Damien, holding him up above the shaking ground along with Red. I guessed that I was on my own now, as they all seemed preoccupied, except for some small help from Jay.

I turned back, leaping over the blistered ground, stepping over all the cracks and standing with my fists raised in front of Seth. My arms caught fire, the gauntlets turning red as they absorbed the heat. I held out my palm, a small ball of magma forming in my hand. I threw it, and it melted against the guard's head. It didn't do a lot of damage but it angered it. I rolled my eyes, bringing down the heat in my hands and drawing my sword. The guard stood, looming menacingly as it approached, spear raised. It swung, attempting to stab my heart, but I dodged to the side, circling around the robot. It extended its arm, sweeping its weapon across the room. I once again dodged, jumping out of its way, but I wasn't its only target. It continued to swing, going for Seth's head. I yelled, thrusting my sword into the guard's face, digging beneath the helmet as I leapt at its weapon, pouncing on the shaft, attempting to break it, but the wood was extremely thick. I drove the point into the floor, letting go of my blade in order to keep the spear away from Seth.

"Defending someone you despise so much... what a peculiar child," a gravelly voice said, seemingly coming from the guard. I was surprised to hear it speak, but also angry at its words.

"It's my responsibility to protect him, and I'm not letting you idiots get that idiot!" I growled, pointing respectively.

"I don't know if I should be grateful or offended," I heard Seth scoff from behind me. I turned slightly, shooting him a glare so sharp I was almost certain knives would materialize in midair.

"Be grateful you're not on my list right now!" I yelled, and he stepped back, shock showing clearly on his face. I doubt he expected that sudden lashing out.

"Are we on the same side, or not?" he groaned.

"Just let me fight in peace," I snarled. "Now shut up, and—" I stopped short, feeling another tremor. I turned to Jay, who looked afraid, glancing around in confusion. If he wasn't doing that, what was?

"Amber! Get out of there!" Damien yelled, a panicked expression on his face, floating in the air. My eyes widened, and I looked back to the guard, grasping the hilt of my sword that was still sticking out of its helmet. I pulled the blade free, stumbling backwards from the force. I grabbed Seth's arm, waved sarcastically, and sprinted over to the boys. A falling stone nearly hit my head, so I shrieked. Jay and Red rushed towards me, pulling me to the exit, everyone now safe on the ground.

"Someone took it? You distracted me," the guard chuckled. "Oh, well. Now you'll all die."

"Not on my watch," I heard Jay grumble. He let go of my hand, turned to face the robot, and held out his palms.

"Jay, no!" Harlequinn looked worried. I wondered what Jay was planning. He took a deep breath and brought his hands together, closing his fists. The ceiling cracked, and closed in on itself, collapsing and crushing everything in the room underneath it, except for us. Dust rolled through the room, the debris settling.

"Everyone, go, now! The Pyramid is extremely unstable!" Red pulled all of us back, rushing us through the hallway. The four boys sprinted in front of me, and I grabbed Red, making sure he was with us. We stumbled, the building trembling, a loud cracking sound coming from above us.

Red yelped, and then pushed me forward. I fell through the door frame and sprawled out on the floor. I barely had time to look back, seeing him just barely miss the door before the ceiling caved in. Rocks crushed his body, the weight of the entire building crashing down on him. I screamed in shock and horror, my brain barely processing what had just happened. I scrambled to my feet, sprinting forward, my breath short and heart racing as I pounded at the boulders covering the door. The walls once again shuddered, and I heard a loud boom.

"Red!" I yelled, pain seeping through my voice as it cracked. Damien approached behind me, trying to help me force the rocks out of the way. "Red? Please... please tell me you're okay!" I screamed as loud as I could, hot tears quickly rolling down my face, but it was no use. There was another tremor, and the ceiling rained dust on us. Damien looked up, worried.

"Amber, I... I'm sorry, we have to go," he said softly, but urgently.

"What? No! Didn't you just see what happened to Red? We have to save him!" I pulled and pushed, punched and kicked, but nothing would get the barrier to move. I stepped back dejectedly.

"I'm sorry, but... we're going to have the same fate as him if we don't leave. Come on." I could barely think, breathe, or move—to a point where Damien had to grab my wrist and drag me out of the hallway, quickly pulling me along. I stared back at the door frame, my jaw trembling, my arms shaking, and my legs weak. I felt broken, useless, and helpless. He was gone... just like that.

My vision was blurred from tears, but I forged ahead. Unless there was somehow a pocket of air, there was no way he was alive.

"We should have gotten out quicker," I whispered. "I knew the room was crumbling, I should have made sure everyone was hurrying out. He saved me, I could have saved him."

"Shh, it will be okay. It's not your fault. Blaming yourself and reflecting on the past isn't gonna do—" he paused, pulling me backwards as a plate from the ceiling crashed down in front of us. "Anything. It won't change what happened. We have to focus on the future, the path ahead. We... we have to tell the hidden village about this as well. I spent quite a bit of time there, and Red seemed to be their leader of sorts, though everyone independent enough to survive on their own. But we also have to figure out who stole the last weapon, and if they're alive and outside or not. We have a lot more to focus on, so... we have to mourn later." I could tell he was suppressing tears, and everyone else's faces seemed glum, even Seth, who was walking slightly behind everyone. I nodded, standing taller, picking up my pace. We burst through the dark hallway, and out the door just as everything crumbled, collapsing in an instant. I held my head in my hands, sighing sadly. Jay stood next to me, putting his hand on my shoulder in a comforting gesture.

"What do we do now?" I said weakly, not feeling up to much at all.

"Harlequinn, look around the debris for any signs of human life. Jay, circle the building and see if anyone or anything escaped. Seth... follow one of them. I'll stay with Amber and think of our next step." The two boys nodded and marched off, while Damien crouched at my side. "Hey... it will be okay. This is why we fight the Kingdom. They created this mess, we have to strike back, and now that we have you... we actually have hope we can do that. You inspired everyone and sparked some hope. You called the Elites, who have been a big help. You're incredible, and you've already gone through so much, taking so much heat and nearly being killed... you're strong. I know it feels bad now, but we have to take a deep breath and find the positives. Okay?" I blinked, barely processing his words, but nodding anyway. As soon as everything registered, I was confused about one thing.

"Wait... this is the Kingdom's fault? Did they create the Pyramid? I thought this was one of our... bases," I questioned.

"When the newer Kings were brought into power, a lot of people tried to rebel. A group of fighters snuck into the castle, stealing powerful weapons and hiding them in places like this. Unfortunately... most were caught later, and corrupted. The King used his dark magic to mutate their souls, turning them into that black matter, and shoving them inside Knights suits, bringing the armor to life, and taking over operations here. But, he couldn't completely turn them to his side, so they attack anyone who comes in."

"Most of them were caught?" I said with a questioning glance. "Does that mean some of them are still out there?"

"I—I guess so."

"Does that mean we could possibly find them? If they got in and stole stuff once, they could know the way again and help us launch a surprise attack."

"That's... actually a good idea. We need to sort a lot out first, but we can try to get in contact with them," Damien paused, smiling slightly. "I'm glad to have you back, Amber. We all are. I'm sure everyone's going to be really excited to see you, especially Aaron. He's barely been sleeping, trying to contact you every second since you talked that one time. We haven't been able to take him on any adventures, it's been so bad."

"Ugh, I feel horrible about that," I sighed, gazing into the dark sky. "I left so many things behind. Everyone at the camp, Aaron, and I... I didn't want to leave you guys so open. I might have made this fight worse, threatening the King..."

"Wait, what?" Damien stopped me, looking at me in shock.

"Oh, you didn't... know about that?" I asked sheepishly.

"Guys!" Harlequinn shouted, rushing towards us. "Jay found someone, come on!" Damien and I looked at each other, then ran around the crumbled Pyramid, following behind Harlequinn. As we rounded a corner, we saw someone pinning Jay to the rubble. They were tall, and seemed to be strong. A mask covered most of his face except eyes, and his shaggy, untrimmed hair hung low. He had small bits of armor on, and a glowing ring on his fist, which was raised above Jay's face in a menacing gesture. His arm flickered, suddenly covered in a thin sheen of glimmering magic, creating the form of a bigger fist.

"One of the weapons!" Damien pointed out. I unsheathed my

sword, praying this would work, and driving my blade into the soft dirt. Flames exploded beneath the earth, curling around my arms and traveling through the ground, covering the distance between us all in a split second, blasting the enemy off of Jay with one fell swoop. I rushed in, grabbing Jay's arm and lifting him up, then turning to face the attacker, who was writhing on the ground.

"What was that?" he screeched, one of his gloves smoldering and a large tear in his clothes on the side of his stomach.

"Fire, you dimwit. Ever heard of it?" I growled, the feeling of anger rising quickly.

"Not really, we use electricity, unlike you savages," he snarled, and I rolled my eyes, lifting my sword as it burst into flames. I held the point to his throat, glaring down at him. "You bunch don't scare me. You're just kids, hiding in the woods and playing pretend."

"Does this look fake?" I asked, smirking as I shoved my sword closer to him. He winced as the heat started to burn.

"I refuse to be afraid of a child, especially one of your... reputation," he hissed, holding his ground.

"I guess we're famous," Damien commented slyly. "Hurray."

"Not in the slightest. Your kind is-"

"Our kind?" I laughed. "Last time I checked, we were humans, just like... anyone else. But I guess that's not true anymore. Hey, if we're not going to be human, I wanna be a dragon."

"Stop this useless chatter! You pests will suffer at the hands of—"

"Who talks like that anymore? And you say we're savages. What century are you living in, dude?" I rolled my eyes, winking at the others gathered around me. This guy had quite the temper, so it would be easy to make him angry, which would make it harder to think or act rationally.

"A century much further in the future than you scoundrels! We actually have light! And defenses that aren't disgusting magic! We have promise, and hope for a future that isn't riddled with death! Just like your friend in there, crushed by a magical trap!" I turned back towards him, barely even able to control my expression. There must have been an evil glare on my face, because he quickly quieted down, sinking further into the floor, his expression dropping.

"And you don't hold the blame for that? You took the weapon, you caused all of this. You have no room to talk. Where you come from, you don't even know what basic decency is. So you have more lights, what does that count when you're talking about humanity? What do you have to brag about that isn't electronics? You have cold, dead, robotic people with no emotion that turn a blind eye to war and death. There's nothing to be proud of," I spat, my face flushing. "And now you've made me angry." I dropped my sword, rage coursing through me as I held my hands above my head, feeling heat spread over my skin as the flame armor I produced before molded itself into me. Wings sprouted from my back as I grabbed the attacker, pulling his shirt and launching myself into the air.

"Whoa—what are you—" He was cut off as I smacked him against a tree branch, shutting him up. The sudden rise made me feel nauseous, as well as my mana quickly draining, but I knew I wouldn't spend much time up here.

"This is your warning, but it's gonna hurt, a lot. Run back to your precious, dull Kingdom and tell everyone what you saw. You won't be on top soon enough—I'll make sure of it. We won't give in, and we'll fight for the countless lives lost in this pointless battle. Oh, and tell the King I said hello, and soon goodbye." I smiled kindly, reaching out and taking the ring from his hand. He struggled in my grip, trying to claw his way out, but I raised my arm, gazing over the trees and towards the castle. I leaned back slightly, and threw with all my might. As soon as he left my grip, I felt my armor falter, and I started to descend. Before I fell beneath the leaves, I heard a boom, and saw smoke start to rise from one of the tallest towers. I went down with a satisfied smile before I reached the ground, fighting unconsciousness as soon as my body hit the floor. I heard yelling, and opened my eyes to see everyone huddled around me, even Seth.

"Okay... where did you go and what happened to you, because I have never seen you, or anyone else, really, do something like that!" Damien exclaimed.

"That was intense, Amber. You threw him into the castle!" Jay laughed. Harlequinn smiled, and impressed and proud look on his face.

"I—I don't..." I couldn't finish my sentence before my head lolled to the side, exhaustion taking over as my eyes fluttered shut.

CHAPTER SIXTEEN

I woke up abruptly, in a place I didn't recognize. I sat up, examining the small cabin I was in. Dust hung in the air, and the wood seemed old, and worn out in a way. A lantern dangled from the ceiling, dimly lighting the room. I was sitting on a mattress, laid out on the floor, a pile of clothes next to the bed. It seemed to be replicas of the tattered clothes I was wearing now, but I didn't get how or why they would give me the same clothes, but I didn't question it for long. I quickly got changed, noticing I no longer had my sword or gauntlets. I groaned in frustration, and looked around for a door or even a window, but strangely, there didn't seem to be either.

"Uh... hello?" I called, hoping that I hadn't gotten captured, and worrying my shouting would draw monsters if any were around. Luckily, there was no such reaction, and one of the walls began to fade, revealing a hidden door. I stepped through, into what seemed to be... a festival?

Fairy lights were strung across the trees, but not lit by electricity. I didn't see the source of power, but I enjoyed the sight of the small, colorful lights. Tables of food were set out everywhere, and there was faint music playing. The crowd wasn't too large but also not too small, and people mingled throughout the village. The sun had set and stars dotted the sky, cheerfully shining through the midnight abyss. I felt a weight on my shoulder, and turned to see Damien, smiling widely.

"You're awake!" he exclaimed.

"Uh, yeah... where are we? And what happened to my stuff?" I asked, confused.

"Oh, we took away your weapons for repairs. The sword needed to be reinforced to handle all the heat your fire emits, and your gauntlets needed to be cleaned and restored. We're in the hidden village though, where Red lived. This party is for him." Damien's face fell slightly as he looked into the trees.

"A... party?" I questioned, wondering how badly I hit my head.

"The people here don't like traditional funerals. Instead of mourning, they celebrate the life and accomplishments of the person. They use this time to create joy instead of reminiscing on a sad event or past. It keeps spirits high, especially with the loss of a figure like him."

"Well, that's a good idea. Celebrate life instead of looking back on death."

"Yup. They have a small area that's set up like a funeral, with a coffin. Though... he's not in it. We couldn't sift through all the rubble, so we..." he paused, putting his hand over his mouth. I nodded, giving him a quick hug.

"I'm gonna go see what's going on over there, then," I said, knowing I should probably leave Damien alone for a bit. He seemed insecure or ashamed of showing emotion around people, and I didn't want to make him feel worse about crying. I wandered the camp, taking everything in before I saw it.

A little arch of flowers was positioned over a casket, half buried in the ground. I stood at the edge of the ditch, gazing sullenly at an empty coffin. Someone sauntered over, standing beside me. I barely paid attention until he spoke.

"How did you know Red?" he asked nonchalantly.

"Uh, I—he arrested me actually," I giggled, reminiscing on our first meeting. "He thought I had enslaved an animal, but it was actually my wolf companion, Aster."

"Ah, so you must be Amber." I turned to face the mysterious stranger, and almost bumped into his hand as I swiveled. His arm was outstretched in a friendly gesture, a soft smile on his face. He was tan, with dusty blonde hair and a tall, lean body. He wore a leather jacket over a simple gray shirt, and denim jeans. He had a casual posture, but a sad look in his blue eyes. I took his hand with a nod.

"That's me," I said, and our arms both dropped to our sides. "How did you know him?"

"I don't know if he said anything about me? I'm Mark. We were platonic partners," the guy said with a shrug. "Not exactly dating, but different than simply being friends. He didn't really experience the type of attraction you usually would in a romantic relationship, but he wanted someone to be closer emotionally with, and do things you wouldn't always do with friends. I was a bit confused about it at first, but I liked him, so I was all for whatever he wanted to do. He helped educate me very quickly." I could see how much he cared for Red by just his expression. His eyes softened, he laughed quietly while he glanced down into the coffin. I felt slightly guilty, and I wondered if he knew what happened. If he knew I was there, but couldn't save Red.

"I'm... sorry for your loss," I choked out, and he pursed his lips.

"He didn't deserve to go out the way he did." Mark sighed, his hands in his pockets. "He always believed in an afterlife, though. He started telling me a lot recently that... when he died, he would try to speak to someone, anyone he could. A god, an angel, someone who could get a message across, and he would tell them that Earth needed help. Things needed to be better in all dimensions. Maybe... now he's gotten a chance to do that. Maybe his death was to make our life better."

"I'm sure he's somewhere, trying to make a difference. He did that when he was alive too. He was always really brave, standing at the frontlines, fighting until he couldn't." Mark nodded in agreement, sighing.

"I wish I was more like him in that way. I'm a coward, I'm always scared and I'm not strong or courageous like he was. Though I'd like to think I'm smart. I'm an engineer, and a master at complex science and even have a good grasp on the magic here. I want to help, I want to do what he was doing, and I heard you're the General, so... if there's anything I can do, I'm open to helping, even if it costs me my life." He turned back to me with a determined look.

"And you said you aren't brave," I said quietly. "Offering to do that is bravery. It's not just being unafraid, but willing to take the risks despite any fear."

"I swear I've heard that before," he said with a smirk. I shrugged nonchalantly.

"Maybe it's cliché, or a common saying, but it's true," I said. "And we'll take all the help we can get if you want to assist. This battle is going to be... very long, draining, and difficult. The King is powerful and has a lot of people working for him. Our only hope is to get as many allies as we can on our side, and launch a massive attack."

"Be careful with who you talk to. In these woods, there are countless tribes, villages, and even some small cities. There are a lot of different people, some who side with the King and his oppressive ways. You'd need a mind reader to tell the good and the bad apart, a lot of them are incredible at acting," Mark sighed, pursing his lips.

"Lucky for us... my friend has telepathy powers. I wasn't aware that some people here would support the King, though. Thank you, that could have led us down a dangerous path," I chuckled nervously. He nodded with a kind smirk.

"Well, I'll leave you be. It was nice meeting you, Amber. I hope our paths cross again soon." Now a much more cheerful expression plastered across his face, he waved as he walked away. I returned the gesture, slowly heading in the opposite direction to look for Damien. After a few minutes I saw Jay and Harlequinn, but I decided it was best not to bother them. They were sitting across from each other at a wooden table, holding hands and laughing. I smiled to myself slightly, before moving on, trying to peer over the crowd. My height made it to where that was nearly impossible, so I stuck to aimlessly wandering in hopes of spotting him. I felt a tap on my back, and turned to face Damien.

"Hey, if you want your stuff back now, here it is," he said, holding my gauntlets, cloak, and the sword inside the sheath.

"Oh, thanks!" I smiled, taking all the items from him and putting them on.

"Have you had a chance to use the cloak yet? We didn't have to repair it at all, but you left it in the fairy realm so I thought I should take it back once you disappeared. It seems to be unused, though."

"Oh! I... honestly, kinda forget about the shield," I admitted sheepishly. He laughed in response.

"Wanna battle? You can try to figure out how to use it properly. It's a bit difficult but I'm sure you'll get used to it soon." I smiled up at him, nodding.

"That could be fun. Powers or no?"

"I think you'd beat me way too easily if you used your power," Damien chuckled nervously. "Let's stick to a regular match, with the exception of your cloak, then we can gather everyone and go home. Deal?"

"Sounds like a plan," I beamed, excited to test myself. "I'll meet you in the forest in a bit, unless you'd like to fight me with your hands." He looked down at his waist to an empty sheath. He groaned, sighing.

"Where did I put that... yeah, it might be a good idea for you to go ahead." We both parted ways, and I headed into the dark forest, the moonlight dimly illuminating the leaves of the trees with a pale silver gleam. I took in the quiet surroundings, happy to be back in a familiar place. I leaned against a tree, listening to the wind pass by and the small animals scurrying on the soft dirt. I perked up, suddenly alert. The rustling I heard wasn't something small, but a very large thing that was far away. The ground started to shake as it approached, footsteps booming. I stumbled backwards, the tree behind me vanishing.

"What...?" I asked myself, steadying my stance. I looked forward, squinting to try to see in the darkness. The forest seemed to be shifting, the dead leaves morphing into thick patches of grass, trees dissolving into thin air and small holes appeared, filling with water. "Not again... how did the change even reach this far?" I yelped, drawing my sword. What was that noise? It couldn't be the forest disappearing- that made no sense. But possibly... a monster?

The grass once again stopped at my feet, creating a perfect line between the grassland and forest. This phenomenon couldn't possibly be targeting, or following me, could it? A small tremor rocked the ground, different from the pounding footsteps. I felt a hot breath on my neck, and was suddenly pushed forward, a strong force throwing me across the border. I screamed, sliding across the ground. I looked up to see a massive Zanzagar, towering over me, its eyes glowing a deep purple. There was something particularly menacing about this specific beast- you could feel its thirst for malicious revenge carried on the soft breeze, an evil presence more prominent than before, radiating off of its skin, every aspect of this creature seemed demonic. A noticeable physical change was that it was bigger than the other Zanzagars, and it was wearing a necklace of skulls. *Human* skulls.

It startled me to see the decapitated heads hanging off of a string, the empty eye sockets looking like their gaze followed my movements. The creature started to move forward, reaching its giant hoof-like hand towards me. I thrust my sword up, stabbing its arm. It shrieked, pulling back and snorting in pain. I stood, nerves starting to shake me, and I was disturbed that my sword didn't dissolve it. I saw lights flickering from the trees behind it, and was reminded of the hidden village. I knew I needed to get this thing away before it possibly killed someone, so... I ran.

I sprinted the other direction, weaving through the dark grass, trying to avoid any ditches. I heard it running after me, getting closer with every step. I made the mistake of looking over my shoulder to see it approaching, then immediately ran into something. I stopped short, falling to the floor with a groan, my sword clattering to the ground beside me. I heard a yelp, and looked up to see a face I recognized, collapsed next to me. He had a slim figure, wearing plain denim jeans and a gray flannel, and he had straight brown hair that nearly covered his eyes, parted to one side, and a slightly squared jaw. Green eyes stared back at me and I pushed away, jumping to my feet. He stood with me, a surprised look on his face.

"Amber?" he said weakly.

"Eli?" I gasped, but before we could say or do anything else, the Zanzagar drew my attention. It raised its leg, bringing its foot down between us. I jumped backwards, once again skidding across the dirt.

"Stay back!" Eli called out, rushing towards the monster. He jumped up, kicking at its thick skin, but the attacks did nothing. He landed beside me with a thud, groaning in pain.

"My knight in shining armor," I scoffed sarcastically, setting my hand ablaze and leaping into the air, using the wind to boost my jump, then shoving my fist directly into the beast's nose. It shrieked, and I landed on its head, setting fire to the coarse hairs on its head. I jumped back down, unleashing a torrent of fire from my palms, blasting the Zanzagar to dust. Eli gaped in astonishment.

"How did you—what?" he gasped, stuttering.

"Magic exists here, blah blah blah. Long story short, you're in another dimension, bad things are happening, don't get in the way and don't try to fight stuff like that. For all we know, you don't have magic and rushing to battle isn't a good idea. Now, we gotta get back."

"Back to what?" he questioned. "Where are we? Why are you here? How can you use magic? That doesn't even exist! Nothing makes sense!" he growled, holding his face in his hands.

"Don't be such a baby," I mumbled. "Calm down."

"I'm two years older than you, last time I checked!" Eli rolled his eyes, and I returned the gesture.

"Doesn't mean you act like it," I hissed. "But, whatever, stay here if you want. It's not just the most dangerous time in this world, you'll totally survive!" I said sarcastically, turning with a flourish. I started to walk back, but I couldn't help stopping, a thought suddenly hitting me. This was the third time a Zanzagar had attacked a newcomer. What could that mean? Why were they targeting people who had just arrived, and how did they find them every time a portal opened? Why were only people I knew coming from the real world?

"I thought you were leaving," Eli called. I scoffed, leaning over and picking up my sword.

"I was thinking," I yelled back, the flat of my blade resting on my shoulder. "See you around. Or maybe not. Probably not," I teased, smirking to myself. A long pause ensued before he spoke.

"Ugh... wait up!" he said, running after me.

"I thought you said you were leaving," I mocked, glaring at him with a pointed look.

"Forgive me for not wanting to die," he mumbled, crossing his arms. He was a foot taller than me, so I had to tilt my head slightly to look him in the eyes, which annoyed me. "I can't believe you're willing to just leave me out here, though."

"I already have one annoyance, I don't want to deal with two," I growled, looking back at Eli. He was scanning the area, shivering a bit. The shirt he was wearing had long sleeves and the night air wasn't cold, so I assumed it was from fear.

"Can you drop the attitude, and maybe explain a little more?" he asked, clenching his jaw.

"There isn't much to explain. This is another dimension, somehow you fell through a portal and got here. Luckily, if I hadn't been standing where I was, you would have been dead," I smirked.

"I could have taken that... thing. What was that, anyway? It was terrifying, and it didn't even look real. If I hadn't touched it, I would have thought it was a hologram or something."

"It's called a Zanzagar. They're vicious, pig-like monsters that for some reason have a taste for new blood. This is the third time they've been hunting people who just came out of the portal."

"The third time? Who else is here?"

"Some guy named Seth," I said disdainfully, knowing full well the two were acquainted and even friends, but keeping up the act. "He's annoying, rude, and a backstabbing liar. Kind of reminds me of you." Eli looked offended for a moment before shaking his head.

"Ignoring that last comment... you know Seth. We go to school together, why are you pretending you don't?"

"Because I've never seen him a day in my life. Must be a different Seth," I rolled my eyes, putting my finger to my lips. "Quiet now. Oh, and you're not allowed to come in."

"Come in where? What are we doing?"

"I said quiet!" We walked the rest of the way in silence before we got to the hidden village. "Don't follow me, or you're dead," I instructed with a stern voice. He put his hands in the air, looking annoyed. I disappeared behind the trees, and heard his gasping and stuttering outside. I ignored all the noise, and went to go find the others.

The festival was being cleaned up, and the sun was starting to come up, slowly rising above the horizon. I found Damien, Harlequinn, Jay, and sadly Seth all grouped together, lifting a table onto a stack. Jay noticed me and smiled.

"Hey!" he waved, and I nodded in greeting.

"We have a problem," I announced, sighing. "There's a new human, from the real world, and another Zanzagar attack. I defeated it, but it was more difficult than before. The monster was taller, and had a skull necklace, so I think it was a different type than the rest, but... I'm worried, because every time someone has come through a portal, there's been a Zanzagar right around the corner." Damien looked shocked, but he put his hand on his chin in a thinking gesture.

"You're right about it being a different type of Zanzagar. Those are called Chiefs, they have thicker skin and more power, so they're harder to defeat. And the portal situation... that is strange. I have no clue what could be happening, though, or why. We should go back to the camp, regroup and figure out our next move." I nodded, almost heading out before wincing and turning back to the others.

"We just have one more problem..."

I led the group outside, to where Eli was examining the trees I stepped through. He jumped back when we exited, passing through the shimmering curtain. He saw Seth, and his eyes widened.

"Seth!" he said loudly, pushing through the rest of us to greet his friend with a handshake.

"Eli! You're here!" Seth smiled slightly. "Finally, I don't have to deal with these people alone."

"I think you forget we're protecting you," I reminded him, trying not to lash out. "We're taking you with us. Let's go."

"No, you can leave. We'd be fine on our own." Seth protested, but Eli looked shocked. "We could survive."

"Come on, the one time I actually offer to help, and now you're saying no?" I crossed my arms, scowling. "There are demons in these woods that wouldn't hesitate to eat you. You're better off with us."

"Guys, enough. Stop your bickering, you're acting like children," Harlequinn scolded, his hands on his hips.

"We... are children," I stated, but my comment only received blank or stern stares. I sighed, crossing my arms. "Whatever. We need to get back to camp, and sort things out. Also, there are a lot of people I want to say hello to."

"What camp?" Eli asked.

"You'll see," I groaned, hoping they wouldn't wreck anything. "Come on, let's go."

"It's a bit of a ways away... Aster disappeared when you did, but maybe if you're back, you can call him?" Damien suggested. I nodded, taking a deep breath and whistling as loud as I could. There was silence for a moment before the rustling of grass caught my attention. A wolf bounded towards me, almost looking like he was smiling as he tackled me. I yelped, but it quickly turned into laughter.

"Hey, boy! I'm back!" I giggled. I looked up to see Eli gaping at the huge dog, and Seth stepped back, still scared it seemed.

"That—what—how... he's so big!" Eli exclaimed. I nodded, standing.

"I never thought I'd see you again," Damien chuckled as Aster rubbed his head against Damien's arm.

"Is he... bigger?" Jay asked, scratching the wolf's ear.

"It looks like it," Harlequinn commented.

"This thing was smaller before?" Eli squeaked. I nodded, smirking.

"He can't carry all of us, maybe two or three, so people are either gonna have to run, or... Damien?" I turned with an expecting glance. He sighed.

"Fine, I can bring some people."

"There's no way you can carry two people," Eli scoffed, crossing his arms. "And I doubt you can run as fast as a wolf."

"I can run as fast as a cheetah if I want," Damien argued, morphing into the wild cat. His ears shortened and moved to the top of his head, fur covered his body and he fell down onto all fours. Sleek yellow fur spotted with black gleamed in the sunlight, and Eli screamed, while Seth stepped back in surprise, somehow still being shocked after spending so much time in the dragon realm, which you would think would be more terrifying than that.

"Show off," I mumbled, giggling. "You can't hold people like that. Are you flying or running?" Damien quickly changed back into a human, and considered my question.

"There's something I've been wanting to try for a while. I think I can basically transform into a perfect copy of things, so if I wanted to, say, be a wolf like Aster..." Damien closed his eyes, placing his hand gently on the dog's side. He trembled for a second, but then grew taller, his back curving and hands turning into soft paws. Fluffy ears and a tail formed, and he morphed completely. The tear in his ear was even the same. I smiled, impressed. He growled softly and Aster howled in response, bouncing in place, obviously excited. "Oh, wait, before we go... Amber, I need to talk to you. Over here?" Damien suggested, padding across the forest floor, gently leading me away from the group.

"Hey, what's up?" I asked, slightly worried. He turned, quickly changing back into a human.

"A lot of things at the camp changed. We got attacked a few times, some people... are no longer with us, and..." he sighed. "The Council was found out. Someone from the Kingdom got into their room, and now they've been forced to disband."

"What? Really?" I exclaimed, putting my head in my hands. "This is awful! Who got in? Did you catch them?"

"It was that one girl Alexander fought. She definitely isn't a mouse anymore," he snarled slightly, the corner of his mouth turning up in a disgusted grimace. "We didn't capture her, though. And the entire camp had to be rebuilt, but... there's not a lot of people now. Some of the less powerful Elites have left, leaving Tigre, Ija, Melioca, Quartz, Shadow and Mirage. We're... really low on recruits, that's why we started going into the woods and trying to get people on our side. It's been difficult, but we've been able to gain allies from three tribes, and a few weapons, like this." He reached into his pocket and pulled out the ring. Now, I could get a closer look at it. There were small engravings on the side, in a language that wasn't English, and the material was a shiny, smooth gold. It didn't look like anything special, but it radiated power.

"Is that the ring from the Pyramid?" I questioned, examining the small object.

"Yeah. This can basically turn your own body into a weapon, as our good friend kindly demonstrated." He put the ring back into his pocket, quickly hiding it. "You can increase your power just by wearing it."

"That's... really cool. But now the Kingdom has a lot of those, don't they?" I scoffed, rolling my eyes. "Well, we'll do what we can. We gotta get back and regroup." Damien nodded, once again shifting into a wolf.

"This war is progressing fast, so it's good to have someone back in charge. We can finally make our move against the Kingdom, and... it's nice to see you again," he said with a smile.

"I agree, I'm really happy I'm back. Now I don't have to be trapped with Seth," I joked, though it wasn't entirely sarcastic. "But it's great to see you guys again, and now I'm definitely fed up with the King. He's hurting so many people... it needs to stop. I'm not forced to stand by and watch anymore, it's time to take action." I looked to the dog with a determined glance, and he nodded.

"They won't stand a chance when they see you coming."

I laughed, nudging him playfully. "Hey, I'll admit, I gotta practice a lot more, even with fire. I'm getting better, but we have a long way to go." We walked back to the group, who was having a small discussion. The talking faded as we approached.

"Hey," Jay said with a wave.

"Hi," I said, returning the gesture. "Is everyone ready to go?"

"I don't even know where we're going," Eli muttered.

"Well, you'll find out," I rolled my eyes, and Aster came up to me, baring his teeth menacingly. Eli backed away slight, and I smirked. "Okay, Jay and Harlequinn can ride with me. Damien, you take Eli and Seth. We'll all meet back at the camp, deal?" Everyone nodded in unison, and I pulled myself onto Aster's back. It was much more comfortable than Berry, and now we were running instead of flying through an abyss. The two boys got on behind me, and I looked back to see Eli and Seth struggling to get up. "Oh, come on... do you need help?" I called angrily. Damien nodded viciously.

"You're pulling my fur. That hurts," he complained, and I sighed, sliding off of Aster's back. "Amber, can you lift them or something?"

"We can get on ourselves," Seth glared at me, then promptly slipped off, and fell over into the dirt. I laughed, offering my hand to help him. He reluctantly took it, and I pulled swiftly, getting him to his feet much quicker than he expected. He winced, holding his arm with his other hand, then stumbled onto Damien's back, clumsily getting up his side.

"What, no thanks?" I asked, scoffing.

"Why should I thank you for almost pulling my arm off?" he said with a pointed glare, raising his eyebrow. I shrugged, slightly amused, before jogging towards Aster, pulling myself up in one swift movement.

"Let's go, then!" I announced, clicking my tongue so Aster knew what to do. He sped off, his wide gait covering much more land in a much shorter time then we could walking or running. We burst out of the forest, Damien and the others close behind. I didn't have to look back to tell, however. I could hear the frightful shrieks rising and figured they weren't very far. My excitement grew as we ran, and I thought of all the friends I wanted to see. Aaron, B,

Alexander, I would even be happy to see Tigre and the other elites. All of them were so close...

We rounded a corner and I saw the broken camp. The walls were almost completely demolished, slowly being rebuilt. The cabins seemed to be intact, but obviously new. The castle was entirely gone, replaced by a smaller building and a few tents outside. We charged through the gate, and I examined the seemingly empty area.

"Hello?" I called, dismounting Aster. Jay and Harlequinn slid off after me. I heard a gasp, and turned to see B, who launched into a hug. I giggled, stumbling and almost falling over.

"Amber! You're back!" she exclaimed, smiling from ear to ear. "I regret the joke I made about you being in my office so much. Please, come any time, just don't leave us like that again." I giggled, and nodded.

"I'm sorry, that wasn't intentional. I wouldn't have left if I had had the choice, but..." I winced, thinking of the attack on the fairy realm and falling into the void.

"I understand. I'm glad you're here now, though!" she beamed.

"Amber?" I heard a soft voice say. I turned to the side to see Aaron, walking towards us from the tents.

"Aaron!" I waved happily, and his jaw dropped. The surprise quickly turned into a grin, and he laughed, running up to us.

"You... you're back! I thought you were dead, after you didn't respond-"

"I'm so sorry, I didn't mean to leave you like that. I... I guess I should explain, now that... we're back... at camp," I said hesitantly. A loud yelp rang out behind the unfinished wall. I turned again to see Damien sliding in, Eli and Seth bouncing around and shrieking. As soon as they went through the gate, Damien turned back into a human, and all three boys went sprawling. I hit my forehead with my palm, sighing.

"Uh... who is that?" B asked, pointing to Eli.

"An annoyance, just like the other one," I scoffed. "Ignore them."

"Wait, is that Eli? Why are you both here?" Aaron asked.

"I could ask the same thing to you!" Eli yelled.

"You all know each other?" B inquired, and I nodded.

"Sadly. We all go to school together, but... they weren't here before, but when the forest started changing, they came with it." I shrugged, and B looked concerned.

"Where are we? What is this? Why is Aaron here? Who is that?" Eli inquired, pointing behind me. I felt wind on my back and turned with a smirk, already giddy imagining the surprised look on Eli's face when he saw the Elite standing (or hovering) behind us.

Melioca floated in the air with an angry, evil look. Her wings were now lined with silver, glittering tinsel-like strands hanging off of the feathers, and her dress was changed too. Blue, layered fabric coated the skirt, different color combinations creating a beautiful gradient. Small blue gems hung from her earrings, now visible since some of her hair was pulled away from her face in a small braid crown at the back of her head. The top of her dress was beaded with pearls in swirling designs, and she had off-the-shoulder sleeves. I was stunned for a moment, but her chaotic, maleficent look was slightly terrifying. I heard a squeak from behind me, and Melioca's eyes widened, almost in anger. She drifted towards the two boys behind me, frozen in shock and fear.

"And you two are...?" she sneered, baring her teeth.

"Have you not met Seth?" I questioned, casually sauntering towards the group.

"No, I haven't had the joy of meeting this rat," she scoffed, turning so she was laying on her back, still floating through the air. "Or the road-kill beside him." I giggled at her insults. The two looked confused, not entirely sure what to do and not wanting to offend this angry, childlike person.

"I'm... I'm Eli. Amber's friend."

"Friend?" I questioned, turning and raising my eyebrow.

"Fine, acquaintance. And... who are—"

"None of your business. Why are they here?" Melioca snapped. I heard a deep chuckle behind her and Tigre walked over, putting a hand on her shoulder and shoving her to the floor.

"Lighten up, kid! They're... kids. Don't take your anger out on them." He smirked flirtatiously in my direction, and I uncomfortably waved.

"I'll do what I want, half-blood," the small girl said, rage filling her voice. She got up, digging her nails into Tigre's skin, drawing blood as he pulled away.

"Ow! How old are you?" he winced, and Melioca smiled triumphantly.

"Older than you," she bragged, tossing her head and walking away.

"We were all created at the same time! Literally! We were born with time!" Tigre threw his hands up in exasperation. "She's impossible," he commented, turning back to us with his hand on his hip.

"Says you," I giggled, and he smiled, revealing a sharp fang on one side of his mouth. "By the way, I'm back."

"I noticed. Where did you go off to in the first place?" he questioned, walking further toward me. I froze, looking around in the crowd of people that were waiting on an answer. "What happened?" he asked, eagerly waiting for my story. I stumbled on my words, unsure if I should tell them the truth. I thought of their land, already chaotic without the help of humans, and from the junk that somehow wound up in the abyss. I didn't want to risk corrupting their world even further.

"I... I fell through a void for a while. A couple of times I passed some islands, but they didn't have anything on them. Seth somehow joined me, and we fell for a long time... then, I popped back up in the fairy realm, and went through the portal. I didn't see him again until the Pyramid," I smiled sheepishly.

"How did you survive that long, with no food and water?"

"I'm... not sure. It didn't seem like much time had passed, so maybe it works differently there. But let's move on from that. I'm back now." Everyone seemed satisfied with my answer, and after various hugs, pats on the back, and a little small talk, the crowd dispersed, everyone going back to their jobs. Except for one face, who stuck by my side.

"What actually happened?" Damien whispered, curiosity shining in his eyes.

"What do you mean?" I laughed nervously. "I told you already."

"Come on, I've known you long enough to see that you're lying. Something was there, right?" he narrowed his eyes, and I sighed.

"What's down there... probably wants to be kept secret. I don't want to risk attacks or even just people exploring. It's better everyone just believes the only thing there is an empty void." He backed away slightly, and nodded.

"I get that. Then I won't press you." He waved, and wandered off. I bit my lip nervously, hoping I didn't make him mad or upset. I felt a small tap on my shoulder, and turned to see Aaron, smiling shyly.

"Hey, Amber."

"Hey! What's up?" I asked with a grin.

"Not much, I just... wanted to say hi again, and hang out. I was really worried when you were gone... it's great to have you back, though." He looked so sad, a sullen frown mixed with anxious shyness, it made my heart hurt. I hugged him, feeling so bad for leaving, even if it wasn't my choice. He seemed surprised, but settled in to my hug, and we stood together for a minute before I backed away.

"I'm so, so sorry. I never wanted to leave, and... apparently it caused a lot of trouble. I—"

"Amber!" I winced, turning to see Damien approaching behind me.

"Can we talk later?" I suggested, but he sighed, crossing his arms.

"It's kinda urgent. Some scouts just got back with a distress call. We're going to the Ice Kingdom." He smirked, but my mind went blank, not knowing what that was.

"Can, uh... can Aaron come with us? I don't want to just leave him again, and he can help." I smiled with a slight begging look. Damien laughed, nodding.

"Sure, we could use his power. But it's going to be a bit dangerous. The Snow Princess has quite a fiery temper, so we're taking Tigre in case things get heated." He giggled at his own jokes, and I stood there with an amused smile.

"Got it. When are we leaving?"

"Soon. Get some food if you need it, but be prepared." I nodded, and he jogged off. I turned back to Aaron, who looked a bit nervous.

"Are you okay?" I asked quietly. He nodded, sighing.

"I just don't know what to expect. No one has ever wanted me along with this type of stuff, even in the Kingdom. I've never had a very important role, so suddenly being thrown into a mission like this is strange." He bit his lip, looking towards the floor.

"Well, now you're with us. We're different, and no matter who you are, you're important, and we appreciate you," I said with a smile, putting my hand on his shoulder. He nodded, the corners of his mouth turning up in a small grin.

"Thanks, Amber. We should get ready." I nodded, patting the belt at my waist, examining my gauntlets, and then putting my hands on my hips.

"Done! Ready to fight some... stuff." I giggled.

"Should I... get a weapon or armor? You guys all seem to have something, but I'm... like this." Aaron gestured to his plain attire.

"Your power is telepathy, right? You can disarm people using your mind, so I think you should be good if we all have weapons. If it ends up turning into a fight, you can just scream at everyone while we attack." We laughed at the image of that.

"I guess... that works. We should probably go wait at the gate, if you don't want food."

"Yeah, I'm good. It's weird. I'm never as tired or hungry here. It's like what I previously needed basically vanishes. Maybe it's the messed up passage of time, I'm not sure."

"Yeah, it took me a while to get used to it. A lot of things can't be explained, thinking about it in logical terms will just confuse you. Trust me, I had a rough couple of months," he chuckled nervously.

"I can imagine. I've always been really involved in fantasy and magic, so a lot of this stuff... it makes sense that it doesn't make sense. I get all of it in a strange way, even though a lot is different from what I usually imagine."

"You did write a lot about magic, didn't you? Sometimes it seemed like you weren't really in our world anymore, like you went off on a fantastical adventure. Now... we're really here." I looked to the sky, watching the white clouds drift lazily across the vibrant blue. I took in the sweet scent of fresh air, the smell the same as if it had just rained. The day was nice, a cool breeze blew away the heat from the blazing rays of the sun. It was peaceful, but I knew that wouldn't last as I saw Damien and Tigre approaching.

"Hey," Tigre greeted with a wink. I brushed off his strange advances and waved.

"You two ready?" Damien asked, leaning casually against the wall.

"It's just the four of us?" I questioned, expecting at least Jay and Harlequinn to come along.

"For now, yeah. It's better if we go in small groups, so we don't attract as much attention, and if things go haywire, not as many people get hurt. We have a long walk, though, we should get going."

"Do we want to take Aster?" I almost called for him, but Damien shook his head.

"The path is complicated. The Ice Kingdom is very well hidden, so you have to know exactly where you're going and follow a precise path. Rushing it or taking animals can ruin the flow, so we wouldn't ever be able to get there." We all started to walk, Tigre slowly following behind us, and Damien in the lead.

"Man, magic is really strange here. It's cool, but a bit weird," I commented, taking a shaky breath.

"Like I said, questioning it isn't a good idea," Aaron whispered, and I nodded. We walked along for a long time, probably upwards of an hour, silently trekking through the forest. Damien kept his head down, mumbling to himself at certain points. All I did was take in the scenery, trying to remember this part of the woods, and the path we were following. It soon became tiring, watching the same thing over and over again. The woods really did seem to be endless.

After quite a while, I could tell we were there. Frost crept along the ground, encasing dead leaves and the bottoms of tree trunks. Everything was coated in a hazy blue, and snow delicately fell wherever the ground was glazed over with ice. The trees inside the little bubble of winter were completely dead, not a leaf to be seen. Few people milled about, but there were plenty of tents and huts set up around the area. The expanse was huge; I couldn't see the end once we got to the edge of the land. What I did see, however, was a giant throne sitting in the middle of the small town. Spires of ice wound their way into the sky, clear like glass. Designs were etched into the smooth substance, creating snowflake-like patterns on the magnificent chair. I marveled for a moment, the throne being the only thing about this relaxed town that stood out. Everything blended in, the same color as the sky even. It gave off a slightly eerie feeling, but we stepped into the bubble.

Immediately, I almost froze. My teeth chattered as I shivered, the intense cold settling on my bones. After a minute the chills went away, and I felt strangely light.

"The magic here will deem if you have pure intentions or not. If you're planning something bad, the cold will freeze your soul and you'll die. If you're peaceful, it will protect you. Hardly anyone comes anywhere near here because of the spells cast on this place," Damien informed me, seeing my confused look. I nodded in acknowledgment.

"Oh," I whispered. "That's... new." I looked to the side, noticing Aaron wasn't with us. I glanced back, seeing him standing behind the blue haze.

"Are you coming?" Damien asked, his gaze narrowing.

"I'm… worried. If I worked for the Kingdom, are my intentions… pure? What if I've been tainted, or something?" he said, shivering.

"You'll be fine. As long as you don't plan on harming anyone here, you won't freeze." Damien shrugged, and Aaron glanced around. I started to become a bit worried, wondering what was actually holding him back. He closed his eyes, stepping forward, holding his hands close to his chest in fear.

"Can you still move?" I asked, getting colder.

"I—yeah. I'm good." He breathed a sigh of relief, steam rising in front of his face. I shivered, crossing my arms. "Are *you* alright?" Aaron asked with a concerned look.

"Yeah, just a bit surprised. I wasn't aware the cold was going to judge my soul. And not to mention, it's freezing here." Everything seemed to glow slightly, the thin layer of untouched snow on the ground barely keeping imprints as we passed over it, like we were floating just above the ground.

"Be careful here. Try not to make eye contact with people. We don't know if—" Tigre started, but he trailed off, his eyes widening in surprise. He froze in his tracks, staring at someone who was steadily coming towards us. He had shaggy, messy white hair and clear blue eyes. He was pale, his skin very faintly tinted blue, and a small splash of freckles across his nose, which was a rosy color from the cold. He was tall, and slightly muscular, but his outfit didn't seem to be fit for this weather. He wore a thin, long sleeved, azure shirt and a fluffy scarf rested across his neck. His pants were made of a similar material, but gray with white snowflakes and snow boots. His hands were red, an almost violent color that made me concerned. Tigre looked at him in shock.

"Frost?" he said weakly, his voice trembling. The guy looked over curiously, a mischievously, childish gleam in his piercing eyes.

"Well, I never thought I'd see you here. Or... ever," he laughed, sauntering over with a slightly amused smile.

"Don't joke. We haven't seen you in thousands of years!" Tigre exclaimed, balling his hands into fists.

"Whoa, hold on. Who is this guy?" I questioned, clenching my jaw.

"He hasn't told you? Good going, Tiger," he chuckled lightly.

"I'm Frostbite. I'm surprised you haven't heard the story of the rogue Elite."

"The... rogue?" I said in surprise. I wasn't aware you even could go rogue with that type of thing.

"Yup. I was tired of being trapped in darkness. Whenever we weren't needed desperately, we hid, sealing away our magic and... essentially sleeping for thousands of years at a time. I didn't want to be caged, so I ran away. In the Ice Kingdom, it's hard to track people; the cold destroys many types of magic. The princess graciously took me in, allowed me a haven as long as I swore to protect her. And now... I'm working for someone else," Frostbite smirked, his gaze no longer playful, but slightly angry or malicious.

"It wasn't that bad. Besides, you abandoned all your friends to work for a child who doesn't understand your true power or what we all are." Tigre shook his head, looking towards the ground.

"I didn't have any friends. Everyone hated me because I liked to do my own thing. I'm more like a kid, not as mature as all of you. Shadow hated me the most; he thinks I don't know how to properly control myself. I do, I just like to play around!" He threw his hands into the air, a condescending look on his face. He took a deep breath, white steam curling through the air in front of his face. "But I'm thriving here now. I told you all I would be fine. My powers haven't been affected, I'm still immortal... life is good." He smiled peacefully, and I noticed how quickly his attitude changed. One moment it was cool, relaxed conversation, then he seemed to get angry, and now... it was like he was half asleep. His energy dropped severely, and his eyes softened, his rage disappearing. It reminded me vaguely of Red, and his quirky personality, at least the first time we met.

"You forgot about us, though," Tigre reminded quietly. "You left us, and we didn't do so well. Word gets around to our enemies, especially if one of our top Elites goes missing. We don't have many people on defense, and in the abyss... darkness is the source of our most powerful enemies. Your Ice Barricade and protection spells were our main source of defense."

"Wait, what?" I questioned. "You can use ice powers for protection?"

"I bet that's also how this place stays so safe," Tigre said with a blank face, his eyes cold. "He can fight like a demon, but his physical spells are even more powerful. He can use Ice Barricade to create a force field, trap enemies, and it's practically unbreakable. Not even the hottest fire can melt it. And the cold that judges your intentions? Another one of his party tricks." Frostbite smiled slightly, obviously pleased to have his abilities bragged about.

"I always told you guys that you needed to upgrade security. I can't be the only one relied on! I'm not reliable at all!" he said with a laugh. "Whatever, what's done is done. I'm guessing you didn't come here to get me; based on your reaction, you didn't even know I was here," He said stiffly, crossing his arms.

"No, this was just chance. We're here because of the war with the King. We're trying to gain allies and take him and his Kingdom down," Tigre replied.

"Well, tough luck. We're a little busy here ourselves. Somehow, the Ice Queen is back."

"She—what?" Damien gasped. He wasn't paying much attention before, but that one name got him to listen. "I thought she was killed, or sealed away hundreds of years ago."

"She was, and that's the problem. You're lucky you weren't here two days ago when she realized what we had done and... now a lot of people are dead because of her rage. We're struggling to keep under her radar, and the princess is basically being held hostage by her. We have no clue why she's here, or h—wait..." Frostbite muttered to himself for a second, before turning to me. "Who are you, why are you here, and where did you come from? The feedback from my spells is... confusing, and you're the source of the bug."

"I'm... I'm Amber. I'm the new General at this camp, right outside the woods. I fell through a portal to get here, but I'm still not sure exactly what happened with that," I laughed nervously.

"So... you're not from this world, but you're human. You're from a place with no magic, yet have incredible power. That doesn't make sense, you shouldn't have any powers, and if you did, it would be weak. You must have upset the balance, you're the reason everything is out of place. You..." Frostbite angrily pointed an accusing finger towards me. "You're awaking forces that shouldn't be awake right now."

"Me?" I squeaked, shrinking back from his touch.

"You shouldn't be here. You're throwing the universe off, and bringing back dangerous entities."

"Wait a minute!" Damien interrupted. "You can't just say that, you have no reason to believe that. There was a prophecy that foretold them coming here, and being the new General of our camp."

"And when was the last time we saw an Oracle?" Frostbite pointed out, a cold glare on his face. Damien paused, at a loss for words. "I'm immortal, I've seen everything in this world, and I know the timeline. I know more than the rest of the Elites, because I've been out in the real world. The Oracle's appearance is also a bad sign. Things that have been sealed away are now breaking out. The Ice Queen is back, and that... that isn't good!" He shook his head exasperatedly.

"Why... isn't it good?" I asked tentatively. "I know you said she was angry before, but she's the Queen, right? The leader of this place?"

"The Ice Queen is similar to the King. She's very malicious and lets power go to her head. She thinks she's above the law and no one can stop her because of her power," Damien said, biting his lip.

"But, wait, if I have fire powers, could I have a chance of defeating her?"

"You have... what?" Frostbite looked at me with an almost fearful expression. I held out my hand, a small flame flickering on my palm. He stepped back, almost hissing in surprise. "Put that away! You'll be arrested!" I quickly doused the fire, the urgency in his voice shocking me.

"Sorry, but... yeah, I have elemental powers. Fire is the element I have the most control over," I said with a shrug.

"And elemental is the four elements, correct? So you have water as well?" I nodded, raising an eyebrow. Where could he be going with this? "Water is in snow, so if we were to protest, you could use her powers against her." I perked up in surprise. I never thought about using the elements to control other things that weren't purely water, fire, earth or air. I put my hand on the ground, feeling the melting snow beneath my fingertips. I concentrated, trying to direct my power into the ground. The snow began to rise, swirling through the air as I directed it.

"I... didn't think I could do that," I commented in awe.

"Great, now we have two oppressive hierarchies to bring down. Piece of cake," Damien mumbled. "I hope you know what you're getting yourself into here."

"Probably not!" I beamed. "But if it helps people, it's worth it. And besides, this is a good way to get the Ice Kingdom on our side, right?" I asked, turning to Frostbite, who shrugged.

"They'd definitely be grateful, especially the princess. She despises the Ice Queen, and getting rid of her or even taking her down a notch would be much appreciated. So if anything, it's a good start," he sneered.

"Then we have a plan," I smirked. "Frost, are you in?"

"First, don't call me Frost. Only Tiger gets to do that. Second, I wouldn't miss this," he laughed, holding out his hand in a friendly gesture. I took it, and we shook.

"Hey, I guess we found ourselves on a team together once again. We're just meant to be!" Tigre giggled. Frostbite rolled his eyes, but he had a slight, amused smirk on his face.

"Don't get too excited. I'm not going back to the Elites, and I'm only doing this for my princess." I raised my eyebrow, and Tigre seemed to have the same idea. Aaron almost choked, and I assumed he was reading Frostbite's mind. Damien, however, looking confused.

"Oh, I see now why you wanted to be here," Tigre teased. Frostbite tilted his head, a puzzled gleam in his bright eyes. "My princess, oh, my princess! Let down your hair!" He laughed maniacally, and I couldn't help but chuckle. Frostbite's cheeks turned red as his eyes widened, his face flushed and he looked embarrassed.

"It's not like that!" he protested, shoving away from our group. "I have a duty to her as a guard. I need to protect those that I serve."

"Right, I bet there's nothing going on between you!" Tigre put his hands in the air mockingly. "No romantic, shared looks as you pass each other. No flirtatious waves, no sweet smiles, no thoughts of her running through your head at every second." As he rambled on, I saw Frostbite's face soften, ever so slightly.

"Tigre, leave the poor man alone," I giggled. "We want him on our side, not trying to kill us."

"Fine, but he knows I'm right." Tigre winked, and Frostbite's expression stiffened.

"We need an actual battle plan, a course of action, not just you teasing me," he pointed out, blushing. "I'll take you to meet the princess. But we'll need a distraction... she's being held in a vault, beneath the ground. I haven't even been able to reach her; she's heavily guarded." I thought for a moment, then looked back to Aaron and Damien.

"What if you two created the distraction?" I suggested. "Damien, you can draw attention by turning into a bear or something, and Aaron, you can do that scream thing. We can get in, and get out."

"Wait, I was just thinking of introducing you all, not planning a prison break!" Frostbite exclaimed.

"Well, we like to think outside the box. Go big or go home, am I right?" I shrugged.

"Is go home an actual option?" he sighed, and I shook my head.

"You're stuck with us, buddy. Welcome to the team," I said with a bright smile. He groaned, but looked like he gave in. "Can you lead us to the princess? Damien can rush in, confuse people, Aaron can scream, then the three of us can run in and steal the princess." I paused, thinking of how strange that sounded when I put it that way.

"You'll be her knight in shining armor. Maybe you can carry her out, like a newlywed couple, running into the sunset." Tigre nudged Frostbite's arm, who furrowed his brows and turned away. Tigre looked almost disappointed, and his expression dropped.

"I'll take you, but be careful. And don't look anyone in the eyes." He started to walk away, arms crossed.

"What did I say when we got here?" Tigre joked. I hadn't been around him much, but he seemed to be in particularly high spirits right now. Reuniting with an old friend must have really made him happy. He wasn't even being creepy or flirtatious. That was replaced by a childish, giddy look.

We followed Frostbite through the barren camp. Snow was everywhere, making it a bit difficult to see. We passed the empty throne, and it felt almost... ominous. I couldn't shake the eerie feeling that someone should be sitting there. Instead, it remained empty, watching over the land, looming silently, casting a slight shadow on the ground behind it. Frostbite turned to face us as we walked, putting his finger gingerly to his lips in a quieting gesture. He took one more step, and sank through the ground. Tigre followed with no hesitation, slipping through right where his friend had. Then it was the three of us left above, a little hesitant. Aaron seemed to be the braver one in this situation as he leapt into the ground, and after seeing him jump down, Damien and I quickly followed suit.

We landed in a humid hallway, the walls coated with wood planks. The air was stuffy, which made it a bit hard to breath. We silently crept along the path, trying to slip silently through the shadows. There was no sound except for our footsteps, the clicks quietly echoing through the tunnels, which made it difficult to be stealthy. I was nervous about the sound, but Frostbite didn't acknowledge it at all as we crept along. I tried to take everything in but there wasn't much, just one long hallway. Up ahead, I heard water flowing, like a waterfall. It got louder and louder as we approached, and the tunnel opened into a large room.

It was well lit, with branches and vines climbing across the walls. Moss spread at the base of the wall, and there were two small ponds on either side of the room, a thin path leading to another door at the end of the room. It was an iron door with bars, and the wall was made completely of stone. Two guards in beautiful, icy armor stood guard, holding what looked like giant icicles shaped like spears. The armor was blue, with spiked shoulder pads, helmets that covered their faces, and whimsical, swirling designs on the metal. They looked like they were dozing off, their heads nodding forward before they quickly snapped back into place.

"Are they tired?" Aaron inquired. Frostbite nodded.

"Probably. They don't get breaks, and they don't switch out. Those two have probably been guarding nonstop for two days," he sighed. Aaron nodded.

"Well, that's good for us. Tired people are easier to influence, I can get in their head much faster and the screaming also shocks them, so... overall, it's more effective."

"That's fortunate," Frostbite smirked, an excited gleam dancing in his eyes. "This will be quick."

"Damien, what animal?" I asked, turning to him. He stuttered for a moment, before shrugging.

"I guess... an ostrich would probably be confusing," he giggled.

"You never turned into a unicorn and danced in front of the camp. This is the second best place," I reminded him with a smug look. He blanched.

"When did Seth ever betray us though?" he asked nervously.

"You weren't with him when I was. Also, he pushed the door closed when we went to rescue the General, remember?" I whispered.

"I thought you were the General," Frostbite commented, looking a bit confused.

"I am, but before, there was... another General. Whatever, Damien, just be a dancing unicorn." He sighed in frustration.

"Fine!" he exclaimed, throwing up his hands. He started to morph, a horn sprouting from the middle of his head, his hands turning into hooves, and a beautiful rainbow mane and tail instantly grew. His fur was clean and white, cropped close to his body. He tossed his head majestically and then trotted up to the guards, whinnying urgently. The two perked up, and seeing the obnoxious horse approaching, raised their hands in unison. Some stone from the wall peeled off, leaving the room completely intact somehow, and then it closed in on Damien with a loud bang. The rock fell to the floor, my friend nowhere to be seen. I shrieked, unable to keep in a scream. Was he... dead?

I stood, frozen in fear, my mind racing while the others leapt into action. Frostbite leaned down and froze the walkway, sliding on the ice so he ran faster. Aaron stood beside me, focusing, but it didn't seem to hurt the guards. They moved slowly, their hands shaking and limbs rigid, but it didn't completely stop them. Tigre rushed in after his friends, the eye on his tiger side glowing menacingly. His claws grew and he snarled, roaring. He slashed at one of the guards, making his helmet spin as Frostbite froze their boots so they couldn't move.

One of the guards raised his spear, pressing down on the middle. It steamed for a second before becoming an ice axe. Tigre and Frostbite kept slashing, freezing, and using brute force, but the guards seemed unaffected. My fear settled inside me, becoming a bubbling pit of rage. I felt my hands start to heat up, and flames burst from my palms, a raging bonfire on each arm. Aaron stopped straining beside me, and yelped.

"Move out of the way!" he yelled, and the two elites looked back to see me, encased in an inferno. They blanched, eyes going wide and faces turning white as they dove to the side. Frostbite flung himself into one of the pools, freezing the top, while Tigre pressed himself against the wall. I screamed, letting the fire flow across the room, racing towards the two guards. The heat was so intense, their weapons immediately melted as I stepped closer. My gauntlets started to buzz, and I held out my hands, flames bursting from my palms in a wave of power. I felt my emotions take over as the heat grew, but the guards didn't run for cover. They held up their fists, prepared to fight, but I got to them first. The blaze smacked into them, digging beneath their armor and setting them ablaze from the inside. It was a little horrifying to watch, but they melted into the floor, their armor sitting in a pool of bubbling water.

Silence followed, a stillness that unsettled me. I heard ice breaking, and saw Frostbite emerge from his pool, the water overflowing from the melted ice.

"So... they were golems," he commented, jumping out of the pond, somehow completely dry. "Fueled by the Queen's power—I'm surprised you were able to defeat them." His voice shook ever so slightly, and he looked concerned, not willing to step near me. I looked down to see my gauntlets were still red, soaking up heat from my arms.

"Did... did Damien...?" I looked around, tears rolling down my face silently. I didn't see him anywhere, and I didn't want to look under the rocks in case it was a gruesome image. I turned away, gripping my face as I tried to not scream.

"Guys!" I heard a small voice say. All heads turned to the ceiling to see... a spider? "I'm right here!" it said, the tiny thing crawling above our heads.

"Damien? What? How did you—what?" I gasped, confused but also overcome with joy. The arachnid jumped, falling towards the floor, changing into a human so the landing was soft.

"Right before they closed me in, I turned into a spider. The stone is uneven, see? So there were multiple tiny air pockets I could hide in. Once they fell, I crawled away. I was going to help, but I saw you and decided it would be best to stay out of the way," he said sheepishly. I breathed a sigh of relief, then launched into a hug.

"I thought you were dead!" I punched him lightly in the shoulder.

"I know, I know, I'm sorry," he laughed. "But we should get on with the mission. We've caused a lot of chaos, and probably attracted some unwanted attention." Frostbite put his hand on the stone wall, and it froze over instantly, a smooth, glossy coat swallowing the stone. He then punched the wall, and it fell apart.

Inside the small room was a girl, probably around eighteen. Her smooth, long hair was an icy, electric blue, and her eyes a similar color. Her skin was extremely pale, almost a blinding white. She wore a crown made of clear ice, the band going around her head and a jewel resting in the middle of her forehead. Her dress was fluffy and looked warm, with many layers, all different shades of blue, and she had on white, elegant gloves. She was curled up in the corner, and as we entered, she looked up in fear before relaxing as she saw a familiar face.

"Frost!" she exclaimed, lighting up, her features delicate and soft, she had a button nose, a round face, and sweet, caring eyes. As she stood, I saw her hair go down nearly to her ankles. She launched into a hug, embracing Frostbite.

"Princess! I'm glad you're safe," he said gently, smiling. "We're here to rescue you. These are some of my friends, they helped me break you out and defeat the golems."

"Is that what that heat was? I could feel it in here! I was afraid I would melt," she joked, pushing her crown back into place. "Hello, everyone. I'm Princess Kiara, of the Ice Kingdom," she announced, holding her head high in a regal fashion, poised and perfect, her lips pursed ever so slightly.

"A pleasure to meet you, Princess," I said, bowing my head. "I'm Amber, the General of a camp just outside the woods. These are my friends, Damien, Aaron, and Tigre."

"Well, it's *ice* to meet all of you." The princess giggled at her joke. "What camp, exactly? Does it have a name?" I paused, looking to Damien, who shrugged.

"We've never called it anything except camp. We haven't had much friendly contact with people on the outside, so we just refer to it as it is, not with a name."

"It had a name before. Don't tell me you all forgot!" Frostbite exclaimed. I looked to him in confusion. "When it was first formed by us, the Elites, we called it Utopia, because it was a safe haven for us and others. I really can't believe everyone forgot," he scoffed.

"That wasn't the official name. Only a few of the Elites called it that, and you were not included," Tigre smirked. "But it was common to call it Utopia."

"So... would we say we're from Utopia? Camp Utopia? The Utopia? Utopia doesn't sound like a word anymore," I said, crossing my arms.

"The Utopia, probably. We don't have time to discuss this now, though. We should get going," Frostbite reminded us. I nodded, and we started off, sneaking through the hallway once again, the Princess at our side. The tunnel ended, and everyone else simply jumped into the ceiling and disappeared. I was the last to follow, but as soon as I reached the surface, something felt... off. Frostbite covered the Princess with his scarf, to hide her face. We snuck through the village, everything seeming still and silent, but it was more ominous this time. The frost in the air seemed to dig deeper, passing through our clothing with ease and gripping to our bones. Even Frostbite seemed to notice, wrapping his arms around the Princess to keep her warm, and everyone else was shivering a bit more. I felt the earth tremble, and looked around cautiously.

"You thought you could get away with her?" a smooth voice echoed through the village. "Nice try, but sadly, you can't escape me." The person giggled maniacally, their voice regal even while cracking up.

"The Ice Queen," Frostbite snarled.

"Yes, it's me, dear. I see in my absence, my daughter has decided to get a little... close... with someone who isn't of royal blood!" The voice rang out cheerily, with a hint of malice. "Let's fix that, shall we?" The ground ruptured, a thick wall of snow growing between the Elite and the Princess. They both shrieked, thrown off of their feet and tossed several hundred yards away from each other. I almost reached out to help, but held back, unsure of what I could do or what backlash my actions could have. Tigre, however, did not seem to think it through as much.

"You hag! Don't touch my friend!" he snarled into the sky.

"Hag? Really? You confuse me for a mirror, darling." She giggled, and the snow once again retaliated, throwing his body into the air like it weighed nothing, and trapping him inside a cube of ice. He froze with a shocked expression on his face. I yelped, surprised at how quickly an Elite was taken out. Two, even. Frostbite was sprawled on the floor, not moving, and the same with the Princess. It was only me, Damien, and Aaron left. I barely dared to move, intimidated and frightened by the sheer power of the Ice Queen. And by her tone, she was just toying with us. "Three outsiders, hmm? Did all of you aid in the Princess's escape?"

"We didn't come here to cause harm. The spells show that, yes?" Damien said tentatively, and the voice paused for a moment.

"You have a point." The snow sped up, swirling in one spot. A figure emerged from the blizzard- an older, put together woman stepped forward. Her hair was white, piled high on top of her head, a crown circling her head, her skin slightly wrinkled, and with piercing eyes. They seemed to be reversed, her pupils blue and her irises a blinding white. Her clothes either blended in with the icy background or were obscured by the stirred up snow, but I couldn't quite make out her outfit in the storm. "But you're sneaking around with the traitors. You must be accomplices."

CHAPTER SEVENTEEN

"We mean no harm," I protested, keeping my voice steady. I stared her down as she approached, a smug look on her face.

"Maybe not to the Princess, or to the village. But to me?" She laughed, gently putting her hand to her lips. "That's a different story."

"How can you tell?" I asked, barely blinking.

"Look at the position you're in, the people you're with, kidnapping my daughter under the guise of kindness. You must've heard I was back from that guard, hmm? Let me guess... I was described as power hungry? Egotistical? Believing I was above the law?" She sighed happily, her tone not at all matching her expression. "You have a bad impression of me. But now, it won't matter, because you'll just be another ice sculpture in my castle." She flicked her hand toward us, the ground shaking and ice growing quickly around us. In panic, I set my entire body on fire, an inferno spitting flames every direction, the heat melting through the snow. The Ice Queen looked up in surprise, shocked to see her attack deflected. I drew my sword, a determined look in my eyes.

"You might want to rethink your plan," I snarled, concentrating my power to my arms. Bands of flames circled my wrists, coating my weapon with a sheen of fire. I tried to focus, not wanting to run through all of my mana at once. The Queen looked almost frightened, the glimmer from the raging blaze reflecting in her light eyes.

"I haven't seen a power like yours in a while," she commented. "Interesting." I waited for her to make a move, but she simply stood there and studied me. I contemplated trying to move the ice and snow, maybe trap her, but I didn't think I could use two powers at once, and if I dropped my fire, she would know something was up, so I held my ground. Damien and Aaron gathered behind me, crouched low to the ground. I didn't know if the Queen was planning something, but I didn't want to wait. I swept my sword in front of me, and a line of fire shot through the air, swirling around the Ice Queen. She waved her hand and the snow around her engulfed the fire, steaming in midair. It wasn't around my body, so I didn't know if I could control the fire, but I tried to reach out, strengthen the blaze and make it burst through all of the water. It complied, flaring up and encasing the ice. I smirked and the Queen yelped, stepping back from the heat.

"Don't play with fire, you'll just get burned," I said, smirking, holding a ball of flames in my palm.

"Oh, dear, wait until I stop playing," she giggled, holding up her hand, which started to glow violently. The world around us shook, and a flurry formed around my head, the cold pressing in and starting to suffocate me. I yelped, brushing away the snow with a flaming hand. Icicles protruded from the ground, the size of my entire body, stabbing up at me. I jumped, wincing as one of the points of the icicles nicked my ankle. A gash opened, blood dripping from my leg and onto the white snow, staining the pearlescent slush with a thick crimson.

The wound seemed too deep and too wide for the small touch, but I didn't question it much. I crashed down to the ground, landing in a pile of snow, both cushioning my fall and trying to swallow me. I struggled in the ice's grip, fire spewing everywhere. I felt overwhelmed with all of my surroundings attacking me. I heard a sound above me, like the crackling of ice forming quickly, an almost musical sound, like a wind chime in a howling storm. The fire around me warmed the little pocket I'd become trapped in, and it was almost soothing. If I hadn't been panicking, I might have fallen asleep, the earthen melody nearly lulling me into unconsciousness, the ground encasing me, pulling at my clothes and skin.

I heard screaming, the desperate cries of a friend. I recognized Aaron's voice, his tearful shrieks, and I tried to move, struggling in the ice. I tried to think of my two friends, clinging to life above me, but the ground filled my head with more peaceful images. Flowing creeks, beautiful sunsets, birds delicately soaring through the air.

"Amber!" Through the snow, I heard the murky voice of Damien. He was enraged, scared, I could feel his emotion through the ground. I felt energized, my veins filled with fire, I no longer wanted the earth to take me. I wanted to fight, I wanted to stay alive and beat this tyrannical monster, but most of all, I wanted to return to my friends. I wouldn't be taken away again, I wouldn't disappear, I wouldn't make them worry. I didn't want to do that to them.

I made the heat nearly unbearable. It clung to my arms, seeping into and out of my skin. I settled back into the blaze, and let it consume me, abandoning any fear I previously had of my powers going out of control, letting it burn away with the ice. The capsule around me exploded, snow going everywhere.

"W—what? How?" the Ice Queen exclaimed, demanding an answer.

"You can't keep me down for long," I snarled, launching myself at her. Just before we collided, I remembered my cloaks abilities, and muttered the spell Damien had told me before. As soon as we made contact, a force field exploded around me, and the Queen went sprawling. I laughed, surprised I had been able to time that so well. I looked down to see I was faintly glowing, a soft red color that filled me with warmth. I noticed the Queen had a similar light, except a much more harsh white. We both had slightly celestial auras around us, which I found interesting. "Giving up?" I taunted, watching her struggle to rise.

"Not in the least!" she yelled, thrusting out her hand once again. The snowflakes in the air turned to ice shards, and rained down much quicker, attempting to impale me. I swept my arm above my head, creating something almost like a shield, melting everything so the worst I got was a slight shower. The Queen took it as a distraction, however, and threw herself at me. I blocked, and we clashed, the red and white colliding so there was a thin pink veil between us. I saw the malice in her eyes as she got close, and it was almost horrifying. The energy around us seemed to be fighting more than we were, each color struggling to overpower the other while the Queen and I battled, each attempting to stand our ground, an unstoppable object meeting an immovable force. I felt powerful, but also threatening, pressure weighing me down, adrenaline flowing through me. She suddenly stiffened, clenching her teeth and looking as if she was about to scream. I snuck a glance behind me to see Aaron straining, and I knew he was trying to help me, using his powers to at least help to incapacitate the Queen.

I pivoted, grabbing her wrists and pulling her towards me, shoving her head into the snow below. She shrieked, and I held out my hand, reaching into the snow, manipulating the water inside to freeze further, creating a cocoon around the Queen's head. The ice clouded quickly, building on itself until layers and layers accumulated, trapping her in a chrysalis. Her arms and legs flailed around, free of the freeze, but her head remained stuck. I giggled, amused by the picture in front of me.

I held my hand in front of myself, slowly closing it into a fist. The snow swirled, and I took a breath, the arctic wind invigorating me, power flowing through my fingertips as a pale blue trail circled around my arm, a slight shimmer being left in the air where it went. I closed my hand, punching towards the ground, and the earth ruptured once again. I heard a painful shriek as the Ice Queen went under the wave of snow, swallowed by the very element she controlled.

It was slightly scary, hearing her screams disappear under the blanket, being thrown into the depths of the Earth. I stood in front of the ground, the dirt below me turned up and a patch of ice missing. I sighed in relief, turning as I heard someone stirring. Aaron and Damien had been thrown to the ground, but they slowly rose. I saw the ice wall between the Princess and Frostbite started to melt as they also got up, and Tigre's cage slowly thawed. The sun shone brighter than before, breaking through the heavy clouds above, which were slowly dispersing.

"Uh... what's happening?" I asked, my voice wavering. The clouds seemed to be breaking down into the strange blue that had been swirling around me before.

"It... it can't be," the Princess said, standing. Her hair was now a soft green, down to her waist and braided with flowers. Her eyes were a similar emerald color, and she somehow gained makeup instantaneously. Gold speckled her face, across her nose, and a pastel yellow color eye shadow was blended in with an orange as beautiful as the color of the sky during the sunset, covering her eyelids. Her cheeks were rosier, and her lips shone with a natural pink. Her warm clothes were now replaced with a shorter, layered dress, still a cool blue. Less vibrant and bright, now dulled down, and softer. Her skin was slightly tanner, and she didn't look like she was made of paper anymore. She didn't have long sleeves, and her dress only reached down to about her knees. She had on comfortable flats, the same color blue as her outfit. Frostbite stood, a look of surprise on his face, blush prominently flushing his face. "I didn't think this would happen," the Princess quietly commented.

"What?" I asked, confused and more than slightly worried.

"The Ice Queen's power kept this land encased in snow, even when she was sealed away. It affected all the citizens, and even me. I thought this was only a legend, but..." she paused, marveling at the sudden burst of nature. Trees regained their leaves, growing back quicker than normal, and all the cold melted away. Flowers sprung everywhere, the tents spread around became overgrown with vines, ponds thawed and the chattering of woodland animals filled the air. Birds flew overhead, squirrels hunted for nuts and sunbathed, rabbits hopped around our feet, foxes slunk beneath the shadows, and countless other animals roamed the new area. "She must be dead. Her spell was shattered."

"This is the Lost Land," Tigre gasped, sitting up in a puddle of water. "You... you lived here the entire time?"

"The Lost Land?" Damien gasped.

"I read about that. There weren't many books in the Kingdom, but the Lost Lands were always a big mystery. I think the King was researching it," Aaron commented in awe.

"What are the Lost Lands?" I questioned, completely in the dark.

"An entire civilization lost to the world. We thought it was completely wiped off the map, but... the reason was unexplainable. It just suddenly disappeared, and people claiming to be from the Lost Lands kept appearing, but the stories were very contradictory. No magic detectors worked near the area the Lands were supposed to be, and it became this giant mystery no one could actually explain. And it was a problem, because the Lands provided a lot to neighboring villages. Crops, seeds, pelts, clothing, even tents or some form of shelter. I was only here once, but this place absolutely amazed me. There used to be a giant temple over there, and guest structures there..." Damien spun, pointing out everything that used to be there. I tried to imagine everything he was explaining, and it seemed like before, it was a beautiful, bustling town. The Princess kept her head down the entire time, her eyes watering. "Now... there's nothing here, or around."

"She took over the cities," the Princess exclaimed suddenly.

"What?" Damien said, looking shocked.

"My... my mother. I was just a baby when this place turned. I remember, though, the rage she flew into. She froze and toppled buildings, casting the entire area in a shell of ice, even spreading it to the nearby cities that we used to help. That's why our land is so big, our expanse so vast. We stole the land, and... we killed them." She fell to her knees, sobbing on the soft grass.

"Your mother did that. There's no we, it was her. She was cruel and unjust, you're not to blame," Frostbite calmly whispered. "You were a child when this all went down. Even if you think it's your fault, you're in charge now. Take this time to make change and right the wrongs instead of being sad about it." I nodded, kneeling beside the two and putting my hand on the Princess's shoulder.

"It will be okay. We're here to help, and we can assist at least a little. Even if you just want advice before we go on our way... we will try." She looked up at me gratefully, her eyes shining.

"Thank you," she said softly. "I... I will try as well. I'll lead my subjects to a better future. We will rebuild, and aid you in your war against the Kingdom. We were once a powerful force as well as a friendly one; the villagers can remember who they once were." I nodded, wrapping my arms around her and giving her a hug. She seemed tentative at first about the touch, but then leaned in, and I could almost feel her smiling.

"I can't believe this... we're in the Lost Lands!" Aaron exclaimed, jumping around.

"Did it have a name before? Or was it always the Lost Lands? If that's the case, it was destined to go missing," I pointed out, a bit confused.

"You wouldn't expect an entire civilization to suddenly disappear even if it was named the Lost Lands. This used to be the Valley, though. It has another name but it's in a language that humans don't understand," Damien commented, brushing back his hair.

"So... all of the disappearance was the Ice Queen's fault?" I questioned. "How did she hide the Valley? People would still go to the same spot and see at least all the snow, right?"

"No, she had spells cast over it so only people who either knew the way or took a very specific path could get here. Remember what I was doing on the way over? I was following that path." I nodded, recalling the strange way we got here. I heard rustling and turned to see all the tents moving. Villagers emerged, bright looks on their green faces. They were all of varying height, their skin made of rough bark in different colors. Their arms were flowering, and leaves grew from their head. They were all... trees.

"What—the villagers aren't human?" I asked, realizing my impression of this place had been totally wrong.

"They used to be ice golems. But they're more like nymphs in their original form. Spirits of the forest, here to protect and nurture this place," the Princess sighed, a slight smile playing on her lips. "I missed seeing them like this."

"Well, this has been a wild ride," Tigre said, stretching dramatically. "But sitting around and talking might not be the best idea, especially if we have work to do."

"I agree. We need to move on, and work on getting more allies. Princess... can we count you and your kingdom as one of them?" Damien asked, turning to her with a small bow. She smiled politely.

"Of course. We'd be more than happy to assist in any of your battles. And with the nymphs now awake... you all should go, instead of focusing on us. They can rebuild fast, and easily. I wouldn't want to hold you here." She shrugged, clasping her hands in front of her.

"I... I appreciate it. If you need anything, please try to find us. We'll be somewhere in the woods," Damien laughed. "We'll check in as well. I promise we won't forget about you all."

"Frostbite, you're not staying, are you?" Tigre asked, a pleading look in his eyes.

"I still have a job here, protecting the Princess. My powers might not be as useful now, but... I won't leave her," he said with a small stomp, a determined expression plastered on his face.

"Oh... well, it was *ice* to see you again buddy," Tigre cackled. Frostbite simply rolled his eyes in response. "I hope our paths cross again soon."

"Same here, old friend." Frostbite tentatively held out his arms for a hug. Tigre beamed, launching into an embrace. I smiled, then turned to Damien and Aaron.

"Are we stopping at the camp before continuing on?" I asked.

"We probably should. We need to regroup, figure out where we're going and who we're taking. Or, maybe we should go on a long mission with no clear direction, and bring more people so we're prepared," Damien said with a shrug. "We'll see."

"Alright. We should get going then. Goodbye Princess, Frostbite." I waved, and they returned the gesture.

"Wait, actually," Frostbite said, putting his hand on Tigre's shoulder. "I need to talk to you for a second." The Elite turned, confused, but followed his friend, a few feet away. They started whispering, and Tigre looked shocked.

"Noted," he said, patting Frostbite's back. "Now we can go."

"What was that about?" I asked as we started walking.

"You don't have to worry about it," he whispered, putting his arm around my shoulder in a protective gesture. "Yet." I turned my gaze up ahead, into the forest, glowing with a golden hue as the sun started to set.

We marched through the woods, trying to hurry and beat the darkness. The sun seemed to be resisting itself, barely dipping beneath the horizon before stopping. Time worked so strangely here, I stopped questioning it.

"Do we have any clue where we're going next?" Aaron asked. "And can I come?"

"I have no idea, and probably," I giggled.

"You helped defeat the Ice Queen, I think you've more than proved your spot with us. And your powers are more universal than others. Like, Frostbite is more powerful in the snow. You said your powers work better on those who are asleep, but it works almost as well on conscious people, so it's useful. Just don't tire yourself out- a move like that must waste a lot of mana." I never thought about how draining it might be to use his abilities. I hoped he wasn't overexerting himself for us.

"I'll be okay. I've been doing stuff like this for a while." He winced, probably thinking back to something horrible the Kingdom made him do.

"You used to work for the King, right?" Tigre nonchalantly asked, though I noticed a glare. Aaron nodded, a guilty look on his face.

"I didn't know what he was doing. He convinced me we were the good guys. Amber, though... we captured them and they taught me that you weren't savages bent on absolute destruction, civilization-less monsters that had rabies and were unreasonable—I will stop now." He flushed under everyone's surprised, shocked gaze. We all stopped, our jaws dropping. "I... don't think that anymore, if that's what you're wondering. But most people in the Kingdom probably do. That is... what we were... taught."

"I—wow. Everyone has the wrong impression, then. Why would

the King plant that in their heads?" I sighed.

"He hates us. He wants to see our downfall, and pitting his subjects against us from the get-go is one of his tactics," Tigre snarled.

"Do we know why he hates us so much? What started this?" I questioned.

"Well, we weren't always at war. Long ago, when the General was a kid, I think he was friends with the King. But it didn't last. People say the King was threatened by magic, afraid of being overthrown, and that's where his hatred came from..." as Damien spoke, a sense of familiarity swept over me. My eyes blurred, and I stumbled, closing my eyes for a second. When I opened them... I was in a different world, a different time, in a barren land.

The foundations of buildings rested in the background, surrounding the shells of previous structures, being upgraded or renovated. A boy who looked to be in his teens stood a little ways away from all of the construction. He sat in the grass, a peaceful look on his young face. He had dirty blonde, wavy hair that hung a bit long on the sides. He had plain clothes, a white long sleeved shirt underneath a brown vest, buttoned in the middle, with dirty jeans and work boots. He sat cross legged, his hands resting on his knees, his dark skin shimmering with sweat. The wind ruffled his hair, the grass brushing against his legs. Someone came to sit by him, in a more relaxed position, lying on his side. He had dark hair and eyes, and a tired look on his face. His outfit was similar, but a darker theme, black and blue instead of white and brown. He was tan, but a much different shade than the boy next to him. Even from here I could tell they were polar opposites, their expressions and color schemes making that apparent. Though I could also tell they fit together, like Yin and Yang.

"I thought you said you wouldn't stop working to play." the dark haired one commented, a smirk on his face. Their face structures were similar as well, soft eyes, arched noses, and round faces.

"This isn't playing, this is resting," the other one informed his friend, or possibly brother with how similar their faces were. "If I don't take breaks, we won't get anywhere. I'll be tired and upset with everything, kind of like you, Luke."

"I'm not like that at all, Mason!" Luke scoffed.

"Don't you have your own work?" Mason giggled, a slight smile becoming prominent.

"That can wait. Unless, of course, you want me to leave," Luke held his hands above his head, looking at Mason expectantly.

"I wouldn't want you to leave, but... we have different responsibilities now. You have a Kingdom to look after, and I have my camp. I was appointed General, and I need to take that seriously. I've been working hard with the renovations, so people can live more comfortably in more modern buildings, and you've been staying around here a lot. Don't you think it's best if you stay with your subjects?" he suggested tentatively.

"I... oh. You really don't want me around, do you?" Luke said angrily.

"That's not it. You're my brother, we're family, why wouldn't I want you around? However, we both have jobs, and mine is taking a lot of my time. It has also made me realize how important getting to know your people is, and that you need to spend time with them and listen to their suggestions or needs. You don't want your Kingdom to fall, do you?" Mason shrugged, his face still calm.

"Is that a threat? I know my subjects well enough, thank you. We're strong, and no one will bring us down, especially not ourselves. My Kingdom will be more successful than your silly camp could ever think to be!" Luke rose, his cheeks turning red. Mason grabbed his arm before he could walk away, anger in his eyes.

"We shouldn't be fighting, we should be working together. My camp has always been a safe haven for those with magic, a place they can stay and train. Your Kingdom is for those without it, a humble city where people can feel at home. We need each other to function, the humans rely on us both. We're separated by two major things, and we both help with one of them."

"Just because you have magic, you're more special then, right? People need you more. I'm less than, my people are less than." Luke looked hurt, an underlying pain that didn't seem new. Mason opened his mouth, shocked at his brother's words.

"That's not what I'm saying. You can't keep acting like this, you're a leader now," Mason said sternly, but it only fueled the fire.

"Yeah, now! The only reason I have a place of my own is because I fought my way to the top. Mom and Dad always said you were born for greatness, destined to rise in the ranks. Did you ever think that you might be pushing people down to get to where *you* want to go?" Luke bitterly spat, tears welling up in his eyes.

"That isn't my fault! You've always hidden away, you didn't care about fame, you only hopped on the wagon once you saw me." Mason's arm started to glow, and Luke shrieked.

"You think I'm jealous? You're so egotistical! You really think you're better because you're the favorite, you have magic, you have Mom and Dad's love!" Luke's voice broke, tears finally falling, his expression showing such pain I almost winced. "You know what? I'll show you. I'll show you the world doesn't need magic, and that I don't need you. I'll show you that we're stronger, better, braver, all without magic!" Luke snapped his arm backwards, making Mason lose hold. He stormed off, leaving his brother alone in the field. A tear fell down Mason's face silently as he held his ground.

My vision switched, following Luke into the construction zone. People were standing around, lifting things magically or by hand. Some flew, most stayed on the ground, but everyone waved or smiled to Luke as he passed. The snarl on his face quickly made everyone back up as he stood in the center of the camp, his clothes starting to billow in a nonexistent wind. A black steam leached into the air, the ground pulsating with darkness as Luke raised his hands. Screams rang out across the camp, and everyone ran for safety. The foundations of everything crumbled, stone and wood falling swiftly, a mushroom cloud rising from the camp as destruction ensued, an evil laugh bellowing in the middle of it all.

I woke up violently, sitting up with a squeal. My heart raced and my breath was short, like I had just run a marathon. Damien, Aaron and Tigre all looked on, concerned and confused glances directed at me.

"Uh... what happened?" Aaron asked, seeming a little scared to say anything.

"I... I don't exactly know. Damien was telling the story, and suddenly... I was in it," I gasped for air, sweat running down my skin.

"You... what?" Damien said, a shocked look on his face.

"I saw two boys, Mason and Luke. I think Mason was the General, and Luke... was the King."

"That's impossible. Luke was the General's brother who died in an accident while the camp was being remodeled. He couldn't have been the King," Damien laughed. Tigre had a sullen look on his face, his eyes turned down.

"Tigre... do you know anything about this?" I asked, poking his shoulder.

"I—uh, no. I didn't even know the General had a brother!" he laughed, smiling nervously.

"He never told me directly, but some of the guards did refer to the King as Luke. Only close friends of his, of course, but... I'm pretty sure that was his name," Aaron added, looking more concerned than before.

"And, when I was in the castle, I saw a portrait of the General. When I asked Aaron, he said it was the King's brother. So... Luke must not have died. I also saw that he caused the accident that the General said he died in." I put my finger to my lips, confused and wondering how much the General lied about. "The General was old, though. Wouldn't the King be as old?"

"He looks pretty young," Aaron admitted. "Except for the scar on his face." I shuddered at the thought of the grotesque mark I remembered seeing.

"What scar?" Damien questioned.

"Half of his face is covered in what looks like a burn scar. Something really bad must have happened to him," I said, thinking back to our battle. "It was disturbing."

"If something had happened, we would probably know about it," Damien said, looking confused. "We've been at war with him pretty much the entire time he's ruled. There haven't been any accidents, and he's really powerful, so he couldn't have been attacked."

"Could he have been… possessed, or something?" Tigre asked. "You know what those demons do to you."

"That's completely possible," Damien said with a shrug. "I'm not sure though."

"What does the demon do?" I asked, almost afraid of the answer.

"There's a creature, a powerful demon, that can take over your body. It feeds off of negativity, but can only thrive in the darkness. It leaves a huge mark as well. One part of its victim's body would be almost entirely covered in dark matter," Tigre said, biting his lip. "One of my friends... was lost to it once."

"The King, from what I've heard and seen, stays in the shadows," I said, sighing. If he was a demon, that explained a lot, but wasn't good for us. "That all fits then. Mason and Luke, the General and the King, were brothers. They got into a massive fight, let it affect the way they ruled and created a hatred for people with magic, on the King's side at least. Then the King got possessed, and now... we have to deal with their sibling rivalry," I groaned, standing up. "We should probably get going. I don't know what we can do with this information, but... now we have it. We have to continue, however." Everyone nodded, and Tigre helped me stand. We started walking, the sun now high in the sky.

I hoped that I didn't collapse again, but I was also curious as the reason why I suddenly saw that. Could it have something to do with me absorbing the General's ashes when he died? Maybe he passed on his memories so someone could find the truth after his passing, so he didn't die with his lies buried, but also didn't have to suffer the repercussions. A bitter feeling crept over me as I considered that possibility.

Tigre and Damien ended up leading, chatting as we walked.

Aaron and I hung back, going at a slower pace, not speaking much. Mottled sunlight burst through the leaves, highlighting some of the floor underneath the glow. It was peaceful, a serenity that was almost unsettling.

"Do you ever miss it?" Aaron blurted out randomly. "I mean... the real world."

"Well, not really. I haven't thought about it much, because of everything that's been happening. And besides... there's not much there to miss." I looked out into the forest, but I didn't even see the edge or the camp yet. I noticed Tigre glancing back, checking on me and looking suspiciously at Aaron. What had Frostbite said?

"Friends?" he inquired. "You had a few at school, we were in the same group."

"I was worried about that at first, but... I have friends here as well. And Damien said that time probably works differently, a minute there might be a year over here. I don't think I'm missing much," I shrugged, not having given this much thought before. "What about you?"

"Well, you all were my only friends, so having you here as well makes it... not as bad. I'm not very homesick, and there's a familiar face within all the chaos and magic." He smiled.

"I'm glad I found someone I knew as well," I giggled. "Though, there's also a problem with it..."

"What do you mean?"

"Eli? And... Seth."

"I thought you forgot Seth. You were acting like you didn't know him, and Damien asked me about it as well."

"I pretended to," I whispered, lowering my voice so Tigre and Damien wouldn't hear. "I panicked, and... now I'm a little stuck. But I do know him, and we don't exactly have a great relationship."

"I know! In the real world, you didn't get along. There was another one, right? Jake?"

"Yeah, him. From the first day, we were at each other's throats, but I doubt either of us can really explain why. We were like siblings in all the worst ways... close only by hatred. That started a lot of fights," I scoffed, though I did feel a bit guilty about what had gone on.

"Yeah, I didn't pay much attention to rumors, but there were some you couldn't avoid. It was like two clans fighting, the school split down the middle," he said sullenly, a concerned look on his face. "Have you ever tried to make up with him?"

"I wouldn't know where to start," I sighed, crossing my arms. "It's not like this happened over time, so I guess that's worse."

"Maybe it's time… you tried to look for an out?" Aaron suggested with a shrug. "I can't tell you what to do, but they're here now. You either have to try to get along or you're letting this get worse, which… affects your leadership."

"I-I never thought about that," I said quietly, biting my lip. "You're right. I shouldn't continue this. I play a part in making it worse. Thank you." I looked up at Aaron with a slight smile, and he nodded back to me.

"If you need me, I'll help you avoid them, if I can. I wonder why they're here in the first place…" he questioned. "You were obviously destined to be in this world, but nothing was said about any others. And they fell through portals as well, right?"

"Yeah, and all three of us were targeted by Zanzagars as soon as we appeared. I had to save Eli from one," I commented, smiling as I remembered the fight and the horrified look on Eli's face. He had tried to help me—not knowing what he got himself into.

"Hmm… when I got here, I was immediately taken in by the King. I didn't see any Zanzagars, so I wonder why all three of you would have the same experience."

"Well, Frostbite said I upset the balance, right? Maybe… I set off something, like an alarm, or it had something to do with the prophecy. He also said I shouldn't have such immense power…" I stared down at my palms, flexing my fingers. Elemental magic was not only rare from what I'd heard, but dangerous. Seth and Eli didn't have powers, and Aaron had a weaker, or simpler one. What was it about me that started all of this? And, why? Once again, this strange land sparking so many questions, none of which could be answered.

"We'll figure it out," Aaron assured me.

"Yeah, right now we should focus on the task at hand, and... hope Jake doesn't suddenly appear," I laughed nervously, regretting my words the moment I spoke. I felt as if something was watching me, taking in everything I didn't want to happen and going out of its way to make me suffer. Maybe a particularly vengeful god had its eyes on me, listening to my words and thoughts, and giggling to itself as it watched me struggle through all of my fears turned into reality.

"Hey, Amber!" I stopped in my tracks, hearing a raspy whisper coming from a... bush? "Over here!"

"Aaron, am I hallucinating or is a bush talking to me?" I said quietly, looking down beside me. He looked just as confused.

"I'm not a bush!" the bush said exasperatedly.

"Uh... Damien?" I called, not taking my eyes off of the foliage. The two halted ahead of us, turning back to see what was the issue. "A bush is talking to me."

"I told you, I'm not—ugh!" Jay's face peeked out from behind the leaves.

"Jay? What are you doing... there?" I giggled.

"I wanted to come find you before you got back to camp, but it got dark almost as soon as I left. I decided to hide here and wait for you." He stood, rising to his full height.

"Oh. Is Harlequinn with—wait." I paused, rethinking my sentence. "Names hold power, right? Are we still doing the letter thing?" Jay waved his hand.

"It's not as important now, especially since a lot of people have... well, died, and the Council has been disbanded. People are more focused on fighting in the moment than using our names against us. It takes a powerful, complicated magic to use names, and now it's less of a threat." I nodded in understanding.

"Well, go on then." I crossed my arms, standing in a relaxed position.

"Sorry to surprise you like this, but we decided to... take

initiative, and set up a little something for the camp," Jay waved his hand, gesturing for me to follow. "It's over here, not far from the gates, but enough so that we're not in danger."

"I'm scared to ask, but what… did you all do?" I questioned, stepping forward. We talked as we walked, and I was surprised at how proud he looked.

"We set up a way for people to ask for our help, an easier way for allies to contact us, and even keep track of where we've been, who's hostile and who isn't, what we don't know, and stuff like that," Jay said with a smile, and I guessed that he had a big part in at least the idea of this.

"How did you do that?" I asked. He waved his hand, and we followed him through a short path in the woods. Near the edge of the forest, a place where you could faintly see the camp, stood a small hut. The wooden structure seemed like it could hold only about two or three people at once, but it looked interesting. There were two boxes on the outside, and maps on the inside, markings already spread across the pages. Pencils and feathers with ink littered the desk space, another box protruding from the wall.

"This is it!" He gestured to the hut. "We have special enchantments on the different boxes so only specific people can access them, either putting something inside or taking it out. The maps mark hostile, unknown, and friendly areas. Right now all we have for friendly is our camp, the hidden village, and I'm assuming now the Ice Kingdom. Hostile is the regular Kingdom, and unknown is pretty much everywhere else."

"Oh, about the Ice Kingdom… it's a bit hard to explain, but it kind of doesn't exist anymore," Damien said sheepishly. "It's a very long story, but the Lost Lands were hidden beneath the snow, basically. I'll tell you more later."

"Dude! You can't drop something like that on me and then leave it for later," Jay rolled his eyes, a slight smirk playing on his lips. "But, alright. I'm too excited about this right now anyway."

"Hey, there's a paper in this box," I pointed out.

"Oh, that's the request box. Someone must be asking for help."

Jay reached in to the box, a slight shimmering field glowing around his hand. He plucked the paper from the bottom, flattening it out so it could be read. "Hmm... there's a small tribe in need of assistance. They're under attack, and their assassins don't have any weapons. They ordered some magic knives, but the delivery has been held up. In return for our help, they'll become allies."

"We can do that easily," I smiled, hope making my heart flutter.

"Maybe, maybe not," Damien said ominously. "We have to be careful with our judgment. Don't let your guard down, and be careful even approaching this. When we help more people, gain more allies, we're more likely to be noticed. The Kingdom can track us down, and follow our trail to here. They may be able to take control of someone who has access to the box, and then lure us into a trap. So... no matter what's happening, be careful." We all nodded, a grim silence sweeping over our group for a second.

"Anyway... let's get back to camp, rest for a bit, and then go help these people," I suggested. "Where are we headed?"

"In the north, there's a small village you can't miss. I've been there a few times," Jay said.

"Alright, let's take some time to ourselves and get ready to head out. Oh, and Damien... do you know much about the spells that are used by actually speaking?"

"Like the one your cloak uses, or the General used to cast a force field?" he asked, and I nodded again. "I know quite a few spells. It's rare we need to use them, not many are for attacking, but I can teach you some if you'd like."

"That would be great. I want to learn as much as I can, be of use in more ways than one. Also, I know the library is destroyed now, but... there was a book that was all about monsters. I also want to learn about that, so I'm prepared for whatever comes out of the shadows." Damien beamed, a proud look on his face.

"I'm glad you're taking that all into consideration. Especially since it was so long ago... I thought you'd forgotten about it," he laughed. "I can definitely help, if you want me to."

"Thank you," I said with a smile. "I don't know how much time we'll have at the camp, but maybe we can practice on the road?"

"We can try. Come on, we don't want to waste any more time here." We started off, walking slightly in front of the rest of the group. Dead leaves crinkled beneath us, everything silent aside from our footsteps. I was excited, adrenaline racing through me. It seemed like we were in the final phases of our journey, of this war. It was all coming to a stop, and I had a good feeling we would be the ones to prevail. Or, maybe it was just hope.

We crept towards the camp, Jay hiding in the shadows the entire time.

"Guys, be careful. There have been a lot of scouts lately, and we don't want to be caught." Jay whispered.

"Scouts? From the Kingdom?" Tigre asked, crouching by a bush, looking angry. I felt like if any of us made one wrong move, he would strike out at us.

"We think so. Some... suspicious people in dark clothing keep trying to get in, or were hanging around the gates. I don't know exactly what their deals were, but... we still have to be cautious," Jay warned, and the group kept going, all of us now crouching and sneaking along. I was nervous, but we made it into the camp, slipping past the giant doors. Only three people were outside, Seth and Eli sitting together while Melioca paced in circles, freezing when she saw us all approaching. She had changed once again, now in an elegant black dress, gray beads lining the ends of the fabric. She had slightly longer sleeves, embroidered with white swirls. Her hair was hanging down, delicately curled, and a pearl necklace rested around her neck, small earrings shimmering on her ears. Her wings were folded behind her, much darker than before, but not pitch black.

"Finally! What took you so long?" she growled. "I've had to take on babysitting, and let me tell you... it's not fun."

"Hey, give them a break," I said gently, and everyone turned to me with a confused stare. "Well, they haven't had the chance to get used to this place, I know for a fact that it's overwhelming."

"Did you hit your head?" Melioca said, drifting over to me and pressing her hands against my forehead.

"No, I'm fine!" I pushed her arms away, glancing towards the two boys in the corner. "Anyway, sorry about that, but we have to leave again soon. We have to go help some people, so we won't be here for long."

"At least take me with you," Melioca suddenly pleaded, grabbing my hands. "I am not fit for watching children. My attention span and temper are both too short."

"Aren't you a child?" Eli protested, throwing his hands up.

"I'm as old as time itself, and I still look younger than you," Melioca glared, tossing her head. "I can't believe I'm asking like this, but... please."

"Hey, we've been stuck here too! And with your attitude, I doubt we've had the best of time socializing." Seth stood, stomping over. "We've been cooped up with an overgrown, bratty bird. If you're taking anyone, it should be us!"

"Bird?" Melioca gasped, shrieking. "I'm an angel, you pathetic excuse for a human! I'll destroy you, if you say one more-"

"Stop it!" I yelled, pushing the two away from each other. "You both are acting childish. Maybe you should come with me, learn to get along."

"What?" The two shrieked in unison. Aaron looked shocked as well, standing beside me.

"How will that help?" Seth said with a glare, but I dismissed him with a sigh.

"Nothing like a good war to create a strong bond!" I said dramatically, waving my hands. The two didn't look amused. "You gotta admit, almost dying with someone definitely brings you close."

"I wouldn't know," Seth said blandly, and I put my hand on his shoulder, trying to get him to stop talking, before Melioca went off.

"Of course you don't, you—" she started, and I shushed her with a tap.

"That's it, go get ready. Just us three, and that's final," I commanded, and they both stormed off, like angry kids who didn't want to go to school. I glanced at Eli, who was still leaning against the wall, but he simply shrugged.

"I'm not gonna get involved," he said wisely, and I nodded. Aaron came up beside me, tapping my shoulder. He leaned in, whispering quietly to me.

"Didn't... didn't you say you wanted to stay away from Seth?" he asked.

"I... I did say that. But that also means we all need to learn to get along, and this might be a good start," I put on a fake, awkward smile. "Or, the day I die."

"And, I also can't come with you. So... I've failed at my only job that I promised you about twenty minutes ago."

"I'm sorry," I winced. "Well... I've made my bed. Guess I have to lie in it."

"Amber, are you sure this is a good idea?" Damien asked, coming up to me. "Melioca is... unstable, and dangerous. Seth will instigate her, and she might end up exploding."

"I'll keep her in check," I said with a smirk. "As well as Seth. I have powers too, I can control this. And if you don't think I can, you should let me prove it."

"I... I have faith in you. You're the General, you get the final say. Just be careful, okay?" He looked at me worriedly, and I nodded. "If you die, I'm gonna kill you."

"Don't worry about me. We'll be alright" I assured him, smiling at his joke.

"Good luck on the mission," Aaron said, though he had a sad grin on his face.

"Hey, at least in this case, *we* can bond!" Tigre jumped in, grabbing Damien's wrist and putting his arm around Aaron's shoulders and winking at me. "Make sure no one... gets into trouble." Aaron looked up at the Elite suspiciously, struggling in his grip, but he couldn't escape his strength.

"Thanks. I'll see you all when we get back." I turned to leave, but Damien stopped me, easily escaping Tigre.

"Wait! You'll need transportation, and a few directions. We

gathered some horses, but the hellhounds got out." He winced.

"Oh?" I said. "Well... I can take Aster." I paused, and whistled loudly. I waited a few minutes in anticipation, but... nothing. I looked around, but I didn't see the wolf anywhere.

"That's weird... he usually responds right away, doesn't he?" Damien asked. I nodded, a little worried.

"Horses it is, I guess. We also need to figure out where the packages would be, right?"

"That will be easier. It should be at the entrance, check in the boxes before you take them though. The note said they ordered magic knives, so I'm assuming that means they're enchanted to never miss a target. They should be glowing, but you can't take your horses through. It's a small, narrow pathway made of branches, with barely any light filtering through. That's why you can't easily miss it - the tunnel is extremely visible."

"I see. We'll just wing it with anything else, I guess," I said, shrugging.

"Great plan, I can see you've thought a lot about this," Damien joked. I lightly punched his arm, smiling.

"We'll be okay. I'll get everyone ready. Can you bring the horses?" I asked, and he nodded.

"I can do that. Aaron, want to help?" Aaron lit up, an excited gleam in his eyes.

"Uh, yeah, okay.," he stuttered, and the two walked off to a makeshift barn in the corner of the camp. I sauntered towards the gate, seeing Melioca and Seth, both with sour looks on their faces. They wouldn't face each other, and Eli smirked in the corner, obviously smug with not having been dragged into this mess.

"Alright, pack your bags. We're leaving soon," I announced.

"Why the rush?" Melioca sighed. "And why did you decide to make me go along with this gremlin? Also, I have no bags."

"Says you! What grade are you in, kindergarten?" Seth spat.

"Are you speaking German now?" she scoffed.

"Seth... I don't think school exists here. Or, if education does, then... it might not be what we're used to," I explained, and

Melioca turned her nose up.

"Yet they know what German is?" Seth muttered.

"Languages exist, you lethargic snail," the angel snarled.

"Both of you, quit it, or else you're riding on the same horse," I threatened. Seth blanched, and Melioca rolled her eyes.

"I'll fly, thank you," she retorted, spreading her wings so they smacked into Seth before she took off, hovering above the camp, gliding gracefully through the air. Despite her attitude, she was very elegant.

Aaron and Damien approached behind us, and I turned to them gratefully.

"This might be a bad idea," I admitted, and Damien chuckled. "But... we have to get through bad situations sometimes. I'll learn to handle it."

"Turning this into a lesson, good thinking," he said, handing me the reins to a horse. "You're practically training yourself now." I smiled, turning to assess the horses. I now held a gorgeous Appaloosa, with a mottled coat spotted with brown and white. Aaron was also carrying a lead, to a white horse with a black star on its nose. "I figured Melioca would want to fly, so we just brought two. They're all saddled and ready to go, so... whenever you're ready, just head north." I nodded in thanks, quickly hugging both of the boys before turning to the gate.

"Seth," I said, gesturing for him to come closer. He approached tentatively, seeming a bit afraid of the horses. "You take the white one." I said, holding out my hand.

"Why don't we take Aster?" he asked, and I bit my lip.

"He didn't respond when I called him. I don't know what's up, but I'm sure it's fine. Anyway, take the reins. You know how to ride a horse, right?"

"Well enough," he sputtered, putting on a brave face. He obviously didn't wanna show any signs of weakness around us. "I'll manage."

"Good," I commented, now realizing how important it was to stay on each other's good sides. I lifted myself up, swinging on to the Appaloosa with one swift movement. The horse shifted its weight, breathing in. I stroked its head, scratching behind its ears, feeling the course hair of its mane. I didn't even bother to turn as I heard Seth struggling to get on, the horse sighing and him grunting as he tried to jump into the saddle. I held out my hand subtly, trying to conjure some wind to gently lift him up. It seemed to work, and as I looked back, he was adjusted properly. I nodded, urging my horse forward, and we started out, trotting through the gate. Melioca glided above us, dancing through the air peacefully. She was going a bit too fast, nearly leaving my line of sight. I burst into a canter, hoping Seth was following close behind. By the sound behind me, I assumed he was.

We headed north much quicker than planned, as I struggled to keep up with the dark angel above us. She looked pleased with herself as she glared down on us. I held out my hand again, keeping myself balanced on the horse, manipulating the air above us to push against Melioca. She shrieked as she was sent sprawling, and I slowed down, breathing a sigh of relief.

"We're supposed to be going the same pace, not playing a game of tag!" I reminded her, shouting above the trees, the thick foliage making it even more difficult to see her.

"Why not just let her get lost?" Seth grumbled. I rolled my eyes, ignoring his comment. I focused on the road ahead of me, trying to make sure I was going in a straight enough line so that we were at least going in the general direction. "How long until we get there?" he said, sounding unsettled.

"I don't know exactly. Probably not much longer." I heard the flutter of wings above us and Melioca flew below the leaves, pulling up next to us and finally going our pace, a scowl on her face.

"You didn't have to send me back thirty feet," she scoffed.

"Oh, I didn't? You're telling me I could have just asked you to stop and you would have?" I pointed out. She sighed angrily and looked away.

"Is that it up there?" Seth asked, looking in front of us. Sticks and branches were woven tightly together to form a long tunnel, three boxes sitting in front of it.

"Must be," I commented, sliding off of my horse. I quickly tied the reins to a tree, and went over to examine the boxes. I opened the lid carefully, and removed the paper on top of the contents. Small knives sat in the box, a light purple hue glimmering over them. "Yeah, this should be it. Grab a box, everyone," I ordered, and they nodded, Melioca touching down on the ground and hoisting it onto her shoulder. I held it in front of me with both hands, and Seth did the same. I looked down into the tunnel, worried the boxes might not even fit. Glancing around the side, it didn't seem to have an end.

"Are we going, or not?" Seth mumbled, and I rolled my eyes.

"Just doing a final check, but yeah, let's go." I started moving forward. We all crammed inside the small tunnel, the boxes and our shoulders scraping against the edges. Melioca struggled to move at all, her wings folded tightly behind her.

"Can't you move any faster?" Seth growled.

"If I could, I would. And besides, we're carrying precious cargo. We don't want to lose or break anything. If we do, what kind of reputation does that give us?"

"What's even in these boxes?"

"Magic knives. There's supposedly a village up ahead that needs them."

"Oh. Please tell me we're not headed into another war."

"No promises," I commented, trying to quicken my pace. I forged ahead, trying to shuffle quicker. We trudged through the mud, the ground becoming thicker, pulling at my shoes. I heard the buzz of insects, and a nearly colorless butterfly drifted past us. I admired the graceful creature for a second, before an arrow shot through the wooden tunnel and pinned it to the other side. I shrieked, the hall opening up to a vast expanse of land. The woods melted away and were replaced by grassy flatlands, combat raging across every square inch within sight.

Blood stained the ground and countless bodies littered the

battlefield. Three giant hawks raced past, a human in armor on each one of their backs, and they all grabbed the boxes. I yelped, surprised to have the packages ripped away, but by the look of their crude, wooden armor, they were the ones whom we were delivering to.

One more person swept in, dropping from above and landing in a crouched position in front of me. He stood, a calm look on his bruised face. He had jet black hair, hanging down just past his jaw. His dark, hazel eyes gleamed with an adventurous, danger-loving shine, the smirk on his face saying the same thing.

He wore a smile, long sleeved gray cotton shirt, and black, well-fitting pants. A plate of wood covered his chest, as well as knee and elbow pads, obviously not protecting him very well. His clothes were in tatters, dark crimson stains everywhere, and his face was mottled with scratches and scars. He was a little taller than me, but it was hard to guess his age. I was just barely able to take in his appearance before he grabbed my waist, holding his hand out and grabbing a thick vine that someone dropped from above. He whooped in excitement as we went flying, and I hung on, gripping his shoulders so I wouldn't fall. We rode into the air, and I noticed Seth was picked up by something similar, though Melioca had disappeared. The vine came to a stop high in the air, and I thought we were going to come crashing down, but the person who swept me up gently touched down on invisible flooring.

We were hundreds of feet up, and it made me nauseous just looking down. I held on to this stranger's arm, a little terrified.

"What just happened?" I squeaked. "And... where is the floor?" He giggled at my comment, and snapped harshly. A wood-like tile appeared beneath our feet, and I blinked, confused. A few feet away, what looked like several hundred people milled about, tending to wounds, sharpening weapons, or getting new armor. Everyone looked ready to jump into battle at a moment's notice.

"That better?" the stranger asked, a small smile playing on his lips.

"Uh... sure, but a little warning would be nice, if you ever decide to sweep me into the air again. I'm guessing you're the people who requested help with the packages?" I inquired, and he nodded.

"I'm glad you got our note. We're losing pretty badly, as you can see." He gestured down below, and I looked over the edge, ignoring the screaming and flailing behind me as Seth landed. It was obvious who was winning, even from this distance. People in real armor dominated the field, leaving destruction and death in their wake. It was painful to see, so many young and old lives taken in an instant, only a few warriors from the Kingdom downed in battle.

"That... I'm so sorry. Why are they going after you like this?" I scoffed. It was hard to believe this could be happening right under our noses.

"We have power, and we've protested the Kingdom and its vile ways. Resistance means death, in these parts," the stranger said sullenly. "I'm Jonas, by the way."

"Amber," I said, nodding in greeting. "I'm the General of a camp a little ways away from the Kingdom."

"A pleasure to meet you. We don't exactly have ranks here, but I'm one of the lead fighters." He bowed slightly, and I smiled politely. Seth let out an exasperated sigh behind me, and I turned with an annoyed expression. He sprawled across the floor, groaning and not even attempting to get up. "Is... that an acquaintance of yours?"

"Sadly, yes," I grumbled.

"And the angel, I assume she's with you as well?"

"That's correct. Where... where did she go?" I asked, surveying the open skies.

"She flew off, right before we came down. Can she defend herself?" I felt bad for laughing but I chuckled, his innocent expression making guilt rise.

"Sorry, but yeah. I haven't seen it personally, but from what I've heard... pray for the Kingdom." I crossed my arms, hoping she was okay despite my own words.

"Well, thank you for your assistance. We appreciate it, and if you have somewhere to be, we wouldn't want to hold you any longer," he said kindly. I shook my head with a small laugh.

"If you need our help fighting, we're happy to assist. I don't think Seth can fight, but he can help heal injured people. If I can find Melioca, that would be great." Jonas had a thoughtful look on his face, staring out to the field below before turning to me and nodding.

"If you're offering, I won't turn down a helping hand," he chuckled. "I can send some hawks out to find your angel friend. Do you need any help getting down?"

"I'll be fine," I said with a smirk. "Thanks. Hurry and find Melioca, we'll need her." I waved quickly, jumping off the ledge before I had time to think about what I was doing. I fell freely for a moment, a small shriek escaping me. I tried to focus, hugging my knees to my chest as my hands caught fire, creating what almost looked like a small shield around me as I came crashing down. The ground ruptured beneath me, a small crater left where I was sitting, flames reaching out and spreading through the cracked ground with a vengeance. I drew my sword, my arms blazing, and I ignored the pain spreading through my legs.

I raced into the battlefield, marveling at the obvious lack of allies. I didn't have much time to scan the plains before the battle came to me, armored attackers rushing forward. I dodged arrows, flung from behind the wall of people, setting fire to the sky in an attempt to clear my path.

I stood, sheathed in flames and smoke, the blaze parting before me as I stepped forward, my cloak flowing behind me. I stood tall, hoping I looked as awesome as I felt. With my theatrics, all attention was drawn to me. The blistering heat of the flames spread through the fields, alerting anyone who hadn't seen my extravagant entrance. I slightly regretted the show, but now I couldn't take it back.

A roar rose up from the other side, some warriors pointing at me like they recognized my face. I cursed under my breath, punching someone at my side, pressing my elbow into their stomach so they fell. I rolled out of the way of a sword strike, dissolved a wooden arrow with a wave of flames, and kicked at someone's legs, making them stumble.

I felt a thud and held back a scream as the sharp point of an arrow embedded itself in my leg. Distracted by the warm blood now flowing down my thigh, someone pushed me down, their blade scraping across my arm. I turned as quickly as I could, holding out my palms and letting out a burst of fire, throwing them back. Someone stepped on my hair, and I yelped, shoving my hands into the dirt and letting the flames burn the grass, rupturing the earth and making everyone close to me fall back.

I tried to stand, fire surrounding me. There were a lot of enemies, and they didn't seem that worried about coming close. I knew I had to make them fear me, run for the hills just seeing the silhouette of my flaming figure, but if this wasn't working, I feared I was out of ideas.

I swept my sword through the air, creating a threatening line of fire that hung for a moment before dissipating, and I grabbed the nearest warrior, smacking the hilt of my blade into their head, knocking them out cold. I didn't want to kill anyone, so I knew I'd have to get creative. I knelt by the ground, not audibly saying a word but mentally reaching out, begging for help.

The world complied, shifting and waving so there was nowhere for anyone to stand properly. Hundreds of men around me flailed and screamed as I stood in the eye of the storm, unaffected, wherever I walked the floor calming in a small circle so my path would not be interrupted. I heard a shrieking from above and looked up to see a horrible image.

Melioca, or what seemed to be her, started to descend on the battlefield. Her eyes were wide and bloodshot, fangs sticking out of her mouth, her neck bleeding like she had been severely hurt. Her wings were pitch black, and her outfit was a full suit of slim-fitting armor, lined with silver accents, the metal a deep, rusty red. She held two long swords, and as soon as she touched the ground, a shiver of fear went through me.

I could barely watch her movements as she soared, making people fall to their knees in pain or removing their knees so they simply toppled over. I closed my eyes, feeling nauseous with the gruesome image in front of me. I held my hand up to the sky, and luckily, they knew what I meant.

A vine tumbled down into my grip and I was lifted off of the bloody ground, back onto the floating island. I hid, not wanting to see over the edge, still disgusted by the image burned into my mind. By the piercing screams from below, the worst wasn't even over.

"She... definitely is a terror alright," Jonas said, holding his hand over his mouth as he turned away, eyes closed tightly.

"Ah, I knew you were too weak to stomach a good battle!" A lilting, joyful laugh came from beside us, and I looked over to see a girl kneeling by the edge, watching the carnage with an excited gleam in her eyes. She had dark skin that shone in the sunlight, and her hair was done up in a curly Afro. She had knives at her waist, and actual armor, metal plating her clothes. She wore fingerless gloves, her calloused hands gripping yet another knife. She had short sleeves that ran over her muscled arms, a silver band swirling up her left bicep. A small chain hung from her neck, a pendant of a beetle dangling over her chest. "That was impressive, kid. I haven't seen someone who could move the earth in a while. While on fire, as well!" she chuckled, showing her teeth. She stood, and I was shocked to see how much taller she was. I nearly had to look up to make eye contact.

"Uh—thanks," I said nervously, a bit intimidated. Her expression softened as she noticed my uncomfortable attitude, and she crouched down a little bit, her hand on my shoulder. The faint scent of honey filled the air as she got closer.

"Thanks for delivering the knives," she commented, patting her belt in reference. "I'm Nadia. I'm assuming you've met Jonas."

"Yeah, though we haven't talked much." I winced, hearing the splitting of skin beneath me. How was Melioca still fighting? Were the warriors like hydras, growing a new head (or body, in this case) every time one was cut off?

"Typical. Jonas, you should have done a better job creating a warm welcome for this girl!" She rose to her full height, sporting a cocky smile as I once again winced, an expression of pain crossing my face.

"I, uh... not exactly a girl," I said nervously. It was still nerve-wracking to correct people, though not as dangerous as the real world. Here, I could fight or even kill anyone that dared attack me, but mentioning it was awkward, to say the least. "Or... or a boy."

"Ah! I'm sorry, forgive me. My point still stands, treat guests with respect!" Nadia announced, and Jonas rolled his eyes.

"We're in the middle of a battle, I didn't have much time. Though, it seems the angel has finished our job for us..." I turned to see Melioca, now back to as she was while we were walking here, gently float up to the island. She landed with grace, brushing off her dress. Small splatters of blood still dotted her face, like red freckles, but it gave me chills. She acted calm, a passive, almost bored expression on her face, as if nothing had happened.

"So, tell me. How have you not taken down the entire Kingdom already, with moves like that?" Nadia laughed. Melioca opened her mouth to speak for a split second, before her eyes rolled to the back of her head and she collapsed. "Whoa!" Nadia rushed forward to grab the angel, cradling her before she could tumble off of the edge.

"That might be why," I winced. "Is she—" I stopped, my hand flying to my mouth as her neck practically split open, blood flowing. "Someone must have really gotten her. Maybe that caused her to lose control and go…" I couldn't even finish my comment, disturbed by the sudden extreme loss of blood and unsure what to even call it.

"Medic!" Nadia called, taking a black cloth out from one of her pockets. She pressed the fabric against Melioca's neck, trying to stop the blood. "She looks really young; I doubt that helps her immense power," Nadia commented under her breath, feeling Melioca's forehead, probably trying to tell her temperature.

"She's as old as time itself. She's an Elite," I said, shaking my head. "She's not young at all."

"For an angel, their powers mature very slowly. A dark angel is the same, and... she seems to be a mix. With the way her outfit and wings changed like that, I'd guess she can easily disguise herself as a light angel, but her dark powers come out when she needs them." Someone rushed over with a bottle of green liquid and a pillow. Nadia grabbed the pillow, lifting up Melioca and gently placing her down, and then pouring the green stuff onto the cloth, which started to steam.

"Doesn't that hurt?" I whispered, but the angel's expression softened, like she wasn't in as much pain. Nadia shook her head, gently brushing a strand of the Elite's hair out of her face.

"She's fine, don't worry. This is certainly a first from what I've seen—a combination of power that's very unlikely in this generation. The only problem is, her powers aren't always active, and her growth is extremely stunted if she's half of two whole beings that already mature at a quarter of the rate of a human." Nadia lifted the towel, and all that was left from the wound was a thin scab. "Rare dragon leaf serum. It's not easy to get, but it heals very fast. If she takes the appearance of a child, that most likely means her powers are that of a child's. So, once she grows up... she'll be able to do ten times what she just did in the blink of an eye, and I doubt she'll get too exhausted from it." She seemed to always be multitasking, even with conversations, jumping between one fact and another.

"Huh," I muttered, surprised and also impressed. I wondered how she could tell all of that just by looking at Melioca. Where did she come across such vast knowledge of angels? Maybe she was one. "Well, it looks like the entire field has been cleared. How did they all get here, though? That was hundreds of people. Didn't you see them coming?"

"We don't usually patrol the tunnel. Most days, it's hidden by powerful magic. Someone interrupted the mage, but we don't know how. He said he was just suddenly in pain, describing someone screaming loudly inside his mind." My eyes widened and

I turned to Seth, who, by his look, was thinking the same thing. "That didn't seem like an option we would have considered, but he wouldn't lie to get out of a job. We assume it was someone with telepathy, manipulating his train of thought."

"Are you sure?" I asked quietly, and she nodded.

"Some others have also said that, and it comes at the worst times, like in battle," Nadia sighed with a disappointed look on her face. "It's cost us many lives. It must be someone from the Kingdom, but we don't know who." I felt bile rise up in the back of my throat, the bitter taste festering in my mouth. I knew one person who could do that, but... it couldn't be him, right? He was on our side. He was my friend. Or... was he? Could we really trust him?

I put my hands to my temples, hating the thought of him even possibly being a traitor. A memory arose, something I didn't think was important at the time. The dream I had, with Aaron in it, the birds warning me of betrayal. My dreams in the dragon realm gave me insight into what was happening above- could that have done the same? I shivered, my mind and heart racing.

"Are you okay?" Jonas asked, putting his hand on my shoulder. I nodded shakily, the cold feeling of dread creeping over me.

"I'll be fine. Well, Melioca took out the people from the Kingdom, and we got you the knives. We should probably head—" my words were cut off by a rumbling, a deep, lengthy sound that gave me chills. A roar echoed across the landscape, and a tall monster lumbered towards us.

Its arms and legs were grotesquely long, and its skin was like quartz. It had sharp nails and a stretched out, horrifying face with a swirl of teeth and beady eyes. It was cracked in some places, moss growing around its head like a crown, and it had a veil of shadows around it. Everyone stopped in their tracks and stared as it approached, entranced by both the horror of its appearance and the fear of another battle. "I guess our job here isn't done after all. Melioca is out, and Seth can't fight... so, I guess *my* job isn't done. Alright." I stretched, drawing my sword and then raising it above my head, bringing my arm down and summoning the fire armor.

Flames encased my body and wings unfolded behind me. I stumbled forward, forgetting the immense mana drop that made me unsteady, and accidentally fell off of the island. I shrieked for a second before pulling up, gliding on the soft wind. I heard whooping and cheering from above and I smiled to myself, shifting my course towards the monster. I felt weak and lightheaded already, so I knew that I had to take a break from the armor. Maybe, if I was able to land on the creature, I could take a moment to regain some mana.

The wind howled like wolves during a full moon, the whipping breeze making it hard to see. I felt more than saw, pressing the palm of my hand down on a cold, smooth surface, which I assumed was the golem's shoulder, or what would count as it. I swung myself over, the flames going out as soon as I landed, crouched down right beside its neck. I felt its body shake as it crashed through the world, the earth below it crumbling.

I caught my breath, trying not to look down as nausea swept over me, my stomach turning at the height. I took a deep breath, staring into the sky as the almost melodic pace of the creature made my eyes droop, the serenity mixed with my drained mana and the slow tempo of the shakes, it was all making me drowsy. I shook my head, weakly standing, quite confused as to how the creature hadn't felt me or attempted to attack me yet. My palm pressed into the soft stone of its body, and something clicked in my head.

This was the earth. Stone was magic resistant, but it was still a part of the earth. I tensed my arm, feeling the warmth beneath this monster's skin, trying to reach down below the layers. I felt a heartbeat, a dull thud, faintly pumping beneath the surface. I put my hand to my chest, feeling the throb of my heart beneath the cloth of my shirt, the rhythms aligning as I closed my eyes, adrenaline racing through me. I heard the footsteps start to slow, crawling to a stop as I struggled to maintain this strange connection, our two hearts beating as one. I didn't even think of dismantling this situation in a peaceful way, but as the creature's heart faded to a stop, I realized that the situation had been diffused.

I wasn't quite sure what happened, but I heard a rumbling and a deep crack as everything slowed to a stop.

Without the beating heart, the monster had no way to stay up. It started collapsing in on itself, its legs suddenly crumbling to dust and the rest of the body quickly falling. I shrieked, my mana too low to be able to fly, and I was approaching the ground quickly, the soft green grass catapulting towards me. I braced myself for impact, not feeling nauseous anymore, though I believed I left my stomach a hundred feet above me. I half expected everything to end out well enough, and someone would rescue me, but my fantasy wasn't fulfilled. At the last second, I realized I was alone in this, but I had an idea.

I muttered the protection spell before I smacked into the floor, rolling away from all the debris, sharp pebbles embedded in any exposed skin. I winced, my eyes tearing up as I skidded, groaning in pain. My gauntlets made sounds as if they were about to break apart, clanging against rocks as the force field faded, only surrounding me for a second, embracing all the impact from the crash, but not leaving me without the after effects from scraping across mounds of stone and rolling around.

Thin lines of crimson slowly grew on my arms and hands, pinpricks of pain spreading all over my body. My face burned and I was sure I had a nasty scrape, but I was so tired, I felt like I was unable to do anything but lie in the broken quartz, not even calling for help. Luckily, our spectacle drew a crowd, and I heard muffled footsteps and shouting. I hadn't realized my ears were ringing, but now it was obvious, drowning out the other noises, a painful shriek that dug into my brain. I felt a hand on my shoulder, a weight that made me flinch in pain, even a slight touch making me wince. In my hazy, blurred vision, I saw Seth running up to me before I closed my eyes and slipped into unconsciousness.

CHAPTER EIGHTEEN

I woke up on the floor, an unwelcome, painful surprise. I stretched, every part of me hurting as I attempted to sit up. My eyes fluttered open and I saw many concerned faces hovering above me, smiles breaking out across many of them as I stirred. Jonas broke through the crowd, kneeling next to me and putting a wet cloth on my head. The cold water felt refreshing, and I didn't notice how hot my skin was until now.

"Thank you," I said weakly, my voice hoarse. "How long was I out?"

"A day or so," Jonas sighed, taking a small bottle out of his pocket. The elixir inside was glowing faintly, a sparkly, light blue hue. He uncorked the small vial, and poured the contents into the cloth. It flowed like honey, slowly and steadily dripping out of the bottle. He then placed the fabric back on my head.

"Are Seth and Melioca still here, or did they leave?" I looked up into the crowd, but I didn't see them.

"No, they're here. They decided to help with clean up duty, after hearing the other choice of chores," Jonas snickered. "Our rule is basically, if you stay here, you have to help out. Seth was ready to leave, but Melioca made him stay. He wasn't going to comply, but it seems like she said something that scared him straight." I giggled at the thought.

"Well, I'm glad they stayed. That would have been a fun journey home, all by myself, in a dark forest crawling with monsters and who knows what else." I sighed, and he nodded.

"Everyone, go back to your posts except the doctors. With our defense down, we need guards. We can't let people get in here," Jonas ordered, and the people around me scattered in a flash. I was surprised at how quickly they moved, and how well they took orders.

"Man, I need you back at my camp," I laughed. "It takes a little while to get everyone organized. Here, you say something and it just goes. But are you still having trouble with the defense?"

"Yeah, the mage still can't concentrate. Which is peculiar, because that means whoever is doing it, wasn't involved in the attack. They're not here, or maybe they're hiding at the outskirts, but they didn't fight." A sense of dread once again crept up over me. Whoever was using telepathy wasn't here, but hiding in the shadows, waiting to strike. I knew I should say something, but I didn't want to believe my own theory or be proven wrong, so I stayed silent, but turmoil bubbled inside me, my heart sinking.

"Well, thank you for the hospitality," I said with a nervous smile, worried my thoughts would show in my expression. "We really appreciate it."

"It's the least we can do, after you obliterated the enemy. And that golem? I don't know what you did, but it crumbled before it could even reach us. You all are powerful, why haven't you gone to the Kingdom yet?" Jonas scoffed, looking into the sky like it was an unbelievable thing.

"Strength in numbers," I mumbled. "We don't want to risk things going south. Melioca can only do what she did for a small amount of time, I don't have all the control I need, we lost a lot of our camp members... it's safer to recruit strong allies. And besides, I heard there's something in the Kingdom that makes people's powers weaker or stop working entirely."

"Ah, that. Yes, I would consider that a problem. You're smart, I would have tried to rush it. Taking it slow must be hard though, isn't it?"

"I mean, we have a lot to do. I wouldn't count this as slow, with the amount of what has happened. It's... a little tiring, if I'm being honest," I chuckled, folding my legs beneath me as Jonas sat at my side.

"Well, we'll be happy to help. Once word spreads of your rebellion, you're bound to get a lot more trouble. And, the battle isn't over after the Kingdom is taken down," he said casually, leaning back on his hands.

"What?" I asked, wondering if we missed something, or what

could be beyond the Kingdom.

"This forest is called the Endless Woods because of how big it is. There're countless monsters lurking in the shadows, demons worse than the King, cities meekly fighting oppression, dictators running some places bigger than five Kingdoms. If you want to help people, you have to dive deeper. You have to continue the fight, and not leave anyone in the dust because they're a part of a less noticed area." I nodded, not having considered the evil beyond the trees. To me, it's always been one enemy, one rival. I somehow didn't consider that there may be others suffering under the control of worse people.

I knew that no one could hear me, but I made myself a pledge. I held my hand over my heart, feeling the faint beat, and I silently promised myself that I would help everyone. I would go to the ends of the earth (or, the forest) and keep searching. Any cries for help, I would answer. I'd use my talent, this gift of a power for good, even if I did end up unsettling the balance of the universe. I'd right my wrongs and set things straight, no matter how hard that would be.

"Yeah, you're right. The fight won't be over for a while." I sighed, closing my eyes and realizing the pain was... gone. I lifted my arm, the bending not hurting me at all.

"You'll need all the help you can get. I'm gonna come back with you, if that's okay," Jonas said nonchalantly, but I almost fell off of the platform. "Nadia wants to, as well."

"I—um, I wouldn't oppose. You've been very kind, and if you're one of the best fighters here, I don't doubt your strength," I laughed. "Do you use magic mainly for fighting?"

"No, I... I actually don't have any powers. I'm most experienced in fist fighting, but I can use almost any weapon." He looked down sadly, and I felt guilty for asking, even though I didn't know.

"Oh, I see. I'm sorry."

"It's alright, the only problem it causes is... not fitting in well, I guess. But it's made me more resourceful, and strong," he said with a look that didn't exactly confirm he was okay with it, but I nodded anyway. "You might want to go round up your friends. If you want to leave, we should go before sundown. You know the woods at night."

"Yeah, I agree. Where are they?" I asked, leaning over the edge.

"Down there." I felt pressure on my back as Jonas lightly pushed me, but I slipped, falling off the platform. He smiled slightly and I screamed, feeling betrayed for a split second, but I saw him jump off as well. Confusion crossed my mind before a hawk passed under me, and I grabbed on to its neck before it flew away. I settled, my heart racing and my breath short from the fear. A bird grabbed Jonas out of the sky as well, and he twirled in the air, the hawk spinning.

"What did I say about warnings?" I yelled, adjusting myself.

"Sorry! We pull pranks on each other sometimes. I guess I should have asked you about that before I pushed you off a floating island," he called to me, laughing. I blinked, quickly overcoming the shock, and smiling slightly.

"That would have been wise! But never do that again, or I'll have to kill you," I threatened with my eyebrow raised, fire dancing on my palm. He nodded, a smug smirk on his face.

"Duly noted," he yelled with a wave, before turning and diving down to the ground. I leaned forward on the bird, and it started to descend, eyes scanning the area around us. I followed Jonas's path, which was a bit hard with how much he was prancing around, dancing through the air as he whooped in excitement. It was funny, seeing him acting like a child on Christmas, that same energetic gleam in his eye, and I was also glad that someone was still able to hold onto that joy, that youthful wonder, the same grin as a kid.

We landed softly, amidst all the wreckage that was slowly being cleared. I immediately spotted Melioca, working above, carrying heavy bits of stone away. Across the field there were countless bags, I assumed all of them holding bodies. Even though their corpses were covered, it was still gruesome, and I despised the thought of this war. Lives were lost, on our hands as well. Did that make us any better than the enemy? Where did we draw the line between good and evil?

A thousand thoughts crossed my mind before I turned, trying not to panic. I saw Seth after a minute, hidden in the crowd because of his height. I felt a bit awkward charging through a group of working people without doing anything, but I forged ahead, knowing we had probably overstayed our welcome.

"Hey," I said quietly, tapping his shoulder. He looked up, sweat beads falling down his forehead, his cheeks red and his breath short. "We're going home."

"Oh, you're awake," he sighed, wiping his eyes. "Now?"

"Yeah, we should get going. Jonas and Nadia are coming with us." I continued with my low tone, not wanting to stir anything if that information could. "Help me get Melioca, will you? We can probably just wave her down." I looked up, shielding my eyes from the glaring sun, the rays making it difficult to see. I held my hand up when I saw a shadow pass over us, assuming it was the angel. The sweeping sound of wings fluttering told me that I was right as she plummeted to the ground, landing with a thud right next to us. I jumped a bit, the harsh noise and sudden shaking startling me a bit. She was breathing heavily, her eyes angry and her fists balled.

"We're leaving, right?" she snapped, crossing her arms. I nodded, taken aback by her attitude. She snarled and whipped her head to the side. "Good. I can't believe they almost got you killed. I'll be by the tunnel."

"We're probably leaving now, so we'll come with you," I offered, but her deadly glare told me she wanted a bit of downtime alone. I held my hands up in a sign of retreat, sighing. "Or, I'll go get Jonas and Nadia."

"They're coming with us?" she said exasperatedly. "God!" Melioca stormed off, the color on her wings immediately deepening, forming into a dark black, like a storm looming over her back. I sighed, rolling my eyes.

"She's not in a good mood," I muttered. I started walking, my feet dragging as I approached Jonas. "Hey, we're ready. Are you gonna get Nadia?"

"I think she's already at the tunnel. Melioca will run into her there, so we're all set."

"We might want to hurry, or Nadia could be dead by the time we get there," I sighed sullenly, and Jonas looked alarmed. He quickly turned, grabbing two gloves off of the back of his hawk, and pulled them on as he jogged. I nodded to Seth, who followed behind us, and we quickly got to the tunnel, now visible. The angel was tapping her foot rapidly, a scowl on her face, while Nadia stood next to her looking proud.

"Are we ready?" she said energetically, hopping up and down.

"Can you calm down? You're being annoying," Melioca snarled. "And loud."

"Fine, we can run ahead and leave you behind," Nadia laughed, a joking smile prominent on her face. Her bubbly personality was contagious, and I soon felt a smile creep up on me as I straightened my back, taking a deep breath.

"You two can," Melioca mumbled something, blushing a bit and hiding her face.

"You're gonna have to speak up if you want us to hear you," Nadia said in a lilting, almost song-like tone.

"I am not a child! Do not treat me as such!" she roared. "You two can run ahead, but... I want to stay with Amber and Seth! I do not want to associate with either of you at the moment!" she said, her eyes tearing up slightly. I was surprised- I didn't think she'd want to be around us either. Nadia and Jonas also seemed shocked, but hung their heads slightly.

"Alright, no need to yell either. Come on Jonas, we'll get a head start," Nadia suggested, waving her hand. Jonas nodded, following after her. I watched their silhouettes disappear into the brambles, and smiled awkwardly.

"Shall we... follow?" I waved my hand, and Melioca stepped forward with a scoff. Seth followed behind her, and I noticed he was unusually quiet. What had happened to these two? Maybe I was dreaming.

The strangeness continued as I noticed the tunnel was much

wider than before. We could walk in a line, all three of us in a row, and still have room. I don't know why they would change it, but... they did. We walked along in silence, an unnerving, almost painful awkwardness.

"Man... that battle was intense," I offered up, trying to spark conversation.

"Yeah, but what does it matter?" Seth shrugged. I blinked, confused.

"Hundreds of people just died. That's definitely something I'd say matters," I argued.

"No, none of it does because this world is made up." He sighed, and I stopped in my tracks.

"How—what? How do you believe that? It's not our world, but this is real. Their lives are real, their families, their experiences. Everyone has a deep history and backstory, they're alive, flesh and blood. Hearts beating inside them, something I'm questioning if you have at this point."

"You're just saying this because you mean something to people here. It's not like you amounted to anything in the real world," he scowled. "You don't really matter anywhere. This place is fake, everything here is fake! You've created a character and now you're invested in this magical fantasy because a few people care, a few people look up to you, unlike in reality." Rage boiled inside me, and I set my hand ablaze, the fire casting an ominous glow in the low light.

"Right. So if this place is fake... I wonder if I kill you, what will happen? Will you wake up, like it was all a bad dream? Will you appear somewhere else in this world?" I asked, a sinister look on my face. I slowly approached him, and he backed away with every step, a glint of fear in his eyes. "What will happen to you, or your body?"

"I... I wouldn't like to test that," he gulped.

"Oh, I'm sure. But I'm curious, so if you don't want me to see what will happen, keep your mouth shut," I snapped, snarling. He yelped, falling backwards into the mud. Melioca laughed, an entertained cackle as I turned away, extinguishing the flame. "Stop laughing," I ordered, and she quieted down quickly, hearing the fed-up tone of my voice. Tears threatened to spill over as I charged ahead, not sure exactly why I was crying. It was more out of frustration than sadness, or maybe it was anger. I didn't slow down, and quickly caught up to Jonas and Nadia, who were laughing before they saw me approach.

"Hey! Are you okay?" Nadia asked softly, seeing the look on my face.

"Yeah, just... I'm done with Seth," I sighed.

"What happened?" She put her hand on my shoulder, stopping so she could stand next to me.

"It's nothing. We should probably get going," I sighed, still unsettled, disturbed and angry. Nadia nodded, putting her arm around me in a hug while we walked.

"Did you all take horses?" she asked nonchalantly.

"Yeah, the hellhounds escaped and my wolf is missing, so we had to."

"You have hellhounds?" she gasped, her eyes lighting up. "And a wolf?"

"Well, *had* hellhounds. And yeah, I found the wolf with my friend, Damien." I saw Jonas's face quickly drop, and he looked over to Nadia, who seemed to be holding a smile on purpose.

"He was starving in the woods, we gave him some food and he started following me around. At one point he disappeared for a while and came back completely healthy, and then stuck by me. I named him Aster, and he seemed to like it." I smiled slightly, thinking of the wolf. He was so small when we first met, I thought he was just a dog, but Tigre thought otherwise.

"Wolves aren't native to this area; it would have to have traveled a long way. How did one get here?" Jonas questioned, putting a hand to his chin.

"I thought the same thing. Unless... how big is he?" Nadia questioned, turning to me with a curious look.

"Almost my height," I giggled.

"Hmm," she muttered to herself, and I saw Jonas looking towards her fondly, an amused smile on his face. "I'll have to see him for myself, but I have a theory—though it's unlikely."

"What is?" I questioned, tilting my head.

"I'll explain once we get back. Or... could you try calling him now?" We paused, and I shrugged, then nodded. I took a deep breath and whistled briskly, the sound echoing through the tunnel and outside into the woods. We waited with bated breath, listening to the quiet hum of the forest around us. Dry leaves crunched beneath something outside, heavy footsteps that padded along quickly, almost in a sprint. I heard a low whine that turned into a howl, and Aster burst through the tunnel, jumping towards me. I yelped, thrown off of my feet by surprise as he pounced, licking me. I giggled, petting his ears. I heard a sharp gasp from Nadia, and then a small squeal of delight as she kneeled beside me, a goofy smile on her face. "He's so cute!"

"He's definitely a wolf," Jonas agreed, standing with his arms crossed.

"And from the looks of it, a lunar wolf. Though... they're usually glowing blue. Maybe if I..." She tapped his head curiously, but he simply looked at her with a wide grin, panting slightly, an innocent gleam in his dark eyes.

I heard muffled cursing and angry footfalls behind us, and even before turning, I knew what was coming. Melioca and Seth hurriedly approached, bickering like children. I closed my eyes, feeling my head start to throb, a deep pain engraved in my skull.

"Why are we stopped?" Melioca sighed, stopping in front of us. "Oh, hello wolf." Aster replied with a sharp bark.

"We found Aster!" I announced the obvious, gesturing to the wolf on top of me. Nadia excitedly did jazz hands next to me, and Jonas smiled.

"And? Let's get going. I don't want to be here any longer," the angel huffed, and Seth nodded in agreement. I rolled my eyes, shoving the dog off of me as I stood, straightening my back. I nodded, climbing on to Aster's back. We all trotted along at a quick pace, soon reaching the edge of the tunnel. Miraculously, the horses still stood in the spots they had been before, whinnying urgently and trying to break free of their harnesses.

"Whoa!" I whispered loudly, petting their snouts gently. The wild look in their eyes was almost painful, so I untied them, handing the reins to Seth and Jonas. "Nadia, you can ride with me or on the horse. Melioca, I assume you'd like to fly?"

"Don't just assume what I want," she protested. "But... yes." I glanced at her, a pointed look in her direction. She sighed exasperatedly before spreading her brilliant wings, and launching into the air.

"The horses seem spooked, not just impatient. Are we sure there's not a monster around?" Nadia said cautiously, examining the woods.

"We can never be sure here," I mumbled. "We should hurry out, though. Fighting on a horse is not a good idea, especially if it's not trained for this stuff. And... I don't know if they are or not, but we shouldn't risk it."

"You're on a wolf," Seth reminded me coyly as he climbed on to his horse.

"Forgive me for being concerned about the horses, and the people on them," I snapped back. He quieted, a somber look on his face as he turned his eyes down. I shook my head and nudged Aster forwards, Nadia gripping my shoulder behind me. She looked at ease, not at all like anyone else's reaction when they first rode Aster. The slight breeze ruffled her curly hair, and a small smile played on her lips. Her other hand gently ran through Aster's fur, brushing through the soft hair. We bounded through the forest, an awkward silence between us. I occasionally checked back to see if she was alright, and if the others were following, but our interactions weren't very frequent, and the long ride made it worse. A wave of relief nearly swallowed me as we broke through the forest, into the sunlight, the camp right in front of us. The gates were wide open, and we burst through, nearly running into B. I yelped, pulling gently on Aster's fur to get him to slide to a stop.

"I'm so sorry!" I apologized, getting off of the wolf's back. B's cheeks were flushed, and she looked surprised, her eyes wide with shock.

"It—it's alright! You guys are back!" she beamed, hugging me with one arm. I sunk into her warm embrace, surprised at how comfortable her hug was. "And you brought..."

"This is Nadia. Jonas is the other one on the horse back there." I pointed, gesturing to the gate, where Seth and Jonas were trotting in. Melioca effortlessly landed in front of them, and immediately walked off without another word.

"It's nice to meet you!" B said with a smile, offering her hand. Nadia shook it, the same expression of happiness on her face.

"Same to you. Are you an elf?" she asked curiously.

"Uh, yes, I am." B sunk back a bit, obviously a little embarrassed. Nadia meant no harm, but I assumed she hadn't gotten many positive reactions on the outside when asked if she was an elf.

"That's incredible! I've never met an elf before. I've heard rumors of your amazing powers, and not to mention beauty, and standing here... well, I can at least say one of them is true," Nadia giggled, her comment not seeming to be flirtatious, or, at least, the intent of it wasn't, but B blushed.

"Oh, thank you," she said giddily, covering her mouth with her hand. "I can show you the infirmary if you'd like, let you see my workspace and... explain what I do. It might not be very interesting, but—"

"Nonsense! I would absolutely love to see it. Lead the way!" Her genuine excitement made me start to grin as well, and the two started off, chattering. I thought it was best not to follow, so I turned back to Jonas.

"Well... Nadia already made a friend," I laughed, and he nodded knowingly. "So, they're off touring the infirmary. Welcome to the camp." I swept my arm in a flourish, showing off... not much. There were a few unfinished cabins, tents still littered the grounds, and the training arena had shrunk massively. It was now a small circle, enough space for two people to move around pretty well.

The ceiling had become a chain mesh that guarded the sky, but it definitely wasn't much to see. I heard footsteps behind me and saw Damien marching angrily towards us, a sour look on his face.

"Amber, what is this?" he demanded, gesturing to Jonas. "And is the other one here?"

"Nadia?" I asked, confused. Jonas didn't look happy either.

"It is you. I thought when they said Damien, they might have been referring to a rat that just crawled out of a sewer. Little did I know, it was a step below," Jonas spat, his arms crossed and a scowl on his face.

"Whoa!" I exclaimed, taken aback. "Stop that, right now. Damien, don't say a word. I don't know what just happened, but… stop! I will not have people acting like this in my camp!"

"Then why do you let Seth and Eli stay here?" Damien questioned. I sighed, rolling my eyes.

"Not exactly my choice. I wonder, who was it that persuaded me to let them come with us and not die alone in a forest?" I pointed out. He huffed in response, not looking towards the newcomer. "What was that about?" I hissed, lowering my voice.

"We met a few years ago. He started saying stuff… I don't wanna talk about it," Damien said angrily, crossing his arms. "This isn't something you can just… fix."

"Well, maybe you should try. You both know what it's about, maybe sit down and... have a conversation. A civil one! I'm so tired of fights like this," I grumbled, rolling my eyes. "And yes, I'm talking about my own as well." I stormed off, hopefully leaving them to talk. I was curious to know what was making them so angry, but at the same time, Damien made it clear he didn't want anyone else to know.

All I knew was, I was tired. The journey had exhausted me, the fighting and me nearly dying didn't help, and neither did Melioca and Seth. I snuck behind all the buildings and tents, and hid in a corner, trying to calm my nerves. I took a shaky breath, sitting down in the shadow of a cabin, my knees pulled up to my chin. I looked down at my shivering hands, and sighed, closing my eyes.

We had a long way to go- I knew I couldn't get this frustrated so easily. I had to take control of my emotions, but at the same time, I hadn't given myself a break since I got here. So I was torn.

"Hey," I heard a rumble behind me, and saw Tigre poke his head out from behind the building. "Are you okay?"

"I'll be alright. Thanks," I chuckled, and he sat down next to me. "What are you doing back here?"

"Oh, I come here a lot. It's quiet, serene. A nice place to... relax, and get away from the world. Even in the midst of war, this is far away from the chaos. It's good to see you back here," he said with a wink, and I nodded.

"Okay... oh, I've been meaning to ask you something. What's going on? What was Frostbite saying? You seem more on edge now," I questioned, leaning back into the wall.

"Well... he said he wasn't sure. He had a suspicion about Aaron-his spell seemed to get some mixed results. He didn't kill him because of that, but he put it like... a present. A fancy box wrapped in good intention, but inside was something more sinister." Tigre looked up, staring at the sky. He was worried, and it was like he had suddenly dropped his act.

"He wanted to hurt someone in the Valley?" I asked, but he shook his head. A horrifying realization dawned on me, and I could tell that Tigre knew.

"Listen, I want to protect you. I thought not telling you would keep you safe, but... then I saw you two. You're so friendly, but I've been noticing flashes of his actual emotion. I don't want you to be played by someone like him." I couldn't keep my gaze still, my mind racing, and my heart breaking. I didn't want to think that he would actually turn on me.

"I... I can't—" I started, my voice cracking.

"I know, I didn't believe it either. Just... maybe stay away. I don't want him to stab you in the back while you're not watching— especially if I'm able to stop it, but I'm not in the right place." Puzzle pieces fell into place as he spoke, so much noise inside my head, I almost couldn't process what the Elite was going on about. I remembered something Seth had said—when he pushed me, it was like a voice in his head was telling him to.

"Didn't Damien say that telepathy could sometimes be used to control people?" I asked weakly, interrupting Tigre. He trailed off, nodding.

"Yeah, they get into your head," he replied, looking worried. I nodded, taking a deep breath.

"I need some time to… I don't know." I sighed, holding my head in my hands. I could vaguely see Tigre nodding, going to stand. He started to walk away, but stopped as angry, brutal screams rang out from the camp. I was on my feet in an instant, gripping my sword hilt. I rushed out from behind the buildings, seeing Ija waltzing into camp, an axe held on his shoulder. He was shouting nonsense, and I couldn't tell if it was enraged gibberish or a different language.

"Ija!" Tigre yelled, running up to him. The lumberjack-like Elite was flushed, his beard moving quickly as he spat, his booming voice carrying across the camp. "He's talking in Norse. This happens when he's angry, but... no one can understand him."

"Where was he?" I asked, exasperated. Damien jogged forward, wincing.

"He was patrolling the woods, trying to find out where those spies were coming from. I guess he... discovered something. No one speaks Norse!" Tigre quickly reminded the giant, putting his hand to his temples. "Someone please... he's gonna go berserk. B? Where's B?" The elf ran out of the small crowd, putting a gentle hand on Ija's arm. His roars softened, and I felt like she just defused a bomb. The Elite was led away, quickly taken out of an area that was more populated.

"What was he screaming about, though?" I inquired, muttering to myself. I looked out the gate, just a glance, but what was out there caught my eye. I stepped outside, feeling the ground trembling.

The forest was changing faster than I'd seen before, the trees flipping in and out of existence, the ground forming, falling apart, reforming and adding bushes or a pit filled with mud. This time, the movement was more destructive, craters forming in the ground, the dirt beneath me crumbling, sending me stumbling back. Trees fell over, booming filling the woods. It was chaos, and watching the madness made my head spin.

"Amber, I'm not sure what we—oh." Damien stopped in his tracks, standing beside me, watching the carnage.

"What is happening?" I whispered, and as if in response, the change stopped. Some trees were left with only half of a trunk, some bushes were so transparent you could walk through them, and the ditches were still left with water and mud, half covered by dirt. A blue light appeared in the midst of it all, a swirling luminescence floating just above the ground. I heard screeching in the distance, the faint cry of what was probably a Zanzagar, but it sounded like much more than one. Pounding hoof beats carried their way through the forest as what seemed like a giant herd approached, no doubt seeking the blue light. I quickly wondered if this meant another outsider, and my heart stopped with the terror of the possibility.

My fears were confirmed as a hand reached through the light, a screaming sound coming from the other side. I sighed, and rushed forward, grabbing the arm and pulling the person through. I barely dared to look as I dragged them into the safety of the camp, quickly throwing them through the gate as I drew my sword.

My body caught fire and I heard another surprised shriek as the person behind me scrambled back in fear. An ominous feeling loomed over me as I anxiously waited for the approach of the Zanzagar herd, the flames around me roaring as if bellowing a battle cry. All my confidence dropped as suddenly the blaze went out, extinguishing without my command. My eyes widened, and I started to panic, my heart racing. I shook my hand, attempting to re-ignite the inferno, but no luck. Perfect timing, as the first Zanzagar burst through the woods, at least ten others following behind it.

CHAPTER NINETEEN

I stretched out my arm, feeling a surge of wind wrap around my hands. My other powers were working, but that was bad news, because I didn't have much control over them. That could potentially help, though.

I jumped forward, still gripping my sword. The air boosted me, throwing me up into the sky, and I came down on the pig's neck. My blade sliced through its flesh, and it burst into dust with a final, pitiful squeal. My hair whipped around as I jumped over to the rest of the herd, rolling across the ground to get to them. I paused for a second, my fingertips resting on top of the ground, and I silently asked for help. The earth responded immediately, spires of stone bursting through the ground and impaling Zanzagar after Zanzagar.

Ashes hung in the air, clouding my vision, but I could see the last monster, right in front of me. It froze, an angry look on its face. I was panting a bit, but I sprinted forward, stabbing the creature in its stomach. I was looking down, but I heard the screech and felt the light dust fall on my shoulders. I stepped back, sheathing my sword and calmly strolling back to camp. Still waiting in the doorway, a terrified look on his face, was yet another person I knew before. He was very tall and lanky, with a soft jaw and dark eyes. His hair was a similar color, a deep brown, and extremely curly. His skin was darker than the others, and he had on a simple, casual outfit. A short sleeved, light green shirt, jeans, and tennis shoes. He was shaking slightly, his eyes wide and confusion flickering on his face. A crowd stood behind him, the members of the camp waiting patiently for me.

"New person," I announced, pointing to the one person I didn't want to see right now. "And, again with the attacks after a portal opens. That's the first time we've seen one, though." I chuckled in the silence, a hush falling over everything.

"Amber?" the newcomer choked out, struggling to speak.

"Jake," I replied entirely unenthusiastically. "Welcome to... this. Don't cause trouble."

"You... fire? Earth? How did that happen?" he said with deep breaths. Eli and Seth pushed through the crowd quickly, and I groaned in frustration. The three stooges had found their way together, it seemed, and now we were in for a lot of trouble.

"Jake! You're here!" Eli said with a celebratory gesture.

"So is Amber!" he hissed in response.

"Yeah, the one who apparently remembers everyone except me," Seth said with a glare, and I flushed a bit. "It's miraculous."

"Great, we have stuff we need to do. If you don't mind—" I started angrily, but was cut off.

"Did I just fall asleep? What was that? What were those monsters?" Jake gasped, and I sighed.

"It took me a while to get used to everything as well. This... isn't our world. And, luckily enough, we get to somehow travel to another dimension, and Amber is still here," Seth said with a snarl.

"I was here first!" I argued, throwing up my hands. "Way before you!"

"And they also have powers, very strong ones, so shutting your mouths would be the wisest option here," Tigre agreed, stepping forward, his hands casually in his pockets. Jake turned to look at the voice, and shrieked, taking in Tigre's strange look. His eyes fell down to the ground where Jake was still huddled, and he smirked, showing off his sharp teeth. I smiled in surprise, nodding a thank you.

"Let's all calm down and get back inside the camp. We need to figure out our next move. Right now, it seems like we have the upper hand in the war, but we aren't sure. We probably need spies or scouts in the Kingdom, as well as people to run the mission," I announced, waving my hands.

"Amber, I think at least you and I should stay behind. You said you wanted to learn more about the monsters, spells, and I think you should spend some time here anyway," Damien suggested, raising his hand from behind a few people. "And... we may also need Seth, Eli and Jake. If they want a chance at surviving here, they have to learn the ins-and-outs."

"I was on board with you there until you decided to finish your sentence," I muttered. "But, as much as I hate it... I agree."

"What are we surviving?" Jake asked, twitching anxiously.

"There are multiple things," I said ominously, with a wink. I sauntered past him, through the dispersing crowd.

"That was mean," Damien giggled, walking next to me.

"Hey, you're laughing," I pointed out with a smile. "Besides, it's true. There's a lot of danger out here, stuff they're probably not prepared to handle."

"You wouldn't have thought you were prepared either. Look where you are now!" Damien said, gesturing wildly.

"Well, I would have died five minutes into being here if it wasn't for you. Then I got back here, and... I got training."

"So they need the same thing."

"They probably don't have powers, so it will be harder," I murmured. "Though, Jonas doesn't either, and he's supposedly good at fighting."

"Sadly, I can vouch for that. He is, indeed, incredible in combat. But against someone with magic like the King's? He wouldn't last. Even the Elites haven't had much luck when they get into a scuffle with the King, past or present. And they just keep getting stronger as the generations go on, so..."

"This is going to be difficult, isn't it?" I sighed. "I have a lot of hope for this, but at the same time, I feel like we're going into this blind. We don't have any idea how the final battle will be."

"We need to start closing in now," Damien reminded me gently. "Test the waters, and then dive right in. We can do this, it just might take a little while."

"I don't doubt anyone's abilities, but I'm still scared we're going to underestimate the King or his army. One thing they have and we don't is technology. I know about a lot of that stuff from my world, but I can basically just identify what things are, I can't build anything." I put my hand to my temples, groaning. "They have the upper hand in many areas."

"Hey, the only one on their side that has magic is the King. If we gather everyone, we'll be fine. We're still working on gaining allies, but we've visited quite a few people who are now on our side. Even if we fail, this is the closest we've been to victory in a long time, maybe ever. You brought us this far, so whatever the outcome, we've made history." I smiled slightly, happy to hear I did at least one thing.

"Hey! Guys!" I turned to meet the familiar voice, and saw Jay and Harlequinn marching towards us, holding hands, their fingers gently intertwined. I lit up, realizing that I hadn't seen the couple in a while.

"Hi!" I exclaimed, reaching out for a hug. After a quick greeting, we all settled down, laughing together. "So, what's up with you two?"

"Oh, we decided to get married while you were gone," Jay said nonchalantly. Harlequinn looked at him with an adoring smile, but I sputtered in surprise.

"What?" I asked, shocked but ecstatic.

"He's kidding! That's in the future," Harlequinn said with a playful nudge at his partner's shoulder. "You have been gone a lot, though. We could have been married."

"I'm sorry, I'm sorry," I giggled. "But I'm settling in for a while. I'm gonna let the others take some battles and I'll manage things here. I now have a lot of combat experience, but... knowledge? That's something I'm lacking a little."

"Oh, so are we back on monsters?" Harlequinn asked excitedly, rubbing his hands together like he had a plot. "The last time we tried to get into that... didn't go so well."

"But we learned something," I said jokingly, with a shrug. "I'm gonna focus on monsters and magic spells that are actually spoken. And, you know... I asked B a long time ago how we could make camp more accessible, and I think I know how." Harlequinn nodded, slowly gesturing something I didn't quite understand. Seeing my confused expression as I desperately wracked my brain for a translation, he laughed softly.

"Learning sign language," Harlequinn explained. "Every night, once the sun goes down, we gather in the training arena and B teaches a class for an hour. Damien actually suggested it not long after you disappeared."

"Oh, I'm glad that didn't get forgotten," I said with a relieved sigh. "I know a little sign," I replied, gesturing the words as I spoke them. "But, apparently, not enough," I giggled.

"You'll catch on quickly. B is a good teacher- she's helped us a lot," Jay reassured me.

"Right now, it's best we move to monsters and magic. Hey... that's a good name!" Damien smiled. I nodded, turning to the couple.

"Wanna join us? I don't know how much you'd need to learn, but if you wanna sit in, you can," I offered.

"That could be fun. We ended up saving the magic book we used last time when everything was destroyed, so... we can take that trip again. Intentionally, this time," Harlequinn laughed.

"Intentionally? Did you not mean to read the book before?" Damien said with a nervous laugh, quieting down when no one responded the same way to his joke.

"I don't know what Amber did, but somehow, we ended up inside the book. We got weapons, and we fought level two monsters when we were only on level one. It was confusing. I think Amber passed out when we came back." I giggled, remembering my exhaustion after that ordeal. It wasn't very funny then, though.

"That... I don't think was supposed to happen. No book we have should do that, unless it was cursed or something. But that would have to have been recently..." Damien started to mumble under his breath, and I put my hand on his shoulder.

"How about we go and study before we question the logic of a magic book?" I suggested cheerily. He smiled, amused, and nodded. We drifted towards the tents that now stood where the castle used to, some rubble still strewn across the ground. No new buildings were in progress over here, not even a cabin. White cloth draped over a few sticks, keeping up the roof while the fabric was nailed into the ground. There were a few tents, the openings all circled around a fire pit, so we each chose one and sat down. Well, Jay and Harlequinn sat together, leaning on each other as they still held hands. Damien pulled the book out of his tent, the same one as before. We spent the whole night going through the book, pointing out the strange features on the drawings, drilling each other on names and abilities, and studying the pages. I wasn't bored for a second, but instead laughing the entire time and engraving the information into my head. We ignored the levels and classes and just dove right into the information. As soon as Damien closed the book, I was out like a light.

I awoke groggily, half lying in a tent. I felt refreshed and much calmer now. More put together, in a way. The sun was just breaking away from the horizon, a warm golden glow sweeping across the camp. Jay was lying on Harlequinn's chest, both fast asleep, and Damien was... gone. I looked around, confused, my vision slightly blurry from having just woken up, and I stretched my arms out, yawning. As I pulled myself up to stand, my ankle immediately withered beneath me, and I winced in pain as the feeling of needles being pressed into my skin erupted, my leg going numb. Everything was silent, so when I shrieked slightly, it carried through the camp, making me feel almost guilty. I didn't want to wake anyone, so I pulled up my leg, bending it behind me as I hopped through camp, balancing on one foot.

I awkwardly stumbled past the tents and onto the path leading towards the gate, crossing the edge and hobbling towards the infirmary. I heard clinking and faint muttering inside as I approached, the wooden door slightly ajar. I peeked in quietly, seeing B standing over the table in the middle of the room, and I was surprised to see how much this place had changed since it had been... destroyed and rebuilt at least once.

It was bigger now, the whole building was more of a rectangular shape, an extension built to hold many beds, three on each side with a curtain in between. There was enough room to walk comfortably in front of and next to all the beds, and the floor was now stone tile. An oak desk sat in the middle of the 'lobby', or entrance. It had a few papers on it, as well as some vials and bottles with various colored liquid. The walls were lined with cubbies, some holding boxes, others paper and more jars. A lantern hung overhead, and some candles were strewn about the room, lighting it nicely. B was humming slightly, a small smile on her face, her light hair pinned back so it wouldn't fall in her eyes as she hunched over. I knocked on the doorframe, hoping not to scare her as I stepped in. Her gaze traveled upwards, and once she saw me, she grinned, straightening her back.

"Amber! He—what happened to your leg?" she gasped, leaning down and pressing on my ankle. I winced, shaking my head.

"I think it just fell asleep," I laughed nervously, and she looked up in confusion.

"Limbs can't... sleep, last time I checked," she said, her eyes narrowing.

"Oh, no, not literal sleep. It's this feeling where your leg, or whichever limb is asleep, goes numb. It kinda hurts to walk when that happens, so I prefer to keep off of it whenever I can," I laughed sheepishly. I didn't think they'd be unfamiliar with terms like that, but I guess I was wrong.

"Oh, I know the feeling then. Why are you here so early, though? I assume it isn't to get your leg checked out?" B joked.

"I woke up before the others, and we studied quite a bit last night, so... I thought I should go ahead and come to you for lessons. On sign language, I mean. I know a little from my world, but... I'm probably really behind everyone else at this point. And either way, I want to help communicate easier, since you're—" I signed deaf, and she smiled, gesturing very quickly. I blinked, not following at all. I signed again, and she flushed.

"Oops! Sorry. I said, yes, that would help. Sign language is my first language, and I can't always hear words correctly when they're spoken to me, even while I'm looking at the person." She repeated the signs while she was speaking, and I tried to connect the signs to her words. "I can teach you now, if you'd like." She reached into the corner of the room and pulled out two foldable chairs, popping them open. I nodded thankfully, sitting across from the elf. We started out slowly, reviewing what I knew and then expanding from there. The building had no windows, so I was surprised when the door opened, revealing the sun quickly setting. Damien's head poked in, a sheepish smile on his face.

"Hey! Amber, no one has been able to find you all day," he said, a relieved expression slowly taking over the grin.

"Oh my gosh! I'm so sorry! I didn't realize the entire day had gone by already. B was teaching me some signs, and... I guess the time got away from me," I said, standing. "Thank you so much for the lessons. I should probably get going, but... thanks." I smiled, trying to sign as I spoke.

"Anytime!" she nodded in response, waving slightly as I walked out the door. The chill in the air made me shiver, a slight breeze going by. Damien looked ahead, a small smile playing on his lips.

"You look happy," I commented as we trotted along.

"Fall is one of my favorite seasons, and the world is finally cooling down for it. Fall rarely comes around, but when it does... I love it," he said, a light in his eyes.

"Wait, what?" I asked, stunned. "Fall is... rare?"

"Yeah? How do the seasons work for you?" Damien asked, looking shocked.

"We have four seasons across the year, but they only come once. Spring, summer, fall and winter. It depends sometimes when they really start to take effect, but they last for a few months. I like fall, too," I giggled. "I've never been fond of extreme weather, so fall and spring are my favorite seasons. I could never decide between the two, but summer and winter were never even in the running. I don't like snow very much, and the heat is awful. The trees are great this time of year, though. I love all the colors and the whole feeling. Snuggling up at fires, having a warm cup of hot chocolate, comfy clothes... it's great." I smiled, the memories and thoughts making me feel comforted.

"Agreed. I wish our world was a bit more like yours," Damien huffed, crossing his arms. "Time flowing normally must be great. You know when the sun will go down, and come up. You know on which side it rises and which it sets. Here, there's a possibility of watching the sunset three times!"

"At least here it's interesting. Normal life for a kid, or even an adult most of the time, is... boring. There's not much to do except worry about things you have no control over. In this world, there's an adventure around every corner, countless battles to be fought that anyone can try to conquer. It's more dangerous, but it's lively. You have a purpose even walking out the door." I sighed, slowing to a stop. He looked back with a concerned expression, as well as a thoughtful look.

"I guess there's good and bad parts to any land, no matter where you go. You'll always wish for something that has no chance of becoming reality, even if you're in a different dimension," he joked, and I snickered.

"Yeah, nowhere is perfect, not for everyone. There's always going to be something someone doesn't like." I sighed, wondering if there was any dimension that was supposed to be 'perfect'. It might end up being creepy, or eerie, how everything would be in place.

"What was your favorite thing to do in your world?" Damien questioned, and I was taken aback a bit. I didn't expect him to ask that, but I pondered for a minute.

"I guess... playing in the woods was fun. That's how I got here, actually," I laughed. "I never had anyone to run around with, though. It made me kinda sad, because I loved being out there but I never had friends with me."

"You said before you liked to write, right?"

"Yeah, and the forest gave me a lot of inspiration. It especially helped that my first big project was about talking wolves," I laughed. "Having a location to write about that was right in front of me ended up being great. What do you like to do?"

"Honestly? I love painting. Simple scenes, like the sunset over the forest or mountains, sometimes even monsters. I helped draw some of the designs in the book we read last night. It's an interest that's... almost indescribable as to why I like it. But... we never have time for hobbies here. There's always something to do. In fact, we should probably go help with dinner." Damien looked down, and I got suspicious. He looked so happy while talking about art, a wistful smile on his face, but then suddenly closed up and got cold. He started to speed off, walking much quicker than normal, but I figured I couldn't do much. Guilt weighed down on my shoulders as I sauntered after him, trying to keep up with his fast pace. The feeling didn't stop as we arrived at the small dining pavilion, all the seats now outside, and I marveled at how few people were left. Tears threatened to overflow as I recounted everything, remembering the bustling, lively building from when I first got here. Now, only a few people and Elites gathered under the setting sun.

It made me sad, but also sparked some hope. We were small, but fierce, and we had allies. You might not even expect an attack from this group, but we were so close to having all the elements we needed to bring the King to his knees once and for all.

I saw Damien, Jay and Harlequinn all sitting together and almost went over before another table caught my eye. Seth, Eli and Jake sat at this one, huddled together as if they didn't want to be noticed. An extra chair sat, pushed away slightly, from the wooden table, their small circle obviously not welcome to any outsiders. Luckily for me, though, I didn't care.

I jogged over, pulling the chair next to me as I sat, smiling innocently as all three turned to look at me. Their hushed conversation immediately died, but I held my ground.

"Look what the cat dragged in," Seth scoffed. "What are you doing?"

"Oh, I'm sorry, I didn't realize it was illegal to sit down," I said with a sarcastic grin.

"Oh, I'm sorry, I didn't think you'd want to sit with us anyway," he snarled in response. I threw my hands in the air, as a gesture of retreat. "Let me rephrase... what are you doing?"

"Just hanging out. Enjoying the night air," I said with a dramatic inhale. "Damien said fall is around the corner, so it's really nice out. I would say it's getting darker earlier, but you never know with the sun here."

"What does that even mean?" Jake said exasperatedly. "The sun doesn't just move around randomly. You're telling me that—" he looked up, pointing to the sun, which was just going down, trying to pass beneath the horizon. Perfect timing, as it started to rise back into the sky, reversing its path. He gaped in surprise, a mixed look of amazement and horror in his gaze.

"Like I said before, this is not our world. Our rules don't apply, even to the sun. Magic is a thing," I said, hoping to exhibit this by setting my hand ablaze. However, my powers stubbornly refused to work once again, so I settled with causing a strong breeze to flow by, wrapping around the table just enough to let them know this wasn't a natural occurrence. "If that doesn't convince you, just look at Tigre! That is not a costume."

"How can we even take your word on that? How do we know this isn't some elaborate scheme?" Seth insisted.

"You assume I have the money to even rent a green screen, let alone the technology to do that?" I chuckled. "How could I pull you into a stage or something even remotely like that without you knowing, without being anywhere near you, without the budget or the people I'd need to make that happen? Seth, you've traveled through the forest with me! You've seen all of this in action. You almost got me killed by a giant shark-jellyfish hybrid in the bottom of a lake trying to save the General, who disappeared in a cloud of smoke when I tried to touch him, reappearing on land moments later!" I exploded, my breathing as short as my temper. All three boys looked surprised, and slightly scared as I settled into my seat, feeling my face heat up as I was sure my cheeks flushed. Jake looked between Eli and Seth for confirmation, but the two also looked flustered.

"I guess... yeah. There's not really any way this could be a prank," Seth mumbled in defeat.

"I tried to fight something here, and it didn't go well. Then it turned into dust in front of my eyes, thanks to Amber, so... I wouldn't say this could be fake either," Eli nodded.

"Thank you!" I rolled my eyes, but Jake still looked suspicious. "Anyway, my purpose of coming over here wasn't to convince you this world is real—"

"Did you have a purpose?" Seth interrupted. I rolled my eyes, a slight smirk on my face.

"Not really, but I did succeed in annoying you all, so at least I was productive," I said slyly, rising from my seat. I jogged off with a small wave, going into the dining pavilion to see if I could help with anything. Tigre was sitting behind a fire pit, a grate forming a grill right above the flames, a tarp covering half his body. A pile of hamburgers sat next to him, on a plastic plate. He looked up as I entered, a deep blush immediately flowing over his face. He looked down at the tarp, and then back at me with an embarrassed smile. His tiger side was covered, all the fur pushed beneath the tarp, I assumed to act like a giant hair net. He looked almost human, aside from his gleaming gold eye.

"Hey, Amber," he said meekly, flipping the burger on the grill.

"Interesting fashion choice," I commented, holding back a snicker.

"You like it? I was thinking of making my own fashion line," he continued the joke, and we both giggled. "So, what brings you here?"

"Looking for work. The tone here has... definitely died down," I sighed. "I almost miss being in battle, as strange as that sounds. At least it's thrilling, and I get to use my powers. So I want something to do, find some way to help."

"We're having a simple dinner, but you can help by giving me company," he joked. "Nah, you can go hang out with your friends if you want to."

"You're my friend too," I reminded him. "And they're your friends as well... right?"

"Yeah, but you seem a lot closer to them, I feel like I'm not really in that circle," he said with a slight glance down, a sad smirk on his face.

"Tigre... we're all basically a family here, even the ones no one likes. Seth, Eli, Jake..." I muttered the last part, and Tigre chuckled. "Point is, the circle wouldn't be complete without every single one of us. Including you!" I said cheerfully, pointing dramatically. His gaze softened and he let out a small laugh, a grateful smile dancing across his cheeks.

"Thanks, Amber," he said, flipping one last burger off of the small grill, and tossing water on the fire. "I'm done now, want to help bring these out?" I nodded, picking up the platter beside him. He grabbed a small stack of what looked to be wooden plates and stood, leading me out of the pavilion. We distributed hamburgers together, each table already decorated with buns and condiments. I wondered how they made all of this, but I didn't question it much. Relish, ketchup and mustard sat in small glass jars at every place, something I hadn't taken notice of before. Everyone happily dug in to their meals, and Tigre and I eventually found our way over to Damien and the others, dining with them as the sun finally set, this time actually going below the horizon.

It seemed more like a party than a feast, but the next day, the mood was severely dampened. People came and went, all giving me and Damien bad news. As more and more villages and people were being helped, the more we found a strange connection between every case. It seemed as if, no matter where we went, this telepathic villain followed us, and none of the people I asked had seen Aaron in days. It was extremely suspicious, and I didn't know how many times I could keep brushing this off.

No one could defend themselves properly, but we were more than happy to help. I wished I could have gotten back into the real action, but Damien insisted on a little more training. We met in the arena early in the morning, while everyone was just waking up. The first thing he did was climb onto the chain mesh above us, dropping in two large sticks, the wood sturdy enough to not break on impact and about as long as swords. I then waited five minutes as he struggled down, standing across from me.

He flipped the stick in his hand, catching it on the other side.

"How about we train your abilities to use your clothes to your advantage? First, the cloak. You've used it once or twice- I heard about when you plummeted off of the golem, you used the force field to keep you from getting killed by the fall. Smart, and it shows that you're getting used to the quick thinking and timing, but you need to practice more, focusing on getting everything exactly right." He stood in a poised position, a sly smile on his face, his arm above his head, holding the stick. I picked up mine from the ground, and nodded. He charged forward quickly, stabbing beside my arm and towards my stomach. I was about to mutter the spell when the stick closed in, and I stumbled backwards, my side in pain. "Too slow. Keep an eye out on your surroundings, don't get distracted. Also, you have to know how long the shield stays up, or how far you can push it. Go ahead, try saying the spell and timing or keeping up the force field."

I focused, my hands spread out in front of me. I muttered the words with vigor, seeing a thin blue sheen slowly cover me. I placed my fingertips on the shield, trying to keep it up, feeling the energy buzz beneath my skin. Despite my best efforts, it only stayed for around five seconds.

"That's not much to work with," I panted slightly.

"Exactly why you have to practice, and keep an eye on timing. You've gotten lucky the last few times you've used the cloak's powers, but you can't rely on that anymore." I nodded, noticing the determination in his eyes. He started to jab at me, and I watched him, trying to study his movements and dodge accordingly. I didn't get hit often, but getting hit at all was bad, especially in life or death situations.

There was no rest for me, as I quickly realized. Damien was taking this very seriously, training me in the day and teaching me spells at night.

"Mutatio animosa, cat!" I yelled, pointing towards a ceramic jar sitting on the small table. It morphed quickly, mutating into a small panther. I leapt back as it pranced away, mewling frantically.

"With that, you have to be a little more specific. So, you probably should have said house cat," Damien winced. "Oh well, it will survive, and it will hopefully not attempt to eat us in the future."

"Sorry," I apologized, smiling sheepishly. "What... what's next?" I had a lot of trouble with the spoken spells at first, but it was fun. There were so many possibilities, but I wasn't able to do much at once, as every single one drained a lot of my mana. I felt much more prepared, though, and I started helping around camp more. The next week, we had hamburgers again, and I enjoyed everything, even the cooking.

As we all ate, a thought popped into my head, one I should have asked before, but I didn't want to risk bringing more attention to the situation. Though, with the reports, I doubted Damien was still in the dark about what I was thinking.

"Hey, where's Aaron?" I questioned. The boys looked up in confusion and concern, and a wave of dread swept over me.

"I haven't seen him," Jay commented, wiping his mouth with a napkin.

"Me neither. He didn't go with you guys on your recent mission... was he here when you got back?" Harlequinn said, and I tried to think. I didn't remember seeing him, which was even odder. He couldn't have gone out by himself, but... a memory fought its way to the front of my mind, and I remembered what Jonas said about the mage. How strange that he also wasn't at camp while that was happening...

My doubts rose once again as I finished my meal, heading to bed early. I claimed I felt sick, and it wasn't entirely a lie, especially once I fell asleep. Dreams plagued me, sickly images flaunting through my mind, horror-filled images that might have only been terrible to me. Pictures barely describable, lonely cities with dust hanging stagnant in the air, faded lights filtered in from above, a crowd of silhouettes surrounded me, no faces visible, evil laughter coming from different angles. A mess so strange that it even

400

confused me within the dreams, and I wasn't sure if it meant something important.

I woke with a start, breathing hard and sweating. I almost believed I was still asleep, because of a melodic whispering echoing through my room, the eerie sound something I didn't think was real. Until I realized, it was real, but not actually in my head. The rhythm made me drowsy, but I fought through my tired daze and stood up, grabbing my sword before stumbling out of my cabin. Obviously I wasn't the only one to notice the strange, foreign words, because half the camp was up and gathered around... Aaron. He stood in the middle of the camp, his eyes closed as he muttered something incomprehensible. I saw angry glares and made out some mumbling through all the noise.

"What's going on?" I asked, my voice hoarse.

"He's been sabotaging us," Damien snarled. "We've helped quite a few people, and wherever we've gone, we got reports of someone screaming in their minds, making it to where they can't protect themselves. Who has that power? Not to mention leading spies here, stealing our supplies, and either trying to kidnap or kill the remaining people here," Damien said spitefully, a glare directed towards Aaron, who stood with a flat expression.

"Aaron, what are you trying to do?" I begged, my hands clasped in front of me. He turned, his eyes showing no light or life behind them. It was as if he turned to stone, no remorse or regret in his gaze. I stepped forward, my hand out to try to grab his arm so he couldn't get away, but he suddenly found his soul as color returned to his face, cheeks flushing and a panicked look in his light eyes. I felt a pain in my head, a shrieking, ringing sound amplified through my mind. I screamed, falling to the ground, clutching my head. I apparently had gotten off better than others, as I saw at least one person faint, then everyone around immediately falling to their knees, rolling around in pain. I forced myself to stand, seeing Aaron sprinting out the gates, into the woods.

I shakily stepped forward, my pace moving as quickly as I could as I tried not to stumble. I moved as if I was drunk. My breathing was as unsteady as my legs, threatening to crumble beneath me at any second as the ringing continued, but strangely receded as I got closer to the gates. After a minute, I could walk properly, but everyone else was still writhing in pain. I gripped the sword at my waist and examined the forest, seeing his obvious trail left behind, a path of crushed leaves guiding the way through the dense trees. I set off, knowing I would have to take care of the others later, at the moment only focused on finding that traitor.

It didn't take me long. He was simply standing amongst the greenery, a sad, pathetic look on his face. Approaching silently wasn't an option, stumbling through all the dead foliage already made my presence known. Stealth was not an option in the forest- the floor was too crowded no matter the season. I stood awkwardly for a moment, watching his unmoving form, before I decided to speak.

"Aaron, I—" I never got to finish. He spun around, grabbed my arms, and walls appeared around us. I screamed and tried to break free, but his grip was strong and the walls formed instantly. Rage took control, and I made a rash decision, one I hoped wouldn't hurt too much. My hands caught fire, red flames flickering up to my wrists. He stepped back, grimacing as he shook his hands, a revolting burning smell filling the small cube. My heart fluttered with hope as I realized my fire was back, at least for now. "What did you do?" I whispered, but he didn't answer. It was ominous, seeing him not talk for so long, especially in this situation. My heart started racing, adrenaline pumping as I reached out and...

I smacked him. My hand flew across his face and with all my might, I slapped him. The sound was almost painful, and my hand hurt so badly, I pulled it back, wincing in pain. Aaron nearly fell over, but resumed his stance, as if he was possessed, or a robot.

"What are you?" I hissed. "You're not my friend. He would never do this. You are not the same person, I don't believe it!" I screamed, almost hysterically. It was so strange, this person I had known for years suddenly becoming like a stranger. A face so familiar, yet I couldn't even recognize him. His silly smile had faded, the light in his eyes was drained, all of his personality was different. It was as if I had known a completely different person, one who I was tricked into believing was somehow this... thing. "You're not real," I said shakily. He stood in the room, unblinking, emotionless. *"You're not real!"* I shrieked, drawing my sword, tears blurring my vision. I didn't know what this was, but I felt crushed. The one person I had from reality, the one I relied on and trusted, the one person I could even stand being around that was from my world... he was the traitor. That dream, with the birds warning me—they were real. They were talking about him.

Aaron.

"Tell me what you are," I growled, trying to keep myself from falling, and bursting into tears. "Tell me, or I'll kill you!" I screamed, my entire body bursting into flames. My emotions went unchecked, my fear and sadness got the best of me. I heard a ringing sound, and my head pounded, a screaming voice making my body freeze. He was trying to attack, incapacitate me. I vigorously shook, my screams echoing around the chamber, pained cries ricocheting around the room. I felt this pain not only in my body, but in my heart. It was like I had been stabbed, everything I knew changing, the camp in danger if he wasn't who I thought he was.

The change came in an instant, a strange force seeming to come over him as he turned, vengeance in his dark eyes. He wasn't the same, almost everything about him was as before, but my brain mutated him, making his face so unfamiliar, even though he hadn't changed a bit.

He was only a monster in my eyes.

Someone I knew, a friend, a companion in the darkest of times. Someone I trusted, and opened up to. Even if this was fake, even if the real him still existed in reality, seeing this hurt me. I still had shared moments with him, I still felt closer to him because of our adventures.

Now, that was over.

With my heart in my throat, I swung my blade. I felt the

resistance as it passed through him, but I didn't look. Tears streamed down my face and I silently screamed, my teeth bared and my entire body aching with the pain of losing a friend. I felt the fire burning my skin, the heat singeing my flesh. I cried out, a small, pitiful shriek before everything stopped. The world halted, but I still couldn't breathe.

CHAPTER TWENTY

"You... you're not... not real..." I fell to my knees, sobbing painfully as the room I was trapped in faded. I heard quick footsteps, and a hand touched my shoulder.

"Amber? Where's Aaron?" Damien asked.

"He's dead," I cried. "He... he's dead." I didn't understand what was happening, my mind so muddled that I went limp, crouching against the floor, whimpering like a hurt dog. I didn't get why he suddenly turned so robotic, what that cube was for, how he even made it. Maybe another person on the outside was trying to get us. It wasn't impossible, we had many enemies, but the thought of that broke me down even further.

I might have fallen into a coma, or my mind and heart were so brutally torn apart that my body stopped working for a few days. Everything was a blur, and I may have hallucinated because one of the rare times I was awake for a few minutes, I saw Seth, Eli and Jake visit me, mumbling what seemed to be apologies, genuine looks on their faces. I didn't remember much except for the pain, only a feeling remaining from the ordeal. Betrayal was the only thought that crossed my mind while my haze carried on.

I once again awoke days later, feeling extremely rested, though tears somehow still stained my eyes. I could feel that my hair was a mess, and trying to brush through it with my fingers ultimately ended up being useless, so I just attempted to flatten it. I sat up in my bed, still wearing the same clothes as before. My gauntlets had been taken off, and so had my cloak and sheath. All of those items lay neatly in the corner, in a nice little pile. I felt a small smile, one where I just barely moved my lips.

I heard a knock at the door, and I looked up to see a few people standing there, peeking through. I waved to them, and everyone stepped inside the cabin. Tigre, Damien, Jay, Harlequinn, even Seth, Eli, Jake and Melioca begrudgingly stood at the door frame.

"Hey... Damien told us what happened. I'm sorry! I knew I

should have been with you. I'm supposed to protect you..." Tigre said quietly. I shrugged sadly, my mind going blank.

"I'll be alright," I said, surprised at how awful I sounded. My words barely came out, my voice cracking and my throat aching. "I don't want to focus on this, or talk about it anymore. I... I want to get back into helping people. I've been out for too long."

"I would say you need more rest, but since you didn't get physically injured, if you want to go on a mission, you should be fine," Jay stated, sitting down next to me. He put his hand on my shoulder with a concerned glance.

"I don't know if that's a good idea," Damien protested. "You just slept for a few days without waking up. We could barely get you to eat. You're probably out of it, and I don't want you getting hurt."

"Why don't we go with them, then?" Harlequinn suggested. "We go in groups anyway. We could take a bigger mission, so we'd need more people. You, me, Jay, Amber and Tigre." I glanced towards the tiger, and saw him light up at the mention of his name, happy to be included.

"We do have that one mission we need to tackle... Kita Naseraeth and her clan. They've been under constant attack by assassins, and Kita's assistant has been begging for help," Jay suggested.

"Kita is an assassin herself. A very high level one. You know her backstory. Can't she take care of them herself?" Damien asked. "Not to be rude, but that seems like child's play for someone like her."

"Who's Kita?" I asked meekly.

"She's a skilled assassin. She's very deadly, and very temperamental. She doesn't like visitors, or even talking to anyone outside her clan. Her motto is kill first, ask questions later," Damien scoffed. "She's impressive, but rash and immature at times. Her background is... complicated. There're a lot of different stories, but the most consistent one is that she was raised poorly by her parents, forced into a life of crime since she could walk. They abandoned her in the woods when she was still a toddler, and luckily, a pack of forest foxes adopted her. Because of that, she has inhuman abilities, and her life as an assassin before led her to be an even more successful one today. She can walk across the forest, barely making a sound, she's quick as lightning and can climb like a squirrel. Her hearing and sight are exceptional, and she has custom made weapons, throwing stars that are enchanted to return back to her either after an hour, or if she wills them to. She'd be an extremely powerful ally, but it will be difficult and even dangerous to attempt to get her on board."

"She sounds like a handful," I grumbled. "Are we sure it's worth it to even go out there? It sounds like she'd be stubborn, and even if we leave with our lives, we won't get her help."

"It's worth a shot. She's like half of an army, stashed inside one person. She's quick, smart, silent, tough and... her clan isn't bad either. All of those women with us would be a huge turning point," Tigre pointed out. "I met her once, sort of. She was very cold and threatening, but obviously, she didn't kill me. Seemed like she may have been close, though..." he looked down, his hand on his chin, seeming like he was reconsidering going with us.

"You haven't been up here in... a long time," Damien laughed. "How could you have met her? She isn't immortal, and she's pretty young, so unless a baby was trying to kill you... even then, she's only around twenty." The mood suddenly fell as everyone looked at Tigre expectantly. Blush crept up on his cheeks, his eyes wide.

"What—what are you suggesting?" he said defensively, crossing his arms.

"Tigre, did you sneak up here? Like what Frostbite did?" I asked. Based on his reaction to his friend, it didn't seem likely, but how else would he have encountered Kita?

"I—wh—how—" he stuttered, looking for a way out. Noticing the stares around the room, he caved. "Fine! A few times, every decade or so... I'd get out of the abyss, go take a stroll. Can you blame me? Frostbite was right, it's boring down there. And when it isn't boring, you're fighting for your life. I can't live going from an immediate heart attack to mind-numbing boredom! Not for long, anyway." Tigre crossed his arms, looking peeved.

"Why did you have such a big reaction to Frostbite, then?" Damien questioned, everyone's attention focused on the conversation.

"I... I was surprised he wanted to leave for good. I always found my way back to the abyss because the Elites are my family, and my closest friends," Tigre said quietly, looking down. "So, I would take walks. Stretch my legs. I ran into the assassin clan, and they're definitely not friendly."

"We'll have to be careful. Strength in numbers comes into play here, so it would be better if we all went," Jay added, switching back to the previous topic.

"Road trip!" I said excitedly. "When can we leave?"

"I don't think any of us has anything else to do..." Harlequinn laughed. "Get your stuff, and we'll get ours. Meet at the gate in, say, five minutes?" With a nod of approval from everyone, they filed out, leaving me alone. Or, almost alone. Seth knocked on the door, not fully stepping into the cabin, but hovering on the stairs.

"Hey, I'm... I'm glad you didn't get hurt. Physically, at least. It would kinda suck if you died, so... be careful," he muttered, an expression I couldn't read plastered on his face.

"Thank you, I think," I said flatly. He nodded awkwardly before descending down the stairs, closing the door softly behind him. I puffed up my cheeks, thinking for a moment. Honestly with him, I'm not sure if he was being genuine, but at least it was a start. I shook my head, trying to clear my mind. I reached down, grabbing all of my stuff and slowly getting ready. When I got to the gate, everyone was already there, chatting quietly. They saw me approaching and all welcomed me with waves.

"It's not that far, so we're gonna walk," Damien explained. "We have to loop around the camp walls and start from behind, though."

"Oh, I don't think I've ever been exactly that direction," I laughed. "Well, let's not waste time. I'm eager to get back out."

"Hey, are you feeling alright?" Damien asked, falling slightly behind the group as we walked along, talking quietly to me.

"I'll be fine, don't worry," I said with a sheepish smile. "Though... I keep thinking about something. Other than, you know... My fire powers stopped working for a while, and I only started being able to use them again when... Aaron."

"That's... peculiar, but can probably be easily explained. You've been focusing mostly on fire, so it's like... Your mana must be separated into what's essentially four different containers. For your fire, the vial is empty. You can't use it for a while, because you've used it so much, you've run out. Everything else is nearly full. As time passes, your mana eventually restores itself, so if you wait a little bit you can use your flames in small bursts. The few days of rest should have put you in a good spot, but it was also after you probably drained your mana again. I wouldn't risk using fire for a little while," he explained. I nodded, a little upset, but I would survive. Fire wasn't the only power I had, luckily.

"Thank you," I said, putting my hand on his shoulder. "I guess I'll have to be more on the diplomacy side, instead of lighting everything on fire."

"Yeah, that definitely sounds like you. Who will you be if you can't destroy something?" he joked, smiling.

"Honestly, I don't know if I could live with myself!" I exclaimed dramatically, putting my hand over my heart. We both fell apart into a pile of giggles, laughing as we headed around the camp.

Behind the stone walls was a vast expanse of empty land. The forest edge curved, and ended just before the front of the camp, but back here? It was flat lands for miles. I didn't see how anyone could hide here, but I still trekked along, not worried about specifications.

The chatter faded as the minutes passed, a hush falling on the small crowd. The sun flicked across the sky, annoyingly casting shadows and then immediately making them disperse, shining full light on the valley. The day was cloudless, the sky was bright and the air was clean, but my mind was chaotic. All the silence let me wallow in my thoughts, bringing up memories I didn't want to face. I was relieved when everyone stopped in front of me, finally getting to the edge of the forest, stepping out of the sun and into the trees. Dead leaves crunched beneath our steps, twigs broke and needless to say, we were not very silent.

"Keep an eye out. They're everywhere, even in the trees," Tigre warned, pointing up just as a bird flew from its perch, startling me. "That's how I got ambushed. It wasn't pretty."

"Nothing with assassins ever is. Most of them are scumbags, to be honest," Jay whispered. "But what else would you expect?"

"Hello!" I heard a cheerful, bubbly voice call from behind me. I turned with a shriek, the others following in defensive stances, our weapons raised. But we quickly put them down when we saw a petite girl standing behind us. Her silky-smooth blonde hair was tied back in a bun, and she clutched a clipboard over her chest. She wore a plain, white, button-up shirt with a black jacket over it, and black pants. She looked extremely professional, and not someone you would expect to meet in the middle of the woods. "I'm Milly, I assume you're looking for Kita?"

"That depends," Damien said, stepping forward. "How do you know her?"

"I'm her assistant, the one who sent the note. Oh, I do wish you'd sent a letter back clarifying the day... she refuses to meet with anyone on Fridays. Normally she's stubborn, and it's hard to convince her to host a meeting in general, but Fridays? Absolutely off limits!"

"It's Friday?" I muttered to myself, but I saw Milly nod vigorously.

"Well... maybe. Kita sometimes makes up the day just to give herself a pass, but I don't argue," the small girl laughed nervously. "Please don't tell her I said that."

"Are you an assassin as well?" Damien inquired, a hint of doubt staining his voice.

"Of course! We all are in Kita's clan," Milly beamed.

"You're very... soft spoken, for an assassin." I commented, hoping I wouldn't in some way offend her.

"People normally don't guess I'm anything other than a mere tool... but Kita doesn't just use me. I have a real job, and I even get paid! I still act as an assassin as well. Kita does have a heart, after all," the assistant giggled. "Anyway, you'll have to come back. Maybe. I don't when Friday ends."

"There's no way we can insist a meeting?" I said, lowering my voice.

"No, she'll be furious. You'll probably be dead before you can get a word out," Milly sighed. "I'll see what I can do. Come, wait here!" She led us a little further into the woods, to a circular wooden table. Five chairs were set out, the perfect amount for our group. We all took a seat, none of us in the mood for talking, so an awkward silence fell as Milly disappeared into the leaves. I noticed she didn't make much noise as she walked, her steps finding their way into any open space that didn't hold leaves. It was impressive, honestly, how flawlessly she did it. I put my arm on the table, humming idly. The boys slowly joined in, tapping on the table, snapping, and I smiled as the melody continued.

However, it was cut off when a knife landed in the middle of all of us. Everyone looked up simultaneously, to see two masked figures leaping through the trees. Black outfits covered their body and faces, but belts with gleaming blades on them were visible. They started hollering, and we all dove for cover, the whooping assassins diving out of the trees and coming towards us. I tried to shove myself beneath the table, but a knife was quickly embedded in the wood beside me, so I thought it was best to move. I struggled to stand, conjuring some powerful gusts of wind to sweep these little things off of their feet. Turns out, I didn't even need to try. Another figure landed in front of us, but this time with features I could actually make out.

She had on a shirt that the sleeves barely went past her shoulders, and something that looked like a dragon pelt was draped over the fabric, scaly armor attached to cotton. A thin belt wrapped around her waist with holsters for metal throwing stars, a pouch no doubt holding more. Her pants were tight-fitting, outlining her lithe yet muscular figure, but the cold glare in her eyes was the most intimidating thing about her. Lavender hair hung down below her waist, tied back in a thick ponytail, her sharp jaw accentuating the slightly terrifying look. She crouched on the table, not smiling and barely blinking, a judgmental expression as she scanned the enemies, and us. In the blink of an eye, she drew her weapons and threw the stars menacingly, catching the attacker's sleeves on a tree behind us. They struggled, but somehow, despite the metal piercing the fabric, their clothes didn't rip and they couldn't get away. The newcomer stood, silently approaching the cowering assassins, her walk so quiet it was eerie. This must be Kita Naseraeth.

"You insolent twigs," she spat, her voice low and menacing, giving me chills. "You're from another clan. You do not belong in my territory. Get lost, and go tell your leader that if he wants rights here, he has to personally talk to me." She muttered some colorful insults, before holding out her hand, the stars returning to her grip in an instant. The two fell from the trees, bark ripping at their clothes as they scrambled away. Kita put her hand on her hip, a cold, unmoving gaze as she turned to our group. We all had our weapons raised, frozen in shock, but as soon as she looked at us, we dropped them. "What do you lot want? Milly tried to get me to come out here, even though it's Friday. That means I'm not in the best mood, so start talking."

"Hi, thank you for seeing, and saving us. I'm Amber, the General of a camp a few miles back. I assume you're Kita?" I asked, holding out my hand in a friendly gesture. She glanced at my outstretched arm with disgust, shooting me a glare that made me shiver.

"That's right, Kita Naseraeth. You're taking a big risk here," she sneered, silently stepping closer, a throwing star held menacingly in her hand. "I should kill you for even stepping in this part of the woods. Especially him!" She threw her star towards Tigre, but she obviously meant it as a warning, because it didn't hit. It grazed past him, taking off a small chunk of fur, and embedding itself in the tree behind him. He yelped, dashing to the side.

"Hey!" he protested, putting his hand on his arm, a small streak of blood growing where the star cut across his skin.

"You disturb me on a Friday, and you bring this ape with you?" Kita demanded, her voice barely rising, but her stare so intense that I did not want to intervene.

"I'm a tiger! That's literally—" his voice faded, his eyes widening as the assassin stepped towards him. A throwing star was held loosely in her grip, and her expression fell. The anger in her eyes was almost indescribable, a raging fire that she didn't let show in anything other than her gaze. She stood perfectly still, not shaking, barely breathing as she held the sharp star to Tigre's neck. I felt as if any noise would cause an avalanche, battle exploding, all of us against Kita. And at this point, I wasn't sure we would win.

I didn't expect anyone to do anything, much less Harlequinn, but he was the one to step in. He reached forward, putting his hand calmly on Kita's shoulder. As soon as he touched her, she whipped around, pivoting so she was behind Harlequinn, wrapping her arm around his neck. She still held her hand to Tigre, so now she had two of our friends essentially held captive.

"Let's be civil!" Harlequinn choked out, slowly being strangled. Jay tried to rush forward, but I jumped in front of him, pushing him back. I remembered what Damien said about not using fire, but I needed to split this up somehow.

I shoved Jay's shoulder, sending him stumbling backwards so he wouldn't approach. Then I dropped to the ground, pressing my hand into the dirt and causing the earth to rupture, throwing Kita off her feet with a scream. With my other hand, I pointed my palm towards the three, conjuring a major gust of wind. I'd never tried to use two powers at once like this, and not these two combined either. I felt my mana quickly depleting, my energy falling as I made the ground tremble while practically forming a tornado. The assassin was thrown away from my friends, struggling to stand as the ground pushed her further and further away from the group. I stopped everything when she was a few feet away and finally thrown onto her back. I nearly reached out to grab Harlequinn and Tigre, but I collapsed before I could, falling on my face.

I think I swallowed some dirt as I crashed, barely able to even lift my head or open my eyes to see what was happening, but from the ruckus, I assumed Harlequinn and Tigre were retrieved. Kita's angry screams soon followed, and I felt someone pull at the back of my shirt, lifting me into the air. The assassin's legs were buried beneath a ton of dirt, and speckles of brown covered her face and arms. Her face was flushed and she had a slight snarl, her gaze even wilder than before.

"We're not here to fight," I said assertively, stomping my foot as I approached her. I kept a stern look on my face, one I hoped would intimidate her, sweeping my arm to the side and clearing the dirt with a burst of wind. Kita quickly picked up a throwing star, spinning it in her hand like she was contemplating how she would kill me. Then... she relaxed. Her tensed-up muscles softened with her gaze, and the star went right back into her pocket.

"Very well. I respect your challenge. Your powers are impressive, I'm assuming elemental?" she asked, her tone now extremely casual.

"Uh... yeah, as far as I know." I stumbled, not expecting her to give in so quickly.

"Milly!" she called, and her assistant dropped from the trees, leaves falling beside her.

"Yes, Kita?" she asked innocently, an adoring smile on her face as she looked up.

"Move Friday to tomorrow. Mark down a meeting with the... camp group. What is your camp called?" Kita said with a smirk, turning towards me.

"I don't think officially, but we—or, some of us, call it The Utopia," I commented, remembering my conversation with Frostbite about the original name.

"Unusual name. You... isn't that the camp that—oh, Milly. You called them here, to persuade me into their little rebellion?" Kita crossed her arms, looking disappointed. Milly shrunk beneath her clipboard, making small marks with a pen she was suddenly holding.

"Does that mean you wouldn't want to help us?" I asked,

concerned.

"I don't trust you, especially not with the wolf you've had stalking me," she scoffed. "I can't believe you thought you could catch me with that. Lunar wolves are exceptional hunters, but so am I." She back flipped suddenly, shooting into the trees, bouncing from one branch to another. You could barely see her shadow as she flawlessly sprinted across the forest, never touching the ground. Something clicked in my mind as I realized she was talking about Aster, who... she now might try to hurt.

"Wait!" I cried out, whistling as loud as I could. Before my breath ended, the wolf dashed to my side, snarling viciously. "He... he's mine, I'm sorry. I didn't realize he'd been following you, and I don't know why he would." I looked around, realizing I lost the dim silhouette of the assassin, and Milly disappeared as well. They really were silent.

"There!" Tigre yelled, pointing above us, where a figure leapt through the leaves.

"No, she's right there!" Jay pointed up as well, then Damien and Harlequinn, and I could see at least twenty shadows, all jumping around us, eyes illuminated eerily. Whispers filled the air, a call I couldn't quite understand but struck an arrow of fear through my heart.

"The entire clan must be here," Damien said quietly. "I've never seen so many in one place."

"Assassins or people?" I muttered.

"Kita must have called them here. Or, they noticed her going out on a Friday—well, now Friday is tomorrow, but they don't know that. Anyway, be careful not to move, or else you'll be immediately hunted down by a lot of skilled assassins!" Milly cheerfully beamed, suddenly standing beside me.

"God, you guys are quick!" I cursed under my breath, nearly falling over in surprise.

"What did you expect? Surely you've heard of our clan. Barely any animals even dare come near here because of us, much less humans," Milly giggled. "All of us are deadly. Watch your step around here."

"Amber, she's right. We shouldn't have come here. Every assassin here could destroy us, and working together, we wouldn't stand a chance. We're obviously not getting Kita on our side—" Damien started. He would have finished if the cyclone of assassins in the trees didn't die down, all the faces disappearing and Kita tumbling down to the forest floor.

"Who says I'm not helping you?" she laughed. "I called them here for judgment. The consensus was that they don't like how easily you give up, you've been here before and you are trouble, you two seem pure, and you... the little leader. Pushing ahead despite all odds, power as worn out as your heart. You're small, young, and you don't have some tragic backstory that hardened you into a vicious warrior, but you still managed to throw me off of my feet. You're determined, and you have strong powers. We may help you... only because that disgusting King doesn't deserve to rule," Kita huffed with an angry glare. She didn't seem to show much emotion except for a terrifying rage, her every move, look, and breath intimidating. "Not to mention the fact that he's trying to put us out of business."

"You're pretty far away from the Kingdom, how do you know about the fighting?" Tigre stepped in, probably at the wrong time, but all he got was a sharp glare.

"We're constantly on the move, we hear things. We know a lot of secrets, including things you don't even know," she bragged, with a slightly proud expression. "Including... the King isn't himself. He was corrupt before, but now, his powers and anger are multiplied tenfold. He's been possessed, a demon slowly taking over his functions. Amber, you fought him, you've seen his face. That's the mark of possession, a significant scarring or mutilation of some kind. That's also the reason he stays out of the light." I was both surprised and not that she knew I had my own run in with the King. He was definitely hard to beat. I collapsed a castle on him and he was still kicking. She was right about the darkness, though. It seemed as if the light hurt him.

"He's been trying to slowly hunt down or disband all the assassin clans in the forest as well. We're already at war with each other, and his constant barrage of attacks isn't helping," Milly said, her face falling. "Some clans are convinced we've sided with the Kingdom and are helping the wretched King."

"So... you're in the same position as us. Well, sort of," I muttered, crossing my arms.

"That's why you have to help us, though," Damien said, stepping forward. "You see everything. We need that type of surveillance, as well as your fighting skills to be able to take the King down."

"Hmm..." Kita paused, her hand on her chin in a thinking gesture. "It would help us. But fighting alongside you makes it seem as if we need help, and you can't keep secrets from assassins, so there's no avoiding that."

"Wouldn't it be a small price to pay? And, you're strong enough you can prove you don't need us to the surrounding clans," I said with a pointed look.

"Alright. We need to discuss more specific terms, but if we have any intent to help, I guess we should tell you of a severely time sensitive matter. The King is hosting a ball tonight to celebrate his birthday. It's a large party, and a prince from another kingdom, very far away, will be in attendance. He's unaware of the war, so the King will no doubt manipulate him to get him on his side. Those people are very powerful, and if he sides with the Kingdom, they will have allies all over the world. I don't think I need to tell you why that's bad."

"We need to dress fancily, don't we?" I groaned. I despised dresses.

"Yes, you're literally going to a royal ball. I've heard enough about you from Kingdom gossip that you're no longer an unfamiliar face, so be careful." Kita shrugged. "If you're going, wear blue. It's the prince's favorite color, and he's more likely to notice a blue outfit, especially since the dress code is black and white. Wear a dark enough color that it still fits in."

"The sun is going to go down soon. Do you know how much time we have?" Damien asked, looking worried.

"About an hour," Kita warned. "And you can't all go. It's very suspicious, as well as I can't fully trust you yet. Amber can go, but I'm keeping the rest of you here to make sure they come back."

"I'll be alone?" I winced.

"Hey, you can do this! You're plenty experienced now. We'll stay here, and cheer you on," Damien said with a smile, followed by the others nodding. "We'll discuss stuff and tell her what we know, all the boring things."

"Where am I supposed to get a dress in the middle of the woods?" I sighed.

"Back at camp, Melioca probably knows what to do. Take Aster, and talk to her," Tigre advised, and I nodded, swinging onto the wolf.

"The Elites are back?" Kita questioned as I started to sprint off.

"I'm an Elite!" I heard Tigre cry as I raced through the forest, bursting through the woods and across the valley.

"We have to hurry, Aster!" He seemed to understand, bounding even faster, panting as we ran. We skidded to a stop in front of the camp's stone walls, reaching the gates just as the sun started to dip behind the horizon. "Melioca! I need a blue dress!" I yelled, sliding off and running into the camp. The angel looked up, a surprised glance on her face.

"Excuse me?" she asked, though she looked excited.

"Long story short, there's a ball in the Kingdom I need to sneak into. The dress code is black and white, but we're rebels, so I'm wearing blue," I joked, but the Elite didn't seem to get it. "Tigre said you could help me."

"Of course I can! How do you think I keep changing into these extravagant clothes?" She asked, gesturing to her dress. All her outfits were elaborate, but beautiful.

"You can… create clothes?" I asked, and she raised her eyebrow, like I was challenging her. She twirled her hand, and I felt my clothes slowly morph around me, exhibiting a power I never knew she had.

"Go check the mirror before heading out. I'll fix anything you don't like," she said, her tone more friendly than I'd ever heard from her, yet still being slightly hostile. I nodded, rushing into a nearby cabin, nearly tripping because I was suddenly wearing heeled boots. I burst through the door, panting slightly, examining my outfit.

I had a beautiful dress, sleeves going down to my elbows and the back was longer than the front, flowing midnight blue fabric. I had a ribbon right above my waist, the fabric tied at my back. A sparkling pattern adorned the sleeves, and going down almost to the middle of my stomach, stopping as it reached the bow. Down from there was plain layered fabric, and my hair was no longer a frizzy mess, but delicately curled in perfect ringlets. I had boots that went up to my ankles, with heels that made me look a lot taller, but weren't that hard to walk in. I even looked like I had a light dusting of makeup, and I was shocked by how incredible my outfit was. I heard floorboards creak, and Melioca stepped inside, admiring her handiwork. "Not too shabby."

"Melioca... this is amazing! Thank you!" I cried, wrapping my arms around her in a hug. She started to protest, but quickly stopped, gently patting my back. "I have to go, but really... I love this dress, and I hate dresses," I giggled. A small smile got through her stone wall of a face, and she looked proud.

"Just... promise me you'll be careful. Do you want one of us to come with you?" She looked concerned, genuine emotion showing through her eyes. My expression softened, and I felt... happy... that she was worried about me.

"I'll be okay, but I don't know what to do if I need to fight. I don't have my—wait, where did my clothes from before go?" I asked, frantically looking around. Damien would kill me if I lost the cloak and gauntlets, and the sword was important.

"Calm down! I thought about that already," the angel said, draping a sapphire necklace around my neck. One stone sat in the middle, surrounded by small blue gems. "This necklace will help you transform if you need it. Just tap the sapphire three times, and your outfit will return. But, it doesn't work for long. I've given you five or six hours. Don't mess this up," she warned, a stern look on her face. I laughed, putting my hand on her shoulder.

"You're amazing, Melioca. My very own fairy godmother," I quickly commented before sprinting out the door, not waiting to see her reaction. Aster was poised to go, and I nearly jumped right on, before realizing that riding a wolf in a dress would be difficult. I guess I had to stick with side-saddle, without a saddle. I had to ride... side.

I begrudgingly climbed up, gripping on to his neck, my legs both on one side of his body. Aster looked confused, but started off slowly as I urged him forward. He tried not to go too fast, probably seeing my awkward position, but my anxiety shot up every step we took. This was time sensitive, so I was scared, but I charged on.

CHAPTER TWENTY-ONE

We arrived at the border of the Kingdom just as the sun set. I left Aster behind the crowded buildings, so I didn't draw more attention to myself. A long line of people slowly filed into the large, obviously remodeled castle. I smirked, taking satisfaction in knowing that I had been the cause of the rebuilding, from collapsing the ceiling to throwing an entire person into a tower, it must have taken a beating. It was wider now, and not as tall. There were no longer doors but a metal gate, with guards surrounding the building. I realized I wasn't wearing a mask, and anyone could easily recognize me, but it seemed to be fine as I walked around.

I slowly shuffled into line, moving with the people around me. I saw a mixture of carriages and cars parked around the area, and true to Kita's word, everyone was in black and white. Expensive suits and extravagant dresses, it seemed everyone had a partner accompanying them. A woman with a gorgeous headscarf stood in front of me, chatting with the person next to her, another woman with long, blonde, shiny hair. The woman with a scarf had a longer, black dress, decorated with pearls, and the blonde woman had a dress that just passed her knees, a white shirt with detailed black roses covering a lot of it.

They both looked happy, but I felt out of place. Young, alone, and in blue. I guess I made myself stand out much more than I wanted to. I felt a soft tap on my shoulder, and turned to see someone standing behind me, a graceful smile on his face. He had long, flowing, white hair that went down to his waist. Piercing blue eyes stared back at me, a sapphire gaze, the color so cold it froze you in your tracks, mesmerized by this person's eyes. He smiled- a bright, friendly smile that was blindingly white, especially against his dark skin. He wore a dark, navy blue suit, and a golden crown rested on his head, a small band embedded with crystals. Small splotches of white mottled his skin, especially around his lips, neck and from what I could see on his arms. He was softly illuminated by the dying light, his poise so regal and his outfit a blue that nearly convinced me right away that this was the prince. Not to mention the crown.

"I'm so sorry to bother you, but... I noticed you're alone. At night in a Kingdom like this, it's not safe! Would you allow me to accompany you?" he asked with a shy smile, holding out his hand politely.

"Of course! Thank you, honestly I was getting a bit nervous," I laughed awkwardly, taking his hand with a small curtsy. He stepped in closer, and I linked my arm around his. "I'm Amber."

"That's a beautiful name! I don't like my name all that much," he admitted, shrugging. "However, I'm the prince of a far off region, so... your highness, your majesty, all that works," he joked, and I giggled, genuinely amused and also excited. He definitely was the one I was looking for.

"So, you came all this way for the King?" I asked, and he nodded.

"This Kingdom has supported my family for a long time, so it would be rude not to make an effort to be here for the King's birthday! My parents are already inside, talking with him I bet."

"Do they approve of someone like him?" I asked, venturing into a dangerous area. "I wouldn't expect anyone to."

"What do you mean?" the prince inquired, tilting his head slightly with a worried glance.

"You haven't heard?" I lowered my voice, ducking my head so that no one heard or saw me. "He oppresses anyone within the Kingdom walls, and tries to take control of those outside of it. He's responsible for thousands of deaths, and is creating war that stretches even into the Endless Woods. And, there's a rumor going around that... he's not himself. Supposedly, a demon has possessed him." I heard the prince gasp, his hand flying to his face.

"I'm not exactly saying you're lying, but... I'm sorry, I can't say I believe everything a stranger tells me. Do you have proof?"

"I think later tonight I will." We reached the gate, both of us hurrying inside, trying to avoid the guard's watchful eyes. I slipped through without a problem, and I slowly walked in, still with the prince. Now, instead of a plain corridor, the castle opened up to a giant ballroom. Marbled floors created intricate patterns below us, crystal chandeliers hanging from the ceiling, casting light across the entire room. Food was set up, long tables with delicacies in every corner. Light violin music rose into the air, the middle of the giant room open for dancing and milling about. I saw no familiar faces, and no one seemed to notice mine as I walked along with the prince. One thing that confused me, however... there were barely any shadows. If the light hurt demons, the King wouldn't be able to show his face in this room. I doubt he would want to either, his scarred face not exactly pleasing to the eye, as well as someone might figure out that he's not himself.

"I love your dress, by the way. Who made it?" he asked nonchalantly, but his expression was secretive, as if he knew something.

"Uh... a friend of mine," I said quickly, nervous from his strange stare.

"It's a beautiful color, Kita really knows what she's talking about," he smiled down at me as if nothing had happened. "Would you like something to drink?"

"Back up!" I exclaimed, slowly lowering my voice as I drew some stares. "What do you know?"

"You didn't—oh, she does love her pranks," the prince chuckled. "I'm good friends with the assassin clan. Don't tell my parents, but the last time I was here, they tried to kidnap me for ransom when I accidentally crossed into their territory. Kita let me go. Apparently the two responsible were unauthorized and made a bad decision. We've kept in touch since then, using a method she learned from that tiger elite when they ran into each other."

"Tigre? And, what method?" I asked, confused, and a little shocked.

"This small bead," he said, pushing back his hair to reveal what looked like a pearl earring. "It's actually a communication device. With the right spell, you can activate it and it broadcasts your thoughts to whoever has another one of these. I think she stole them, actually."

"But why would she be pranking me by sending me here? If you're friends, didn't you already know about the King's antics?"

"No, I had no clue, but now I'm sure I can trust you. All Kita said was that you'd be wearing a blue dress, but I wanted to be safe. She must have wanted you here, but she never wastes an opportunity to have some fun," he smiled, probably reminiscing about her antics. "They're planning something."

"What could they—oh. Oh no..." the final battle was approaching much quicker than I expected. She must have sent me here tonight to meet with the prince, and have me at the ready in the Kingdom. "Do you have people on your side who can fight? Anyone from your region?"

"I practically brought an army. They're waiting for my command, to attack or to halt. Why?"

"Tonight, the King's reign ends. I have a feeling they're planning on launching an attack, and that's why they wanted me here. Melioca, the friend who made this dress for me, gave me a necklace that basically holds my old clothes, so I can get them back for fighting," I said, hovering my hand over the sapphire. "We just have to wait until they get here. This is an attack he won't survive, trust—" I was shocked by the cold feeling of hands pressing down on my shoulders. My breath halted along with my heart, as I saw in the corner of my eyes... the King, a mask over his marred face. The prince next to me scrambled backwards, holding his hand out threateningly.

"I don't think I've had the honor of properly meeting you," he said slyly, grabbing my arm. "May I have this dance?" I couldn't tell what his plan was, but I stiffly nodded, and he swung me out into the middle of the floor. The prince watched helplessly, his hand at his ear.

"It... It's very bright in here," I choked out as the King spun me around, forcing me to dance to the music. I didn't entirely know what he was doing, but he led, so I didn't have trouble.

"Indeed. A bit harsher than I think is needed, but what can you do?" he said with a shrug. I practically had to lean back, watching him with fear. He wore an elegant suit, and seemed strangely calm, like he knew what we were planning.

"You could… ask someone to tone it down?" I suggested, confused.

"Ah, I wouldn't want to ruin the fun. The planners worked so hard." The King spun me around, and I hastily followed his movement, trying not to take my eyes off of him.

"A little constructive criticism never hurt anyone," I commented, and he nodded wisely.

"In that case… what criticism would you give me? You seem to be very opinionated on how I rule my Kingdom. So, let me hear your ideas," he hissed, bending over, leaning to look me in the eye.

"Opinionated is an understatement," I sniffed, pulling away from him. "You know what you're doing wrong."

"Do I?" he asked, and my face dropped. His expression became so vulnerable for a split second that it was like he reverted back to his youth.

"You really are Luke, aren't you?" I asked quietly, noticing other people catching on to the dancing, couples flooding the room as the music sped up.

"I haven't heard that name in a long time. Tell me, how did you stumble across this piece of history? I thought I did enough to erase it."

"Your brother, Mason. He died, but he gave me what I needed to figure out the connections between you two." I expected the King to be at least a little distraught, knowing his brother was dead, but he simply looked ahead, emotion unchanging.

"I expected him to kick the bucket, if that's what you're wondering. That wretched excuse for a hu—" he started coughing, choking on his own words. He wiped his mouth, gulping. "He found an heir."

"What was that?" I asked, holding back from asking if he was alright.

"He left too quickly, I assume," the King responded, ignoring my question. "Left you with too much on your shoulders, giving his burden to a child who wasn't ready, leaving you in the dark to fend for yourself. He's lucky he didn't make another demon."

"You don't choose when you die," I reminded him, but he shook his head. "Are you saying it wasn't an old age thing? He said he was over four hundred."

"We weren't born that far apart from each other, and look at me," he said with a gesture. "You don't think anything else was remiss? You don't believe he was involved with any wrongdoing— even when he abandoned your camp, your friend, and you." I noted him saying friend—not friends. He must be talking about Damien.

"No matter what he did, you're worse. Look at what you've done—how many people you've killed," I glared up at him as we shuffled around the floor. "You've enslaved your people here. You've made everyone suffer, including yourself. You can't be *happy* here."

"And you can't predict my emotion," he spat back. "You can't possibly understand the anguish I've gone through just to get to where I am, the things I've done to rise through the ranks of this harsh world."

"Maybe I can't. But I can imagine how it is to lead—you don't know *my* story, do you?" I said, lowering my voice. I didn't want information to get out that I wasn't from this world, but to one-up the King, I could give a little backstory.

"Oh, trust me, I've had you watched from the shadows," the King scoffed, like I had insulted him. "You may have noticed the figures following you, the strange frequency of demons flooding to your doorstep, the… unfortunate accidents that keep happening." He gripped my wrists, like he was threatening me.

"You can't be behind everything that—" He cut me off with a skeptical look, and my eyes widened.

"You know my secret already. You should have figured out that I have control over demons. The monsters in the woods are under my control; just like how this city is. I have a much bigger reach than you could ever imagine, outsider," I could hear the music slowing down, like the song was coming to an end. Everyone around us started to halt, and I panicked, unsure of what to do. "I know of the prophecy. I know what you are, and where you're from. You don't deserve to rule—I've only been doing my duty, keeping away the pests that may make the world a worse place." The King pulled me close, whispering in my ear. He was strong, and I couldn't break away from him.

"Let go of me," I quietly demanded, listening carefully for the notes dancing through the air to cut off, hopefully freeing me.

"Let's do this again sometime, shall we? Go ahead, scheme with your little rebellion. To kill the King on his birthday—how cruel, don't you think? Then again, I wouldn't put anything past your bunch." I felt his grip loosen, and I ripped my hands away from him. Looking up, he had a smug smile plastered on his face. He definitely knew how to make people feel useless.

I backed away, fear still making my heart race, like his words had dug into my ears, his breath traveling into my soul. Even if he wasn't strong, intimidation wasn't a weakness of his.

"Amber, what happened?" I felt a tap on my shoulder, and spun around as steadily as I could, minding the heels. The prince stood behind me, looking concerned. "What did he say to you?"

"It doesn't matter. We need to get everyone here—and I mean *everyone*." I felt like I had to glance over my shoulder, watch my back. The King was gone, disappearing back into the crowd that now mingled as soft violin rose into the air.

"It'll take a little bit. Here, have a drink while I talk to the others." He handed me a silver cup, one filled with a deep red liquid. He then stepped towards the wall, holding his hand to the side of his head and whispering something. I held it to my lips, slowly taking a sip, surprised at the fruity flavor.

"Wait, is this alcohol?" I asked, examining the liquid. "Because I don't think that's legal."

"We need help, yeah. I—it's punch," the prince replied, looking at me as if the answer should be obvious.

"Okay, but is that a yes or…" I was ignored as he turned back to his call. I shrugged it off, looking back at the crowd.

"They're on their way, but it will take a little while," the prince said after a minute. "Shall we dance? It would look more natural than two kids standing around at a ball."

"Oh—you're right. Sure." He held out his hand, and I leaned back, leaving my cup on the table before we spun onto the dance floor. It was much more casual than when I danced with the King; and there were fewer threats.

I should have known that we would have drawn his eye, though. Me, dancing with the son of two people who supported him? It must seem suspicious, more so than standing on the sidelines after all.

"Sorry to interrupt," a chill went down my spine, a cold hand on my shoulder, the deep voice resonating, but maybe it was just in my head. "May I steal your partner for a second?" I could almost feel him smiling; but it wasn't an offer.

"I, uh… Of course, your majesty." The prince backed up, letting go of my hand. He looked like he wanted to apologize, but couldn't before the King swung me around.

"I didn't expect him to be a part of your plan. How cruel! Turning my allies against me?" He looked down to me, like he knew I was afraid, but I held my posture.

"Maybe he wasn't your ally. And besides, everyone would rather fight for the good guys. You aren't doing yourself any favors by becoming a dictator." My eyes narrowed, a sneer forming on my lips.

"You're brave, I'll give you that. I can see why Mason assumed you were the rightful heir."

"Assumed?" I challenged, taking a deep breath to calm my nerves.

"You can't possibly entertain the thought of me believing you're fit for the role of General. You're weak minded, and you don't have enough courage to do a bad thing for the sake of your dwelling.

How are you supposed to rid the world of tyranny if you can't bring yourself to kill a human?" We spun, and it felt like the outside world was becoming gray around us, like everything had stopped, slowly turning to stone.

"I'll do what I need to," my mouth filled with a bitter taste as I remembered Aaron. "Maybe I already have."

"Oh, yes, him. The power of telepathy usually strengthens your mind, but his will shattered under a small bit of pressure." The King chuckled, and I resisted the urge to slap him. "That seemed to put you in quite the situation. I could *feel* your pain… it was hard to watch."

"What, did it remind you of your parents abandoning you for your older brother?" I said, regretting the words as soon as they left my mouth. He let go of my hands, an enraged expression on his face, bringing his palm down on my cheek. I fell to the floor, the clap echoing through the suddenly silent room, and I cried out as I skidded across the floor, right towards the prince. He leaned down next to me, pulling me up.

"You scoundrel!" a woman exclaimed, walking up to the King, her heels clicking on the floor. She wore a puffy black dress and a crown similar to the prince's resting on her head. She held a white purse delicately in her hands, a shocked look on her face. A man dressed in a white suit came up next to her, his hand on her back.

"Those are my parents," the prince whispered, helping me up. I clung to his arm, trying to look helpless, wanting to stir up a rebellion in the room.

"How dare you touch a child?" the woman exclaimed, slapping his arm with her purse. "You are vile! We will be taking our business elsewhere, thank you very much!" she exclaimed.

"Your majesty, you don't see the whole story," he stumbled out, glaring at me. "This child is at the front of a rebellion—turning traitor against the very Kingdom that they call home."

"This is not my home!" I protested, holding my cheek, the skin burning beneath my touch. He looked confused for a moment, as if he didn't understand my protest.

"You insufferable pest—you'll be tried for this!" he screamed, stepping menacingly towards me, hands raised in a motion to grab me.

He never got the chance. The wall exploded next to us, shrapnel and debris spilling into the dust-filled room. A chandelier snapped and fell, crashing to the floor as a panic started. People screamed and forced their way out of the castle, the prince's guards coming through the door and a hoard of rebels bursting through the hole in the wall. Damien led the charge, everyone from the camp behind him, and following them, I saw the assassins, some nature golems from the Valley, Frostbite skating in behind them with the princess on his shoulder, and countless others I both recognized and didn't. We had grown so much without me even realizing, I was shocked to see the amount of people rushing in.

The King must have been as surprised as I was, because his hands fell. Kita spotted me, sprinting my way, a horrifying gleam in her malice-filled eyes. She jumped on the wall, running sideways for a moment before leaping behind the King, using her stars to slash at the back of his neck, landing and immediately swiping at his feet, throwing him off balance and making him tumble to the floor. He screamed in pain as others pounced, Frostbite covering him with a layer of ice, Damien changing to a hawk and pecking at his face, Jay picking up all the remnants of the shattered wall and levitating them, bringing them down to impale the King. Harlequinn watched with pride, a small smile on his face.

The room had been completely evacuated, the shock and terror from the sudden charge making everyone flee. I tapped the sapphire around my neck three times, my clothes reappearing as I stood, my cloak flowing behind me and my blade held threateningly in my grip. I heard screams as the attack against the King continued, but... something was off. I winced as a golem raised its fist, smashing down on the ice encasing him, a frost filling the air. Everyone went still, and I wondered, could this really have been over so quickly?

I was definitely mistaken, and I felt foolish for thinking a powerful demon like him could be taken down so easily. Dark shadows started to spread across the floor, a bubbling liquid that burned the ground like acid. They quickly coated the walls, burning away what was left of the castle, until we were completely exposed to the world, the night sky shining diligently above us. The King rose like a cliché vampire, standing while barely moving. He laughed, a rolling snicker that burst into an evil cackle.

"You think your puny army can stop me? You fail to believe I'd have one of my own!" he shrieked, turning his scarred head to the sky and whistling, an unnaturally loud sound that, once the echo faded, you could hear a drumming from the woods. Monsters and demons spewed forth, clinging to the ground and drawing themselves forward, thousands upon thousands of creatures headed for us. We only had about a hundred people in our rebellion, including the prince's army that stormed the castle when it existed, but now everything but pieces of the floor melted away.

I saw a staircase leading down into the ground, all of it made of stone, and I tried to make a run for it, but the shadows grabbed me. I heard shrieks as the others were no doubt being encased, my sword clattering to the ground as I froze up, my skin going numb. I assumed the King was just going to dissolve us, but he shocked me once again. All of us were thrown into the air, screaming and yelping, all being separated and catapulted to different areas. I soared through the cold sky, watching the Kingdom's bright lights fade as I was shot the opposite direction.

My vision blurred as tears threatened to fall, not from sadness or anger, but from the wind stinging my eyes. I could barely see, but I knew I was far, far away. I felt myself start to drop and turned, almost unable to make out anything, I just barely noticed myself quickly nearing the ground below. I realized that I was falling towards another valley, the flat land spanning for miles. As I got closer and closer, I tried to focus on timing before activating my cloak, holding it in midair. It shattered as I smacked into the grass, and I rolled to the side, but it definitely saved my life once again. I crouched, hugging my cloak around me, adrenaline pulsing through my veins, sweat beads pouring down my face.

I heard the howling of monsters in the forest, quick footsteps padding towards me; disgusting, hungry growls as the creatures noticed their prey was too weak to even stand. I was an easy target, out in the open, recovering so I wouldn't get sick the moment I moved. I didn't look up, but I felt the earth moving, vibrating in a way where I could feel every footstep, I could see every stride, and I could envision the horrendous mob forming around me. My shaky breaths created some steam that danced in the air, illuminated by the moon's bright rays. The monsters didn't seem to be moving anymore, possibly confused as to why I wasn't doing anything.

I tried to stand, holding out my arms threateningly. I felt the wind swirl around me, the earth almost bubbling beneath me. The monsters seemed hesitant to attack, suddenly gaining brains. A few broke away from the smart crowd, rushing at me, knives and claws bared. I felt a scratch at my back as something kicked me down, nearly sending me into the blade of something in front of me. I turned to the side as I fell, but it got my shoulder, and I landed with a thump, pebbles embedding themselves in my skin.

I got up, kicking at the monster in front of me, sweeping its legs out from beneath it. It fell, but a flaming creature behind it leapt over its stunned body, pushing me back, further into the crowd of monsters. The fire burned my arms, and I screeched, slamming into something. The ground below me rose up in spines, crushing a few monsters around me, but for every one down, there were ten more to replace it.

My face got kicked into the ground, something stabbed me in the back, I felt an arrow drag across my skin, nothing was going well. I tried to fend off the hoard, but seeing me on the floor encouraged all of them to attack. I was piled on by creatures, only getting a break for a second when I feebly pushed them away, wind swirling around me.

I felt a hot breath going down my neck and panic quickly swallowed me. I looked around me, feeling my heart starting to race. My head spun and my vision blurred as panic took over. I was surrounded, and my friends were nowhere in sight. My sword was gone, the sheath around my waist just reminding me of the nonexistent weapon. Heat rose at my fingertips, and I felt a stinging, burning sensation that I wasn't trying to conjure. My emotions were getting the best of me, and my powers were reacting. I felt sick, so worried that my stomach began to turn. The crowd started to close, menacingly stepping forward, all weapons and claws raised, the enemies a strange mix of monsters I'd never seen before.

"Damien!" I shrieked the first name that came to my head in a pitiful attempt to call for help. My eyes darted from side to side as hopelessness consumed me, losing faith that anyone was there to save me. We were miles from civilization, and we didn't have many allies in the first place. I tried to take a deep breath, but it turned into hyperventilation, my breath quick and short. Fire crawled up my arms, and seeing the blaze, everyone charged.

All I remember is heat as I fell further into the floor, prepared to give in. This entire fight had been useless, people died for this cause and here I was, unable to continue what they gave their lives for. Tears fell down my cheeks as I sunk into the ground, the earth cracking beneath me. Flames crawled through the ground, exploding in the space around me and creating a blazing inferno, bursting up from the ground with an angry roar, reaching high into the sky, encasing me and the crowd.

Water swirled around me, moisture taken from the air, my sweat, the plants, rocky debris pulled violently from the ground and ripped into the sky, strong wind colliding with the fire to create something like a tornado, devastating the land below. Everything was brought together, my powers raging in an extravagant display around me, feeling the pain I had endured all manifesting in this disaster. Searing heat met freezing water, invincible bedrock collided with unnaturally strong bursts of wind. Smoke hung in the air, screams rising from every direction, and I let out my own shriek, all my mana draining in an instant, the disaster around me raging on as I fell into unconsciousness.

I awoke in a deep pit, the dirt and stone seemingly curling around me, creating what almost looked like a shield. The edges were smoothed down, dripping slowly. My head pounded, and I felt weak, though I tried to stand anyway. My legs withered beneath me, but the dirt rose from the floor, catching my almost limp body and carrying me above the hole. As I rose into the air, I gasped, marveling at the damage.

The area around me had been decimated, thick black smoke hanging in the air, grass smoldering, and a hole hundreds of feet wide that reached down to smoldering bedrock. There wasn't a soul in sight, but not a single remnant littered the ground, and the gruesome thought of a destructive force so powerful, not even bones would be left behind, terrified me. I looked down at my hands, trembling as I wondered... that was me? I did this? Now I knew what Damien was so afraid of when he said we needed to keep my powers in check, but did he expect something like this?

It was hard to take in everything, and I nearly reached the clouds before I could see the damage fully, the thin, cold air making me realize how hot I was. My skin steamed within the vapor of the clouds, and I felt a chill go through me as I quickly cooled down. I assumed this was the consequence of all my built-up emotion, being let loose in a flurry of mass destruction.

"Amber!" I heard my name, my head snapping towards the call. I saw the small figure of... Damien, maybe, running towards me. It sounded like his voice. "How did you—oh god." His voice slowly faded as he looked down, noticing the giant pit below my tower of dirt.

"I... I didn't mean to," I called down, the earth below me crumbling slowly, sliding me down harmlessly to the ground. It was as if I didn't even need to control it or ask for help, even my presence on the earth enough for it to read my thoughts, reflecting what I needed.

"I'd hope not. This thing is huge! How did—you got attacked, didn't you?" he said with a worried look.

"Yeah, they all came out of the woods. I felt sick, and I guess all the stress and panic overwhelmed me. I exploded, and my powers seemed to use themselves. Everything activated at once! I don't even know how I'm standing," I admitted. "But I feel fine, like nothing ever happened." I glanced down at my torn clothes, a lot of blood flowing down my face, arms and legs. It didn't hurt, and somehow I didn't feel tired from the explosion.

"That should be impossible, but let's not discuss technicalities right now. I'm lucky we landed near enough to each other. I was just far enough to see the corner of the explosion, and I flew here. I was around ten miles away and I could still feel the heat." Guilt stung me as Damien looked up slightly, fear shining in his eyes. I didn't want him to be scared of me, but... I was scared of myself at this point. "Any way you can do that again, aimed right at the King?"

"I don't even know if I can use my powers right now, and I don't exactly want to check in case something goes wrong. We do need to head back, though. I'll fight as much as I can with a sword. If I can find it..." I sighed, putting my head in my hands.

"Ever since we found you, I've been thinking. You might have started with an overflow of power, too much mana to even be contained by separate sources. That's why intense emotion makes you explode, so letting go of all of that overflow might now allow you to use your powers normally. Elemental magic is strong, but normally not strong enough to blow up this much. I didn't know how to justify this before, but I'm thinking this world knew more people would be coming, and since you stumbled in first, you inherited their magic. That's why they have none and you have so much," Damien suggested with a shrug. My eyes widened, and... that made sense, in a weird way that never would in the real world.

I held out my hand, watching as a flame danced to life in my palm, waves of wind swirling around it gently, mist sprinkling over my hand as debris from the explosion slowly floated up, hovering over all the other elements. I was surprised, and pretty shocked, but ecstatic at the same time. "That's... interesting. I guess you're right, though."

"Ready to go kick the King into another dimension?" Damien said with a smirk, holding up his fist. I giggled, bumping my hand against his. We both turned backwards, not even able to see the lights of the Kingdom from how far away we were.

"We need to get there, fast. You can shape shift, but... I want to try something," I said, remembering Frostbite's dramatic entrance from earlier. I spread my arms out like I was trying to balance, the earth moving and turning beneath me. It rose up, dirt gripping my heels as I sped through the valley, shrieking as I was launched. I heard laughter behind me and Damien followed, morphing into a hawk and trying to keep up. I whooped in joy, giggling until I could see the looming buildings of the Kingdom once again.

"Look!" Damien called, and I followed his gaze to see Tigre, Jay and Harlequinn still fighting where the castle once stood. They were struggling within the shadows, desperately fighting off the King and all the monsters around him. I skidded to a stop right at the border, sneaking around the buildings. Damien quietly morphed back to a human, following me closely.

"What's the plan?" I whispered, leaning back a bit.

"I'll distract the King from above. You try to grab the others and lure them away so we can form a better plan," he suggested, and I shrugged, nodding.

"Everyone else must have been thrown pretty far away... he's trying to separate us so we're weaker. Reassembling who we can is a good idea." I turned, going around the opposite way as Damien advanced forward. I could see confusion on his face before he held out his arms, slowly transforming into what appeared to be... a buffalo? A thick coat of fur covered his body and his short legs propelled him forward. He charged, and I almost laughed at the picture of an animal like that going after a possessed King.

Ignoring the bubbling laughter, I ducked my head, sprinting low to the ground as Damien distracted the King. He snorted and bellowed, drawing all attention to him as I crept towards the boys. All three were within a foot of each other, so it wasn't difficult to grab them and run. I held my finger up to my lips in a quieting gesture, so when I approached, they wouldn't make any noise. Tigre was the closest, so I tapped his shoulder to make him notice I was there, immediately shushing his shriek. Jay and Harlequinn glanced over as well, seeing me and smiling. The King was so distracted, his shadows started to loosen, his energy more focused on charging buffalo. I grabbed at the Elite's wrist, wrenching him free from the grip, accidentally pulling too hard and stumbling backwards. I reached out for Jay to steady myself, but he also jumped out, grabbing Harlequinn as we all tumbled down. What I didn't notice, however, was that I slipped down the stairs going into the basement.

We all fell, shrieking as we tried to regain our footing, but it didn't work until we were down the entire flight, resting on the stone floor. The screams quickly fell into giggles, as we all forgot where we were for a moment, caught up in the sheer silliness of it all. Our explosive laughter stopped as soon as it started, however, Damien crashing down next to us. The ceiling was covered by the shadows, and small lanterns illuminated the room around us. The basement was entirely made of stone, a large room with a pillar in the middle.

I heard a strange sound, a pulsing coming from the mottled black and gray spire in the room. Looking around, I saw a hundred or more minions roaming, a mixture of humans and monsters, all carrying various weapons, dapper suits and ski masks covering their faces. They turned as they saw us, bearing teeth and brandishing their knives, swords, and even shovels. I gulped, fear coursing through me.

We all stood, Tigre growling viciously, Jay and Harlequinn holding up their fists threateningly, Damien turning into a wolf, and my hand burst into flame. The pause didn't last long, all of us throwing ourselves into battle, war cries ringing from every angle. I punched a monster, my flaming fist going right through its stomach as it dissolved with a scream. I ducked an attack from behind, sending a line of fire right towards someone I couldn't quite see. The blaze in my hand flickered, and I cursed, putting it out. I looked around for another weapon, and I had an idea. I gently touched the floor, my fingertips barely reaching the stone as it softened, molding around my arm. I brought my hand up, and a spire of rock formed in my palm, a jagged edge like a sword. I planted my feet, pivoting so I was turned the other way.

I held up my hand, slashing left and right. I tossed the blade to my left hand, and threw it behind me like a boomerang, using the wind to aid me, and I heard grunting as it struck down a few of the monsters in the back. It flew into my right hand, and I stabbed it into the ground, getting carried away by the excitement. I stumbled to the side a bit, nearing the strange pillar, and my sword suddenly melted back into the ground. In my surprise, I was tackled, pushed against the stone so suddenly and with so much force, I heard a sickening crack. I screeched, looking into the cold eyes of a man wearing a black mask. He shoved the back of my head into the wall behind me, placing both of his hands firmly on my face. I could just barely see the battle raging behind him.

"You should really die already," he chuckled. I struggled against his grip, but he was too strong. I wiggled and writhed to no avail. I would have to use my powers. I smiled slightly, excited to see the look on his face once he saw me flaming. I reached out to grab his arm, and... nothing. No fire. He started to laugh maniacally, throwing his head back. "Did you already forget? You're inside the castle! That doesn't work here!" He continued to throw his head back in amusement, sounding like a hyena on drugs. Nearly giving up, I noticed the space between my lips and his hand...

I did what I had to. I bit him. Clamping down on his hand as hard as I could, driving my sharp teeth into his flesh, the metallic taste of blood quickly filling my mouth. He wailed, backing away, his gloves beginning to turn crimson. "You—you evil child! You *bit me!*"

"And I'll do it again! Get away!" I bared my teeth, even going as far as to snap at him. I saw him flinch, and before he could reach out to hit me, I swept my leg at his, throwing him off balance and stepping on his fallen body, driving the heel of my boot into his stomach. He coughed, spluttering and spitting before I kicked the side of his head, knocking him out but not killing him. I surveyed the battle before me, trying to keep up with what was happening. Damien slid towards the enemies, but stopped short of their feet. One stabbed at him and he barely scrambled away

"What's happening? My powers... they aren't working!" He tensed his muscles, attempting to change into something. The entire time, Jay hadn't been levitating things, but he was getting distracted trying to. Harlequinn jumped to the rescue every time he was nearly stabbed, tackling people and clawing at them. Tigre was simply on the ground, growling so ferociously at anything that tried to come near, no one even wanted to take a step towards the struggling Elite. A deep laugh echoed through the cavern.

"Oh, yes. Bedrock! What an amazing magic suppressor. You have about as much magic as you did in the void. Amber, you should know how hopeless this fight is now." The King chuckled evilly, rolling in on a cloud, similar to the way Shadow moved. I stifled a laugh, a secretive smile spreading on my face

"Really? Well, I guess we have no hope. We're out of luck. End of the line!" I exclaimed dramatically, now more hopeful than before. I focused, trying to remember Berry, the fight on that corrupted island, and I felt my arm warm up slightly as my hands burst into flames. I still struggled and the fire wasn't as strong as I could make it, but I had power no one else had. I heard a shriek, and saw the King's eyes widen. I guess I'd surprised him.

"How did—" he started, but I cut him off.

"I don't know how you knew where I was, but you obviously missed the fantastic ending. I defeated that overgrown lizard with ease, and I'll do the same to you!" I yelled, my powers sensing the vigor and conviction in my voice and roaring to an inferno. I felt the heat rise, but this time, it wasn't an uncontrollable blaze even I was afraid of. This was entirely me, not my rage personified.

He was right in front of me, the scar on his face almost seeming like it was trying to peel off, a fearful gleam in his eyes. He held out his hands, dark spears colliding with me, passing through the flames. I sidestepped, casually dodging the first two, bending the stone out of the ground and creating a rock shield around me as he threw more. The ground pulsated beneath me, and I stumbled, nearly getting thrown. Both of us were emitting so much energy, even the minions scrambled back. All other battle halted, and it was just the two of us, wreathed in shadows and light. In such close quarters, I knew it would be dangerous, so I directed my fire up, into the ceiling.

The blaze exploded, creating a massive hole, and I quickly grabbed the King before he could react. He screamed as I took hold of his wrist, jumping up and propelling the both of us into the sky, like shooting stars amidst the clouds. We hovered for a moment, taking in the chill before I shrieked in anger, punching my flaming fist right into his eye. In return, he reached out, darkness trying to strangle me, constricting around my throat. I struggled to breathe, forcing my hand further into his face, trying to act on a frankly nonsensical plan. We tumbled around in the air, shadows covering me, the King's skin hissing.

He kept knocking my hand away, and I felt myself start to slip away from consciousness. I couldn't breathe, my air running out, and the darkness pressing against me, finding its way into my wounds. I struggled for air, feeling like worms were crawling into my skin, and I choked, raising my arm, using the last of my strength to punch the King. My fist sunk deeper into the deep scar on his face, and I really hoped I wasn't wrong.

However, my theory soon came to life, truth shining through as the shadows started to peel off of the King's face. This wasn't about beating him. With his strength and defense, there wasn't much of a way I could. But removing the demon festering inside him was the one thing I could do. My light would be able to take him out, sear away the infiltrator and bring back the General's brother.

"Luke!" I yelled, choking as I forced the words out. The King seemed surprised, his grasp loosening, and I threw my head back, visions coursing through my mind.

Luke and Mason, the General and the King. Together as young boys, playing in the field, then they were older, chasing after a boy and a girl, prancing through the Kingdom's intricate buildings. The brothers shared hot chocolate, told each other stories, sat by the fire and read. Always together, memories flashing in my mind as if they were my own, a montage created from something real. Bits and pieces of a story, fitting together like a puzzle piece. But it wasn't all happy. I saw Luke, bitterly glaring at Mason through a window, eating fancy food in a restaurant with a girl while his brother counted the few coins that they had left. Mason got more achievements, earning medals and being praised, while Luke sat in the background, fuming. He was never enough, he wasn't able to compete. He was minuscule next to his brother. He never could do enough to top his own family. He didn't share the spotlight, so he turned to the darkness.

"My crime is, sadly, now yours to fix."

The words echoed in my head, and I once again saw the General's withering form, on the bank of a lake. I knew what he meant now. He created a monster, not intentionally, but by negligence and ignorance.

"Mason?" I heard the King's fragile voice, flickering between his deep, gruff tone and one that sounded like a broken child.

I broke free of the flashback, staring at a no longer scarred face. My power flickered, and we fell, both silent. I gazed in shock at his young face, no different than from my memories. The demon must have corrupted him from the very beginning, preserving his youth. But the shock didn't prevent us from plummeting, and we quickly came dangerously close to the ground. Thinking fast, I pulled Luke closer towards me and yelled the spell to activate my shield. It didn't absorb all the shock, and I let out a yelp, landing on some debris. Luke bounced away from me, my strength fading as pain coursed through my body. We landed right beside the opening in the basement, and as I looked down to check on my friends, I saw the enemy, human and monster alike, slowly disappearing.

"Amber, no!" Damien called, sprinting towards me, breathing

heavily. "Everyone, get to them!" he yelled, waving. It took the boys a moment to snap out of their stupor, but they all quickly shuffled upstairs, kneeling beside me. Damien put his hand on my back, a concerned look on his face, but I crawled forward, towards Luke. He was sprawled on the ground, his hair splayed out behind him, barely breathing. Scratches marred his face, and his body trembled.

"Who—is that actually the King? It looks like you punched the age off of him," Tigre joked, and I looked back with an unamused stare. "Sorry, bad timing."

"We need to help him," I muttered, my throat burning. I felt like now I had a mark, a deep shadow pressed into my skin. I could barely even see, but I knew we needed to get him back to camp. "Tigre, Jay, Harlequinn, can you try to look for the others? The ones that were thrown in the attack. They could be miles away, but we need to find them. I'll take Damien and Luke to the camp, get B to help."

"Isn't this our enemy?" Jay said, looking baffled. "He ruined our lives for years! He was a literal demon just a minute ago!"

"You once told me no matter what, we have to help people, even if it's just for the sake of showing them we're better. That applies here, too," I said with a stern glare. He backed off, his hands in the air.

"Get on," Damien said, turning into his version of Aster. "You three, you got the General's orders. Let's go." He grinned, showing his teeth, but the others grumbled, running off to do what they could. The boys departed, and I weakly grabbed Luke, pushing him up onto Damien's back. It was difficult, and took a minute, but we finally got situated. I paused, trying to stand, my limbs weak. Damien offered a hand, and I gently took it, pushing myself up.

I surveyed the area, looking at the carnage. The Kingdom was deserted, lights going out and buildings toppled. I remembered my sword, and I groaned, hoping I hadn't truly lost it. As soon as the thought crossed my mind, it clattered to the floor at my feet. I looked up, seeing a dark figure racing past. Sadly, that was not the weirdest thing I had encountered here. Happy to finally have my blade, I sheathed it and climbed on to the wolf's back. We went slowly, trying to make the ride as smooth as possible, but it was excruciating waiting for the minutes to pass. Luckily, we weren't too far and quickly passed through the gates.

"B!" I yelled, sliding off of the wolf's back, crumbling to the floor. "B, please help!" The elf poked her head out of the infirmary, my yelling drawing the attention of everyone. A small crowd gathered, confused as to why I was carrying a young boy back from the battle.

"What's going on?" she asked, quickly scooping Luke into her own arms and laying him on a bed.

"This... this is the King," I said tentatively, and she gasped, flinging herself away from him.

"Please! He was possessed by a demon the entire time. He's actually the General's brother, but he's innocent. His actions weren't him... just a demon infesting his mind." I pleaded with my eyes, clasping my hand together in a begging motion. B sighed, resuming her position next to the bed, begrudgingly rolling her eyes and starting to work.

"Amber!" I heard someone at the door, and looking over, Jonas poked his head through. "I think you'll want to see this."

"B, I know you can help. Please, do what you can," I said with a small smile, right before I sprinted out the door, trying to keep myself up. People were still gathered, all pointing and gasping, looking outside. My heart skipped a beat, worry taking over me as I pushed through the crowd, hearing a strange, pulsating sound.

Blue light bathed my face as a portal slowly opened, a swirling vortex right in front of me. I could just barely see the real world through the veil, my school not having changed a bit, the people in the image barely moving. "It... it goes back home."

"Home?" Seth said, popping out of the crowd. "We... we can leave?"

"It looks like it. I don't know if any time would have passed, but... you should be able to resume normal life," I said, almost in a haze. My thoughts were interrupted when I heard footsteps, and looked to the left, seeing Tigre, Jay, and Harlequinn already leading the rebellion back to camp.

"Guys! You're—wait, that was quick."

"Luckily, they could all only be thrown so many directions. Most of them had already met up and headed back!" Harlequinn said cheerfully. "What's this?"

"A portal. Back... to my dimension," I said nervously. I felt a hand on my shoulder, and looked back, seeing Damien with a sullen look on his face.

"Do you want to leave?" Damien asked, his eyes watering. I looked back towards the swirling portal, the place that could take me back to my home. I turned to see everyone from camp waiting on my decision, the numbers small. The sad smiles on all of their faces made the decision for me.

"No. This place is my home now. I'll find another way to visit my friends. You guys need me here." Damien looked surprised, then launched into a hug. I could hear celebrations throughout the entire crowd, even though some were confused cheers, people from outside the camp not entirely understanding the situation.

"I don't know about you guys, but I'm out!" Jake said, holding up two fingers in a piece sign before jumping through, flying back into the real world. Eli soon followed, and Seth tried to as well before I grabbed his shoulder.

"Hey, wait. I... I wanted to say I'm sorry for anything that happened. And, please don't say anything about this," I said, biting my lip. I didn't want to end this on a sour note, my mind still hectic with the thought of our argument.

"I'm sorry, too. I won't tell a soul—besides, I already said they'd think I had finally gone mad. I'll make up an excuse for your absence. See you on the flip side," he said nonchalantly, though the emotion in his eyes was something I hadn't seen before. He leapt through, and I sighed, letting out my breath.

"Uh... time to celebrate?" I suggested, and my comment was followed by cheers. We all piled into the camp, laughing joyfully and finally letting our worries go. The battle was over.

Caught up in our festivities, no one noticed the sly figure of a creature, unrecognizable by anyone even if they had seen it, slip through the portal, hissing in determination, darkness following behind as, once it was entirely through, the vortex closed.

ACKNOWLEDGEMENTS

I'd like to thank everyone who encouraged me to get this far.
My family and friends who supported me through this process,
and helped me achieve more than I thought I could.
Thank you to my teacher, Mrs. Stephanie, who helped me get
through a writer's block that prevented me from putting this
story on paper.
Thank you to Sam Jackson, who drew the cover and helped me
with the final push I needed to get this book out into the world.
Thank you to Diane J. Reed, who gave me advice and an inside
look into the writing world to help me along.
Here's to all the people who read the book before it was
published, who gave me feedback and helped to edit.
Thank you to everyone who was here from the beginning and
stayed to the end.

Made in the USA
Lexington, KY
13 December 2019

58558927R00245